"Please forget that."

He stepped closer to her. Too close. He'd intended to overwhelm her with his height, overturn her senses with his nearness. Instead, he fell into her gravitational pull, as though she was the sun and he was a celestial body destined to be burned by it.

In an effort to regain control, he cupped her shoulder with his hand, grazing a path with his thumb that caused his throat to tighten. "Forget the way you kissed me?"

He moved even closer. There was barely an inch between them and no telling where his body warmth ended and hers began, just that the air between them snapped and crackled as if on fire. "The press of your lips against mine was an experience I've no desire to forget."

She swallowed and, for a brief second, he would swear he saw her sway toward him. Then she took his hand and removed it. "I *saved* you," she said, stepping to the side and leaving a gulf between them.

He tried to hide the sense of loss with a cheeky grin, turning to lean against the dressing table, his arms crossed. "And I saved you, so we're even."

She took a fierce breath. "You wouldn't have had to save me if you hadn't dragged me into that refuse-ridden water to begin with." Her eyes sparked. "Would it have been so hard to let go of me?"

"Impossible."

Praise for
Samara Parish and
the Rebels with a Cause series

"Parish wields a deft hand with dialogue, characterization, and plotting."
> —*Library Journal* on *How to Win a Wallflower*

"This is sure to win the heart of any hopeless romantic."
> —*Publishers Weekly* on *How to Win a Wallflower*

"Readers will be eager for more."
> —*Publishers Weekly* on *How to Deceive a Duke*

"Dazzling." > —*Booklist* on *How to Deceive a Duke*

"Historical romance fans will be happy to find another strong-willed, science-minded heroine and the duke who loves her, and they'll look forward to the next story in the series." > —*Library Journal* on *How to Deceive a Duke*

"A sparkling new voice in historical romance delivers a satisfying story of love on the edges of the beau monde."
> —*Kirkus Reviews* on *How to Deceive a Duke*

"In this dazzling debut, Parish gives historical romance readers everything they could ever desire in a novel...[A]n extraordinary romance that succeeds on every level."
> —*Booklist* on *How to Survive a Scandal*, starred review

While the Duke Was Sleeping

Also by Samara Parish

How to Survive a Scandal
How to Deceive a Duke
How to Win a Wallflower

While the Duke Was Sleeping

Samara Parish

FOREVER

New York   Boston

Forever
Hachette Book Group
1290 Avenue of the Americas, New York, NY 10104
read-forever.com
@readforeverpub

First Mass Market Edition: February 2025

Forever is an imprint of Grand Central Publishing. The Forever name and logo are registered trademarks of Hachette Book Group, Inc.

The publisher is not responsible for websites (or their content) that are not owned by the publisher.

The Hachette Speakers Bureau provides a wide range of authors for speaking events. To find out more, go to hachettespeakersbureau.com or email HachetteSpeakers@hbgusa.com.

Forever books may be purchased in bulk for business, educational, or promotional use. For information, please contact your local bookseller or the Hachette Book Group Special Markets Department at special.markets@hbgusa.com.

ISBNs: 9781538757734 (mass market); 9781538757741(ebook)

Printed in the United States of America

BVGM

10 9 8 7 6 5 4 3 2 1

To my husband—my home—and to our roots,
so lovingly tangled.

And to my grandmother, who taught me the love of books.

Acknowledgments

Writing can be such a collaborative effort if you want it to be. I'd like to thank those who helped shape this book. Justine Lewis is one of the greatest friends a girl can have. Her feedback at various stages of draft both improved the story and kept me sane. I am so lucky to have her.

Much of this book was written sitting in a university pub with Charlotte Anne and Adrienne Marie as we punctuated our words with industry gossip and grand plan-making. I also need to give a shout out to my sister, who is always willing to read and give her thoughts from a reader's point of view, which is so valuable. She's my beta team of one.

Thank you to my agent, Rebecca Strauss, for her ongoing support and guidance. Our relationship is one that I greatly value, and it gives me great hope for our future.

Thank you to my publishing team: my editor, Madeleine Colavita, Maggie Smith for her enthusiasm, and my publicists Dana Cuadrado and Caroline Green, who are such great advocates for my stories.

As usual, my husband listened to me for hours on end as I gossiped about my imaginary characters, and he stepped in at every deadline to take care of the house and our fur family so that I could focus on my writing. Not all writers are so lucky to have that support and I will never take it for granted.

Finally, to my Smut Club, Tanya Nellesteine, Jacqueline Hayley, and HM Hodgson, who have welcomed me with open arms even though I'm not particularly smutty. The giant marble cock is dedicated to you, xoxo.

While the
Duke Was
Sleeping

Chapter One

St. Paul's Cathedral, London. December, 1893.

Adelaide just couldn't bring herself to give a fig about this wedding. Not now, at least. Not after a night spent attending to her mistress's pre-wedding jitters. Not when she'd been run off her feet for a week wrapping jewelry, packing trunks, and pressing gowns that would become unpressed the moment they were folded and sent three blocks to the duke's residence.

In an hour, she might care, when the celebrations were in full swing, and she could sneak off for a moment on her own. She would either care or be asleep.

"It's exciting, isn't it?" A lad approximately her age sidled up next to her, his hands stuffed in his pockets. "A big wedding. All those people watching. All them guards." He pointed to the red-coated Coldstream Guards arranged in precise lines along the cobblestone road that led to St. Paul's Cathedral. The tall bearskins, admittedly, were impressive.

She plastered on a smile, not wanting to disappoint him. "It's very exciting."

The lad smiled and snapped his heels together, giving a jaunty salute. "Joshua Thompson, at your service."

Sighing internally, she dipped a short curtsy in response. "Adelaide Rosebourne."

"Are you part of the bridal family's service?"

"I'm Lady Cordelia's maid." She held up her sewing bag filled with needles and thread, damp cloths, dry cloths, hairpins, even a tin of peppermints and a small flask of Madeira. She was prepared for anything that might need fixing before the bride entered the cathedral.

Joshua's smile broadened. "You'll be joining the duke's household, then. Welcome. You're going to love it. We're a tight-knit group—a family, really." He leaned across and shoulder bumped her in an overly friendly manner.

"I am looking forward to it." It was only half a lie. She *was* looking forward to changing households. She'd been at the Duke of Thirwhestle's residence for six months now, and she had itchy feet. She'd joined service for the money and the chance to stare at the same plastered ceiling every night instead of the procession of cracked, thatched, or wooden roofs that came with whatever room she'd rented for the month.

But pleasure in the regularity of the Thirwhestle servants' quarters was hard to come by when it was accompanied by the regular snoring of her bunkmate—a bunkmate who was excessively curious, wanting to know every detail about Adelaide, like her star sign, and her favorite author, and where she'd live if fortune befell her and she never had to work again.

In a two-bedroom cottage with a walled garden and a dining table so heavy it could barely be moved six feet, let alone across the country. With no snoring bunkmates.

As lady's maid to the Duchess of Hornsmouth, Adelaide would have her own room and a significant increase in her wages, bringing that cottage dream a little closer. Assuming she could put up with Cordelia long enough.

"What's your favorite meal?" Joshua asked. "I'll have cook prepare it in welcome."

"Pork pie," she said, picking something at random. "Excuse me."

The hubbub of the crowd had swelled. All of London seemed to have come to catch a glimpse of Cordelia as she traveled through the streets toward her nuptials. As three carriages came into view, flowers were flung toward them and promptly crushed beneath the heavy, oversized wheels.

Out of the first vehicle tumbled a dozen small children, dressed in pouffy skirts and short pants tied with pink ribbons. The bridesmaids exited the second. Cordelia's parents, the Duke and Duchess of Thirwhestle, climbed out of the third, and, after a suitably dramatic pause, Cordelia followed.

She immediately scanned the crowd, her gaze falling on Adelaide. 'Get here now,' she mouthed.

Adelaide rushed over, ready to dispense whatever her mistress needed.

"It doesn't fit," Cordelia hissed. "You made it too tight."

Adelaide swallowed the retort she'd like to make and simply said, "It fit yesterday, my lady. And it fit an hour ago."

"I cannot *breathe*."

The bridesmaids were corralling the page boys and flower girls. The duke had strolled over to where guards on sleek horses kept the crowd at bay, and he was accepting flowers on his daughter's behalf.

"Turn," Adelaide said. She pulled at the buttons, pretending to loosen the dress even though there was nothing she could honestly do. "You can breathe. If you couldn't, you'd have passed out before you even left your bedroom."

"This is not what I would have worn. My father chose this dress." She held out a hand. "Peppermint, please."

Adelaide withdrew a candy from her bag. "You look divine. I have never seen anyone so beautiful. You make a stunning bride. Hornsmouth is very lucky."

Cordelia's lips thinned. "Indeed. *He* is lucky. What a shame we are not all so."

"*Such* a shame, my lady." *Rein your opinions in, Adelaide. This is not the time.*

Still, it rankled. If she was in Cordelia's place, there wouldn't be a moment of dissatisfaction. The Duke of Hornsmouth had eight different estates across the British Isles and the blunt to service them. She would never again prick her thumbs remaking a dress that had been remade a dozen times over because food had been scarce, and she'd dropped yet another inch across the bust. She would never have to choose which tavern was the safest to rest her head in that night.

She would have a home—four walls that never changed— and she could settle in it permanently. Marriage to the Duke of Hornsmouth would give Adelaide everything she'd ever wished for.

But Cordelia was not Adelaide. Cordelia was the privileged daughter of a duke—impulsive, impassioned, and impossibly stubborn.

There was a crunching of gravel as the duke joined them. He took his daughter's elbow. The drumbeats picked up pace, and the pulse at Cordelia's throat quickly matched the insistent *rat-da-tat*. For a second, Adelaide thought she saw genuine fear in her mistress's face—a more raw and vulnerable expression than Cordelia had worn in all the time Adelaide had known her.

The duchess also joined them and poked her daughter between her shoulder blades. "For heaven's sake, girl. Stand up straight. You're embarrassing us." She turned to Adelaide with a sour look. "You are dismissed."

Adelaide hurried out of the way.

"Cor, she's a stunner," Joshua said. "The duke is going to be very pleased."

"He might be." Until he experienced Cordelia's petulance firsthand.

Joshua turned to Adelaide and frowned, his gaze flicking between her and her mistress. "You know, the two of you look remarkably alike."

"That's true." They shared the same coloring and were of roughly the same height and figure. She was saved from having to further comment by the sudden cessation of drumming. From within the cathedral, organs sounded.

The Duke of Thirwhestle gripped his daughter's arm as they climbed the stairs, her ridiculously elaborate dress dragging along the plush carpet.

"How is she standing under the weight of that dress? Those jewels are paste, surely."

"Not paste," Adelaide replied. "The bill for that dress would make you faint." As Cordelia walked out of sight, Adelaide looked around. The ceremony would last an hour or so. She had to be at the duke's residence by then to meet Cordelia's needs before the reception began.

"Oh, Lord." Joshua took hold of Adelaide's shoulder.

As she looked to see what had caught his attention, the crowd erupted.

"Oh, Lord" is right. Fuck.

Cordelia had her skirts gathered in her hands as she tore down the steps. Alone. She had the frantic expression of a fox being run down. Her gaze landed on Adelaide and Joshua, and she veered toward them.

Adelaide met her halfway. Over Cordelia's shoulder, she could see the Duke of Thirwhestle emerge from the cathedral, enraged.

Cordelia's fingers dug into Adelaide's in a death grip. "Get me out of here."

Adelaide had a split second to make a choice. The duke, or the girl alone, breaking free from decisions that weren't hers.

She picked the girl. She would likely come to regret it.

Right. Option one. Carriages.

No, that won't work, Adelaide. They couldn't take any of the finely sprung carriages before them. Each belonged to a member of the *ton* who would never keep the girl's location a secret.

Option two. A hackney.

The street had been closed for the wedding, but if they could make it to the Briarstone Inn, there would be plenty of vehicles for hire. Adelaide always had her meager savings sewn in the hidden pockets of her dress. She could pay for a cab. So she wrapped one arm around her mistress's shoulders and used the other to push through the crowd.

"Make way. Coming through. Make way." Caught in the heat, the smell of sweat, the bodies pressing inward—memories of the riot in Paris flashed through her mind. She'd not meant to get tangled in it. She'd deliberately stayed away from the area. But when the protest had broken past the wall of horse guards, the city had quickly ignited. Adelaide, only five blocks from the tavern that had been her momentary port, had been buffeted around, at times getting caught in the river of people storming toward the Palais Bourbon, ending up further and further away from where she had meant to be.

The story of my life.

That same sense of chaos filled her lungs as she attempted to break through the crowd that was pressing in to glimpse the runaway bride. "Back off," she yelled as grubby hands reached for Cordelia.

Finally, they broke free.

An enclosed cab—door still unpainted where a crest had been sanded off—stood at the edge of the road. The driver was eating an apple, paying no attention to the goings-on around him.

"Oi!"

At Adelaide's yell, he looked up from the pamphlet sitting on his lap. His frown disappeared as he set eyes on Cordelia and the ridiculous wedding dress so encrusted with jewels that it sent shards of rainbow light across everything in its path. "Doing a runner?" he asked. "Where are you going?"

Where are you going, Adelaide? Where will you be safe?

She paused for a moment to take stock. There was one thing that she knew how to do really well. One thing that was as easy as breathing. "Take us to the docks."

She knew how to leave.

Cordelia had already clambered into the carriage and was twisting her arms backward. "Get me out of this dress. *Now.* Get me out of it." She yanked at the fabric, as if she could tear the buttons free herself. She was more likely to dislocate her shoulders than undo the fastenings.

"Turn." With Cordelia kneeling on the floor between the seats, Adelaide made quick work of the buttons.

Cordelia grabbed the hem, cursing as parts of it caught beneath her knees, bunching the yards of silk carelessly as she tried to drag it over herself. Adelaide felt Cordelia stiffen as the dress got caught around her head. Then she thrashed like a fish in a bucket.

"Hold still."

The dress came off and was discarded in a giant ball by the door. Adelaide then set to work on the laces of Cordelia's corset. The process was hampered by the way Cordelia had hooked her fingers around the lace edge, pulling it away from her body as hard as she could, making it that much more difficult for Adelaide to tug the laces free.

Once the garment fell away, Cordelia, now dressed only in a chemise, bustle, and petticoats, dragged in a long breath. Then another. "Where are we going?"

"Where do you want to go?"

"Somewhere my father can't find me, and where my likeness will not be splashed across the gossip pages. I just need a few weeks free... just until the speculation dies down."

"The continent, then. We can be lost in a heartbeat once we land."

"France?"

"France, Italy, Spain."

"And you know how to get about in those places?"

She'd spent the first twenty-five years of her life getting around those places, and every other corner of Europe. Hence why she was so determined to settle, even if it meant putting up with Cordelia until she had the funds saved. "I can get by. What money do you have on you?"

Cordelia held her hand to the necklace at her throat. "I have only this—and that, I suppose." She gestured to the pile of silk, ruffles, and jewels that had been discarded on the carriage floor. "But you cannot make me wear it again. I'm serious, Adelaide. I will not. You'll have to swap dresses with me."

Adelaide looked at the overly ornate dress. She'd seen the dressmaker's bill. The gown cost more than two years of Adelaide's salary. She looked down at her own simple dress that had been remade and repaired a dozen times over.

At least you share the same coloring.

Chapter Two

England smelled different. Everett Montgomery—Monty to his friends, Rhett to his family, that rogue Montgomery boy to the grand dames of the *ton*, and plain old sir to the people he'd met during his five years on the continent—noticed the scent immediately. There was a sourness to London docks other cities didn't have. On the continent, a wharf was synonymous with the sharp smell of saltwater, a brisk breeze, and a sense of hope.

The Thames carried with it the scent of the refuse that floated scum-like on the surface of the river. There was no breeze; the air hung heavy, and Rhett had little sense of hope. He'd been summoned home by his brother, the Duke of Strafford, ostensibly to spend Christmas with the family, but Rhett knew better. He'd been summoned to account for his behavior.

To ensure that Rhett actually returned, the duke had cut off his finances. So here Rhett was, back in jolly, freezing old England.

"Bloody 'ell, Montgomery. Get out of the bleedin' way." The ship's bosun stood with two of the crew, a ripped sail furled and balanced on their shoulders.

"If you'd won the last hand of piquet, I would help you

with that." Getting under the skin of Pat, the crew's third in command, had been Rhett's primary source of entertainment as they'd sailed across the North Sea.

The bosun frowned. "I thought the duke was waitin' for you. Shouldn't you get goin'?"

"The duke can wait." *Not for that long, though.*

Rhett was willing to prod at his brother's limits, but he was too reliant on his quarterly allowance to poke too hard. If he angered his brother, he might very well be forced into work. He shuddered. He was not cut out for the dull, dutiful existence of a clergyman, but a life in the military—its structure and rules and hierarchy—was not a life for him either.

No, he had to meet his brother displaying an appropriate amount of chagrin and with a good argument for why his adventures on the continent should continue. Maybe he could say he was writing a book or getting a hands-on foundation of geopolitical issues for a future, not-ever-really-going-to-happen-for-a-man-like-him career in politics.

"His lordship might wait," Pat said, "but we won't. Get movin'!"

Rhett looked over his shoulder. Behind him the entire crew was waiting, arms full of cargo, for him to get off the bloody ship. Every man but the bosun was rolling his eyes or sniggering at his reluctance to set foot on English soil.

"It was a pleasure, gentlemen." Rhett saluted the men he'd eaten, gossiped, and gambled with for the past week. Then, when Pat's frown deepened further, he grabbed the bosun's face and planted a firm kiss on his cheek before skipping out of reach.

The crew cheered, and Pat's cheeks turned bright red, but with a sail on his shoulder, he had no way of clipping Rhett behind the ears, an admonishment that had played out a dozen times in the past few days.

Rhett laughed, hoisted his pack on his shoulder, and walked the gangplank with a swagger that belied his nerves. However lighthearted he might try to appear, the upcoming confrontation with Peter weighed heavy. If he didn't play it just right, his fun on the continent would be over.

Rhett scanned the dock for the ship's captain so he could say his goodbyes and give his thanks. The grizzled older man was just at the edge of the gangplank, arguing with *the most stunning woman in existence. Damn.*

Rhett was an expert in the fairer sex. He'd wooed women in France and Spain, Germany and Italy, even as far away as Russia. But never had he set eyes on a woman as beautiful as the one who was currently waving a finger in the ship captain's face. Her strawberry blonde hair, locks of which had escaped her boring chignon, could be Scottish or Irish. Her delicate features could be French. Her bold stance and wild gestures reminded him of Mediterranean women.

He'd escaped England to see all the beauties Europe offered. How ironic that the most beautiful of them all had been waiting for him back home, looking completely out of place—a perfect bloom amid the mud and trash and dead fish for sale.

Instead of continuing down the jetty toward the wharf, he veered toward her instead, placing himself at the captain's shoulder. Up close, she was even more magnificent. Her blue eyes flashed like the excess of jewels sewn into her dress, which caught the morning sun and refracted rainbows onto the dark and dirty docks. She had a smattering of freckles across her cheeks—an unusual sight in a highborn woman, but one that made his fingers itch to trace them. Long, deep red lashes framed her eyes.

"We can finance our passage at twice your usual fare," she said. "We need only a few hours to have the blunt ready."

The captain crossed his arms in the same bullish stance he used when Rhett, or any of his actual subordinates, got caught messing about. "I dunnae care for the blunt. I willnae have unmarried women aboard my ship."

The vision was unmarried. *Huh.* Surprisingly, that made his day better. Married women, especially those who were shackled to old men, were more fun. Their affections were more free than those of young women on the marriage mart. But he was illogically pleased that no one had claimed this beauty as their own.

"Only unmarried women are forbidden?" The chit appeared to swell with anger, though when Rhett looked down, he could see she'd simply risen onto the balls of her feet and leaned forward. "You superstitious jackass. You cannot truly believe my sister and I would be bad luck."

"Bad luck, bad juju, ill fortune. Whatever way ye wish to describe it, yer nae coming aboard. I willnae anger the seas."

The woman huffed; a lock of hair got caught in her breath, flying upward. "But if we were men, you would allow us onboard?"

"Aye. If ye were men. Or if ye had husbands to accompany ye and ward off any tempting thoughts my men might have."

She stood still for a moment, inhaling deeply as though she was preparing to breathe fire. "Damn you, you gullible prick."

The captain turned white. Even Rhett was taken aback by such language coming from a young, well-bred woman. Taken aback, but bizarrely aroused.

She shifted, as though done with this conversation and ready to leave. Before she could, Rhett grasped her elbow, ignoring the frisson of energy that shot through his finger-tips. "Can I be of service, my lady?" *Any kind of service?* There were a hundred ways he could think of to serve her.

The young woman pursed her lips. Her gaze arrested him

entirely. "Do you have the authority to force Captain Jenkins to let me on his ship?"

Rhett looked back over his shoulder to where Jenkins was glowering. "I do not have that power, no."

"Do you have a boat of your own that can take my sister and me to France?"

"I, uh...No I don't, my lady. However..."

She raised a hand to cut him off. "Then you cannot be of service."

Her dismissal should not have cut the way it did. People had been dismissing Rhett his entire life. He was the second son of whom no one expected anything, and that had created a thick skin.

But her words pierced through it, drawing blood, as did the way she turned back to the captain as though Rhett wasn't worth thinking about. "Are there any captains who don't share your ridiculous superstitions?"

Jenkins brought a hand to his eyes and peered at the long line of ships that were tied to the wharf. "None that are sailing today."

Rhett nudged the captain with an elbow. "My lady," he murmured and then threw the woman his most charismatic smile, the one that never failed to make a woman snap open her fan, the one that was sure to win her over.

She didn't flutter her lashes or go pink at the cheeks. Instead, she rolled her eyes, blew the loose strand of hair from her face, and looked to the heavens. "Lord save me from—" Her eyes widened, and she stepped forward, grabbing him by his lapels.

Well, all right. Unexpected, but I'll take it. He reciprocated her embrace, catching her by her waist. As he did, there was a yell from above, and she threw all of her weight into spinning them away from the gangplank.

He was vaguely aware of the giant barrel that whooshed past his head and the splintering of wood exactly where he had been standing. He tried to right himself, but the turn was unexpected, and the press of her body against his had his balance off-kilter.

Together, they stumbled. He held onto her when he should have let go. He could see what was about to happen but had no way of preventing it.

They tumbled into the filth that was the Thames.

He should've closed his mouth. He should've worn a coat that was less heavy. He definitely should have expected her ear-piercing shriek.

"Why, you miserable cur." She gagged and then spat. He prepared himself for a further, well deserved, tongue-lashing, but the outrage on her face turned to panic. Her head bobbed lower in the icy water. She moved her arms frantically, but it took a moment before he realized she could not free her legs from her voluminous skirts. She was kicking and kicking, but she was going down anyway.

It took four strokes to reach her. She latched onto him, trying to push herself up using his shoulders, but all that did was push him under. It took but a second for them both to go down.

He couldn't see through the muck, but his hand collided with what was definitely a well-formed breast, and he wrapped an arm around her chest. His lungs and eyes burned. He used all his power to kick him, her, and her ridiculously heavy gown to the surface.

When they surfaced, she was spluttering and gagging. The men on the deck had thrown out a rope, and Rhett pushed her toward it.

She grabbed hold with desperate hands, and the men on the jetty towed her to shore. Once they'd hoisted her from the water, they stood back, offering handkerchiefs and wine from a distance, the latter of which she uncorked and drank directly from the bottle.

There was no rope thrown for Rhett. His legs were tiring from the additional weight of his sodden clothes and shoes. "I'll just make it back on my own, then, shall I?"

Adelaide heaved in breath after breath, choking and sputtering each time. She could kiss whoever thought to give her a bottle of cheap red wine, the bitter taste of tannins and strong oak going some distance toward masking the sour filth of river water that was at the back of her throat and up her nose. She could even feel it in her ears.

She accepted a handkerchief from a sailor, who remained as far from her as he could. Adelaide didn't blame him. She'd never smelled worse in her life.

As she blew her nose to clear out all the muck, a body crashed to the ground beside her. *Him.* She balled her fists by instinct. The bastard had almost killed her. If he had simply released her before he fell, then her lungs wouldn't now be on fire. She wouldn't be freezing. She wouldn't have pulled a muscle in her shoulder trying to fight Cordelia's skirts. She wouldn't smell like the lavatory of a dockside inn.

She turned to him, ready to unleash her fury, but stopped when she saw him roll over onto his side, his coughs still ejecting splatters of water, his eyes closed, and his muscles limp as though they'd exerted all the energy they were capable of and had given up.

Merde, Adelaide. You can't yell at a man in this state. Even if he did almost kill you. Besides, technically, he had also saved her. One might not completely erase the other, but it counted for something. She wiped a sodden lock of hair out of his eyes. "Sir? Are you okay?"

His coughing had stopped. His entire countenance was now limp. His lips were the palest shade of purple, and panic shot through her.

"Sir...?"

The ship's captain cleared his throat. "Montgomery," he said. "Everett Montgomery."

Adelaide leaned over him, cupping his head in her hand. "Mr. Montgomery, can you hear me? Are you alive?" She leaned closer to feel for breath. That was when he opened his eyes, when her lips were two inches from his and her gaze could go nowhere but to him.

"No," he rasped. "I am certainly dead. For what other explanation can there be for the sight in front of me but that she is an angel?"

"Oh, good God." Adelaide pushed away from him. "He's perfectly fine."

The ship's captain was shaking his head. The crowd of sailors sniggered.

"I wouldn't say *perfectly* fine," Everett said as he sat upright. "My boots are ruined, and all the effort I put into styling my hair this morning was completely wasted."

"Well, that is what you deserve for dragging me into the river." There was an uncomfortable flip-flop in her chest— not the good flip-flop she usually felt in the presence of handsome men like him. It was a wet and slimy flip-flop. *Oh no. Oh, please no.* There was something in her dress.

Mr. Montgomery clearly hadn't noticed her panic— despite the fact that she was gagging—given he continued to argue with her. "*You* were the catalyst for that dunking," he said, "given you were the one who pushed me off-balance."

Damn the man. Damn both creatures, the one squirming between her breasts and the one in front of her. "To save your life," she said as she reached a hand down her bodice. *Ack.* It was cold and squishy. With a churning stomach, she grasped it and yanked it away from her, tossing it at Mr. Montgomery's feet. "You would have been killed by that barrel had I not acted."

He shifted backward, nudging the wormlike creature with his toe. "Which might have been preferable, to be honest. At least if I'd been flattened like a human meat patty, I would not be covered in filth." His teeth chattered and Adelaide handed him the half-empty bottle of wine.

The ship's captain cleared his throat. "You both seem well. Miss, I apologize for not being able to assist you with your trip. Montgomery, good riddance." He drew a circle in the air, gesturing for his crew to keep moving.

"Well, isn't that gentlemanly?" Adelaide muttered. There were two other handkerchiefs that had been tossed toward her. She handed one to Mr. Montgomery and used the other to wipe her face and hands. The rest of her would have to remain sopping wet until she returned to the inn she and Cordelia had taken a room at.

"Oh, God damn." *Cordelia. She is going to combust the moment she sees the state of this gown.*

"Do you always take the Lord's name in vain in such a public manner? Most of us just do it in our heads, you know."

She rubbed her temples, hoping to ease some of the tension that had sprung up. "Most of us aren't about to face the reckoning of a lifetime."

Everett snorted. "Don't be too sure of that. A reckoning is the sole reason I'm home." He pushed himself up to standing and turned to her, giving her his hand and a rueful smile— a peace offering of sorts.

She took it. It was surprisingly warm, given the river was freezing. His fingers were lightly calloused, and his grip was strong. The fumes from the muck that covered her had clearly gone to her head because as she squeezed his hand in return, she felt a dizziness, and her chest constricted. As he pulled her upward, she was forced to rest a hand on his shoulder to keep her knees from buckling, and he caught her around the waist.

His brows furrowed in concern, and his fingers tightened at her hip. "All joking aside, are you well? Should you be standing? Can I fetch you some fresh water?"

She swallowed. Her entire body flushed hot, and it leaned toward him, completely unbidden. "I'm fine. Just a little lightheaded. I need to get out of these clothes and away from the stench before I vomit."

The corner of his lips quirked. "Stomach bile can only improve things, don't you think?"

She shouldn't giggle. Not when she was covered head to toe in refuse. Not when she was about to experience another Cordelia scolding. Not when she was facing unemployment and an uncertain future—but she couldn't help the little snort of amusement that escaped. Near-death experiences tended to undermine the gravity of almost every other catastrophe.

"Please, allow me to escort you home," Everett said, with a steadying hand still on her hip. "It is the least I can do given I pulled you into the river with me."

She hesitated.

"I don't bite, I promise. At least, not without permission." He winked, drawing another smile from her. "And I will leave you safely at your front gate."

She sighed. "It's not that. There is no home for you to escort me to, hence the attempt to gain passage to France." *And that plan is kaput. What the hell are you going to do now, Adelaide?*

"Your home is in France? What part?"

She shook her head. "There's no home there either." She'd

never had a home, as such. As a child, she'd moved from town to town with her father, going wherever the work was. They'd take rooms above a tavern, and he would do any odd job that came his way while she took on mending work. As she grew older, she'd spend the evenings at a table telling stories while he drank himself under it with the few coins men tossed in her direction. They never stayed in one place long enough to call it home. Inevitably, her father got caught trying to swindle someone, and they'd have to hotfoot it out of there immediately. Life had never been still or steady.

Everett cocked his head, the furrow between his brow deepening. "You are a very peculiar person, and I still don't know your name."

He didn't need to. The less she shared, the better. Sharing led to connection; connection led to disappointment. No one got to keep the people they cared for. Not forever. That's why one invested in bricks and mortar.

"You can call me Della."

Yet still she said, *What the hell, Adelaide?* She gave false names wherever she could, yet the nickname that no one had called her in years was what had slipped out. He had gotten a foot under her defenses without her even noticing. The last thing she needed right now was to entangle herself with another human, even if said human was devilishly attractive despite the muck covering him. He was also the kind of amusing that never failed to disarm her. Men who could make her laugh were very, very attractive.

"If I'm not escorting you home, may I at least escort you off the wharf?" He held out an elbow, and she placed a hand on it, trying not to gag at the slime that covered his sleeve.

"Thank you. I appreciate your help. Let's go—*whoa.*" Her legs immediately tangled in the layers of wet petticoats and underskirts that had almost drowned her earlier, and she went down *hard*. Only Everett, yanking on the arm she'd given him, stopped her from whacking her chin on the brine-soaked wood. "Damnation." She shook her head as she scrambled to a sitting position. Her ears flamed hot with embarrassment.

Everett squatted so he was eye to eye with her. "Are you all right?"

"Fine," she mumbled. This was the first time she'd worn such an elaborate dress. It had taken her a minute to navigate the skirts when she'd first put it on. The soaking was an added complication she hadn't considered. "I didn't think..."

Everett smiled. "That your dress has murderous intentions? No. Most people don't assume that. Can you stand?"

"I can stand," she said, accepting his hand as he levered her up. "I'm just not sure I can walk." She leaned over and tried to bundle the skirts, but she couldn't even reach the inner layer that had entwined itself around her legs, plastering them together. "God damn it."

Everett snorted. "Your vocabulary is to be admired. What finishing school did you go to?"

"The school of life, Mr. Montgomery."

"Call me Rhett."

"Rhett." It suited him. It was far less stuffy than Mr. Montgomery.

"There are two solutions to this problem," he said. "I'm not sure you'll like either."

"I'm listening."

"The first is that I carry you to that tavern at the end of the wharf. It will have a bathroom of questionable cleanliness where you can extricate yourself from your clothes."

Oh no. Not a good idea, Adelaide. He is too good-looking and funny and kind for you to let him carry you. The river had plastered his clothes to his body, and even through his shirt, waistcoat, and jacket, she could see the definition of hard muscle along his arms and chest. It had been a long time since Adelaide had been pressed up against a man, and Rhett was exactly the kind of man she would choose, had she the time and freedom. But Cordelia was currently sitting in a small room above a dockside tavern, and the longer it took Adelaide to secure them passage out of London, the more of Cordelia's whining she'd have to face.

"What is option two?" she said, hoping her voice didn't sound as strangled as it felt.

He shrugged. "I help you disrobe here. I'm very good with petticoats. I can get them off faster than any lady's maid can."

She rolled her eyes. "You sound very certain."

"It's a fact. There was a competition last year, and I wiped the floor with everyone else."

Don't ask, Adelaide. Just don't. But she couldn't help herself. "What kind of establishment hosts a petticoat removal competition?"

It was Rhett's turn to flush bright red. "That's not really relevant to this current situation, is it?"

Ha. She knew very well the type of establishment in which he'd made a name for himself.

Adelaide looked around. Sailors were trailing to and from the ship like lines of ants, carrying cargo off and returning with empty arms to reload. Each one that passed looked at her and Rhett with unbridled curiosity. There was no way on this good earth that she was going to allow Rhett beneath her skirts with such an audience, even if the purpose was innocent.

"Fine," she ground out. "Carry me." She put her arms around his shoulders, trying to ignore the frisson of energy that went through her. *Get a grip on yourself, Adelaide. This is not the time for untoward thoughts.* But they plagued her anyway, heating her from within.

Rhett wrapped an arm beneath her skirts and swung her against his chest. "*Ooof.*" He stumbled forward, causing her to grab onto his neck with both arms, convinced they were both about to plow headfirst into the jetty.

He steadied himself, though, and she shot him a scathing look. "For what it's worth, you are not supposed to grunt when you pick up a woman. It's not at all flattering."

He smiled ruefully. "It is not you. You are a delight to hold. It is the weight of the Thames, which has hidden itself in your skirts. Did we leave any water in the river? I didn't check."

Adelaide rolled her eyes. "Shall we get going? The sooner I'm out of this dress, the better."

"*Agreed.*"

She snorted. He was a practiced flirt. No doubt he'd charmed his way through Europe, and now he was charming her, which was delicious, actually. No one had flirted with her in months, not since she'd given up writing travelogues to become a lady's maid. It had been such a rotten, stressful day that perhaps she was entitled to some diversion. So she let her body loosen and allowed herself to sink into his arms.

However off-balance he'd been when he first lifted her, he had no difficulty carrying her and Cordelia's dress down the jetty. His arms remained strong, and his stride was long and sure. It was nice to have someone caring for her for a change. The only thing she'd change about this particular moment was the scent that surrounded them.

Whatever Rhett might smell like in normal life—and she suspected it was divine—it couldn't cut through the putrid odor they shared. The sailors they walked past gave them a wide berth. But as long as she took short, shallow breaths, she could almost ignore the smell and just enjoy the feeling of being in someone's arms again.

Chapter Three

Carrying beautiful ladies was one of the few tasks at which Rhett was almost guaranteed to shine. He'd carried them from ballrooms after they'd swooned; he'd carried them across meadows after they'd conveniently turned an ankle. He'd carried them to bed. But even he wasn't delusional enough to think he was making a positive impression on the woman currently in his arms. Quite besides the fact that he reeked, his boots squelched in a way that said "child playing in puddles" more than "gallant rogue," and the threshold he'd just crossed was not into a candlelit bedroom but the seediest, most disgusting tavern in England.

He could feel her tense in his arms.

"This place is...disgusting," she said.

"Which is why we're here. No reputable establishment would let us enter."

She sighed. "That's probably true."

It was definitely true. The wet footprints he was leaving on the grubby stone floor were crime scenes in themselves. He strode directly to the back of the room, where he kicked open the door to the bathroom.

"Sorry about the smell," he said.

"At this point, does it even matter?" she asked.

Rhett smiled. Most ladies would tear strips off of him for taking them to such a place. This mystery woman was, at least, pragmatic . . . and quite likely not *ton* at all, despite the dress. She was an enigma.

He tried to find the least urine-stained piece of floor to set her down.

She steadied herself with a hand on his arm and his insides flip-flopped unexpectedly.

Before he could say anything charming or witty, the door behind them crashed open and a drunken sailor entered, the fly of his trousers already unlaced. His enigma looked away, drawing a hand to her eyes to block the view.

Rhett wished he'd had that same luxury. The man's shriveled todger was already exposed when Rhett grabbed him by the shoulders and pushed him back the way he entered.

"But I need to take a piss," the sailor whined.

"Find somewhere else." Rhett slammed the door shut, but then thought better of it and pulled the door wide again. The sailor hadn't gotten far. He was so drunk he was still processing his eviction. "Hot water," Rhett said. "Lots of it. A dress, if you can find one, and one of the kitchen maids. I'll make it worth your while."

The sailor's eyes narrowed. "How much worth my while?"

"I'll pay your bar tab," Rhett responded.

"Righto." The sailor shuffled away. Whether he had the cognitive function required to act on Rhett's demands remained to be seen. Rhett would give it ten minutes, and if there wasn't at least one steaming bucket of hot water in sight, he would find some other means of acquiring one without leaving her unattended.

"All clear," he said to Della. She lowered her hand and gave him a funny look.

"What is it?" he asked.

"You are ... thoughtful, Mr. Montgomery."

He blushed. That wasn't the type of compliment he was used to getting. Uncomfortable, he scratched the back of his neck. "We'll wait for water and a kitchen maid to help free you."

"And you?"

"Will stay here until she arrives and then guard the door. I make no promises about the direction my thoughts will go in."

The woman snorted. "I'm sure I can guess."

His instinct was to find a wall to lean against. Women liked leaning, or so he'd heard. Leaning on walls, leaning on desks, leaning over them. He was his most impressive at a sixty-five-degree incline. But there was no wall fit to touch. "So tell me," he said, crossing his arms instead. "What brings a woman like you, in a dress like that, to the London docks?"

She shifted her gaze to her sleeves, which she tried to tug back into their original puffs. "I am seeking passage to the continent."

Obviously. "So you said to the captain. Passage for you and your—"

"Sister."

She was concise—yet another divergence from his usual female companionship. "And does your sister also wear her fortune sewn all over her body?" He would tease her out from her armor before the afternoon was through.

She sighed and rolled her eyes. The buckles were undone, at least. "No. She has more common sense than that. She is more like you. Her clothing is functional rather than decorative."

He drew a hand to his chest in what was only part mock outrage. "Are you suggesting that I am frumpy?"

She wrinkled her nose. "Not at all. Clearly, you are the epitome of style. Forgive me. I don't know how I overlooked it."

He took a step back, brushing down his lapels and trying not to wince at the glutinous feel of them. "I would have you know my coat is made of the finest German wool. It is—was—a good portion of my fortune."

She smiled and it drove away a little of the cold, at least. "It is a very fine coat, despite its current state."

"Thank you. It has been with me for many adventures. Alas, I think it has seen its last. At least it went out saving the life of a beautiful woman."

She flushed pink and diverted her gaze, running her fingers across her brow, as though his compliment was having precisely the effect on her that was intended. He could win her over.

There was a knock at the door, and Rhett straightened, stepping in front of her to block the view from the main room of the tavern.

A young girl opened the door. A dark line streaked across her hairline where sweat had mingled with dirt and dust. Two buckets of steaming water were at her feet, a shirt and pants were draped over her arm. "I was told I was needed in here, sir."

Rhett nodded and took a bucket of water in each hand. He stepped out of the way so the young girl could attend to Della.

The maid only got a few feet into the room before she stopped dead, her nose wrinkling. "No," she said, taking a step backward. "Lord, no." She untied her apron and tossed it at Rhett's feet along with the clothes. "Good luck with that, sir." Then she slammed shut the door behind her.

Damnation. "I...uh." Rhett turned around, grimacing.

"I'm not sure what to do here." He didn't know this woman well enough to strip her of her clothes. Not that you needed a person's entire life history to do so, but you did need enthusiastic consent, and usually some kissing first.

The woman closed her eyes and sighed. "It will have to be you."

Rhett's heart rate picked up, and he swallowed hard, trying to keep his inner desire from having any external expression. "Pardon?" He was surprised the frog in his throat let the words out.

"Don't tell me Mr. 'I can remove women's petticoats in under ten seconds' was all talk." Her gentle teasing loosened the parts of him that had frozen.

"I never promised to do it in less than ten seconds," he said, struggling to remove his wet coat. "In fact, I'm not sure I can divest you of this monstrosity in ten minutes. But I'll try."

She turned her back to him, giving him free access to the dozens of tiny buttons that ran from her shoulders to the small of her back. They were damn fiddly ones—the kind he didn't enjoy working with even when they were dry.

She sensed his hesitation and simply said, "Tear them. Otherwise, we'll be here for hours."

He could not think of a single woman of his acquaintance who would take such a practical attitude toward the day's events. He searched through the maid's apron and thankfully found a pocketknife.

Before he could take it to her dress, some basic tidying was needed. At some point in the dunking, or in the chaos afterward, most of her hair had come undone, with only a couple of pins to hold up what remained. Gently, he tugged them out, and the locks flopped down. He stuck the pins in his pocket, then he took all her hair, combed through it gently with his fingers, parsed it out into three lengths, and braided it. Then he gently placed it over her shoulder.

She picked up the braid and studied it. "Where did you learn to do that?"

"I have three sisters," he said, picking up the knife. "I can braid hair and pour tea. Teddy bear teatime was taken seriously in our playroom." The thought made him smile. He'd been avoiding coming home, and he was not at all excited about his upcoming conversation with Peter, but damn, it would be nice to see the girls again.

The knife was blessedly sharp and cut through each loop that constrained a button with relative ease. With each slice, more of her underclothes were revealed. The chemise was plain, rough cotton, completely incongruous with the quality of the dress. The corset was equally thin and austere. The mystery of her deepened.

He worked swiftly, trying to ignore the swell of his cock as more of her was exposed to him. Her shoulders were practically bare. The wet fabric was practically transparent. Once all the buttons were free and he'd undone the ties of the small horsehair bustle, there was nothing to keep him from viewing her perfect form, accentuated by the way the fabric clung to her skin.

"Should I cut away the petticoat too?" It was well and truly tangled around her legs. No wonder she couldn't move two steps.

"No," she said forcefully. "I can save it with a good wash."

Rhett doubted it. There was nothing he was wearing that he didn't plan on tossing into the fire. A laundry maid would have to scrub for hours to get the filth out, and he wouldn't subject the lass to that. It was odd, though, that Della was so willing to take a knife to her elaborate dress but was determined to save cheap underclothes.

"I'm going to unwrap it from you, then," he said to her. "I'll have to put one hand on your thigh and reach between your legs with the other."

She nodded her consent, a flush of pink creeping up her chest.

He knelt down, keen to hide the jerk of his erection. Her skin felt clammy and cold beneath his hand, but when his other hand grazed the inside of her thigh to grab the hem of her skirt, warmth touched them both.

Gods. The sooner he was out of this misery, the better. He needed to address his own needs—a freezing cold bucket of water intended to do more than sluice away the muck.

Finally, her skirts were unwrapped, and he untied the knot around her waist. Rhett kept hold of the fabric as she stepped out of it. She turned to face him, her cheeks red, one arm crossed over her chest, the other covering what it could of her drawers. "Thank you," she murmured. "I'll keep the rest of the clothing on, I think."

Rhett swallowed. "That's a good idea." To avoid looking at her, he studied the floor where they stood. The buckets were no longing steaming. He tested the temperature and then raised one. "Turn around."

She did so, and having her back toward him with her round derriere so perfectly displayed did nothing to cool his ardor. He dumped the water over her head. It cascaded off her in rivulets, running down her bare skin and dripping off of her chemise.

Torture. Complete fucking torture. He handed her the soap so that she could clean herself properly, and then turned away. Some visions he didn't need to capture as memories. Such memories might drive him mad.

"I'm ready now," she said.

Thank the Gods. He picked up the last bucket of water.

He was more targeted this time. He poured slowly, making sure that the water rinsed every inch of her.

As she stood under the stream, she turned, raising her head so that he could rinse her face. Her lips were angled perfectly. It would take no effort at all to lean down and press his lips to hers. Instead, he clamped them shut. She was so damned close, and this was, without a doubt, the most intimate he had ever been with a person. He'd slept with many women, he'd bathed with some, but never had he performed such ministrations.

"Thank you," she murmured as the last drop of water hit the puddle at their feet. Her hands were crossed in front of her chest. Clearly, she was just as conscious of her transparent underclothes as he was.

This would be the time for a witty remark, something to make her laugh and hide just how discombobulated she made him, but the English language seemed to have disappeared from his brain. He didn't enjoy feeling this...bare. Naked was fine. Naked was as good an armor as a joke. Bare was a state he refused to be in.

He picked up the clothes the kitchen maid had left. They'd been sitting on top of a towel, which was now so piss-stained from the lavatory floor it was unusable. He handed the shirt to her, and she tugged it on, struggling where her wet skin caught hold of the fabric.

Deftly, she buttoned the collar. Rhett was certain she intended to look more demure all done up, but the sight of her in an oversized man's shirt that barely existed was more erotic an image than her practically naked had been.

He wanted it to be *his* shirt she was wearing. Not the particular shirt on his body right now, but a future, clean shirt.

He wanted her, not just because she was the most stunning woman he'd ever seen, but because throughout this entire ordeal, she'd remained calm and practical; she'd even found humor in it. There wasn't a single woman he knew who would have responded with such good grace.

He had no idea why she'd been wearing that damned dress. It had fooled him at first glance. She'd appeared like a high-society miss, but that wasn't possible.

She got to work on the buttons that closed the fly front of the trousers and then rolled the waistband over itself until it somewhat fit on her body. He couldn't take his eyes off of her fingers—long and nimble. They moved quickly with a softness that immediately made him imagine them hooked around the buttons of his trousers.

He dragged in a deep breath.

"Thank you," she said once she had rolled the hem of the trousers so they wouldn't drag on the ground.

"Think nothing of it." *Don't stop thinking of it.* The gods only knew he wouldn't.

Then she stepped closer to him, and his mouth ran dry. The hairs on the back of his neck prickled. When she rose onto her toes and reached her lips to his, he stopped breathing. Her kiss was soft and sweet, but not unpracticed. She deepened it with no hesitation.

His instinct was to wrap an arm around her waist and draw her to him, but he hadn't gone through hell trying to get her clean just to cover her with his filth, so he kept as much distance between them as kissing would allow. By the time she had finished, there were stars in his vision, and there was a good chance he was about to swoon. He inhaled, and by the time oxygen filled his lungs, she had put several feet between them.

"Thank you, Rhett. Good luck with your reckoning. I'm sure it can't be worse than what you've already faced today."

He tried to revert to his usual roguish self, but her kiss

had left him feeling as though nothing fit well anymore. He faked a satisfied smirk. "Everything I've faced today led to a beautiful woman kissing me. I could be smitten by all the world's gods simultaneously, and it would still be worth it."

She laughed, a truly joyous giggle. "I'll carry that thought with me as I face my own reckoning." Carefully, she gathered her spoiled dress and rolled it into a giant ball, trying to keep it well away from her body.

"How can I see you again?" he asked as he realized she was leaving. Because, gods, he wanted to see her again. Not a single liaison had ever left him feeling so addled.

She sighed and looked genuinely disappointed. "It's not in the cards for us. I do not know where I'll be a day from now. But wherever it is, I'll remember you."

And with that, she walked out of his life.

Chapter Four

Stupid, stupid, stupid, Adelaide. Why did you kiss him?

Because he was handsome and funny and had tended to her with a care she hadn't felt in a decade. Because as he'd braided her hair, she'd felt a peace that she was entirely unused to. When she traveled, she always had a part of herself ready to flee at a moment's notice. She never entirely relaxed. Even once she'd taken the position of lady's maid, there was always that preparedness to leap into action at Cordelia's whim.

With Rhett's fingers combing through her hair, her entire body had gone limp. A decade of alertness had disappeared in the space of minutes. No man had ever made her feel like this. There was something calm, and sure, and content about the moment despite the fact that they were in what was likely the seediest tavern in England. She could not imagine a more disgusting place to kiss a man, yet she had.

Stupid, stupid, stupid, Adelaide. She had enough on her plate. She didn't need the distraction.

Yet still, she wondered. How hard would it be to find an Everett Montgomery in England? Once she'd settled things and Cordelia was again ensconced in the bosom of her family, once Adelaide had put aside enough money to be free, could she—would she—find him again?

She trudged up the stairs of the Briarstone Inn and knocked on a door with the three-two-three pattern they'd discussed previously.

Cordelia opened it. "What in heaven's name happened to you?"

"It is a long story."

"Adelaide, you reek."

"I am aware; and trust me when I say I smell a lot better than I did an hour ago."

"Impossible," Cordelia muttered, standing aside so that Adelaide could enter. "You smell like a rotting cat that took a dip in the Thames."

Cordelia wasn't far off, but Adelaide did not have the energy to explain it. Besides, then she'd have to explain Rhett, and she didn't want to share the memory of him with her employer. That was hers to keep tucked into her chest.

"What time does the ship leave?" Cordelia asked. "Are you sure you know what to do once we reach France?"

"There is no ship leaving today that will take us, my lady."

"*What?*" Cordelia's shriek raised all of Adelaide's hackles. "Where are we going to go? What are we going to do? We cannot stay in London, Adelaide. Someone will find us."

Adelaide took a deep breath and faced her mistress. "Would that be the worst thing?"

Cordelia looked like a stunned fish. "What are you suggesting?"

"Perhaps we should return to your father's house." It had been Adelaide's first instinct to flee, but first instinct and rational thought were two very different beasts. Now that she'd had time for the latter, sending Cordelia back home seemed the wisest move.

"No. He will be too angry. And somebody will see me. The papers are likely waiting outside my house. I cannot go back until the gossip has died off."

"My lady, what you're asking of me is a great deal." Certainly, it was more trouble than this posting was worth. Had Cordelia gone through with the match, she would now be the Duchess of Hornsmouth, and Adelaide's wages would have doubled. Now she was left wondering what other roles she might be more suited to that could bring her dream of her very own home to fruition.

"This is your fault." Cordelia stood with arms akimbo. "You are the one who told me to leave Hornsmouth."

Adelaide took a step back. "Pardon?"

"Last night. You said, 'Why are you even going ahead with it?' "

Fuck me. "It was three in the morning. I'd spent an entire night listening to you elucidate the duke's same four faults. I was tired, and I spoke out of turn."

"You did."

"I didn't think you'd heard me."

"Well, you were wrong, and as I walked down that aisle, your words echoed over and over."

Good Lord, Adelaide. What have you done?

Cordelia narrowed her eyes. "It is your fault as much as it is mine that we are here, so you must help me."

That ratio of responsibility seemed miles off, but if there was even a sliver of blame to put on Adelaide, she couldn't throw Cordelia to the wolves. One certain wolf, in particular. "Fine. We will hide out for a week until London finds something else to talk about, but then we will return to your father."

"A month."

"A fortnight only."

"You underestimate how many people will enjoy my fall from grace."

"A month then, but you must guarantee my wages."

"Done."

"Fine."

Adelaide stalked to the fireplace and tossed Cordelia's dress in, shuddering at the sharp hiss as damp fabric encountered flame. The fire dwindled. She pulled on the rope that would call one of the inn's maids. She needed proper clothing and more wood. She could pick the jewels off Cordelia's dress from the ashes.

As she waited, she paced the room, searching for a solution other than sailing to France. She thought back to all the maps she'd studied while looking for new towns and experiences to write about. They needed somewhere no one would think to search for them. A small village, not a city. Everyone would expect them to go where Cordelia could still have her luxuries.

Berwick. It doesn't even make it onto most maps.

"I know somewhere, but you cannot go as yourself. It would create too much gossip, and that would travel to London no matter where we hid."

"If you're about to suggest that I be *your* maid—"

"Sisters," Adelaide interjected before Cordelia could say anything that would make the day harder. "We will travel as spinster sisters who are looking for a cottage to let."

"A cottage? You want me to stay in a cottage?"

Adelaide rolled her eyes. "Where did you think we were going to stay? Even if we had made it to France, we still would have had to lie low until the gossip died and you were ready to face your father. That was never going to be in a manor house."

Cordelia flopped back on the bed. "This is the worst day of my life."

Cordelia was fully dry, wearing Adelaide's nicest dress, still smelling of the jasmine oil Adelaide had put in her bathwater before the wedding. But sure. *Cordelia* was having the worst day.

Later that night, as she stared into the flames and tried not to inhale, she felt an overwhelming sense of wanting. Not to be anywhere but here, which was a familiar feeling, but to be in one place specifically—in London's most disgusting bathroom with Rhett Montgomery.

Not a single hackney cab would take Rhett home, especially given his pack was sitting at the bottom of the Thames along with the diary he'd been writing in and his money pouch. When the tavern had realized that he had no way of paying for the soap, water, and change of clothes they had given him, they'd booted him out before he could get clean. He'd walked three hours in wet boots, his heels rubbing raw, until he'd found someone willing to overlook his bedraggled state and lease him a horse on the condition that he purchase the saddle at an exorbitant price once he reached the duke's residence because there was no way the reek of the river would come out of the leather.

The entire time, he was thinking of the beautiful woman whose kiss had completely undone him, which was ridiculous. As far as his semi-naked encounters went, that one was tame, but it had left him with an unbearable needing.

Which meant to say that his mood was worse than his odor by the time he reached his brother's London residence.

"You can forget about coming into my kitchen," the duke's cook said, waving a spoon at him.

"Mrs. Brown, surely you wouldn't reject your most beloved Montgomery sibling?" He gave her the same cheeky grin he used to give when he swiped hot biscuits from the bench. She had always *tsk*ed but would let him walk away with a handful anyway.

Not today. "I reject that god-awful stench and the way you're dripping it onto my porch. Get off with you. Go around and use the front door like a proper gentleman."

Rhett sighed. "Bennett has already denied me entrance." It was hardly the homecoming he'd been expecting. Usually, he was feted with open arms by family and staff alike, but the butler didn't want a single drop of the river to land on the polished marble floor of the foyer and had shooed him away.

"Then go to the stables and get hosed off. You can't be smelling like that."

The stables, where he'd just been. Where the groom had taken one look at him, muttered a brusque, "My lord," and then quickly found work well elsewhere.

"Can I at least have a biscuit? I'm starving, and there's not a single cook on the continent that can measure up to your baking."

Mrs. Brown flushed pink and tucked the wooden spoon into the front pocket of her apron. "I'll send someone to the stables with a plate. Now get going before the very presence of you contaminates tonight's dinner." She turned her back on him and motioned for the kitchen maids to return to their work.

As he headed toward the stables, he kicked along a pebble. "Welcome home, my lord," he muttered to himself. "How wonderful to see you. The house has been dull as dishwater without you."

Not that the house would have been dull, exactly. He had three sisters who lived at Montgomery House, and the younger two could certainly create as much havoc as he did. But he liked to think that he added a certain joie de vivre to the stately home, and that his presence had been missed.

Instead, even the horses shied away from him as he entered the stables.

Damn it. He stripped to his smalls and dumped his ruined clothing in a pile. It would need to be tossed onto a fire. There was no salvaging any of it.

He took a battered metal pail from the corner of the stables and placed it beneath the pump outside. Dumping one bucketful of water over his head did practically nothing to the grime that had affixed itself to him. At this rate, it would be half an hour before he was clean enough to step foot in the house.

He'd just filled a third bucket at the pump when his middle sister sang out from behind him.

"Rhett!" Jacqueline might be of age, but deportment training had done nothing to curb her liveliness. She could still be heard before she was even seen. "Bennett said you're home and that you need a change of—" She stumbled as she caught sight and smell of him. Pressing a hand to her lips, she blanched, crinkling her nose as she did so, causing her spectacles to slip. The hand at her mouth caught them before they could fall to the ground. "Oh, good God. What happened to you?"

What happened? He'd been pitched into the Thames by a beautiful woman who had smelled like lemons in that moment before they'd hit the water, and who had left him yearning. *Yearning*, for heaven's sake. Like an unworldly pup.

"It was an unfortunate mishap," he said. That said, if he could do it over again, he would do exactly the same. He would treasure that kiss until he was old and failing.

"I cannot even put into words how bad you smell."

"Thank you, sister." What would life have been like as an only child? "Shouldn't you be out paying calls or something? Or is this season as dull as the last?"

"This season has not been cut short like last year's, more's the pity. You could have ruined this one too." Jac hugged the shirt and trousers she carried to her chest. "Being out is bollocks."

Rhett snorted. London society was bollocks. She wasn't wrong. But if he had to be in London, tickling those bollocks made for an enjoyable pastime. "Finagle me an invitation to whichever ball you're attending tonight, and I promise you some fun."

The duke wanted to see him promptly, but escorting his sister to a ball was a perfectly reasonable excuse to delay his travel to the Strafford country estate where his brother was residing.

Gritting his teeth, he closed his eyes and dumped the bucket of water over his head.

"What the jumping jacks have you been doing? You smell like you've been rolling around in a pig's wallow."

He didn't need to open his eyes to know who spoke. It wasn't enough to have one sister catch him in such a state—wet, filthy, and wearing nothing but drawers. His youngest sister, the least likely to let him live it down, was also witness to his debacle.

He wiped the water from his eyes with the back of his hand and fixed Edwina with a mock glare. A full decade younger than Rhett, she had a sharp tongue that had not yet been dulled by society's demand for propriety. "Rolling around? You speak as though I'm an animal."

"You are an animal, brother. You're naked in a stable, washing in a bucket." Winnie snorted—horselike, he might add.

"I am not naked, and you are insufferable." She would bring this moment up whenever she wanted to score a point for the rest of their lives.

"Oh, believe me, I'm suffering," Winnie continued. "Every

creature within a mile of you is suffering. Perhaps Bennett will make you sleep in the stables tonight, and the horses can take your room."

If he had anything near him, he'd throw it at her. Especially if it was something that had accompanied him into the river. But all he had was the bucket, which he needed if he was going to wash the muck from him. He settled for sticking out his tongue.

And that dignified expression was the first thing his twin, Margaret Montgomery, now Lady Titteler, saw as she rounded the corner of the barn, one hand holding a plate of Mrs. Brown's warm shortbread. She had a wide smile on her face that warped as she wrinkled her nose.

"What happened to you?" she asked.

"An unfortunate mishap, apparently," Jac replied.

"I fell into the Thames."

Because his younger sisters were confirmed devils, they dissolved into a pile of giggles. "Shall we place bets on how it happened?" Winnie asked when she could compose herself. "I think he lost a bet with one of the crew he'd been traveling with, and they tossed him in."

Jac shook her head. "It was a prank that backfired. He tried to toss someone else in, and he slipped."

"Maybe Lord Baltiford heard Rhett was returning home and was waiting for him when the ship docked."

"Maybe it was Lady Baltiford, who, I heard, is still peevish that Rhett left in the first place."

Rhett scowled and pumped furiously to fill another bucket. The sooner he was clean and dressed, the sooner he'd not be at such a disadvantage. "Next time you wonder why I spend my time on the continent, remember this moment."

Jac and Winnie continued to giggle. Meg sighed. "That's enough, sisters. Edwina, go fetch a horse blanket." She crossed to Rhett, ignoring the filth she stepped in as she neared, and planted a firm kiss on his cheek. "Welcome home, brother. You've been missed."

At last, someone cared. It was always Meg. He and his twin were closer than two people ought to be. "I'd hug you," he said.

She stepped back. "Don't you dare touch me. Don't touch anything."

Rhett looked longingly at the plate of shortbread she still carried. Every second, the biscuits cooled further.

She rolled her eyes and held one up so he could take a bite.

"Gods, that's delicious," he said through a mouth of crumbs.

"I'll make sure Mrs. Brown sends a plate to the drawing room when you come inside. Then you can tell me all about your travels now that you're finally home."

There was the slightest hint of reproach in her tone. He should write more when he was away. He was a terrible correspondent. He could never quite capture his adventures properly when he put pen to page, so he had given up trying. Meg was a constant source of news and a tether to the family that he didn't reciprocate nearly enough.

She handed the plate of biscuits to Jac before returning to the house.

Deliberately, with a satisfied smirk on her face, his middle sister took all three remaining biscuits and stuffed them in her mouth at once.

"You devil child." For months, he had been dreaming of Mrs. Brown's shortbread.

Her mouth was so full, the grin she gave in response barely looked human. Winnie *hmph*ed as she handed Rhett a coarse, wide blanket from the stalls. No doubt she, too, had been looking forward to a biscuit.

He wrapped the blanket around his waist, never taking his eyes off Jac. "You are going to pay for that."

She backed up a step, and then a second, but there would be no escaping him. He launched forward with all the speed of a man used to sparring in a ring. She dropped the plate to flee, but she was seconds too late. He bent down, and caught her around the stomach, flipping her over his shoulder.

"Ew. No. Put me down. Your filth is going to transfer." She pounded on his back with his fists. "Rheeeeeett."

Her screams were like finding a proper ale pie in some hole-in-the-wall café in Greece—a sweet, sweet reminder of home. With a satisfied smirk, he dumped her in the mud by the pump.

Three hours and two entire cakes of soap later, Rhett was sitting in his favorite armchair by a roaring fire, a full plate of biscuits and a pot of tea on the table next to him. However apprehensive he was about his upcoming conversation with the duke, this was bliss. Distance made one appreciate the little touches of home more.

Meg entered. She dropped a quick kiss on Rhett's damp curls and then sniffed.

"I know," he said before she could mention it. "I lathered my hair a dozen times."

She reached into her skirts and pulled out a small bottle of perfumed oil. "Here. This will mask it until it fades."

"Thank you." He uncorked the bottle and tipped a generous amount of oil into his hands. It had the sweet summer scent of jasmine. He rubbed it over his fingers and then through his hair. For good measure, he scraped at the remnants on his palm with his fingers, hoping to dislodge the smell that had taken up residence under his nails.

Once she'd settled her skirts around her comfortably, Meg folded her hands in her lap, looking for all the world like their mother had years ago. "Why are you home, brother? There's no wedding, christening, or funeral."

Rhett shifted uncomfortably. "Can't I come home simply because I wanted to see my family for Christmas?"

She smiled. "You can, by all means, but you haven't. You missed the last five Christmases, after all."

There was no point in keeping anything from his twin. He could hedge his words as much as he wanted to, she would still extract the truth from him. She was tenacious that way.

"The duke called me home. It seems he's become dissatisfied with my life of late."

"I can't imagine why that would be," she said dryly. "Perhaps it has something to do with all the women. Or all the wine."

"Which you only know about because I write you."

Margaret narrowed her eyes. "Occasionally. You write me occasionally."

He'd walked right into that jab. "Yes," he conceded, "but my point is that my international adventures are always discreet. Unless you've been gossiping where you ought not, the duke does not know about them."

She shook her head. "They are not as discreet as you think, or have you forgotten Finland?"

Rhett shifted uncomfortably. Getting arrested for public indecency had earned him a postal tongue-lashing from his brother. "That was one time. He knows of nothing else."

"That one time caused havoc here in England. We were forced to leave London early to avoid the gossip." Meg was looking at him with an expression of disapproval he rarely received from her, and it made him want to squirm in his seat.

"I've done nothing so feckless since." At least, nothing that had made it across Europe.

Meg *tsk*ed. "Perhaps it's the *nothing* that Peter objects to. You've been gallivanting around the continent for years now with no sign that it's leading anywhere. At some point, you are going to have to give up this nomadic lifestyle and come home. Find a career. Find a wife. Add another branch to the Montgomery family tree."

The thought sent a shiver down his spine. The entire purpose of traveling the continent was to distance himself from the family name. He told no one that he was part of *that* Montgomery family, the Duke of Strafford's Montgomery family. Hell, half the time he didn't give a last name at all. Being the perpetual lesser brother in England was hard enough. He refused to be so elsewhere.

"I have no wish to come home, Meg. I can't think of anything more suffocating."

She frowned. "You'd rather drink your way through Europe? Still? It might have been justified in the beginning after what that woman did to you, but are you not coming to find it tiring?"

"No, I'm not." Rhett studied his fingernails to avoid looking at his sister, else she would see the truth. Exploration had once created a near-constant state of gratification, but now it was peppered with moments of ennui, and those moments were stretching in duration.

It terrified him.

If he was a disappointment in England and disenchanted on the continent, what else was there for him? A wife and family? Hardly. Women didn't want black sheep. They wanted the golden goose, or golden ram. Whichever. Rhett had experienced it firsthand. The memory of it was burned into his brain—him, standing with a dozen tulips, ready to propose like an utter fool, and Lady Meredith Moylan caught whispering to her friend.

"Three weeks, and he has yet to introduce me to the duke. How long do you suppose I'm to feign interest before I find another way?"

It had shattered something within him. She hadn't wanted him; Peter had been the prize she'd truly sought. Of course he was. He was the duke, and Rhett was not.

Rhett had no plans to repair those broken bits of himself. They could stay where they were, stacked into a barricade.

"I have no intention of coming home or marrying. I'm completely satisfied with my life as it is."

Meg narrowed her eyes. "But what about children?"

Rhett slumped in his chair with a carefree shrug. "I'll be the *fun* uncle. The duke can be the responsible one. He does responsibility so well, don't you think? No point competing with that."

There was no point trying to compete with his brother at anything. Peter would always be richer, taller, and titled. Peter was the one who women sought for marriage and who men sought the good graces of. Rhett was merely valued for his familial ties.

"What of a career then?"

Rhett cocked his head. "Careful, sister. You are sounding like our brother."

"I don't think Peter is wrong."

He tugged at his upstanding collar, his pulse ratcheting up. "There is nothing I'm good at, other than excess. Everything I try, I fail at. Now, I beg you to drop it. I will experience disdain enough from Peter. I do not need it from you too." In frustration, he unknotted his string tie and cast it aside.

There was a long pause, and Rhett could see his sister tally up the pros and cons of pressing him. Evidently, she landed on peace, rearranging herself in her seat and putting on a bright smile. "I think Peter has decided to take a wife. He wrote last week and asked if the duchess's suite was up to snuff."

Rhett pondered the consequences of that. Once Peter married and had a son, Rhett would not even be the heir. Would that be an improvement or a further embarrassment?

Jac and Winnie both entered Meg's drawing room, Jac also freshly showered. She scowled as she took a seat on the settee across from him. "I had to throw out my slippers, you know."

Rhett nudged the plate of biscuits toward his sister. "I'll take you shopping for another pair. Unless the duke has closed your accounts too?"

"No."

Well, that was a relief. "Good. While we're at it, I need some new boots. I might have survived a dunking in the Thames, but they didn't, and I do not have another pair."

Jac sniggered. "Who trips into the river? Were you drunk?"

Rhett drew himself up and tried to look impressive. "If you must know, I was saving a life."

All three girls exchanged dubious glances. "Whose?" Jac asked.

"I do not know her full name." And for that, he was truly sorry. "But she was beautiful, and if I hadn't risked my life, the outrageous dress she was wearing would have drowned her. I'm surprised she could even stand upright under the weight of all those jewels."

There was a collective gasp. "He's not talking about..."

"You don't think..."

"Surely not..."

"It's possible she left England," Winnie said. "I might, under the circumstances."

All three sisters nodded in agreement, but they apparently didn't feel the need to enlighten him.

"What are you talking about?" If it had something to do with his enigma, he needed to know about it.

Jac turned to him. "Did she have red hair? And was about yea high?" Rhett's heart yammered unexpectedly as his sister stood and held up a hand just above her own head.

"She did. She was. Do you know her? Who is she?"

Winnie leaned forward, hands clasped in excitement. "Brother, you met Lady Cordelia Highwater. Who, as of this morning, is the most infamous debutante in London."

She didn't look infamous. Ridiculous gown aside, she looked as fresh as new snow. She also wasn't a debutante, and she was definitely not *ton*. She was too practical; she was too quick to utter the words "gullible prick," and she had kissed him in a filthy tavern.

"She was supposed to be Her Grace, the Duchess of Hornsmouth," Jac said. "But she fled from her wedding this morning. One moment, she was at the altar, and then the next, she was running like demons from hell were after her. It was splendid to watch."

Winnie frowned. "I missed all the excitement. I wasn't invited because I'm not out. It was the biggest scandal of the year, and I was stuck at home."

For once, the gossip didn't intrigue him. He had thought his sisters could shed light on who Della was, but the two could not possibly be the same person. She had a mouth that could make a sailor blush and a forthright demeanor that was devilishly attractive. Perhaps she was an actress.

"Did she say anything to you?" Meg asked. "Did she give any clue why she was leaving London?"

"All she said was how grateful she was that I saved her life and that I was her hero." Never would he admit to his sisters that the only reason the woman had been in the water was because *she* had saved *his* life and that, in return, he'd pulled her into the river with him. No sane man gave his siblings that kind of ammunition.

"Perhaps she will seek you out," Jac said excitedly. "In gratitude. Perhaps she'll come for tea, and then we can discover what truly made her flee her wedding."

"She is not coming for tea," Rhett said gruffly. She had kissed him and then left. Perhaps it was for the best. The kiss had been unlike any other, and that was not good. After Lady Meredith, he'd decided that serious relationships were not for him. Serious anything was not for him. He didn't have the talent for it, so he would take his pleasure where it was offered without strings attached.

Which was why this stupid fluttering in his chest was a problem. Something about this woman had him off-kilter. Perhaps it was her beauty. Perhaps it was her unexpected manner. Perhaps it was how easily she had walked away. Rhett was a sucker for women who didn't want him.

He would hope that she'd found better luck elsewhere on the docks and was now many, many miles from him. "You're mistaken. The woman I met was absolutely not Lady Cordelia Highwater."

Chapter Five

One week later.

"Bloody hell. You *killed* him?" In the six months that Adelaide had been working for Cordelia, she'd witnessed much that made her roll her eyes. But never could she have expected the body on the floor. She'd been out running errands when she'd heard gossip that the Duke of Strafford was paying a call on the two new sisters who had taken up residence in Honeydale Cottage.

"They're not sisters at all. One's the daughter of a duke. Our duke has gone to propose."

Fuck. How had their secret gotten out? Adelaide had been so careful. She'd constructed believable aliases and minimized Cordelia's contact with people. They'd only been in town for a matter of days.

Adelaide had exited the general store as quietly as she had entered, her mind racing through all possible scenarios and exit strategies just to find the one situation she hadn't anticipated—a dead man in the sitting room.

All blood had drained from Cordelia's face, and her hands were twisted in the practical, secondhand woolen skirts they'd purchased from a farmhouse two days into their trip. "I don't know," Cordelia said. "I *might* have killed him? Be a darling and go see."

Examining bodies was certainly not part of Adelaide's duties, but in for a penny, in for a pound.

Squaring her shoulders, she marched across the sitting room to where the Duke of Strafford lay slumped on the floor, his head at an odd angle by a chair, one arm caught awkwardly under his body, his legs spread-eagled.

Adelaide crouched over him, slipped two fingers just below the edge of his tie, and pressed them against his throat. *Th-thump.*

She exhaled swiftly. "He's not dead."

"Oh, thank goodness."

There was a rustle and a soft *thump.* Adelaide looked over her shoulder to see her mistress sitting on the rug, her back against the doorframe, staring up at the ceiling. Relief was perhaps the most sensible expression Adelaide had witnessed on Cordelia in the past week.

Adelaide turned back to the duke, who was as grim in repose as he had been when he'd called on his new tenants three days ago. She wasn't particularly keen on being present when His Grace woke, but what were her other options? The man was unconscious on their sitting room floor and required some form of care, which Cordelia clearly wasn't capable of providing.

Adelaide put a hand on his shoulder and shook it gently. "Your Grace?"

Nothing.

She shook more forcefully. "Your Grace." Still, there was no response. She turned to Cordelia. "What did you do, my lady?"

Cordelia scowled. "I shoved him, but it was not my fault."

Of course it wasn't. Nothing was ever Cordelia's fault.

"It's true! He was spouting all sorts of nonsense about how our marriage was such a *practical* option and how he'd already drafted an announcement to *The Times*. And, when he grasped my hand, I took umbrage. I pushed him away from me. I had not noticed that dratted cat sneak in. The duke tripped over it, and his head smacked against the edge of the chair."

Adelaide scanned the room quickly for the offending animal, a scrawny white cat with one blue eye and one brown that had latched on to the sisters the moment they'd taken up residence, nudging, purring, and pawing for food. It had taken a post behind the lace curtain, peering out with a scowl on its face. The curtain flicked as the cat's tail swished.

Once she'd satisfied herself that the stray was fine, she turned her attention back to the duke and the god-awful, centuries-old piece of furniture that had come with the cottage they'd rented only days ago. "He smacked his head on that?" Bloody hell. That thing looked as though it could take out the god of war himself.

Adelaide leaned over the duke once more, this time running her fingers through his sandy tresses, exploring his skull until her hands found it: a lump the size of a robin's egg. When she pulled her fingers away, the tips were covered in sticky red blood. There were plenty of injuries that she was capable of dealing with: snakebites, burns, deep lacerations. She'd even helped set a broken arm in Rome. But head injuries were well beyond her self-taught medical skills.

"I think it's time to send for the sawbones and the duke's man of business."

Cordelia shook her head. "No one must know that he was here."

Adelaide searched for a little more patience. "My lady," she said calmly. "The duke arrived on horseback. He'd have traveled through half the village to reach this cottage, and I don't for a moment believe that he did so unseen. Keeping his visit secret will be impossible. Not to mention that he will likely call the constabulary the moment he wakes. You assaulted him."

Cordelia tugged pins from her hair and hurled them across the room. Pins Adelaide would no doubt need to collect. "This is all his fault. What an incredibly arrogant, dense, and demanding jackass to *assume* I'd marry him. To have an announcement all written up before he'd even broached the idea with me. My life is *over.*"

Adelaide rolled her eyes. "Your life is not over. At least, not any more than it was yesterday. When the duke wakes, you'll apologize for striking him, and then you'll carry on as you were."

"And if he's already sent the announcement? Have you forgotten why we're in this back-of-nowhere town?"

It was hard to forget the sight of Cordelia tearing down the church steps or how she'd grabbed Adelaide's hands so tightly her fingertips had left slight bruises.

"What was he thinking?" Adelaide muttered, standing and pulling a handkerchief from her sleeve to wipe the blood from her fingers. Cordelia was beautiful, an absolute vision to behold, but they'd spent no more than ten minutes in each other's company yesterday, certainly not long enough for either of them to get any sense of the other. Especially so, given every word out of the girls' mouths had been a lie.

"Apparently, he found me quite convenient. He has no interest in engaging with London's marriage mart, and given he and my father discussed a potential match *when I was fifteen*, my appearance was a timely solution. Of course, I *must* be flattered by his interest. What possible reason could I have to turn down such a match, given he is a duke, and I am a duke's daughter?"

That was the part Adelaide didn't understand. "How did he know who you are?" They'd lied about their true identity to everyone they'd spoken to. Cordelia had even done a passable job of acting like a normal person rather than someone who was waited on hand and foot.

Cordelia stared at her toes and scrunched up her nose. "I wrote my true name on the leasing document."

It took everything Adelaide had in her not to drop her head into her hands. "Why?" she asked when she was confident she could mask her annoyance.

"It was a legal document. It would be wrong to lie on something so official."

The girl had no sense. You told what lies you needed to in order to survive, official document or not. "There is no escaping it then. The duke knows. His man of business surely knows, and it won't be long until the entire town knows." Already, the news had spread to the general store.

"What are you going to do about it?" Cordelia asked, finally crawling to her feet.

What was *Adelaide* going to do about it? She bit her lip for a long moment until she was composed enough to answer. "I will call for a doctor and send someone to his home so they can bring a carriage to transport him."

"And after that?" There was a thread of unease in Cordelia's tone.

Adelaide sighed. What came after that seemed bleeding obvious. Could the girl not see it, or did she see it perfectly well but hoped otherwise? "We wait for him to wake up. You apologize for nearly killing him, and we hope he takes it no further."

"And if he does?"

"We send for your father and let the dukes duke it out, I suppose."

Cordelia took a step backward. "No...no, no, not possible. I can't go back. All of London will stare. *Two* failed engagements!"

"I hardly think this one counts." Adelaide gestured to the unconscious duke. "You never even agreed to it."

Cordelia shook her head, eyes filling with tears. "It doesn't matter. If the duke has already sent that announcement to *The Times*, we won't catch it. London won't care that it was a misunderstanding. The gentleman is *never* to blame."

Adelaide wasn't a monster; her mistress's distress wrenched at her heart, but Cordelia lived in a fantasy land. She crossed the room and put a comforting hand on Cordelia's shoulder. "My lady, the uncomfortable truth is that there are consequences to your actions. You left the Duke of Hornsmouth at the altar. You knocked this one unconscious. People are going to stare at you until there is a better scandal to gossip about."

Cordelia huffed, as if the entire situation was an imposition on her and not, actually, the natural fallout from her own behavior. "This is going to ruin everything."

Adelaide sighed. "Why don't you go upstairs to rest, my lady? The village is only ten minutes' walk. I'll go."

Cordelia shook her head. "No. You stay with it...him. In case he wakes up. You should handle it. You're unnervingly good in a crisis."

It took the better part of an hour for Cordelia to return. During that time, Adelaide sat on the chair responsible for taking down the Duke of Strafford. Now and then, she checked his pulse. Despite his state of unconsciousness, it remained steady.

"This is most inconvenient," she said to him, as she scratched the stray cat beneath the chin, taking comfort in its soft purr. "And entirely avoidable. Would it have been so difficult to woo her? Just a little?" There was nothing quite as effervescing as a little courtship. Even the overly formal, highly supervised courtships of the *ton* held a touch of magic. Had the duke put even a *soupçon* of effort into his proposal, he may have succeeded.

Perhaps.

Cordelia had yet to reveal her true reasons for leaving Hornsmouth at the altar. Having one jagged tooth, an estate in the Scottish highlands instead of lowlands, two left feet, and a fondness for cigarettes was not reason enough to set one's entire life on fire. But every time Adelaide broached the topic, Cordelia pressed her lips tightly together and left the room.

"Blimey."

Adelaide's head snapped up. She'd been so lost in her musings, she hadn't heard the liveried footman enter. A few seconds later, another footman entered.

"Lord. Did you ever see such a thing?"

"He's not dead," she said as she stood, unease coursing through her. It was one thing to have an almost-dead duke at one's feet. It was another to have witnesses to such. Visions of being locked up for murdering an aristocrat flashed through her mind.

"Of course not, m'lady." The first footman shook his head. "We didn't mean to suggest such a thing."

"I'm not a—" She was interrupted by the entrance of even more people. A younger woman ducked in front of the two lads. An older woman prodded them forward so she could get a better view. A man with all the appearance of a butler but the expression of a gossipy kitchen maid stood with his mouth hanging open.

"What a turn of events."

"He'll wake with a crooked neck, for sure."

"Jesus, what happens now?"

"And the poor bugger had just gotten engaged."

Looks of speculation, hesitation, and titillation morphed into pity as the crowd glanced her way. "Apologies, m'lady." *Surely they don't . . .* "This isn't what you think. I'm not—"

"Make way. Now. *Excuse me.*"

A wave of relief hit Adelaide as Lady Cordelia pushed through the gathered crowd, a frown on her face. The duke's man of business and a white-haired fellow carrying a doctor's bag followed on her heels.

Adelaide quickly crossed to them. "His pulse is steady," she said to the physician. "But he has not responded to me at all."

The doctor reached out a hand as if to clasp her comfortingly on the shoulder, but he pulled back before he'd made contact. "I'm sure he heard you, my lady. The soul can tell when our loved ones are nearby. It brings comfort even through the dark."

"Oh. I'm not—" She looked at her mistress, waiting for Cordelia to set the doctor straight.

Cordelia patted Adelaide's arm, her smile sweet, but her eyes flaring. "The doctor is right, Lady Cordelia. The duke can surely hear you. Your presence must give him great comfort."

What on earth?

Conscious of the many pairs of eyes on them, Adelaide smiled wanly and took Cordelia by the arm, dragging her to the corner of the room farthest from people. "What are you playing at?"

Cordelia grasped Adelaide's hands, fairly crushing them in her own. "This is a *disaster*. Every wretched part of it."

"I am well aware," Adelaide said, shaking free. "How does pretending that I'm you help the matter?" It didn't.

Absolutely no good could come from this. She wouldn't do it.

"I cannot face him, and one of us must."

"Or we could leave," Adelaide whispered. "Right now, Cordelia. The moment his body is taken from this house, we could pack our things and get out of here." Staying would be foolish. Leaving would probably also be foolish, but at least it would give her time to come up with a solution.

Cordelia shook her head. "For heaven's sake, Adelaide. Would you simply stay with the duke until he wakes and convince him to retract our betrothal announcement? Then we can find somewhere else to hide, and everything will be well."

That blasted betrothal announcement. The upper classes truly had no sense. Masquerading as a lady of the *ton* and confronting an arrogant duke with a blistering headache was the most asinine idea she'd heard. Not even her decision to run with the bulls in Pamplona had been as foolish as this.

"Would you like anything else from me, my lady?" she asked in a tone that clearly conveyed how ridiculous a request it was.

Cordelia narrowed her eyes. "Convince him not to tell anyone about how he came to be in this state. I would not survive that gossip, Adelaide. No man would want to marry a criminal. I'd be ostracized for the rest of my life."

"Fine," she said, relenting. "But once this is done, we are returning to London. You cannot run from consequences forever."

"Excuse me, my lady."

Cordelia turned, a smile on her face, and was about to respond when she caught herself, her smile freezing, and she took a deferential half step behind Adelaide.

"Yes?" Adelaide responded, rolling her eyes.

The woman in front of her stood tall and proud, soft gray wending its way through her chestnut hair, which was pulled back into neat and simple bun. Her dress was a well-made, conservative outfit that indicated a senior member of staff in a peer's home. The woman curtsied, a gesture that sat ill with Adelaide. She was nothing but a lady's maid. No one should show her such deference.

"I am the housekeeper at Strafford Abbey. Mrs. Hillston. I'm sorry to be meeting you in such circumstances. I'm certain His Grace would have rather introduced you to the staff in a proper manner." She glanced over to where the doctor was instructing the young footmen, a laborer, and what looked to be a coachman as they transferred the duke onto a door that had been taken off its hinges.

"I appreciate you introducing yourself, Mrs. Hillston. It certainly is an unusual circumstance." It wasn't difficult to put on the soft affect of the upper classes. Mimicking her surroundings had been the key to surviving as she traveled on her own. In every city, she'd blended in, finding safety in being unremarkable, unmemorable, which was fine. She forgot others just as quickly as they forgot her. People were transient, momentary things.

Cordelia looked askance at Adelaide's newfound accent but said nothing.

"The doctor said you can ride in the coach back to the house if you're prepared to squeeze in beside them."

Hell no. She would face the duke on Cordelia's behalf, but she would do it with an open door in sight and a good ten feet between them. "Oh, I don't think that's—*oof.*" She stumbled forward as Cordelia jabbed her in the back. Adelaide shot her mistress a glare.

Cordelia simply smiled sweetly. "You should go, my lady. If the duke wakes, you'll want to be the first thing he sees."

Chapter Six

Rhett was in a foul mood even before the carriage pulled to a stop outside his brother's country house.

Enduring a full day's ride with his sisters, who didn't understand the meaning of traveling lightly or quietly, had pushed him to a knife's edge. To add to the insult, they'd missed the bloody turnoff. "Not again, ya bleeding maggot," the coachman had sworn.

It was almost as if the tiny village of Berwick was deliberately obfuscating its presence. There was no paved road turning east, not even a signpost to suggest that if you turned down the semi-worn track between two old elm trees, an hour later, you'd find yourself at the smallest ducal estate in England.

Rhett had a good mind to douse both trees with red paint in order to make his next journey easier.

"At last," Winnie said, taking the outrider's hand so as not to stumble as she exited. "We were in that carriage *forever.*"

"A day's ride is hardly forever," he replied as he climbed out of the carriage after her. It was a quick trip compared to some treks he'd been on. But his sister rarely left London, so Rhett could see how she'd feel this had been a marathon journey.

"I need tea," Jac said.

"I need a chamber pot," Winnie replied.

"That's because you didn't heed my warning and instead insisted on having tea at our last stop."

Winnie poked out her tongue. Rhett turned away from his sniping sisters to help Meg out of the carriage. He held out an arm, and she took it, walking with him up the stairs. Winnie bounced along behind them as the driver and footman who had accompanied them untied the luggage from the top of the carriage.

When the siblings reached the top step, the door was still firmly closed.

"That's odd," Jac said.

"Quite." Rhett rapped on the door with the metal head of the cane he carried with him.

There was no response. He frowned and rapped again. This time, the door flew open, but it wasn't the household's familiar butler in the doorway. Instead, an unknown maid stood there, her cap slightly askew, her gaze flicking over her shoulder before returning to Rhett and his sisters.

"May I help you?"

Rhett and Meg exchanged glances at the lack of formality. "We are here to see my brother," Rhett said. "The duke," he added when the maid continued to stare at them without an ounce of understanding.

It was a further few seconds before the maid's eyes widened, and she flapped her hand about, fanning her face. She still made no move to clear the doorway.

"Do you think we might come in?" Meg asked.

The maid flushed red and stepped aside, drawing the door open fully. "Of course. My apologies, my lord, my ladies." She looked toward the stairs as though she'd suddenly faced a four-headed monster and was waiting for salvation from up high. The only thing to come down the stairs was a pair of gossiping footmen, so immersed in their conversation they didn't even look up to see who was at the door.

Rhett crossed the threshold and, when he realized the maid wasn't about to do it, he helped his sisters out of their traveling coats, took their bonnets and pelisses, and walked them over to the coatroom at the edge of the entryway. "Where is Daunt?" he asked as he shucked his own coat and hung it up. The butler should be at his post or, at the very least, the underbutler should be there in his stead.

"Mr. Daunt will be down directly, my lord. Apologies. With everything that's going on, the house is in quite an uproar."

Jac leaned forward. "Do tell. What is going on?"

The maid blanched, and Rhett's stomach tightened. She crossed to the bellpull by the door and yanked it so hard Rhett expected it to tumble from its fastenings.

There was a frustrated sigh from above. "I cannot see what could be so important as to require my..." Daunt, the butler who had managed Strafford Abbey for as long as Rhett had been alive, trailed off. "My lord. My ladies." He wrung his hands. "I forgot we were expecting you today."

Forgot? That seemed decidedly out of character. "Is my brother in his study?" Better to get this argument over with so they could enjoy Christmas together.

Daunt swallowed hard. "No, my lord. The duke is... occupied."

"Please send word that Lady Titteler, Lady Edwina, Lady Jacqueline, and I are here." Rhett turned to his youngest sister. "Didn't you need the lavatory?"

Winnie narrowed her eyes. "You are a devil," she hissed, flushing pink with embarrassment. She turned to the butler. "If you could have the family rooms opened, that would be much appreciated. I will head there directly." She shot her brother a look that could have felled a Siberian sled dog before hastening off.

The butler continued to wring his hands, as though the instructions he'd been given were beyond the run-of-the-mill requests made of the head of staff.

The footmen, who had been so engrossed in their conversation earlier, had paused at the edge of the room and were looking at the siblings nervously. A chambermaid, who had entered with a pile of laundry in her arms, froze. The housekeeper walked in, saw the three siblings, and raised her eyebrows.

Something was amiss. By the way she narrowed her eyes and crossed her arms, Meg sensed it too. "Daunt. Mrs. Hillston. Is there something that we should know?" she asked.

She received a soft, faint smile from the housekeeper. "You must be hungry after your journey. I'll have the kitchen prepare some food."

Rhett recognized a deliberate nonanswer when he heard one. He was an expert at them. Whatever was afoot, the senior staff were too loyal and too well trained to spill. Rhett would need to wrest it from his brother or wring it from a footman.

Peter's study at Strafford Abbey carried the weight of the dukedom: the century-old desk that still had a patina of age despite careful attention from staff, the thick tomes on the shelf about everything from agricultural development to estate law, the piles of accounting books that took up the left half of Peter's desk, and the giant portraits of the previous dukes hanging over them.

It was heavy and burdensome, and it kept Peter tied down. Rhett would suffocate under his brother's responsibilities. He preferred the freedom to up and leave when he wanted, with just a fresh change of clothing and a destination in mind.

Traveling the continent was the only time Rhett had

felt like his own man rather than the lesser version of his brother. Not that he resented Peter. Someone had to make sure the estates ran properly and their sisters were provided for. Rhett was simply grateful that it wasn't him.

He eschewed the chair in front of his brother's desk and took the more comfortable armchair by the fire, crossing an ankle over his knee and looking into the flames. He'd put off the encounter as long as he could, escorting Jac to Almack's and a half dozen balls, taking Winnie shopping for a new fan, reticule, bonnet. He'd sat with Meg on the lawn seat in their Mayfair garden and listened to all the ways she was going to dress down her husband when he finally returned to England.

But he couldn't put off the inevitable forever. One of two things was going to happen. Either Peter would be satisfied with a metaphorical rap over the knuckles and Rhett's promise to find a worthwhile reason for his travels, or the duke would cut Rhett off, forcing his hand toward the army or the clergy.

The army. No, the clergy. No, the army. Damn it. Neither. Rhett could not do it, and none of the other careers he'd tried his hand at had fit either. He'd made a terrible student, frustrated at the extent to which historians looked backward when life was forward. Speculating on the market had been a disaster. All he'd achieved had been the loss of twenty thousand pounds in the space of a year. He had eschewed safer stocks and bet on the young, the visionaries, the disruptors, the people who represented what Rhett wished he was. Peter had understandably refused to continue supporting that endeavor.

Even Rhett's attempt at becoming an artist had failed. He was, according to some of the greatest artists of their time, too reluctant to show his belly, and only in raw honesty could one succeed artistically. And so he traveled. His purpose would show itself, or it would not. Either way, he would have a good time searching for it.

A footman entered. Rhett didn't recognize the lad, but it had been five years since he'd stepped foot on the estate.

"My lord?" The footman stared at him with the expression of someone who'd asked a question more than once.

"A brandy, thank you." Regardless of the man's question, brandy was an appropriate answer.

"I'll have one of those as well."

Rhett rolled his eyes and looked to the doorway, where Jac had just entered. The footman hesitated and then looked at Rhett for direction.

"What was your name?" Rhett asked.

"Thomas, my lord."

"Thomas. A quick lesson for you. Looking to a man for permission when my sister makes a request will not end well for you."

It was true. Of all of his sisters, Jac was the most odd by society's standards. She was bold and refreshing and a lot of fun, but not your typical duke's daughter.

Almost as proof of it, Jac snorted, and Thomas—quick boy that he was—didn't miss a beat. "One finger or two, my lady?"

Jac beamed. "Two, please." She took one of the remaining armchairs in the room, gathered her shawl about her, and snuggled in. "I take it Peter hasn't made an appearance?"

"Not yet."

Rhett swirled the brandy around in his glass, watching as the liquid stuck to the sides, hanging on as though it were fighting the pull to keep up with the rest of the drink.

"You are more contemplative than usual, brother."

Rhett threw back his drink, polishing the full drink off. "Yes, and it's doing me no favors. Tell me a story, Jac."

Jac arched her brow. "What about the story of the man who posed naked for a horde of artists, causing his brother to have a conniption and go mute for days?"

Heat crept up the back of Rhett's neck. "It was France. It's what one does in the artistic center of the world."

Jac giggled and waved at his crotch. "You didn't even attempt to cover your parts. They were on display for the entire world to see."

"Hardly the entire world." Though definitely too much of the world if his sisters had seen them. Never in a million years would he have deliberately given them that kind of ammunition. Those sketches were supposed to have remained private. "In my defense, it was an afternoon lesson by a grand master. I was assured that no painting would come of it."

"No painting, maybe. But at least four of the sketches made their way to London. Peter spent a fortune collecting them all."

Rhett dropped his head in his hands. His brother was going to roast him alive for that. "Did he really go mute?"

"I think he feared what might come out of his mouth had he opened it."

There was a disapproving *hmph* from the doorway. Andrew Gray, the duke's man of business and a longtime family friend, furrowed his brows. "How much did you pay the artists for such a flattering representation of your nether regions?"

Rhett straightened and gave his friend a wicked smile. "No bribe necessary. That was all me. I can provide references, if you like."

Jac rolled her eyes. "That is far too much information, both of you." She stood and met Andrew halfway, clasping his hand in affection. "Andy, it's good to see you. We're waiting for Peter. Would you like brandy or tea? I'll ring for some."

Andrew took on a grim countenance. "I can't stay, I'm afraid."

Jac cocked her head. "Whatever you're off to do can wait. Peter won't mind you catching up. You can couch your gossip in business terms if you like."

Andrew shook his head and swallowed hard.

"What is it?" she asked. "You're acting strangely."

Rhett stood. His gut was screaming at him. The servants' odd behavior, Daunt's reticence, Andrew's stiff bearing. He and his sisters had walked into something. "Yes, Andrew. What is it?"

"Your brother. There's been an accident."

As his sisters rushed forward, Rhett's feet locked in place at the foot of Peter's bed. The girls immediately grasped Peter's hand, leaned over him, brushed the hair from his forehead, and peppered Andrew with a dozen questions.

"What happened?"

"When did it happen?"

"How did it happen?"

"What did the doctor say?"

"Is he going to be all right?"

"Will he wake?"

"How long has he been out?"

"Has anyone tried forcing orgeat down his throat? He hates that stuff. He'd wake from the dead to avoid it."

"Shush, Edwina. Don't say dead. Don't jinx it."

Still, Rhett stood silent, taking in the sight of his brother—always so strong, so stalwart, so steady—lying unconscious. Peter was pale, paler than Rhett had ever seen him. His shirt hung open at the collar. Someone had removed his waistcoat and jacket and replaced them with a robe. Probably the duke's valet with Andrew's help. Rhett knew firsthand how hard it was to change someone out of clothes when they were nothing but deadweight. It was usually him being assisted when he was too drunk to even change himself.

There was a slight smear of blood on the shirt. His sisters hadn't yet noticed it, and it was enough to spur Rhett to action. He joined the girls at his brother's bedside and leaned over, tugging at the robe until the stain was hidden.

"What happened?" His voice came out strangled, tangled with an emotion he could not identify.

Andrew had waited in the doorway, giving the family some space, but now he came forward, resting a hand on Jac's shoulder. She rested against him, and Rhett wondered when the two had gotten so close.

"We're unsure of the circumstances of the accident." Andrew looked pointedly to the other side of the room, toward the window, and all three siblings followed his gaze.

Rhett's heart swooped at the sight of her. His stomach flip-flopped before settling into a pit.

What the devil?

Pressed against the back wall, caught mid-shuffle toward the exit, was *her*. The woman who had haunted his dreams every night for a week. Every time he'd found himself bored, his mind had turned to her, to their brief meeting, and he'd imagined all the ways it could have gone differently.

Chief among those daydreams had been her twining a hand through his hair, looking at him adoringly, promising future encounters. There was nothing adoring in her expression right now. She looked like a deer caught in the sights of a wolf.

"What are you doing here?" His words were terse, his tone gruff. Not by choice; the timing was bollocks. He wanted to see her again when he could devote all his energy to uncovering what it was about her that had him so arrested. This was not the time. This was not the place. Peter... Why the devil was she in Peter's bedroom?

Even her freckles paled. "Rhett. I... Uh... I was not..." Her speechlessness was unexpected, given she'd had words aplenty at the docks.

His sisters looked at her, looked at him, looked back at her, their brows furrowed in confusion.

Della swallowed. "Excuse me. This is a time for family." She stared firmly at the floor and marched across the room.

It was instinct, how quickly Rhett moved to block the doorway to prevent her exit. He'd lost her once before. He wasn't ready to lose her again. Timing be damned. "Why are you here?" he asked, straining to keep his fingers from reaching out to her.

When she wouldn't answer, Andrew cleared his throat. "She's Peter's fiancée, apparently."

Rhett's entire body went stiff. Andrew's words left a ringing in his ears.

She closed her eyes and shook her head, clearly frustrated.

His sisters launched into their infernal babbling once again, crowding around her.

"Peter said nothing about being betrothed."

"He's betrothed?"

"Why hasn't he written to us?"

"When was the last time we received a letter from him?"

"He could have come to London to introduce her. It's not *that* far."

"I tell you, the postal service has been subpar for a year now."

"Did he consult with any of us on the matter?"

Della stared desperately at the door, and then up at him, pleadingly, her hands twisted in her skirts.

"Who are you?" asked Jacqueline.

The babbling stopped as all sisters stared at her, waiting for an answer.

"She's Lady Cordelia Highwater," Andrew said when she said nothing.

The girls gasped. Rhett's jaw locked tightly. *No, she's not.*

Chapter Seven

Oh shit. The words had been bouncing around her skull from the moment the whirlwind of a family had burst through the door. Now, surrounded by them and their shocked expressions, cut off from the room's only reasonable exit point, and faced with him, Rhett, the man who'd thrown her into England's most disgusting body of water, *oh shit* became *fuck, fuck, fuck. You're in it now, Adelaide. God damn it.*

"Lady Cordelia Highwater? *The* Lady Cordelia Highwater?" the youngest of the sisters said. "The one who—"

"Shush, Edwina." The eldest looked a full decade older than the others, but she didn't act it as she rammed an elbow into her sister's ribs. "Lady Cordelia, how lovely to meet you. We did not know Peter had chosen a bride. Forgive our surprise."

Adelaide slipped on her lady-of-the-*ton* persona, took the woman's proffered hand, and gave it a little squeeze. "It is a pleasure to meet you too. I'm only sorry it's under such circumstances. If you'll excuse me. I need some air." She turned to face the man who had, quite frustratingly, stalked her thoughts for the past week, and drew forth her coldest, haughtiest stare.

It hurt him, she could tell; but he didn't protest. He merely raised an eyebrow and stepped aside.

With an appearance of calm that she did not feel, she left the room.

Adelaide burst into the cottage she and Cordelia shared knowing two things. First, they needed to leave. Now. Second, the universe was once again having a laugh at her expense. What else explained the sudden appearance of the man from the docks, whose touch had ignited a wildfire of wanting?

All her senses—physical, emotional, logical—had been turned upside down the moment they'd hit the river and those damn skirts had dragged her below the surface. She counted on those senses. They had kept her alive all these years. But even being back on dry land hadn't centered them. Only on the long walk back to Cordelia that afternoon had she begun to feel in control.

Now, a week later, her senses were jumbled once again, and a disturbing thought threaded through her. Perhaps it was not almost drowning that had caused her awareness to tumble and bounce. Perhaps it had been him.

Which was one more reason for them to leave immediately. There could be no safety when her senses were misfiring.

"How did it go? What did the duke say?" Cordelia asked, leaping up from the chair.

"He said as much as an unconscious man could, which is nothing." She scanned the room for things that needed to be packed, snatching them up in panic.

Cordelia paled. "He still hasn't woken?" she asked as Adelaide pushed past her to the room where their second-hand trunks were stored.

"Despite the doctor's best efforts."

"But he hasn't worsened?" Cordelia asked, trailing behind.

Adelaide dumped the items into the trunk with no care for neatness. "You mean, worse than showing no signs of life other than a heartbeat? No."

There was no sign that Cordelia had even registered Adelaide's distress. If she had, it was apparently so inconsequential to her that it didn't deserve acknowledgment. "You need to go back," she pressed. "You must be there when he wakes."

That was a terrible bloody idea. Adelaide took Cordelia's hands in hers. "It is time to admit to your role in the accident, apologize, and return to London."

Cordelia shook her head. "My father will be furious. I cannot face him."

The duke would be furious. He would scream and rant and likely lock his daughter in her room until he found another peer to take her. But he wouldn't allow her to go to jail, and he would do his damnedest to protect her reputation. It was also his, after all.

"At least you have a father to face," Adelaide said. "You have a family who will shield you." She would give anything to raise her father's ire again.

"You don't understand," Cordelia pleaded.

"I don't understand?" Adelaide was tempted to give her mistress the dressing-down she deserved. To explain just what it was like to be without a family, to have no one but one's self to turn to in a crisis. But sharing her past would give too much away. She gave nothing of herself unless she had to.

Cordelia narrowed her eyes. "If the duke wakes and you are there, this whole mess can be swept under the carpet. If you have him retract the announcement before it's published, no one needs to know how he came to be unconscious, or of his ridiculous betrothal suggestion."

Adelaide pinched the bridge of her nose. "It is too late for that, my lady. Your supposed betrothal is already public knowledge."

Cordelia shook her head. "Only the servants know. They are inconsequential."

Spoken like a true aristocrat. Alas, servants were neither inconsequential nor the only problem. "News has spread farther than that, my lady. The whole town knows."

"A tiny town that no one can even find?" Cordelia huffed, crossing her arms. "You will make it right."

"My lady, his family knows." Members of the *ton* might not gossip about their own kin, but nor would they accept a quick brush under the carpet without a full account of what had happened.

"His family?" Cordelia's voice faltered.

"He has three sisters. They are … loud, and they were displeased to discover their brother had entered into a betrothal without their input."

"Oh, heavens."

Adelaide paused for no reason she'd admit to before adding, "He has a brother, as well." The temptation to keep that knowledge secret was stupid. Cordelia would know the truth, and there was no point wishing to keep Adelaide's thought-stalker to herself. He was not hers to keep, and that wasn't what she wanted anyway. She was an island. That was better. "At least, I assume it is his brother," she continued, trying to sound normal as she spoke of him. "They have the same honeyed hair, though the younger has no grays."

Cordelia nodded. "Lord Everett. Has he returned to England? That will set the cat among the pigeons."

"How so?" Adelaide tried to mask her need to know with polite curiosity.

"He is extraordinarily popular with married ladies. All of them. I cannot discuss him further. It—he—is inappropriate." Cordelia's cheeks flamed red.

Disappointment coursed through her. Rhett was one of *them*, the men who played hearts like a deck of cards—obsessively attentive for a night and then discarded on the table when the sun rose.

You've had your share of them, Adelaide. No more. "That makes it even more important for us to return to London." She needed distance between them. "We don't want your name associated with such a man, and as of now, he thinks I am you."

That should have been it. Adelaide wished that had been it. But Cordelia was like one of the alley cats of Cyprus, obsessively gnawing at the issue. She would attempt to hold Adelaide to their bargain, regardless of how foolish it was.

"That makes it all the more important for you to stay and settle this with the duke the moment he wakes. If his family thinks he's betrothed, there's no way we can keep that from the London gossips without the duke's intervention."

This was madness. Utter madness. "I will not continue this charade," she said, checking beneath the bed for any items that might have been accidentally kicked under it.

Cordelia crossed to the trunk and started to pull items from it. "You will, because I'm asking you to, and you work for me."

And *that* was one of the greatest challenges of becoming a lady's maid. Sure, there was a guaranteed income, roof, meals, and even clothing, but it came at the expense of Adelaide's ability to say "To hell with this; I'm leaving."

When she was traveling from town to town, no one told

her what to do. But now she had an employer whose good-will and willingness to disperse wages she was reliant on. So she kept a smile on her face as she said, "You hired me to help with your hair and your clothes and to keep you company when needed. You did not hire me to lie to the family of a man you may have murdered."

There. How many times had that sentence been said sweetly?

Cordelia was unswayed. "Then let me hire you for that."

"Pardon?"

"I'll concede that what I'm asking of you falls far outside of your role as a lady's maid. That's true. But if you do this for me—if you stay until he wakes or he dies, and you keep me out of jail and off the front pages of the newspaper—I will pay you an obscene amount of money. Enough that you will never have to work again."

Adelaide scoffed. "You don't have a cent, except for the jewels you were wearing as you ran, and they aren't worth what you're asking." She slammed shut the cupboard door and stormed to the kitchen. The necklace alone was worth a bloody fortune—more than enough to lease a cottage for the next decade. But she didn't want to do it, damn it.

Cordelia followed, like a nagging little duckling. "Like you said, I'll have to go back home eventually. My father will compensate you handsomely for your troubles, and if he doesn't, then I will sell what I need to in order to do so. You have my word."

Selfish and spoiled as Cordelia was, Adelaide believed her. The duke *would* pay well; he wouldn't risk Adelaide spilling the story to the constabulary or the press. But was all the money in the world worth walking back into that house and risking her freedom? If the duke's family caught her in a lie, they might assume the duke had met with foul play rather than foolishness. If they were angry enough, *she* could be the one imprisoned.

Worst of all, she'd have to spend time with the duke's family. The duke's brother. The thought of being alone in a room with Rhett again rasped like sandpaper on skin. There would be no kissing this time, no gentle touches or witticisms.

Sensing Adelaide's hesitation, Cordelia interjected. "I know you're putting money away. I know that's why you applied for a lady's maid position when you clearly had no experience. Think about whatever you're saving for before you decide to turn down my offer. You might never get it otherwise."

Adelaide froze. She'd gone into service after six months of editors who had dallied on their payments. A lady's maid's wages were only marginally more than what she'd made writing, but the pay was regular, and if she wanted to someday lease her own home, she couldn't continue to dip into her savings for food and board.

And she wanted a home.

After an entire lifetime of moving from one place to another, she wanted somewhere she could put down roots. She wanted to own an entire bookcase, rather than the two or three novels that she exchanged whenever she reached a new town. She wanted an armchair that wasn't worn from a thousand different arses. She wanted it worn from just one arse—hers. She wanted to sit beneath a tree she'd planted that had grown tall enough to give shade.

With the kind of money Cordelia promised, she could lease a home in a village somewhere, with a garden she could tend to and rooms full of furniture.

But was it worth the risk of facing Rhett Montgomery again?

Rat-a-tat-tat. Both women jumped at the unexpected knock. *Rat-a-tat.*

"Are you going to answer the door?" Cordelia asked.

Adelaide swallowed. There could be a half dozen people outside, each with a dozen different reasons for being there. Perhaps the duke had died, and the staff had come to let his fiancée know. Perhaps he'd died, and there was a constable there to arrest her. Perhaps he had died, and the sisters had come to grieve with company. Perhaps the duke lived... perhaps.

"Fuck it." She stormed to the door, counting on her intuition to guide her from there.

"What is it?" she asked, yanking the door open. *Fuck.*

Rhett stood there, leaning against the doorway, one hand gripping the frame.

"Mr. Montgomery," Adelaide said, casting her eyes downward as though if she couldn't see him, this moment couldn't happen. "I'm sorry for your..." She stopped. The duke wasn't dead. Speaking as though he were would only invite bad fortune. "...these current circumstances."

His eyes narrowed. "Are you sorry? Tell me, Lady Cordelia, what is it you have to apologize for?" His tone had sharpened, whet on a stone of suspicion, and Adelaide's heart rate increased.

"Your household is in turmoil; most empathetic creatures would feel sorry for that."

His expression darkened. "And for your own turmoil?"

He was talking of her supposed betrothal. Were she truly engaged to the duke, her own life would be in a state of upheaval, her heart would be cracking. So, she schooled her face into an expression of grief. "I'm sorry for that too." Sorry she'd been embroiled in all this business.

There was a long pause as he studied her.

"How can I help you, Mr. Montgomery?"

He flinched. "It's Mr. Montgomery now? No more Rhett?"

Rhett was the rogue on the docks, the man who'd made an awful day bearable, the happy memory she'd turned over in her mind a hundred times since then. The lord in front of her was anything but. He was furious, and he was hurt. *Wounded dogs bite, Adelaide. Keep your distance.* So, she kept her silence too.

"Why did you lie to me?"

"I have never lied to you. Not once."

"Why didn't you tell me who you were?"

"Because it was inconsequential."

"It is hardly inconsequential when you belong to my brother."

Adelaide drew herself to her full height plus some. "I belong to no one."

Rhett rubbed at his face. "Of course. I did not mean to imply actual ownership…Damn it. You are my brother's fiancée." He ran a hand through his hair. "You were not mine to kiss," he said, his voice unsteady. "Yet it is all I have thought about."

She leaned against the doorway, her body close enough to feel his warmth, but not touching. Not again. She was so tired, and he was looking at her for an explanation. She had no words for him. None that he wanted to hear. None that would not embroil her even further in this mess.

After a moment of silence, he shoved his hands in his pockets and stepped back. Her body protested the distance. It was colder without him. His face had shuttered. The rogue was gone. "Meg insisted I let you know you are welcome at Strafford Abbey, and that you mustn't leave because the duke's overbearing sisters have overrun the place."

"She said overbearing?"

There was a ghost of a smile. "I may have editorialized somewhat. But they are keen for you to visit tomorrow so they, we, can learn more of you and how you came to be engaged to our brother."

Adelaide swallowed hard. She could tell him the truth right now. After all, up to this point, she hadn't lied. She'd stayed quiet through Cordelia's blatant mistruth and hadn't corrected any misunderstandings, but she'd not truly taken part in this sham.

Cordelia would be furious, and there would be no keeping it from the London gossips. Adelaide would lose her job and most likely any chance at another position within the *ton*, but she wouldn't have been complicit.

But telling the truth would mean giving up the money her employer had promised, and accepting that a home of her own was far off. She would be stuck in service, or wandering, for decades.

She stared at him, at all the various consequences he represented. "I'll see you in the morning, Mr. Montgomery. Please send word if the duke wakes before then."

Rhett stalked down the hall, down the stairs, and out into the night. His breath fogged in the cold air, obscuring the light from the local village.

"Brother." Jac stood in the doorway, her robe hugged tight around her. "Are you well?"

"I'm fine, Jac. I just needed some air. It felt like the walls were caving in."

"Didn't you just spend a week on a ship?" she asked, joining him on the landing. "Aren't the cabins tiny? However did you manage?"

It wasn't the size of Peter's bedroom that was the problem. It was the weight of the person in it. Who'd have thought a person could suck out more of the air while unconscious than they had when they were awake?

"Ships are conduits to adventure, Jac. It doesn't matter how small they are; they're giant with possibility."

Jac rolled her eyes. "How very poetic of you. Next, we'll discover that you spent your time in Germany writing poetry with Otto Schwarz."

Rhett could feel the heat creep up his neck.

"Rhett!"

"One cannot travel to Weimer and not pay a call on Schwarz. It's what one does in the land of poets."

His sister clapped a hand over her eyes. "Lord, Peter is going to have a conniption. He'll wake from this episode and then pass out all over again. Tell me you are not the subject of one of Schwarz's poems."

Rhett put his hands in his pockets and shuffled his feet. He felt no shame about that hedonistic week and was rather chuffed that Otto had chosen to write about it. But that didn't mean he wanted his younger sister to know the steamy, graphic details.

"Tell me which one it is."

"Never."

"I must know."

"It's bad enough that you've seen those infernal sketches of my member; you do not need to hear it described in lavish prose."

Jac stared at him mulishly.

He changed the topic to the one that was tumbling over and over in his mind. "What did you make of Lady Cordelia?"

Jac shrugged. "It was hard to make much of her when she escaped from the room almost immediately. Not that I blame her. Winnie was making so much noise."

Rhett raised an eyebrow. Of all his sisters, Jac was the

loudest. It was as if she assumed other people's hearing was as bad as her eyesight, and she yelled to compensate. "I invited her back tomorrow so that we can meet her properly."

That wasn't the truth. The girls might want to "meet her properly," but Rhett wanted answers. He didn't for one moment believe that she was the Duke of Thirwhestle's daughter. No young lady of the *ton* had such a mouth for profanity and for kissing. Even his sisters, who were as sensible as young ladies got, would not acquiesce to a stranger disrobing them, regardless of how few other options there were. They would have rolled home like a pig in a blanket before stepping foot in that tavern.

"She accepted?" Jac asked, clapping her hands. "Thank goodness. I'm half-mad with curiosity. Is Peter the reason she left the Duke of Hornsmouth at the altar? I never thought he could inspire that kind of passion. He's so…staid. I always assumed his wife would be equally…"

"Dull?"

She glared at him. "Conservative."

There was nothing conservative about Della. He couldn't stop the corners of his mouth from inching upwards as he recalled the stream of profanities she'd leveled at the ship's captain.

His smile faded, though, with the reminder that if she was who she said she was, she was bound to his brother. Once again, Peter was given freely what Rhett coveted simply because he was a duke and Rhett was not.

It wasn't Peter's fault, though. Arguably, he was in a worse position. Women would say and do anything to become a duchess. There was no lie they wouldn't tell. No level they wouldn't stoop to.

Rhett may not be husband material, but now that he was aware of that, he could enjoy his affairs knowing exactly what women wanted from him—a flirtation, a romp, and that was all. Peter could never *truly* trust a woman's motivations.

Della, if that was her real name, absolutely could not be trusted. He put a hand on his sister's shoulder. "You are sure that she is Lady Cordelia, aren't you? She is the one you saw running down the aisle?"

"Yes," Jac said confidently.

"And you were wearing your spectacles?"

Jac frowned, a crease forming between her brows. "I don't see what that has to do with anything."

Rhett exhaled, running a hand through his hair. "It has a lot to do with the current situation, Jac. We know nothing of this woman or her motivations. She is likely not who she says she is. Even if she is Lady Cordelia, for all we know, she's just another title hunter."

Jac screwed up her nose. "I know what I saw, and didn't you see her too? How many redheaded women could have been fleeing London in such an ornate wedding dress on that very day?"

Jac made a good point. The evidence pointed to Della truly being Lady Cordelia, but he didn't like it. It didn't sit right.

"You're so cynical, brother. If all she wanted was a title, she could have married the Duke of Hornsmouth. No, I'm convinced this is a love match."

He didn't believe it. The woman who kissed him a week ago couldn't possibly be in love with someone else. Surely. Yet Lady Meredith had kissed him, and Peter had been her target all along. "You don't find it strange that none of us knew Peter was betrothed? That he hadn't told you or Meg?"

She shrugged. "Peter has never exactly shared his feelings with us. Besides, Andrew says our brother has been talking about marriage for months. I don't know how the relationship between Lady Cordelia and Peter began, but I'm so glad it did."

Rhett wanted to be happy for his brother. He wanted to have as much faith as Jac did, but he didn't. Something was off. He didn't know what was wrong, but he would find out.

Chapter Eight

"His Grace is standoffish," Cordelia said, nestled in her bed, rubbing the sleep from her eyes as Adelaide, who had been awake for three hours already, took to her own hair with a curling tong. "Prior to Lady Jacqueline's coming out last year, he rarely attended social events, even though he was in town while parliament sat. When he does attend, he refuses to dance or even engage in discussion beyond a minute or so, much to everyone's frustration."

"Everyone's?" Adelaide asked, catching Cordelia's eye in the mirror.

She pursed her lips. "The women of the *ton*, at least. He's one of the few eligible dukes left. The others are married, ancient, or missing half their teeth."

Adelaide arched a brow. "Except the Duke of Hornsmouth." He was young, powerful, and he could have been Cordelia's.

Cordelia grimaced. "Except Hornsmouth. I suppose he has a full set of teeth, even if one is wonky." She turned her gaze to the bedspread, fingers tracing over the pattern.

"And he's not ancient." It was possibly unkind to push when Cordelia had made it clear she had no interest in discussing her former fiancé, but Adelaide still could not quite come to terms with Cordelia's decision to forgo the security that would have come with being the Duchess of Hornsmouth.

"He's not ancient." Cordelia bit at the words, spearing Adelaide with a haughty look. "But Strafford is more handsome, if not quite so rich, and he has an air of mystery about him, which makes him *the* most sought-after guest. Far more so than Hornsmouth. And there is nothing left to say on the matter."

Message received. Adelaide nodded. Discussion of Hornsmouth would end. They would focus on the task at hand—teaching Adelaide everything she needed to know about the Duke of Strafford and his family so that she could pull off the subterfuge convincingly. "But Strafford is rarely in London."

"Yes."

Adelaide gently pulled the hot tong from her hair, taking the curl and pinning it tightly to her head for it to cool in shape. "And his sisters?" That was the greatest risk in all of this, that someone in the house would know what Cordelia looked like and spot the ruse. His sisters posed the greatest threat if they'd attended the same balls as Cordelia.

Cordelia slipped her feet into her slippers, hugged her robe around her, and crossed to her cupboard to rifle through the meager number of dresses they'd purchased over the past few days, paid for with cash they'd acquired pawning a couple of jewels. Cordelia held one out, considered it, and tossed it onto the floor. It would take Adelaide hours to iron out those creases.

"I've never spoken with his sisters. Lady Margaret is Lord Everett's twin. She married an archaeologist several years back, and then he left her to pursue his work almost immediately. It was all anyone could talk of, but it occurred before I was out."

Adelaide thought back to the moment the duke's family burst into his rooms. All three of the sisters bore a resemblance to Rhett, but he and Lady Margaret were almost identical. She was a shorter, softer version of him.

"Lady Jacqueline came out last year, but we've never interacted. She's...bookish. She was invited to everything, of course. She *is* Strafford's sister, and it was the only surefire way to have him attend an event, but she seemed utterly uninterested in the whirl."

Quel horreur. Cordelia's problem was that she had always been a duke's daughter. Her good graces had always been sought, and she'd always been the center of the whirl. By the tone of her voice, it had never occurred to her that anyone would not choose those circumstances. But Lady Jacqueline was also a duke's daughter, and it appeared this one did not care to conform. Adelaide liked that and was grateful for it. If Cordelia was right, Lady Jacqueline's lack of interest in society meant she would not notice that the Cordelia who had been at her brother's bedside was not the same Cordelia who had spun about a ballroom.

If her mistress was wrong?

She would deal with the resulting problems when and if they happened. Besides, Lady Jacqueline was not the sibling foremost in her thoughts.

"What about the brother? Have the two of you spoken?"

Cordelia wrinkled his nose. "I am not an attractive, married woman of the *ton*. Lord Everett had no reason to speak with me." There was a sourness to Cordelia's tone, as though hope and disappointment had mixed like milk and juice, turning rancid. "Besides, I've never met him in person. He spent the past years gallivanting around Europe. According

to the rumors, he was even more debauched on the continent than he was in England. A rake in the truest sense of
the word. He'll notice you; you're pretty enough. But once
he discovers that you're me and not a candidate for his bedroom, he'll put you out of his mind."

The thought stung. She hadn't been able to put Rhett out
of her mind since his hands grazed her thighs in the gentlest
way. How deflating it would be if he could dismiss her so
easily.

Adelaide shucked her robe and stepped into her petticoat, wrapping the strings of it around herself and deftly
tying them at her waist. Her stays were front lacing, and she
needed no one's help to fasten them. The dress was another
matter. They'd bought it for Cordelia, who'd refused to wear
anything simple. As such, it required a second person to fasten the dozens of small buttons that reached from the small
of her back to her neck. "You'll need to help me," she said.

Cordelia gave her an arch stare.

"This was your idea. If you want me to pretend to be you,
then there will be times you must pretend to be me. Or we
can cancel this entire charade and return to London."

Cordelia's lips thinned, but she made a circling motion
with her finger, and Adelaide turned.

As her mistress fumbled with the buttons, Adelaide
stared at her reflection in the mirror. With the exception of
that jewel-laden monstrosity of a wedding gown, this was
the finest clothing she'd ever worn. It was a simple day dress,
nothing a proper lady would think twice about. Cordelia
owned three dozen of them in different shades back in London. But the fine muslin was soft beneath Adelaide's fingers.
The lace at the neckline and waist was pretty. The gentle
bustle gave her a curvaceous shape that made her feel rather
special. Women who wore dresses like this worried about

how full their dance card was or who to invite to a country party. They didn't worry about how to remove punch stains from satin.

"Spill nothing on it. I only have three now."

"I will be careful," Adelaide said, turning to face her. "With any luck, the duke will wake this morning. His body likely just needed a solid night's sleep. I'll go in, make the request, and be out before anyone else in the household has woken up."

"Good morning, Your Grace."

The duke didn't stir. Adelaide looked at the butler who, after quickly masking his shock at her appearance at such an early hour, had escorted her to the duke's bedroom where a footman leaned against the back wall, his eyes drooping. Mr. Daunt coughed, and the lad sprang upright, eyes darting side to side, widening in surprise as they settled on Adelaide.

She couldn't blame him. It was beyond unusual for an unmarried woman to enter a man's bedroom, but the situation was hardly normal. No one could honestly believe something untoward would occur when the duke was still unconscious.

"Has there been any sign of him waking?"

The butler shook his head. "None, my lady. We've had someone watching over him at all times, but he hasn't so much as shifted."

"How lovely it must be to sleep so soundly." She regretted the words the moment they left her mouth. The man was unconscious with a head injury that her mistress had given him. He might not ever wake up. Still, Adelaide couldn't remember the last time she'd gone more than a few hours without waking. She'd thought that she'd sleep better once she took a permanent position, but staring up at the same roof night after night had made her uneasy.

It had to have been because the roof was not her own. The only other explanation was that having a fixed address wouldn't satisfy her at all, and that was not possible.

"Can I get you anything, my lady?" Mr. Daunt asked.

"Tea would be lovely, please." He exited, and Adelaide left it thirty seconds before she turned to the footman in the corner, who was eyeing her curiously. "There's a draft," she said, rubbing her arms for effect. "Would you fetch a blanket? Several, in fact."

He hesitated, looking first at the duke, and then out the door after the butler.

"I promise, the duke is in no danger from me." She gave him her most winning smile. *Just leave, damn it. I have no desire for a witness.*

The footman shuffled foot to foot. "You're to marry the duke? When he wakes, I mean, my lady?"

Somehow, Adelaide didn't let her winning smile crack. She knew what he was thinking. If she truly was to marry the duke, then she would be his mistress. Her words would carry more weight than even Mr. Daunt's. But she was not his mistress yet. She was a stranger imposing upon the household at a turbulent time.

She raised a brow in her haughtiest possible manner. "On the very off chance Peter wakes in the few minutes it will take to fetch a blanket, I will ring for Daunt." Her use of the duke's given name was a deliberate move to imply an intimacy that didn't exist.

"Very well, my lady," the footman said, fooled by a clever turn of phrase. "If you swear to ring the moment he moves."

"I swear it." My God, she was good at lying. If the duke woke, she'd ring no one. She'd need every second alone with him that she could wrangle.

Indeed, the moment the footman left the room, she

hurried to the duke's bedside, where four armchairs had been dragged. "Wake up." She took him by the shoulders and shook him. Hard. "Your Grace, I really must insist." But though his head lolled to the side when she released him, there was no sign of life.

She took his head in her hands to straighten it and paused. "I'm terribly sorry," she whispered, and then she slapped him gently. When he didn't respond, she slapped him a little harder, wincing as she did so, even though she knew she'd not hit him hard enough to hurt.

She looked about the room for something, anything, that might be a solution. There was a pitcher of water on the duke's desk. *Bloody hell, Adelaide. Only a truly terrible person would even consider it. Or a desperate one.* She needed the duke to wake now. She needed to resolve the matter before his siblings woke and an awkwardly uncomfortable situation became an impossibly complicated one.

Taking in a deep breath, she dumped the water on his face. He didn't move. Didn't flinch. Didn't react at all to the shock of it, or the rivulets that now ran down his brow, his cheeks, and his jawline.

Damn it. She slumped into the chair closest to him and stared. He was good-looking. Perhaps even as good-looking as his brother, if she considered it logically. But her stomach didn't twist for him the way it did when she looked at Rhett. She didn't shiver at the sight of him. She'd had the unusual chance to see both men dripping wet, hair plastered to their face, and it suited the younger brother much better.

Adelaide's gaze traveled to the small table by the bed. Needles, thread, and a half-done embroidery were neatly piled there. On the chair next to her was a woman's handkerchief, creased and crumpled as though it had been twisted, straightened, and wrung again over and over.

His sisters had clearly set themselves up by his bedside last night. "Your siblings love you," she said, trying to ignore the envy that slid down her spine. She would give everything to experience that constant affection. Almost. "I hope you don't die—truly, I do—but if you did, you would not die alone."

Adelaide would be alone. If she passed today, Cordelia might feel sad for a moment, until she felt frustrated at the inconvenience of having to train a new lady's maid, but no one would sit by her bedside. No one would lay flowers on her grave. Life would move on as if Adelaide hadn't existed.

It was partially her fault. Logically, she knew that if she wanted people to love her, she had to allow them close enough to do so, but what was the point? In every instance, she'd had to leave—either because her father or her work demanded it—and the friendship had been lost. It was far safer to eschew friendships entirely, even if that meant being jealous of the duke. Given the pinched faces of the servants, the uneasy chatter in the halls, the somber pall that rested over the house, he would be well mourned.

She swallowed back the lump that had formed in her throat. "I hope you know how lucky you are to have people who care for you. Not everyone gets to have that."

Some people were destined to travel this mortal coil alone. For her entire childhood, it had just been her and her father, and he'd hardly been doting. Most days, she hadn't been sure he hadn't forgotten her. She'd been sixteen when he passed. Since then, it had been just her trying to find a spot on which to settle, somewhere where she felt she could put down roots, but nothing had felt right. So, when publishers would ask her to write a piece about some far-flung city, she would acquiesce, thinking perhaps her next destination would be the town that she needed.

She shook her shoulders, determined to throw off the maudlin cape that had fallen over her. "For what it's worth, I never meant to lie to them. This whole debacle is all Cordelia's fault. That girl doesn't have a shred of sense. I'm sure had she told the truth and waited for you to wake, we could have resolved all of this without the lies."

There was no response from the duke. Not even the flicker of an eyelid. There was, however, one drop of water on the very tip of his nose, so perfectly balanced it had yet to fall. Adelaide took a handkerchief from the cuff of her sleeve and leaned over him, dabbing his nose, cheeks, and brow free of the damp she had created. "If you would do me the favor of waking right now, I would really appreciate it."

There was a cough, and Adelaide jumped. "Lady Cordelia," Lord Everett said, his hair mussed, his eyes blurred, his body heavy with sleep—or a hangover, if the slightly pallid tone to his skin was any indication. The duke's man of business stood close behind. "I did not expect you over so early."

She had hoped to be in and out, job done, before the family woke. "I'm an early riser." She gave him a weak smile. It was the truth. She was often up before the sun. When she was traveling, an early start to the day could be the difference between a hot dinner and bed that night, or an apple and a hunk of cheese in the corner of some farmer's barn.

"Well, that is unique amongst the *ton*," Rhett said, suspiciously.

"I know, you all lie abed until midday."

He quirked an eyebrow, and the duke's man of business frowned, as though they had noticed the way she'd distanced herself from his peers. Proof, if they had caught it, that she didn't belong. That she was an impostor.

Rhett smoothed out his expression and crossed the room to stand beside his brother. "No change?"

"I'm afraid not," Adelaide said.

She held back a sigh as the sisters tumbled into the room in a kaleidoscope of colorful robes, twisted hair rags, and wails. Adelaide stood, ready to leave.

"No *change*?" the youngest said as she threw herself on the duke's bed, burying her face in his neck. The eldest one, Margaret, put an arm around Adelaide's shoulder, pulling her close and patting her comfortingly, as though Adelaide was a grieving family member, which, she supposed, she was meant to be. She raised the damp handkerchief to her eyes and dabbed away nonexistent tears.

Good Lord, you need to get out of this situation, Adelaide.

"Why is Peter wet?" the youngest asked, sitting upright, her brow furrowed in confusion.

Oh heavens. The empty pitcher was right there, all the evidence one needed to realize she'd been torturing a helpless man.

Margaret tensed, her fingers digging into Adelaide's shoulder. "He hasn't got a fever?" There was a thread of anxiety in her tone.

The man of business pushed past the siblings and bent over the duke, putting the back of his hand against the duke's forehead, then cheek, then forehead again. "He doesn't seem to be hot, but he's clearly been sweating throughout the night."

All three of the girls started talking at once, getting progressively louder as they each strove to be heard over the others. The end result was an unintelligible cacophony. What Adelaide would give to be the duke, separated from the chaos by unconsciousness.

"Jac." Rhett ran a hand through his hair. All three ignored him.

"Lady Pallsbury had a fever for three days last season. She swears it was the leeches that saved her."

"Should we open a window?"

"Has someone sent for the doctor? We need the doctor."

"Remember when Jac was three and had a fever? The doctor piled her with blankets so she could sweat it out."

"Someone fetch a blanket."

"We should bathe him. If he's been sweating all night, he'll be smelling ripe in no time."

Rhett sighed. "Winnie."

"You know, I've never seen Peter sweat before."

"There are bound to be leeches in the woods, surely. There's a stream that runs right through them."

"Can a person not sweat at all?"

"Oh, wouldn't that be marvelous? I swear, there comes a point where the ballroom is so crowded I can barely breathe and sweat drips right down my drawers."

"Oh, good Lord," Rhett said. "Jac! There are some images I do not want in my head."

Adelaide caught the eye of the Mr. Gray, the duke's man of business, who she'd met just days ago when signing the cottage lease. He shook his head at her, as though he'd given up swimming against the tide. He had the duke's wrist in his hand, his finger pressed against the light blue veins. "Peter's pulse is quickening."

Of course the man's pulse was quickening. Not even the dead could be unmoved by the caterwauling.

"Somebody call for a doctor," the youngest wailed.

"We should have given the doctor a room. It will take an hour to fetch him. What if Peter doesn't have an hour?" Margaret started fanning her face.

For heaven's sake. "The duke likely just needs some fresh air and some quiet," Adelaide said. "Perhaps we should try staying silent, just as a precaution." It was a long shot, and more for her benefit than the duke's. She didn't know if the duke's siblings could even be quiet.

Adelaide strode to the window and thrust open the curtains. The morning winter sun was pale. She cracked the window just enough for cool, crisp air to flow through. She inhaled deeply. The air inside the room had turned suffocating when the siblings had entered, and for a moment, she could forget they were there and simply enjoy the quiet she was used to.

But only for a moment. The sisters had collectively held their breath, as though it was the only way to keep from speaking. Once that breath was exhausted, they exhaled.

"He looks better, don't you think? The fresh air is helping."

"Quite. He has some color to him."

"Peter has always been pale. He spends far too much time indoors. Rhett, put your arm to his. Compare your color."

Rhett pinched the bridge of his nose. "I will not compare my arm to his. It's hardly fitting to compete with a man when he's indisposed."

"I do think you are more tanned. It is to be expected, I suppose, when one spends all their time shirtless."

"I do not spend all my time..." He huffed. His sisters were baiting him, and he knew it. Adelaide could see him rein in his frustration.

"According to the newspapers, half of Europe has seen you in a state of undress."

"Remember the Trevi Fountain? He was found sitting shirtless in the water, asleep against the stone."

Rhett shook his head, as though fighting back a retort. He lost. "I was *not* shirtless. My shirt might have been transparent when wet, but it was on my body, so it still counts."

An image of Rhett assailed her. Him almost naked, a soaked shirt clinging to him, revealing every ridge of muscle and the shadow of hair on his chest. Good God. Despite the crisp breeze coming through the window, heat crept over her.

Adelaide couldn't help herself. "You seem to have formed a habit of being wet, my lord."

Rhett threw a sharp glance over his shoulder at her. "Let's not start on who was responsible for my last soaking."

"The same person who prevented you from being squished like a bug?"

Mr. Gray *tsk*ed, drawing the room's attention. "His heart rate went down, then it rose again. I believe the quiet helped."

"Well then," Margaret said, shooing her siblings from the room. "Quiet is what he'll have."

"Why does she get to stay?" Edwina asked, gesturing to Adelaide.

Because I have no hope of a private conversation with the duke unless you are gone.

"She doesn't," Margaret said. "Lady Cordelia is joining us for breakfast."

"Oh no. Please. That is unnecessary. I ate before I came."

"Don't be silly." She took Adelaide by the arm. "You are family now, and family eats together. Besides, we want to know everything about you. We will leave no stone unturned."

Which was exactly what Adelaide was afraid of.

Chapter Nine

Lady Cordelia stopped short at the door to the breakfast room, forcing Rhett to come to a stumbling halt. Her spine was straight, and he could see the tension in her shoulders. Her hand curled around the doorframe. *Odd.* She hadn't hesitated on the docks when a barrel was literally barreling toward them. She hadn't hesitated when the only solution to her problem was to have a strange man undress her, and she hadn't hesitated to act this morning when his sisters had begun their bewailing.

So what was it about a simple family breakfast that had her refusing to cross the threshold?

He put his hand on the small of her back, trying to ignore the frisson of energy that coursed through him, and gave her a little push. Her shoulders rose, as though she'd taken a deep and bracing breath. Then she followed his direction and walked to the table, where his sisters had already claimed their usual spots, leaving two seats free across from each other.

He held out the chair for her to sit, and she blushed, the pink of her cheeks matching her strawberry blonde hair. She murmured her thanks, her demeanor a world away from

the woman he'd first met. Hell, this wasn't even the woman
who'd been in Peter's room that morning. This woman was
exactly what one expected of a duke's daughter. Quiet,
demure, polite. He didn't like it. It sat uneasily with him, like
bad salmon. He much preferred the self-assured woman he'd
been dreaming about for the past week.

As he sat, he studied her. The dress was obviously different from what she'd worn at the docks. It flowed over her
curves instead of enveloping her. It was not weighted down
with a king's fortune in jewels. For a moment, he questioned
whether the woman on the docks and the woman in front
of him were even the same person—but the constellation of
freckles across her nose was identical. It was also impossible
for another person to have her eyes; they were light blue and
flecked with dark sapphire. The way his body thrummed at
the sight of her was the last bit of confirmation he needed—
in his twenty-eight years, no other woman had stirred such a
deep and all-consuming reaction in him. Just having her in
the same room caused his stomach to tighten and his cock to
twitch.

Damn. She was his brother's bloody fiancée—supposedly.
Potentially. If her claim was true. If it was, then when Peter
woke, Rhett would be faced with a lifetime of damnable
attraction toward a woman he could not have. Either that or
she was lying, which, for no discernible reason, cut just as
deep.

Regardless, he would go to the continent again, put as
much distance between them as he could, and hope this
swirly feeling in his belly disappeared.

"So, Lady Cordelia."

Della winced as Jac addressed her. "Call me Della,
please," she said as the footmen carried breakfast on covered
trays.

Jac grinned. "Della. Perfect. Our brother has said nothing about you. At least, Peter hasn't. Rhett waxed on about your first encounter." She waved a fork in Rhett's direction, and, not for the first time, he wished for the power to extend his leg the extra three feet necessary to kick her under the table.

Cordelia looked up at him, her cheeks pink, no doubt curious about how much of their encounter at the docks he'd shared with his siblings. He shook his head to tell her he'd not shared everything.

She loosened a little and turned to his sister. "There isn't much to tell."

Jac snorted. "That can't possibly be the truth. One moment you're walking down the aisle in front of all of London, about to marry one of the most powerful men in the country—beautiful dress, by the way—and the next, you're betrothed to my brother and sitting at his bedside. There are many steps between point A and point B, and I want to hear all about them."

Cordelia gulped and reached for her tea. "You were all at the wedding?" she asked, taking a sip and looking for all the world like she was trying to hide behind the cup.

Meg wrinkled her nose. "Jacqueline was. I was keeping Edwina company. She was very sore that she'd not received an invitation."

Winnie narrowed her eyes at Cordelia. "Only young women officially 'out' were invited."

"But one would think you would know that," Rhett said, stabbing the ham on his plate. "Given it was *your* wedding. It was *your* invitation list."

"My father oversaw the invitation list," Cordelia said carefully, holding her butter knife suspiciously tight. "And my mother organized the rest. It had to be done 'just so,' and I had little input in the matter."

"And you were willing to hand over the reins of what was supposed to be the happiest day of your life?" he drawled.

"Rhett," Meg snapped. "You're being rude." She gave him the "don't screw this up" glare she'd been giving him for decades. His twin seemed determined to like Cordelia. She'd been far too welcoming this morning.

"Besides," Jac added, "it was hardly the happiest day of her life if she didn't go through with it. I certainly wouldn't want to spend my days planning an event I didn't want to be part of."

"May we discuss something else?" Della asked.

"Of course," Meg said.

"Absolutely," Winnie added. "Tell us how you met Peter."

"What made you fall in love with him?"

"How do you know she's in love with him? That's presumptuous."

"It is not. Why would she marry him if she's not in love with him?"

"Jac has a point. If she didn't want to marry for love, she could have married Hornsmouth and saved herself the scandal."

"Fair. Well?" All three girls turned to Della with such determination, Rhett was surprised their teeth weren't bared.

For a moment, he felt a gut-wrenching urge to rescue her from his sisters' interrogation. It was like the panic he'd felt when that blasted dress had pulled her beneath the water.

She looked at him, eyes wide, as though she could count on him to save her again.

He popped the ham into his mouth. Foolish. She would soon come to learn that he could not be counted on. Besides, if his sisters didn't interrogate her, he would do it himself.

"What was the first thing you noticed about him?" Winnie prompted.

"About Peter?" She dragged her eyes from Rhett.

"Of course Peter. Who else?"

She swallowed, and her eyes flicked back toward Rhett. "His horse."

"His *horse*?" That was clearly not the response Winnie had been looking for.

"It was standing outside the cottage, munching on the few winter plants that were blooming."

"Oh, Praxis. Yes, he is a fine animal."

"I own his brother, you know."

"Did Alastair put Zeus out to stud again this year?"

"Yes. They bred him with Lady Mottram's filly."

"Oh, excellent. That should be a good pairing."

"So, Lady Cordelia, do you like horses when they aren't eating your flowers?"

Cordelia's eyes pinged from one sister to another as she tried to keep up with the conversation. It was to be expected. Spending time with this family required either the ability to track multiple concurrent threads or the willingness to ignore his sisters completely.

"Had you spoken with Peter before your arrival in Berwick?" Rhett asked, trying to get the questioning back on track. What he was really asking was, *Will I find any evidence of your connection to my brother in his personal effects?* Peter was a stickler for holding onto things. He kept every letter, every Christmas gift, every crossed-off to-do list. Every thought he had was recorded in one of his many diaries. If this supposed engagement wasn't a sham, there would be some trail of it somewhere.

Cordelia looked at him. "No. We had never met until I arrived in Berwick."

"And you came to Berwick because . . . ?"

"I needed somewhere to go. Somewhere I wouldn't be found. This seemed like a good spot."

She wasn't wrong. No one would come looking for her here. "And it's a coincidence that you found this place—a town so small it doesn't feature on maps, a place so hidden I can rarely find it despite having lived here, a place where there is a single, wealthy duke, who happened to own the cottage you leased?"

"Goodness, Rhett," Meg said, her brows furrowing. "You are in a mood this morning."

"I was woken up early." He threw an annoyed look at Cordelia.

"Rhett is not a morning person," Winnie added. "He will lie abed until midafternoon if he has the chance. It drives Peter mad."

"The duke prefers more productive lifestyle choices?" Cordelia asked.

There it was, the inevitable comparison, the perfect duke and his feckless, irresponsible younger brother. Best not disappoint. "What need do I have to wake before my body tells me to?"

"Your body might tell you to wake earlier if you didn't stay up until morning," Meg said wryly.

"Or if you didn't ply it with so much liquor when you were awake that it needed to force you into unconsciousness so it could have a break," Jac added.

Their words stung, though they shouldn't. They were mild compared to many descriptors of him. He'd heard them over and over, even before they were true, so he might as well live up to them. In the mornings, his head pounded, worse and worse as the years went on, making an excellent case for changing his libertine ways. But what would he possibly change them to? Not the army. Not the clergy. There was no room for a second son in the House of Lords. No estate for him to manage. That was probably for the best.

He'd be a terrible duke. That fact had been pressed upon him from time immemorial.

There was no role for him here in England, so he'd gone elsewhere.

Della cleared her throat, looking from person to person, clearly uncomfortable. "Perhaps I should leave. This feels like a family discussion."

"You're marrying into this family," Winnie said. "You might as well get used to us."

"You're an only child, aren't you?" Meg said.

Della nodded. "Yes."

"You're lucky," Winnie said.

Meg frowned. "You don't mean that. She doesn't mean that."

"What's it like to grow up alone?"

"She was hardly alone," Jac said. "She had her parents, at least one nanny, a governess, and a house full of servants."

Cordelia ignored them. "It was . . . what it was," she said, slathering a thick layer of jam on to toast. "I moved around a lot. I met many, many people, but then they would leave, or I would leave, and I'd rarely see them again. There was never anyone around long enough to form close bonds with."

"Except for your parents."

She looked up and forced a smile to her face that didn't align with the sadness in her eyes. "Except my parents."

It was a sad way to live. Rhett's siblings might drive him batty ninety percent of the time, but he wouldn't give them up for all the respect in the world—not even Peter. He couldn't imagine a childhood that didn't involve fishing in the stream together, or competing to create the longest daisy chain, or sneaking out at night to watch for shooting stars.

Everything had been shared—beds, toys, books, meals, dreams. While Rhett might have fled to the continent to escape the family name, never, not once, did he want to escape his family.

Meg reached across the table and took Della's hand. "Well, now you have us. Thank goodness. We're so lucky you came into Peter's life, and now of all times. I'm so grateful to you."

Della shut her eyes, her head shaking almost imperceptibly, as though being included in the family was painful.

It was painful for him too. All the wayward fantasies he'd had of her had been dashed. "Yes, we're all *so* grateful," he repeated tightly. The words sounded bitter despite his best attempts to make them sound otherwise.

"You should come and stay with us," Winnie said, clapping her hands together. "Then you can spend as much time with Peter as you like."

Della's headshake this time was firm, mirroring Rhett's own objections. "Oh, no. I don't think that's a good idea. No. I don't have a chaperone."

"Meg can be your chaperone," Jac said before Rhett could agree with Della and direct the conversation elsewhere. "She's a married woman, and the servants won't talk. Besides, what sort of impropriety could happen when Peter is sleeping?"

Cordelia looked at Rhett, her cheeks flaming red. It was as though all sorts of improprieties were tumbling through her mind. Perhaps it was their kiss. Perhaps it was the way she'd stood almost naked in front of him, and he'd held his breath the entire time. Perhaps she'd been as muddled and turned about by it as he had.

Perhaps she was having improper thoughts right now—because damn, there were a lot of improprieties that could occur with the two of them under the same roof, Peter's presence or not. Rhett's cock twinged as images of her bare skin under his fingertips ran through his mind.

She swallowed hard. "I think it's best that I remain at the cottage."

Yes. Perfect. The last thing Rhett needed was this woman under his roof. She inspired all sorts of feelings in him—suspicion, anger, envy, lust. She was a walking catalyst for the deadly sins. He couldn't live with her for days on end and not come out of it as a damned man.

"Don't be silly," Jac said, oblivious to her brother's discomfort. "At least this way, you'll be here the moment Peter wakes. He'd want that."

Della pursed her lips.

No. Don't do it. Don't say it. I'm not sure I can bear it.

She avoided looking in his direction as she said, "Thank you. I'll stay."

Chapter Ten

Peter didn't need to be awake in order for Rhett to feel the weight of the duke's disappointment. It hung over his shoulder like a specter, silent and judging. On more than one occasion, the ghostlike presence had set Rhett's heart racing. He'd left his brandy on the table and run upstairs to Peter's bedroom, convinced his brother had passed. Each time, the duke had been lying peacefully, unmoved from his previous position. The footman in the corner would bow and say, "Nothing has changed, my lord."

But it had all changed, and he couldn't put his finger on why. In theory, if Peter woke at this moment, Rhett could go on living his life as he always had. He'd still need to plead his case regarding his allowance, but a near-death experience could only relax the duke's unrealistic expectations, surely.

Yet still, it felt like nothing would be the same again. Facing his brother's mortality had shifted something within him. Everyone would die at some point, and their lives would be collected as memories and judged, even if the judgment was unintentional. Even if the worst did not come to pass and Peter lived, Rhett had this dreaded feeling that life as it had been was no longer possible.

For the fourth time that morning, Rhett approached his brother's room, prepared to be devastated. The door was open, and the footman was gone. Instead, *she* was pacing before the window. The sunlight caught her strawberry blonde hair, turning the edges gold. It shone through the delicate muslin of her skirts, exposing her silhouette and her long legs that he was far too familiar with.

Rhett swallowed. She was every bit as arresting as before. His heart thudded off-kilter, and his cock twitched. He adjusted it to sit beneath the waistband of his trousers. Never had a woman had such a visceral effect on him. Why the hell did it have to be this woman? His brother's fiancée. Lady Cordelia Highwater.

Supposedly.

Dukes' daughters didn't argue toe-to-toe with ships' captains. They didn't kiss strange men in strange taverns. They didn't gnaw on their thumbnails the way she was doing. They certainly didn't mutter obscenities, in French or any other language, yet here she was, quietly cursing.

More importantly, Rhett certainly wasn't attracted to single young ladies of the *ton*. There was nothing about a milquetoast debutante that raised his blood pressure or his cock. Not anymore.

That he was attracted to this woman meant that she was not who she said she was. It was clear as day to Rhett, even if his sisters refused to see it. Whoever she was, she had an agenda, and he would discover what it was.

Rhett coughed, drawing her attention. Her face smoothed over into the polite expression of a proper young lady. A less observant person might not have noticed that split second of conscious thought before the mask appeared. He'd noticed. He noticed everything about her.

"Lord Everett," she said, curtsying perfectly. "I hope I'm not intruding."

Of course she was intruding. This was a deeply personal family emergency, and she'd inserted herself into it for some unknown reason that he was determined to ferret out. Rhett's best option was to be as smooth as she was and catch her in a lie.

He bowed with all the grace he'd show the queen. "Lady Cordelia. Your presence could never be an intrusion. You are most welcome."

She arched a brow. *Damn it. Too smooth.*

"Thank you, my lord. I am glad. Your butler had my things put in a room down the hall. Is that agreeable?"

"The room with puce-colored wallpaper and a hideous stuffed bear's head with gilded teeth?" he asked as he strolled into the room as casually as he could. "Daunt must like you." *Daunt should have known better. Putting her in the family wing was inappropriate.*

"I wanted to be close by, in case..."

"In case my brother carks it?"

The woman purporting to be Cordelia flushed, backing into Peter's desk. "That is a crude description."

"I wouldn't have thought a woman willing to call a ship's captain a gullible prick would be so easily offended by language."

She closed her eyes and shook her head, the pink flush creeping up from under her collar deepening. "Please forget that."

He stepped closer to her. Too close. He'd intended to overwhelm her with his height, overturn her senses with his nearness. Instead, he fell into her gravitational pull, as though she was the sun and he was a celestial body destined to be burned by it.

In an effort to regain control, he cupped her shoulder with his hand, grazing a path with his thumb that caused his throat to tighten. "Forget the way you kissed me?"

He moved even closer. There was barely an inch between them and no telling where his body warmth ended and hers began, just that the air between them snapped and crackled as if on fire. "The press of your lips against mine was an experience I've no desire to forget."

She swallowed and, for a brief second, he would swear he saw her sway toward him. Then she took his hand and removed it. "I *saved* you," she said, stepping to the side and leaving a gulf between them.

He tried to hide the sense of loss with a cheeky grin, turning to lean against the dressing table, his arms crossed. "And I saved you, so we're even."

She took a fierce breath. "You wouldn't have had to save me if you hadn't dragged me into that refuse-ridden water to begin with." Her eyes sparked, adding to the roiling flame within him. "Would it have been so hard to let go of me?"

"Impossible." The truth was out of his mouth before he could stop it. It would have been impossible to let go of her then, and if she hadn't stepped away just now, it would have been likewise beyond his capabilities. He shook his head and took advantage of the distance she'd created to back out of her orbit. She was a charlatan or his brother's fiancée, neither of which included a future of continued kissing. Rhett turned away from her, toward his brother, guilt immediately washing through him. *Pull it together.* "Has there been any change?"

"None," she said, her voice evening out. "Not a flicker of movement other than the steady rise and fall of his chest."

Rhett crossed to the bed and took Peter's hand. "He's not drenched in sweat. That's a good sign."

She sighed as she came to stand beside him, though she kept her distance by several feet. "He wasn't drenched in sweat earlier."

He turned to her, eyebrow raised.

"There was a pitcher of water by his bed. I thought it might wake him."

The image of his brother, one of the most power-ful men in England, being doused in water by this slip of a woman was one he wished he'd seen in person. Peter would be horrified. Genuinely aghast. Dukes were never so maligned.

Rhett chuckled hard enough that Cordelia, or whoever she was, looked at him askance.

"When he wakes, I will relish teasing him about that."

"If he wakes." Trepidation wove through her tone, and for a brief second, she raised her thumbnail to her teeth, before catching herself and clasping her hands behind her back. Would her plans fall through if his brother passed, or was she genuinely worried about him?

"My brother is stubborn and arrogant, and he always gets what he wants. He'll come through this. Death is no obstacle to him."

"We all die eventually," she whispered.

We all do. He'd be wrestling with that thought all morn-ing, and with what it meant. She didn't need to know that, though. "How encouraging," he drawled. "Thank you."

She shook her head, rubbing at her temples. "I apologize." She reached out and grabbed his hand, giving it a comfort-ing squeeze. "Of course your brother will come through. Ignore my comment. I am a cynic."

Her hand in his felt nice, natural, as though it was meant to be. The reassuring look on her face actually brought him a measure of peace. Then he remembered who she was, or perhaps wasn't, and he pulled his hand from hers.

"A cynic at your age? After one season? I thought young debutantes all had fantasies about love and knights and horses. Although I suppose a duke is the going dream of the day, is it not?"

"My fantasies are…different." She tucked her arm around her body.

He shouldn't ask. He didn't want to know, except he desperately did. "What are your fantasies, Lady Cordelia?"

She didn't answer.

"Come now. We're to be family, are we not?" *Curse the thought.* Did it make her stomach roil as much as it did his?

She paused, frowned, and he could tell she would not answer.

"Come on, Della." He bumped his shoulder against hers. "Tell me a truth."

She shifted uncomfortably before relenting. "A bookcase that stretches across an entire room that not even ten men could move in a cottage that's all my own where I can forget the rest of the world exists." There was a wistfulness to her tone, a sense of yearning that wrapped around his heart like ivy and squeezed.

Every instinct in him wanted to rescue her from whatever had caused her to want to hide away, to tease apart her desire to be alone and replace it with himself.

Which was how Lady Meredith Moylan had done it. She'd played Rhett's emotions like a violin, winding him taut, dragging her stories over him until he was playing her tune. The difference now was that he could recognize a fraud when he saw one.

"My brother owns several such homes, which I'm sure you know."

She recoiled as though he'd raised a fist. "Are you calling me a fortune hunter?" The outrage was genuine. *Blast.*

He liked women. He loved women. At least, he loved the ones who were married, or who didn't know that he was brother to a duke, or who were related to Rhett and had no ulterior motives in talking with him. He took no pleasure in offending one. If a man spoke to Rhett's sisters in such a manner, Rhett would hoist them up a flagpole—if he was feeling generous and didn't thrash them instead.

"I'm sorry," he said, leaning toward her. She stiffened. "Forgive me," he said. "That was rude. Please stay. Meg has taken Winnie into town; Jac is writing letters to whatever mystery person she's been obsessed with. I could use the company."

She glanced at him sideways. "You don't want some alone time with your brother?"

"Given he's currently such a charming conversationalist?"

She smiled. "Fair point." She took the embroidery from a chair by the bed and sat, arranging her skirts so they lay without creases. The embroidery she barely glanced at before placing it on her lap.

He had options. He could take the seat next to hers or one of the others that were placed in a semicircle around the bed. Remembering how easily he'd slipped into her orbit earlier, he left a chair free between them.

"What would you like to discuss?"

"Tell me more about you."

Her smile faded. The rest of her expression shuttered, as though preparing for a storm. "There isn't much to know."

Which was the evasive response he'd expect from someone not being honest about who they were. "Come on now, surely you can share a little of yourself given we've both seen each other at our worst."

"Was that our worst?"

"Perhaps not in character, but it had to be the worst we've looked or smelled, unless you have a rollicking good story to tell me."

Cordelia laughed, and it caused his stomach to swirl. "No, that was definitely the low point in my hygiene."

He shifted. "Tell me about your family."

Her shoulders tensed, and for a moment, he thought she'd refuse. She was certainly hesitant to tell him anything. Finally, when she realized he wasn't about to fill the silence, she relented and sat back in her chair.

"I don't have a lot of family."

That rang true—as far as Rhett knew, the Duke of Thirwhestle only had one child and had no siblings himself.

"My father was absent, even when we were in the same room. One time, he so completely forgot about me that he left me behind and was half a day's ride away before he realized and had to turn around."

"The servants didn't notice you were missing?" It was hard to believe this goddess of a woman could be overlooked.

"We weren't traveling with a large retinue."

"I hope he was profusely apologetic when he returned."

Cordelia gave an unladylike snort. "Hardly. It was, of course, my own fault. He was never responsible for his actions. That would require being honest with himself when he wasn't honest with anyone."

He heard the truth in her words. Not just because of the rawness in her voice or the ways her eyes drifted, as if remembering the neglect, but because Rhett had met the duke once, and that was all it took to know that he was not a good man.

"I'm sorry," he said. "That sounds…difficult."

She started, eyes focusing as she returned to the present. "Don't be. Difficult family is better than no family. It's hard to be alone. But it makes you self-sufficient, I suppose."

She was self-sufficient enough to run from her own wedding, setting fire to all the bridges behind her. Was that why she was here? Had she gone out into the world this past week and realized it was harder to get by on one's own than she'd thought?

She shook herself, and her expression shifted to one of neutral politeness, as though for a moment a mask had slipped, and she was now firmly replacing it. "And what of your family, Everett?"

"Rhett, please. You called me that once."

She softened. "Rhett, then. Is yours a difficult family?"

"Are you curious to know what you've gotten yourself in for?"

"It's always best to be prepared."

He drummed his fingers on the arm of the chair, juggling his own feelings with what his brother's betrothed might want to hear. "My sisters, once they love you, will love you forever." It was their best trait. It was what set them apart from others. It was something he had yet to master.

"And His Grace?"

"Loves with equal strength, though it manifests differently." That was half of the problem. If Peter cared less about Rhett, he wouldn't be so doggedly determined to see Rhett ensconced in a traditional, acceptable career. The trouble was that while the duke cared about Rhett's happiness, he simply did not know Rhett well enough to know what that happiness would look like.

It was difficult to blame him. Peter had barely reached his teens before the dukedom was thrust upon him. He'd suddenly had estates to look after and four siblings to care for. Winnie had not even been a month old. His attention had gone where it was required. Rhett had been ten, old enough not to need or want his brother as a parent. The two had always been friends, peers almost, looking for ways to avoid their annoying little sisters. Then their parents had died, and

Peter's duties had pulled him away, and somehow, a gulf had developed.

At some point, Peter and Rhett had become strangers. Strangers who loved each other for no reason other than blood.

"There are worse things than being loved too much by one's brother," she said.

She was right. Damn it. He shifted uncomfortably in his seat, keenly aware of the privilege in his problems.

"Perhaps Peter needs some quiet."

"If you wish," Della said, picking up the half-completed embroidery that Winnie had given her.

He faced forward in his chair, pretending he wasn't off-kilter. The conversation hadn't gone to plan. He was supposed to be interrogating her, drawing out the truth of her motivations, confirming that she was a fraud. Instead, all he'd discovered was that she could stir thoughts in him he thought he'd eliminated years ago.

Chapter Eleven

Good Lord, embroidery was ridiculous. Adelaide would much rather have stockings to mend or a dress to cut down and reshape. These constant stitches for no purpose other than to look pretty might keep her hands busy, but her eyes and mind were left to wander to the two men in front of her.

There might be a way to wake the duke. It wasn't ideal; she couldn't do it on her own, and if it worked, she would have company when the duke woke. Lord only knew what kind of quickstepping she'd have to do in that situation. But sitting here, doing nothing useful, chafed. It gave her far too much time to study the honeyed curl of Rhett's hair, the way his long fingers drummed against the arm of the chair he lazed in, the cut of his trousers tight along his muscled thighs.

Adelaide squirmed. She'd seen more of the world than most people. She'd watched men in Italy, Prussia, even the Middle East. There were handsome specimens everywhere—tall, lean, and hard, with chiseled jaws and smoldering eyes. There were shifts in appearance across the continent, and she had appreciated the beauty in every change, but no man had stirred her the way Rhett did. Heat hadn't flashed over her skin, her insides hadn't clenched, there'd been no warmth pooling between her legs.

She certainly hadn't been moved to drop her guard, even if it was only for a moment.

Good God. She needed to do something productive, or she needed to leave. Staring at him was leading to madness.

"I have an idea."

"You have a what now?" Rhett looked up, his hazel eyes smoldering.

Ignore it, Adelaide. Pay no mind to the stupid, distracting flip-flop of your belly. "To wake your brother. I have an idea. It's a long shot, but it might work."

His brow creased, and he leaned forward. "I'm listening."

"He needs to move. His body is as stagnant as his brain is. Perhaps if we get the first moving, the latter will too." It made sense, according to her admittedly rudimentary understanding of the circulatory system. The more one moved, the faster one's heart beat, the more oxygen traveled to the brain. It was why she'd gotten so lightheaded running with the bulls in Pamplona.

Rhett cocked his head. "What exactly are you suggesting?"

"We get him out of bed. Walk him around the room." A walk outside would be better, but she had no desire to maneuver an unconscious body down and up three flights of stairs.

Rhett snorted. "Walk him? Like a dog?"

In her mind, it was more like a horse with colic, but sure, a dog. Whatever. "Walk him, drag him, get his blood flowing in some manner."

He looked at her as though she'd suddenly sprouted six heads, leaning back in his chair as if one of those heads would bite. "That sounds like lunacy."

"Do you have any better ideas?"

He snorted again. "No, and I'm quite taken with this one, to be honest. Peter would hate it."

Most people would hate being manhandled, but when there were no other options, one had to be practical. "Well, then. Let's give it a go. It can't hurt." She stood and tugged sharply at the duke's blankets.

Oh.

Her ears burned immediately. That same embarrassed heat crept across her chest. Someone had changed the duke since yesterday. Under the blankets, he was wearing only a thin nightshirt, untied, his graying chest hair on display, and his legs were naked below mid-thigh. The fabric was so thin and so soft that it settled across his waist and crotch like a whisper, obscuring *nothing.* Adelaide caught a fairly good impression of the duke's, ahem, member before she turned away, her gaze colliding directly with Rhett's smirk.

"First time seeing your fiancé's assets? Do they live up to your expectations?"

She swallowed, trying desperately to seem unaffected. Still, she couldn't help her gaze traveling south, toward Rhett's waistband and below. Were both the Montgomery brothers so well-endowed?

"The duke's assets are perfectly fine," she said, once she trusted her voice not to break. "I'm sure he can put them to good use."

Rhett's eyes narrowed.

Why the devil did you say that? Great work making an already awkward situation worse, Adelaide.

He was annoyed. If she didn't know better, she would venture as far as *jealous.* "My brother has been a veritable monk for years. I'm not sure his assets continue to work."

She snorted. "Well, I dare say that of the two of you, his are less likely to be worn-out."

Fuck, Adelaide. You do not need to voice every thought

that comes to mind. What was it about this man that loosened her tongue?

Loosened your tongue for all sorts of purposes. Her already-burning cheeks ignited, and she fanned herself. *Double fuck, Adelaide. Control your thoughts.*

If Rhett noticed her increased embarrassment, he didn't show it. "*Nothing* is worn-out, thank you very much." There was ire in his tone.

"If you say so," she said primly, trying to ignore the desire to say *prove it.* "Here, help me lift him." Adelaide circled the bed until she was standing opposite the only conscious lord in the room. She leaned over the duke, one arm lifting his shoulder, the other shoving behind his back. Rhett sighed and did the same. Against the duke's nightshirt, their fingers touched. She would have sprung away from him if she could, if the deadweight of an unconscious man didn't have her practically pinned.

"On the count of three," she said, gritting her teeth against the discomfort of Rhett's touch. "One, two, three." They heaved until the duke was sitting upright, but the momentum was too much. First his head tipped forward, and then his torso, until the duke's own head was squished in his lap.

"Huh," Adelaide said. "He's remarkably flexible."

Rhett snickered. "I wonder if he could, you know, to himself."

She furrowed her brow. What the devil was he talking about? Before she was forced to admit her confusion, he crudely popped a tongue into the side of his cheek.

"Oh. *Oh.*" She shook her head. It was a gesture Adelaide knew well. One didn't spend as much time in taverns as she had without learning the different cultural references for fellatio.

She laughed before catching herself and switching back into her Cordelia mask. "That was a grossly inappropriate thing to say in front of a lady. You should be ashamed of yourself."

"Apologies, my lady," he replied. Funnily enough, it didn't sound at all like an apology.

Adelaide circled the bed. "Let's try to do this without the lewd commentary, shall we?" But what Rhett had said couldn't be unsaid, and she wondered if it was, in fact, possible for a man to, you know, to himself. Wouldn't that be convenient? Women were limited to their own fingers, and while they could get the job done, they certainly didn't compare to a skilled tongue.

Rhett crouched next to the bed and laid one of the duke's arms across his shoulders. Adelaide leaned over and took hold of the other.

"*Sur le compte de trois,*" Rhett said, waggling his eyebrows. "*Vous parlez français, n'est-ce pas? La plupart des dames le font.*"

Once more, Adelaide got the feeling that she was being tested. "Yes, I speak French. It's a mandatory subject in all finishing schools."

Rhett *hmph*ed. "Just curious."

It wasn't just curiosity, though. He didn't trust her. Nor should he. That first afternoon when they'd met had revealed the truth—she was not a lady of the *ton*, however she might have been dressed, and she was going to have to work hard to change his mind now.

She smiled prettily as they hoisted the duke into a standing position. "*Möchtest du auch mein Deutsch testen? An mea Latinus?*"

Rhett raised an eyebrow. "German *and* Latin? That must have been one exceptional finishing school."

Damn it, Adelaide. Too far. "I've always had an interest in languages," she said, trying to cover her misstep.

"Odd. Most young women are more interested in less cerebral hobbies."

She raised her own eyebrow. "Are you calling women stupid?"

Rhett flushed. If he could have hidden behind his brother, Adelaide rather thought he would have. "No. Of course not. I have three sisters, two of whom could run intellectual rings around me. I'm simply saying that in my experience, young ladies are more interested in gossip and ladder climbing than they are in languages."

She shifted under the weight of the duke's arm. "I have no interest in ladder climbing." She didn't need a husband. All she needed was enough money to lease her tiny home, a place where she could stay forever if she wished. If she could convince the duke not to press charges against Cordelia, she would have that. A husband would only complicate things. The romance would end as they inevitably do, yet she would still be stuck with that person for the rest of her days.

Rhett reached across to prop his brother's head upright. It fell backward, the duke's mouth hanging open like a Japanese koi fish searching for food. "All young ladies are preoccupied with the *ton*'s hierarchy," Rhett said, frowning and tugging on a lock of the duke's hair.

"And I am at the top of it," she replied sounding as much like Cordelia as she could. "I am a duke's daughter. There are no more rungs left for me to climb. Now, shall we continue? Enas. Dýo. Tría."

Rhett held up a hand. "What are we doing on the count?"

"We walk," Adelaide said with some effort, gripping onto the arm that hung over her shoulder. The duke was heavier than he looked, a deadweight threatening to make her fall. And she wasn't even bearing all the duke's weight. Rhett was grimacing under the strain of his half.

"Righto."

As they stepped forward, the duke's legs remained where they were. After a few more steps, they reached the point where the duke's toes dragged on the ground behind them and his head hung forward. What little support he'd had for his own weight was gone, and Adelaide's knees almost buckled. Still, with a grunt, they continued until they were at the wall.

"Now we turn," she said. *But how the devil will we do that?*

"This is ridiculous. If only Peter were awake to feel the weight of his humiliation."

"If your brother was awake, that would solve so many issues." And create new ones, like Adelaide's need to plead for mercy on Cordelia's behalf. "How do we turn him?"

Rhett closed the gap between himself and the wall, leaning his back against it, shifting so that his brother effectively leaned on him. The duke's face was buried in Rhett's neck; Rhett's arms wrapped around his waist to keep him upright.

"Aw. Sweet, brotherly affection," Adelaide said, leaning forward with her hands on her thighs, panting, grateful for the brief respite from the load.

"Hilarious. What do we do now?"

"He's heavier than I expected. I could get your sisters."

"No. They would not help. They'd stand there and taunt me."

Adelaide stood, arms akimbo. "Why would they do that?"

Rhett scowled. "You are an only child. You would not understand. Could we simply drop him here? Perhaps the loss of dignity will jolt him into consciousness. He couldn't bear to become a pile of nightshirt and bare limbs."

"We can't leave him on the floor." She needed the duke to feel kindly toward her when she asked for his forgiveness.

"Then let's take him back to the bed."

Sending him back to bed would achieve nothing. The duke would still be unconscious, and she would be stuck here, waiting for him, distracted by his impossibly good-looking brother. If the duke didn't wake up, Cordelia risked going to gaol for murder, and Adelaide would never have the home she wanted. She shook her head resolutely. "We've barely given this time to work,"

"It will not work." Rhett was becoming exasperated. "The concept is sound, but *he* isn't doing the moving; we are. The only blood rushing is ours."

Adelaide rubbed her temples, trying to ease the tension forming there. "You're right. We need his limbs to be functioning."

"And how do you suppose we do that?" He shifted against the wall, and the duke shifted with him. He tightened his arms to prevent his brother from toppling over. The teasing expression he'd worn earlier hardened.

Adelaide scanned the room for a solution. The embroidery Cordelia had given her was still by the bed, but that couldn't help. The only other items in the room were a few chairs, a dressing table, a wardrobe, and a lamp.

"Hang on a second," she said. She threw the wardrobe door open. There, neatly folded, was a stack of scarves. She grabbed as many as she could.

"Ditching me for a stroll outside in this weather? Craven woman."

"Ha ha." Adelaide dropped to her haunches and looped one scarf around Rhett's ankle.

"What are you doing?"

She tightened the scarf around the duke's ankle, binding the two brothers together.

"Whoa. What are you doing?"

She looped a second scarf around their knees, making

sure the knot was tight. "When you move, he moves. You will be as one."

Rhett rolled his eyes. "You realize I've spent the better part of my life trying to get distance from the duke?"

"And yet here you are at his bedside. Look how far all that running has gotten you." Her cheeks flushed as she reached between Rhett's thighs. His cream-colored trousers were tight and left little to the imagination.

"I wasn't running. I wanted to find myself."

She tugged the knot tight. "Did you find yourself, my lord, amongst the saloons of Europe? Did the wine and the women guide your way?"

Rhett looked at her askance. Of course he would. Young ladies might hear such gossip; they might even whisper of it to their friends, but they would never confront a man about it directly. *Damn it, Adelaide.*

"No. Not yet." He gave her a wry smile. "That is why I must get back the moment my brother is well. My raison d'être lies somewhere across the seas."

"If years of traveling hasn't led you to discover your purpose, perhaps the path is not on the continent. Perhaps it's right here."

Rhett snorted. "Unlikely. Now, are you finished?"

There were only enough scarves to tie the two men's legs together. The duke was currently slumped over Rhett's shoulder, head against the wall.

"When we move, his arms and torso are going to go flailing. They always do," Rhett said. "I won't be able to keep him upright on my own."

Adelaide smiled. "Do you have a lot of practice moving unconscious bodies?" She, herself, had only ever moved a couple and even then, they were passed-out drunks spread-eagled with a person holding each limb. This was an entirely different endeavor, and she would take whatever insight Rhett had.

"I have some experience. There was one night in Moscow…"

"Dead body or unconscious?"

Rhett grimaced. "Unconscious, but you're probably best off not knowing the details."

Adelaide *tsk*ed. "You won't tell me your deepest secrets?"

"Will you tell me yours?"

She shook her head. She didn't even share the shallowest of them if she could help it. Already, he'd drawn too much from her. She'd never discussed her father with anyone.

"Well, since I won't be solving the mystery that is Lady Cordelia Highwater, let's get back to work." The words were said jovially, but she could sense his disappointment.

Rhett hooked an arm under each of his brother's shoulders in a giant bear hug and took a step away from the wall. The duke immediately sagged at the waist, his almost-bare arse sinking toward the floor. His cock flopped forward, clearly visible from behind, and Adelaide tried not to look. Rhett stumbled, and she raced to prop the two of them up with her hands firmly on the duke's shoulders.

"You'll have to do more than that. Hold him around the middle."

Adelaide wrinkled her nose. She could hardly refuse. This had been her idea. Trying her damnedest not to blush, she placed both hands on the duke's arse cheeks and pushed upward until he was flush with his brother.

Rhett grimaced, clearly as uncomfortable as she was.

She wrapped her arms around both of their waists, interlocking her fingers against the band of Rhett's trousers. A hot spark grazed her fingers where the warmth of his body met hers. When she looked past the duke's shoulders, she saw a flush creep up Rhett's neck. He was staring at her the way a lion watched his prey, like he wanted to devour her. Like he'd stared at her the day they met. He'd been a gentleman. He'd adverted his gaze whenever he could, but he'd not been able to hide the smoldering in his eyes. It had made her feel beautiful and powerful and shaky with lust.

"It is hot in here, isn't it? It's not just me?"

Rhett swallowed and nodded. "Let's just move."

"All right. One. Two. Three." They both stepped forward into each other, the duke squeezed in the middle, before they both stepped back and almost tumbled. "We'll go left first," Adelaide said once she'd regained her balance. "One. Two. Three."

Once again, they both moved in opposite directions and almost fell as the duke's body weight exaggerated the mismatch in balance.

"*Merde*," Adelaide swore before she could stop herself.

Rhett raised an eyebrow. "Your finishing school must've had a curious curriculum."

"Our French teacher had a colorful vocabulary when she was upset. Now, will you just follow my instructions?"

"You said left," Rhett said indignantly.

"Why would you assume I meant *your* left instead of mine?"

Rhett frowned. "I . . . uh."

"Because everyone always defers to the son of a duke."

He scowled. "You speak as though you're not the daughter of a duke."

Damn it, Adelaide. You need to be more careful. He will trip you up. "It was a comment about your sex, not your breeding."

"Of course." But once again, he didn't believe her. His tone was placating, not accepting.

"Let's just get moving." The sooner this exercise succeeded

or failed, the sooner she could get out of there. "*My* left, on three."

This time, they moved in synchronicity, taking small steps toward the window. Each time Rhett lifted his foot, he did so exaggeratedly—a kind of high-step march that looked ridiculous and made it bloody difficult to balance the dead-weight between them, but it was sensible, given the point of the exercise was to get as much of the duke's blood pumping as possible.

After reaching the window, the bed, and the window again, Rhett huffed. "How long do we need to do this for?"

"Ten minutes should be sufficient. If your brother hasn't woken by then, then the exercise is clearly not working."

"Ten minutes." Rhett rolled his shoulders and shifted so the duke was leaning across his other shoulder. "Then you are going to have to entertain me, Lady Cordelia. Distract me from the fact that in all my years of life, I've never been this close to a man in his bedclothes."

"But you've been this close to a man out of his bedclothes?"

"Well, there was this one time in Munich," he said, starting his high-step march toward the bed once again. "Actually, at least thrice in Munich...Every September, it hosts this enormous celebration."

Adelaide snorted as memories of previous Oktoberfests played through her mind. "Last year, they put one of the carnival tents near a brewery tent," she said. "Did you know elephants were so fond of beer?"

"You saw that?" Rhett stopped with no warning. Adelaide's grip on the duke faltered as she kept going. "Damnation," he said. "All I saw was the aftermath. Entire caravans trampled, monkeys loose, clowns trying to put the tent back together despite being too drunk to stand."

Oh, the clowns. If it weren't for the furious screaming of the ringmaster in the middle of the street, Adelaide would have thought it was a skit, the way they continually fell, pulling the tent down on top of themselves. She was about to say just that when she caught herself. Lady Cordelia had never left England, let alone attended Oktoberfest.

"I didn't see it. Though I would have loved to. I read about it in a travelogue."

"Oh, of course. I don't know what I was thinking." Rhett's expression fell, as though he'd been looking forward to reminiscing.

"I, for one, would like to have seen the expression of the farmer who rolled home from the event to find an elephant stripping his cherry tree. How would we even attempt to catch such a creature?"

"You would attempt to catch it? Truthfully?"

"You would not?"

"*I* would try to catch it, if only to have a good story to tell. But I would not expect a young woman to do so."

Adelaide continued to shuffle backward, trying not to fall. "Well, perhaps not all young ladies are so straitlaced. Some of us are more than capable of catching elephants, metaphorically. Perhaps next Oktoberfest, if I'm out that way."

His brows furrowed, and she realized she'd slipped. "That is assuming my third cousin, the crown prince, extends an invitation."

Rhett narrowed his eyes. "You are a singular woman, Della. Your contradictions intrigue me."

Was that an accusation or a compliment? Either way, this lie that Cordelia had dropped her in kept expanding, and as it did, it was no longer just Cordelia's lie. Every time Adelaide embellished it, it belonged more fully to her. Her mind flew back to her father, to their midnight departures whenever his lies caught up to them. She had never wanted to be like him, yet here she was, lying to someone she genuinely liked. Her lies were not little and white. They would have consequences. They would cause hurt when the truth came out. Perhaps there was a way to resolve the situation that would still save Cordelia's reputation without further compromising who Adelaide was.

"Are any of us honestly what we present ourselves as?" she whispered.

Rhett remained silent, waiting.

"The truth of the matter is—"

A loud gasp cut through the air. "What are you doing?" Margaret, Jacqueline, and Edwina stood in the doorway, their eyes wide, hands to their mouths.

It wasn't a total overreaction. The scene must look somewhat odd. Adelaide and Rhett were practically embracing, her fingers locked at his waistband, him staring at her intently. Between them was the duke in naught but his bedclothes, hung against his brother like a sack of potatoes.

"It was her idea," Rhett said, levering the duke's body onto hers and stepping back. He'd forgotten about the scarves, though. First, he fell to the floor, then his momentum brought his brother crashing down on top of him. Adelaide tried to slow the duke's body, to minimize its impact. All that did was bring her down onto them both.

"Oof. Ow. Bloody hell." At the bottom of the pile of limbs and torsos, Rhett groaned.

With the help of his sisters, Adelaide scrambled off the two men. In the process, the duke's nightshirt shifted, leaving his bare arse exposed to the room.

"No, no, no, no, no, no," Edwina said. "We do not need to see this."

Margaret bobbed down to tug on her brother's clothes,

giving him a modicum of privacy. "Everett Montgomery, our brother is *sick*. He needs rest and care, not to be part of one of your irresponsible pranks. How could you? At a time like this?"

"It was not a…" He tried to shuffle his way out from under his brother, but between the duke's weight and the bindings at their legs, he was well trapped.

"It was not a prank, and Lord Everett is right, it was my idea," Adelaide said, quickly working on the knotted scarves.

The sisters stood, arms akimbo, skeptical looks on their faces.

"We were trying to boost his circulatory system. The blood flows around the body and to the brain, so we thought that if we could get him moving, blood might flow more freely." She released the last of the knots and stood.

Jacqueline gave her a long, assessing stare. "That sounds like it makes sense. What an interesting idea. How did you learn so much about the human body?"

The real Cordelia knew nothing of the human body other than what she could see, and judge, on the outside. She took no interest in anything other than gossip and the acceptable pastimes of a young woman. Adelaide had never seen her with a novel, let alone a newspaper or a work of nonfiction. There was no good reason for her to understand the circulatory system.

"It was just a guess," Adelaide said weakly.

Rhett grunted again, still spread-eagled on the floor, unable to move. "If you lot are quite finished?"

"Sorry, brother." Between the four of them, the girls rolled the duke to the side, only barely maintaining his modesty. Rhett dragged in several deep breaths.

Edwina shook her head. "Peter is going to kill you when he wakes. You know that, don't you?"

Chapter Twelve

In Rhett's mind, the difference between small towns in England and small towns in Europe was charm, namely the fact that European towns had some. Berwick was small. The streets and buildings were narrow. Except for the Christmas wreaths on the doors, it lacked color, and its inhabitants were standoffish.

But here he was, seated in the village's only pub, drinking weak-as-piss ale in a futile search for normalcy. The barman had been polite, but when Rhett had tried to banter with him, he'd awkwardly ducked his head and found a spot at the other end of the bar that needed intense cleaning.

Every time a new person would enter, Rhett would give them a wide smile, throwing his arms open. "Bonjour. Ciao. Privet." Truly, he'd welcome conversation with anyone; it would make him feel more like the man he'd made himself into over the past few years and less like the feckless Lord Everett, which was all he was when he came home.

But each person who entered gave him a wide berth before clustering in little groups where they were *clearly* gossiping about him—looking at him without actually looking at him, no matter how hard he tried to catch them doing so.

"What's for lunch?" he asked the barman. Up at the

house, he'd seen the footmen laying out a full spread—soups, cheese, pheasant, pickles. Along the sideboard had been an array of pastries and cakes with enough clotted cream for him to indulge in his usual two-thirds cream, one-third cake concoction. Meg must have had a word with the kitchen staff.

But he hadn't stayed, despite being starved. Instead, he'd escaped to the village.

"Haggis."

Great. Wonderful. Of all the kingdom's staid culinary delights, they were serving the one that turned his stomach. Perhaps he should just grit his teeth and return to the house. He could have a footman bring food to Peter's study. It was stocked with plenty of decent brandy, although Rhett had developed a penchant for gin while he was abroad.

Perhaps if he entered through the back garden, he could avoid his sisters and all of their many questions. For some reason he could not fathom, given they'd expected nothing of him before, he'd become the person his sisters went to for answers—of which he had none. Zero. *Aucun.*

I don't know when Peter will wake, Winnie. I don't know what's wrong with him. I don't know what will happen if he passes, Jac. I don't know if Lady Bertram will consider this an acceptable reason to miss next season. I don't know how I feel about any of this, Meg.

I don't know. I don't know. I don't know. And that lack of knowing only made him feel even more worthless.

The only person not asking him questions was Della. She'd stayed quietly in the corner of Peter's room waiting for him to wake, making fast work of the embroidery in her lap and deftly palming off all attempts by his sisters to engage her in conversation. She was firm in her rejections but sweet in the delivery. She was poised. Calm. Collected. Gods, she was exactly like the lady she claimed to be.

Except the lady she claimed to be wouldn't try to catch an elephant, damn it. He was mad with attraction to her, but if she was who she said she was, she was already spoken for *by his blasted brother*.

The doorbell jangled, and Rhett looked up, keen for a distraction. *Ugh*.

"Avoiding anyone in particular?" Andrew asked as he took a seat beside Rhett and gestured for a pint of ale.

"Can I not avoid them all?"

Andrew frowned. "For the next hour or two," he said, his disappointment clear. "But you cannot spend your time idling right now. After lunch, there is work to do."

Rhett took a big gulp of the dreadful beer. "Work?" Rhett didn't work. Not how Andrew meant it. He would climb a rigging or help shoe a horse. Hell, he'd even muck out stables; there was something satisfying in manual labor. But Andrew wasn't asking him to pick up a shovel. The estate was well staffed. He knew exactly what Andrew wanted. There was a pile of it on the desk in Rhett's room that he refused to look at. The sight left a pit in his stomach.

"With Peter out of commission—"

"Don't say it." *It was never supposed to happen. He was the spare. A backup only in case the proper duke perished.*

"Rhett, you can't run from your duty."

"I'm not running." Which was a lie. He'd escaped the house as soon as he could and was dragging his feet before returning. That was why he was trying to make conversation with anyone who was willing. It gave him a legitimate reason to avoid going back.

"If Peter doesn't wake, if he passes..."

"The sawbones said he'd be fine."

"The doctor said there was a fifty-fifty chance of his recovery."

Rhett drained what was left in his glass and gestured for another. "I like those odds."

Andrew's lips thinned. "I don't, and as Peter's man of business, I have a responsibility to him and to the estate."

"Great. Excellent." Rhett accepted the tankard a barmaid offered to him. "You do it. You've been helping him manage the dukedom for years, ever since we were children."

Andrew had been Rhett's father's ward. He had grown up in the same schoolrooms and dining rooms, played games on the same lawns, climbed the same trees, paddled in the same lakes, all the while knowing that when he was older, he would be the family's solicitor or estate manager or some equally important caretaker of the Strafford domain.

Andrew had been groomed for his role in the same way Peter had, while Rhett had been left to his own devices. Hell, Andrew would be a better duke than Rhett ever could be.

"You know what needs doing," Rhett said, "so do it. I'm unnecessary."

Andrew *tsk*ed. "You are quite necessary," Andrew said. "I can advise, but ultimately, the duke decides."

"And the duke *will*, when he wakes. Until then, you have my permission to act as you see fit." Because even if it was for the shortest period of time, Rhett would screw it up.

"Everett." The censure in Andrew's tone grated.

Rhett slammed his tankard on the bar top, the thud of metal against wood making Andrew flinch. "Not a single person thinks that I'm fit to be the duke, not even you, so why are you pressing this?" He went to stand, but Andrew grabbed him by the shoulder, holding him firm.

"If people think you are irresponsible and incompetent, it is by your design. You played the fool even though you weren't one. You sought the moniker."

Rhett clenched his fingers around his tankard. He had

no biting response to the truth. It hadn't been conscious, at least not at first. Negative attention had been preferable to no attention at all. Eventually, he'd realized that pranks and smart-alecky quips were easier than trying and failing.

He wasn't good at numbers. He had trouble concentrating on the dense reading his professors liked to set. He found dead people boring. The only thing he was good at was alive people, but that wasn't a subject he could be graded on. He'd scraped through with a degree only because of Peter's influence, and he'd entered society already labeled a scoundrel.

None of his attempts to be anything different had succeeded.

If Peter died, and that was still yet to be determined, then Rhett would work out what the hell to do with this whole mess, but until then, there was no reason the conscientious and respectable Andrew Gray couldn't step in.

Andrew squeezed Rhett's shoulder. "If Peter dies, his titles fall to you. You don't have the option of declining them."

Rhett shook his friend's hand off. "Philborough hasn't set foot on his country estates in decades. English lords swan around Paris and Florence with a woman on each arm every summer."

Andrew ran the edge of his tankard in circles on the bar. "That's true. Plenty of lords let their estates run into the ground with no care for the people they're supposed to be responsible for. But that's not in you. You are not that self-centered, no matter how hard you pretend otherwise."

Rhett swallowed. He might not be that self-centered, but he was also not his brother, and stepping into Peter's shoes would only bring about comparison. He could be something else, maybe, if there was something he was good at. But he couldn't be the duke.

"Your faith in me is misplaced. If you'll excuse me, you've rather spoiled this drink, as unlikely as that sounds, given its quality."

There was a billiard table in the back corner of the tavern. If no one would play with him, he'd play on his own. He turned away from Andrew to see an older man in worn farmer's overalls gripping his hat in front of him. He had one foot turned away, as though ready to change his mind about approaching.

"My good man," Rhett said, trying to put him at ease. "I'm in desperate need of a playing partner." He gestured toward the billiard table.

The man shook his head. "N-no thank you, my lord."

"Then will you join me for a drink?" he asked, tipping his glass. "The more of these I have, the better they taste."

The man took a step back and looked at Andrew. Andrew shrugged and nodded toward Rhett, giving tacit permission for whatever came next. Which was not a great sign of things to come.

Rhett clamped down on the desire to squirm. "How might I help you?"

The man cleared his throat. "My condolences for your brother, my lord."

"Condolences are for the dead. My brother is still very much alive."

The man's eyes widened, and he crumpled his hat in his giant hands. Rhett immediately regretted making him uncomfortable. "Apologies, my lord. I only meant that I'm very sorry for the situation. It must be a difficult time for you and your family."

Rhett grimaced. The entire point of escaping the house was to escape the situation. It was bad enough that Andrew had imposed on his reprieve. Now complete strangers were dragging him back toward that which he was avoiding. "Thank you for your concern—"

"Gregory, my lord. Gregory Smith. I'm the local smithy. One of them, anyhow."

Rhett nodded. "I shall pass your well wishes on to my sisters. I'm sure they'll be very appreciative." Desperate to be thinking about anything but the house, its inhabitants, and the unwanted future that was threatening, Rhett tried to turn the conversation to something that had no stakes at all. "Have you lived in this town long, Gregory?"

"All my life, my lord."

"Please call me Everett."

"My lord Everett."

Rhett sighed. "That's not exactly what I…" On the continent, he rarely told people who he was. He would simply say Everett Montgomery, and people would call him that. In the most formal situation, they might call him *sir*. Not *my lord*. He would never be comfortable with the moniker, but explaining that felt like far too much effort.

"Never mind," Rhett said. "I've ordered the haggis. Tell me, should I leave before it arrives, or am I going to be able to eat this meal without embarrassing myself?"

Gregory smiled widely. "It's the best haggis on this side of Hailsham."

They were in the very south of England. "Is it the only haggis on this side of Hailsham?"

"That may be, my lord." Gregory's cheeks flushed.

"I guess I'm in for a treat, then." Beside him, Andrew snickered. *Fabulous.*

Gregory looked pained, more uncomfortable than even the worst serving of haggis could justify. He regarded Rhett with an apprehension that Rhett wasn't used to. Rhett was friendly. He had a welcoming face. People weren't scared of him, yet here was this burly man ducking his head and shrinking into himself as though he were a schoolgirl.

"What can I do for you, Gregory?" Because there was no way this man had approached for a casual chat.

"Now that you mention it, my lord Everett...It's my daughter. She's reached a marrying age. It's time I think about her future."

Rhett patted the man's shoulder. "I'm flattered that you would consider me, Gregory. But I'm not currently looking for a wife. Not that I doubt she'd be an excellent lady of the manor. I simply don't plan on settling down and have no manor for her to run, if you know what I mean."

Rhett could feel Andrew's disgruntled stare boring into the back of his head. He shifted on his stool.

Gregory's ears flamed red to match his cheeks. "Pardon, my lord Everett. I wasn't propositioning you."

Rhett shrugged. "If you were, it would have been the first proposition I've had in a week. It's a shame. Maybe I'm losing my appeal." Rhett turned to Andrew, determined not to stumble under his friend's disapproval. "Am I as handsome now as I was before I left England, do you think?"

Andrew rolled his eyes.

Frustrated, the smithy interrupted. "My lord, she will not *listen*. Samson and I have arranged a splendid match for our children, but my daughter will have none of it. Julia claims to love a *Blanchfield*." Gregory spat on the ground.

What did he think Rhett could do about it? Granted, he'd sat in a bar giving advice to many a man down in his cups, but there was a level of expectation that Gregory had that was unfamiliar. "That is a conundrum," Rhett said, trying to pretend that he was talking to a drunk sailor in a bar off in Lisbon. "I don't envy your position. I'm still at a loss as to how I can help."

Gregory took a step forward. "Talk with Julia, my lord. Make her see the folly of her reasoning. A Smith can never marry a Blanchfield."

Rhett knew better than to tell a woman her reasoning was daft, and in his experience, most women's romantic decisions weren't easily swayed by a man's opinion or their parents' feuds. "I do not imagine that my thoughts will hold much weight with your daughter."

Gregory furrowed his brow. "But you're the lord while your brother is indisposed, are you not?"

No, he was definitely *not* the lord. "I hardly imagine my brother involved himself in such affairs while he was conscious." He looked at Andrew, who appeared more frustrated than was reasonable.

The smithy's confusion deepened. "The duke would always hear our complaints. No problem was too small for him. His guidance was very much valued."

Of course it was. Perfect Peter was perfect. "I'm not my brother, Gregory. I'm sorry to disappoint." He stood and slipped a coin on the bar. The town wasn't a safe haven, but neither was the house. Perhaps he could sneak back in without his sisters noticing. There was a door that led from the gardens into Peter's study. He nodded to Gregory to be polite, not acknowledging the man's stunned expression. As he exited, he heard Andrew speak.

"It's been a trying day. His lordship is tired. You can discuss it further with him tomorrow."

Ha. Now Rhett knew where not to come for a meal tomorrow. He would find somewhere else to hide.

Fuck. Adelaide rifled through the many, many papers on the duke's desk, looking for the betrothal announcement to *The Times* that the duke had supposedly written. There was no reason for the duke to have lied about it. It wasn't in his bedroom, so it would either be here or on its way to London. Lord help her if that was the case. If the newspapers printed it, not only would it mean Adelaide wouldn't be able to hold up her end of the deal, it would also mean that Cordelia's family would know where she was. Then there would be a very angry, very awake duke to deal with, as well as the unconscious one.

She flipped through the ledgers, looking to see if the letter had been slipped between the pages. There was nothing there except proof the duke was doing his job. The incomings and outgoings were carefully tabulated, and the estates were in the black. The dukedom had several properties, though none were pulling in significant income. They existed on what looked like industry investments. The duke had licensed the design of multiple technologies and was using the profits to prop up his estate without laying off any staff or evicting tenants who were behind on rent.

Cordelia could have done much worse than marriage to the Duke of Strafford. He was a man of honor. He looked after the people who relied on him. His family were kind people, and he offered financial security. Cordelia had been—continued to be—a fool for not leaping at his proposal. If she were given the opportunity, Adelaide wouldn't turn it down.

Perhaps, if the duke woke, Cordelia could be convinced to see reason. Although, after the failure of this morning's attempt to rouse him, Adelaide was less sure the duke would wake from his comatose state. What that would mean for the rest of them was anybody's guess. The siblings had asked blessedly few questions about *exactly* how the duke fell. If he died—which he surely would without a proper drink soon— would they insist on an investigation? If they did, Cordelia's scheme would be revealed the moment anyone from London became involved. It would make her look guilty. It would be hard to convince anyone of her innocence. Adelaide would appear just as culpable.

If he weakens, or if he doesn't wake in two days, you will have to leave, Adelaide. Drop Cordelia at her father's front door and find a ship that will take you to France. Pay a man to pretend to be your husband, if that's what it takes.

Adelaide loved the continent. She was only in England because English ladies' maids were paid well compared to the work she had been doing. She didn't mind if her house with a garden and heavy furniture was on English soil, French, or Spanish, so long as she had a place of her own where she could put down roots.

But without Cordelia's money, there would be no roots. She would have to go back to eking out a living through her travels, and all the uncertainty that went with that.

No. Nein. Nunca. You must find this bloody announcement. You must wake the duke, and then you can leave all of this behind for your own piece of this earth.

With no sign of the announcement in the ledgers or the stack of letters, Adelaide turned her attention to the drawers. The top one was locked, and she pulled a pin from her hair, unbending it until it formed a straight stick. With one eye closed and her head cocked, she slid the pin into the lock, jiggling it until she heard a soft click. Modern drawers had locks that took a long time to pick. Funny that the most powerful men held on to ancient furniture that afforded next to no protection.

The drawer held journals, beautifully bound and full of the duke's delicate, almost feminine script. She flicked through them quickly to see if there were any loose papers, keeping her eyes averted from the words. It was bad enough she was rifling through the man's things. She wouldn't rifle through his thoughts as well.

Nothing.

She lifted the last journal. Beneath that were several loose sheets of paper. They were too thick to be plain old letter paper. The duke didn't strike her as someone who wasted good paper on a notice to *The Times*, but a betrothal was a rather special announcement. Perhaps he had more sentimentality than she gave him credit for. She picked up the first leaf and turned it over.

Not an announcement.

Adelaide's heart rate quickened, and there was a sudden, unwelcome, hot swirl in her belly. She'd seen naughty sketches before. If you knew where to look, you could buy entire magazines of them, and she knew where to look. But never had a single sketch turned her mouth dry and set off such a ringing in her ears.

Rhett was spectacular naked. Spectacular. The strong line of his jaw was rendered in sharp charcoal and reflected in other lines—the deep v of his collarbone, the shadows that cut across his chest beneath curving muscle covered with a dusting of hair, the hard rope of brawn from his waist to his groin that traveled past interlocking abdominals. From between his long and lean thighs jutted his cock, semi-engorged. Surely the artist had taken liberties with *that*.

She snatched up the remaining pieces of paper and flipped each over. Rhett, naked, from multiple angles. Unless it had been a concerted effort between the artists, no liberties had been taken at all with his member. In each sketch, the artist's focus was clear—one rendered his eyes in perfect brooding clarity. Another captured the sardonic quirk of his lips. A third was focused on form, with each muscle drawn in detail. Regardless of focus, all of them captured the same thing, a beautiful, giant cock, sketched so perfectly that she could imagine the shaft—how silky it would feel beneath her fingers, what it might feel like pressed up against her.

She sagged against the desk, using one of the papers to fan herself, trying to get her temperature to a reasonable level. She was not unpracticed in the art of sex. She'd had a handful of lovers who'd satisfied the urge when it became distracting. They'd been fine enough specimens, but none of them compared to the man on the pages in front of her.

Bloody hell. How will you ever look him in the face now, Adelaide? She could just picture it, walking into the duke's bedroom, seeing Rhett there with his sisters, and her eyes immediately dropping to his crotch. *Damn it. Why do fashionable men have to wear such tight trousers?* There would be no tearing her gaze away from that, and there would be no hiding her sudden interest from him. He wasn't a prude, so he would likely find it amusing. He'd sat for the sketches, after all, though why his brother had them was beyond comprehension. Unfortunately, this new scrambling of electricity across her body would give him even more power over her.

"Damn it."

The hairs standing up on the back of her neck were the first sign that something was about to shift, then the door behind her that led out into the gardens clicked. The hinges were too well-oiled to squeak as it opened, but there was a slight *whoosh*, and then a current of cold air swept into the room.

"Della? What are you doing?"

Chapter Thirteen

Bloody hell. It had to be him. She looked down at the sketch in her hand. There was no telling if her racing heartbeat was due to what was drawn there or the fact that she was about to be sprung looking at it by the figure in question. She quickly folded it and shoved it into her pocket. There was no hiding the others that were spread across the desk. She neatened them and pivoted.

Rhett looked beaten down. Gone was the devil-may-care twinkle in his eye. His shoulders were slumped, and his tie was limp and creased, as though he'd been tugging at it. He looked like a man—*Whose brother is on the brink of death, Adelaide. Is it such a surprise?*

But beneath the exhaustion was something more concerning—suspicion. He was the one Montgomery sibling who still regarded her with wariness. As he should. She would, in his place.

She cast around for an excuse for her presence. There was no good reason for her to be snooping through the duke's things. Her gaze landed on the wall-to-wall bookshelf next to her, stacked full. "Your brother was in the middle of a book. We were comparing notes. I thought perhaps I would read it to him while he slept." A quick glance at the book-case would reveal her lie. There were no novels there, only non-fiction.

"You're looking for it on his desk and not his shelf?"

She shrugged. "I rarely put a book back on the bookshelf before I've finished reading it. It sits beside my bed, or on the coffee table beside the chair, or—"

"On your desk." Rhett nodded. "Fair point." He crossed to stand next to her, and a frisson of energy zinged across her shoulders, making her shiver.

"Was it here?"

"Was what here?"

"The book you and Peter were reading together." Again, a tone of misgiving.

Bloody hell. She shook herself, trying to focus on the matter at hand and not the sensations coursing through her at his nearness, not the memory of those sketches or the memory of their kiss. Not his enormous... Her gaze drifted down. How had she *not* noticed it before? Had his dip in the Thames caused some shrinkage? Was it something about the light in this room? There was only the fire to cast a glow rather than the dozen lamps in the duke's bedroom. Perhaps the way it created shadows down one length of the shaft...

"Hello? Della?" Rhett waved a hand in front of her face. "My eyes are up here."

Good God, let the floor swallow you whole.

"What did you find?" he asked.

She opened the desk drawer, turning to block his view of it. "Nothing of interest," she said, shoving the rest of the sketches to the bottom of the drawer beneath the notebooks. "Just the duke's journals." She took the topmost one and held it up.

"Well, that certainly *is* of interest." Rhett snatched it from her hands. Unlike Adelaide, he seemed to have no problem spying on his brother's thoughts. He flipped to the last page covered in writing, swallowing hard as he read, his lips pursing as though he'd been force-fed ouzo. What was written that caused such a reaction?

"My brother was excited to marry you," Rhett said stiffly. "This was written yesterday." He snapped the journal shut and tucked it under his armpit. "You really were betrothed."

"You doubted it?" she asked, trying not to let on how hard her heart was beating or just how much he'd rattled her.

"How could I not? The family knew nothing of it, my brother is not the type to behave rashly, and you...are not what you seem." He shook his head. "I need a drink."

There was already a bottle of brandy and several glasses arranged neatly on the table that sat at the center of a semi-circle of chairs. One for each sibling, she realized. The duke would welcome them here, into his personal space. One more reason Cordelia was a fool.

The nearby fire threw a warm glow against the dark leather. He took a seat, setting the journal down beside him, and leaned forward to grasp the decanter. "Drink?" he asked, holding a glass in her direction.

"No thank you. I should check on your brother." The less time spent with Rhett, the better.

"You haven't found the book."

"I'm hardly going to find it sitting with you drinking, either."

"True." Rhett gazed into the flames, swirling his glass. He was hurting, that much was abundantly clear, and Adelaide had never been a person who could walk past someone in pain.

"Very well. One drink won't hurt." She took the seat opposite him and accepted the glass of brandy he offered.

It was smooth and left a delightful burning trail down her throat. A little mewl escaped her. The duke's stores were stocked well. Rarely had she the opportunity to enjoy such a decent spirit.

Rhett stared at her contemplatively. "Was it love at first sight? Was my steadfast, boring brother who has barely shown any interest in women suddenly overwhelmed by your beauty?"

"I am not beautiful." Cordelia was. She had all the features of a classic stunner. Adelaide was a much plainer look-alike.

Rhett scowled. "You've a beauty that turns men's minds to mush. You know that."

"I...No. I did not know that." She couldn't help a little smile as his compliment tucked itself into a corner of her brain.

"Well, you do. I wouldn't have thought Peter would be so susceptible to it, but here we are."

Adelaide snorted. She didn't know if the duke thought Cordelia pretty or not, but his reasons for marrying her had been driven by his brain and no other organ. "Your brother thought the marriage would be practical. It was ever-so convenient that we had arrived in Berwick, because he had no desire to spend next season courting a bride."

Rhett coughed and spluttered, holding a fist to his lips. "You cannot be serious," he said when the choking had eased. "Of course you are serious. My boneheaded brother would look at someone like you and see a solution to a problem rather than a blessing. And everyone considers him the *good* Montgomery brother."

That was a strange phrasing. "Are you not a good person, Rhett?"

He sighed. "I am irresponsible and dissolute, feckless, a

good-for-nothing, a rogue, according to society, and that was perfectly fine. No one expected anything else until now."

"What's changed?"

Rhett swirled his glass. "If my brother doesn't wake, then I will be the duke. I am to step into his shoes despite being a fraction of the man he is. I will disappoint them all."

"Are you so certain of that?" She couldn't explain why she didn't think it would be true. She didn't know him, and everything his sisters had said about him supported his theory. But he'd treated her too kindly, too respectfully, for her to believe his words, even though he clearly didn't trust her.

"Am I certain that I will disappoint? All the evidence points in that direction. Peter gave me a hefty sum to manage once. He was testing me, trying to determine if I could be trusted with one of the smaller estates."

"And?"

"And I lost twenty thousand pounds in a year." He threw down the drink he had and poured another.

She took a small sip of hers. "On women and booze?"

"On investments that didn't pan out."

Adelaide shrugged. "Investing is a risky business. Plenty of prospects don't pan out."

There was violence in the way he swirled his drink this time, brandy reaching the lip of the glass. "My judgment is poor, and I can't manage finances properly. It was a good thing I didn't have an estate full of people counting on me. Peter needs to wake. I have none of what is needed to do this job."

Her heart hurt for him. It was awful to hang on to such regrets. "You care. That's not nothing."

He paused, glass halfway to his lips. "Pardon?"

"You don't want to disappoint people. That means you care about doing right by those who will rely on you. That's more than a lot of lords have going for them."

Rhett shifted in his seat. "This is all far too maudlin. It presumes my brother is going to pass, and I assure you, he won't. He won't risk the dukedom by dying. Is there really no gin in this room at all?" He pushed out of his chair and strode to the shelf that was crammed full of bottles of all shapes and sizes.

She twisted in her seat so she could still see him.

Rhett was taking each bottle by its neck, reading the label, and then casting it aside on one of the nearby shelves. "Tell me a truth, Della."

"What do you want to know?" she asked cautiously.

"Do you find my brother attractive? Is that why you plan to marry him?" Was that jealousy she heard in his voice? Rhett snatched a bottle and waved it at her. "Ah. Gin. Would you like to try some?"

Adelaide looked out the glass doors that opened into the back garden. The sun had set; the sky had turned blue-gray. It would be dark in a matter of minutes. "Sure."

"You haven't answered my question," Rhett said as he poured clear liquid into two glasses.

Della pursed her lips. "He's good-looking enough. More so than most men. Less so than others. He seems the responsible type and kind. He would be a sensible match for any woman."

Rhett's expression darkened and, with a drink in each hand, he returned to the fireplace. He stood scorchingly close to her and handed her a snifter. He smelled of bergamot and salt. It reminded her of a warm summer's day on a Greek island. It would be so easy to reach up, to brush her hand against him.

When he took the seat next to her instead of the one opposite, she swallowed hard. There was a loud pop and crackle from the fireplace that had to be a coincidence, but it felt ominous regardless. "Yes, marriage to him would be sensible, and women have done many insensible things to 'land' him. Women have stooped to many levels to be the next Duchess of Strafford."

There was too much pain in his voice; he stared too deeply into the clear liquid for his thoughts to be entirely with his brother.

"That must have been difficult for him," Della said.

Rhett scoffed. "Sure, it's been difficult for *him*." He sighed and shook his head, bringing his attention back to the present moment. "That's not fair. It has genuinely been difficult for him. He's had very little to do with women since Lady Meredith."

"Who was Lady Meredith?"

He grimaced. "I thought she was the love of my life, but her eyes were on my brother the entire time."

"I'm sorry." She wanted to reach out a hand to hold his, to show him he was not alone in having lost, but there was too much distance between them, so she settled for a condoling smile.

Rhett downed the rest of his drink. "I'm not sorry. I rode the wave of my brother's pity all the way to Rome, then Amsterdam, Minsk, Zagreb, Budapest, Moscow. It was a full year before he started back up with his "you need employment" spiel. By that time, I was far enough from England to ignore him."

"You were running."

He shook his head, closing one eye to look through the empty glass. "I wasn't running. Not at all. I was exploring. I was like Columbus, but I was looking for...I don't know. I thought I'd know when it presented itself, but maybe it has been and gone, and I didn't even recognize it."

She shifted in her seat, swinging her legs over the arm

of the chair and leaning her head into the soft, worn leather. "What would it have felt like, this thing you were searching for?"

"Like the right key in the right lock. Or maybe as though I'd just had a good meal. Can the soul be hungry, do you think?"

She'd never thought of it in those words, but it was absolutely the sensation she felt. "Yes, it can. The soul can be starved."

He cocked his head, staring at her as if he was trying to see beyond what she was. "Tell me, Della. What is your soul starved for?"

It was a question she would not normally answer truthfully. She would obfuscate or straight-out lie, but her normal shield seemed to give way when Rhett looked at her. He had so easily showed her his vulnerability; was it so wrong to show hers?

"Stability. I've had none for as long as I can remember, not in people or places. I'm tired of floating on the tides. I want to be still. I want to build myself a lighthouse."

He took a sip of his drink. "A lighthouse sounds lonely."

"So is floating." It was her turn to feel uncomfortable at the serious turn of the conversation. She'd already revealed more of herself than she should have. She put aside the gin and locked her defenses back into place.

"Tell me about one of your adventures, Rhett."

"Something true?"

"Of course." No doubt his genuine stories were as entertaining as fiction.

There was a long pause, and he wrinkled his nose. "I am searching my memories for a story that is suitable for a young lady of the *ton*."

Adelaide laughed. "Don't censure anything on my account,"

she said. "I can handle a story with questionable behavior."
She snuggled into the armchair, rolling the brandy snifter
full of gin between her hands.

"Are you certain you won't swoon?"

She furrowed her brows in mock outrage. "I've never
swooned in my life."

"Never?"

"Never."

"Well then, let me tell you about a fortune teller I met in
Athens."

Bloody hell, that is so inconvenient, she thought as she
closed the door on the duke's study. It was bad enough that
her skin sang in Rhett's presence; she didn't need to *like*
him too.

Their time together at the docks had not been an aberra-
tion. He was as cheeky and amusing today as he had been
then. For an hour, he'd regaled her with tales from his travels, all ones that might have shocked and horrified proper
ladies of the *ton* but that, in truth, Adelaide found hilarious.
She, too, had swam naked in the sea at Ålesund during the
winter solstice. How could one not?

Adelaide smiled at the memory as she strolled down the
hallway, her feet silent on the thick carpet. She desperately
wanted a place to settle. The trials of a nomadic existence
were always top of mind, but Rhett's stories had reminded
her of the joy travel had brought her over the years. She'd
experienced things most other women wouldn't. And when
Rhett repeated the phrase, "you really had to be there…"
with a thread of disappointment in his voice, she understood
that too. Sometimes, she'd really needed someone else to be
there so they could reminisce together.

Perhaps once she had leased her home and finally settled

in one place long enough to purchase something large and heavy, she would return to the continent occasionally. It wasn't something she'd considered before. For years, all she'd dreamed about was becoming as still and stable as a Brittany lighthouse. But perhaps she could be a lighthouse and still float upon the canals of Venice during Carnival.

She nodded at the footman who stood in the foyer's corner. Having anyone bow to her felt uncomfortable, but if she was going to maintain her cover, smiling as though it was her due was imperative. On the long sideboard were two salvers. The braided silver twisted into an intricate Celtic knot on each side, at the center of which was a stone—jade for the incoming post and moonstone for the outgoing.

Her heart leaped at the site of several missives waiting to be taken to the general store for posting. She probably looked like a snoop, picking up the pile and reading through the addresses, but it was a necessary evil. Jacqueline had over half a dozen letters waiting to be sent, three of them to a single recipient, but there was nothing in the duke's pretty hand. The sudden sense of relief she'd felt dissipated. *Damn it.*

Taking a deep breath and pretending that she wasn't about to ask a completely impertinent question, she turned to the footman. "Is this your usual posting?" If the footman's role was to wait in the foyer until a member of the family needed help, then surely he would have seen if the duke had dropped a letter off to be posted. "Before his…incident, the duke spoke of sending our betrothal announcement to London. Do you know if that occurred?"

"I couldn't say, my lady."

"Was yesterday's post mailed, or was that missed in all the excitement?"

"I don't believe there was mail sent yesterday, my lady."

Then the announcement was likely still in the house. That's *if* it existed in the first place and Cordelia hadn't been confused amid all the chaos. She crossed to where the footman stood, noting the tiny sharpening of his posture.

"It would be tasteless for such an announcement to take place under the circumstances, don't you think?" she asked. "If you or any of the household staff run across it, please deliver it to me for safekeeping until His Grace recovers. I will remember your support."

Perhaps it was underhanded to use her supposed future role as the man's employer to her advantage, but two dozen eyes keeping watch for the announcement would be better than hers alone. "I'll be with the duke, if anyone should find it."

The duke remained as silent and still as he had that morning. Her attempt to get his blood pumping had been futile. He was losing color in his face, and his lips were pinched and dry. *Of course they're dry, Adelaide. He's had naught to drink in a day.*

A man could last three days without water; she'd read that somewhere. As long as he wasn't exposed to the elements, he could last three days. One of those days was already up, with no sign of change. Adelaide rang for a footman.

"Fetch a bucket of ice chips. Snow, if you've no ice on hand."

"What are you doing?" Margaret asked as she passed the footman and came to sit by her brother's side. She enveloped his hand in both of hers and raised it to her lips. Rhett's was a close family. They cared about each other a great deal. What a blessing it must be to be part of something like that.

"Your brother needs liquid. It's been at least a day since he drank anything."

A crease formed between Margaret's brows. "Of course. I hadn't thought of that at all. He must be parched."

Adelaide moved to the other side of the bed. "Help me sit him up. The footman will be back with ice shortly. If we give it to him lying down, it's just as likely to go down his windpipe as it is his throat."

Together, with much grunting and a little Gaelic cursing, the two women had him in a seated position.

"Here," Margaret said. "Let's prop him up with pillows; it will be easier than dragging him backward." They gathered the pillows that had been stacked neatly against the wall and shoved them behind his back.

By this time, the footman had reappeared with a silver bucket full of ice and tongs.

"Thank you." Adelaide scrambled off of the bed and took the bucket from him.

The duke's head hung forward, his jaw slack. "You hold him," she instructed.

Margaret did as she was told, sinking her fingers into her brother's hair and pulling back until his head was level. "My family can be a lot to contend with," she said as Adelaide took an ice chip from the bucket and placed it in the duke's mouth. "I hope we aren't scaring you off."

"I'm still here, aren't I?" Not for the reason Margaret thought. She was here until the duke woke, then she would leave. Adelaide eased her pressure on the duke's jaw, allowing his mouth to drop open. The ice that had melted in his mouth dribbled over his lips and onto his bed shirt.

"Merde."

"Poor Peter. He'd be horrified to see this. I'm going to have to swear my siblings to absolutely secrecy about this whole ordeal."

"Let's try tipping his head further back." Adelaide popped a few more ice chips in the duke's mouth and closed his jaw. "None of your siblings seem the type to keep this under wraps."

Margaret sighed. "That is so true. Jacqueline might be prevailed upon, but Edwina would probably just blurt it out unconsciously. And Rhett..."

Adelaide's heart hiccuped weirdly at the sound of his name. "Rhett would...?"

"I don't know. He and Peter aren't close. There's a rift there that doesn't seem to be mendable."

"Closeness requires a willingness to be vulnerable. I can understand a reluctance to do that. I've never mastered the art, personally." Though Rhett had been remarkably open with her. Was she the exception, or was it Peter?

There was a long pause before Margaret said, "Well, I do hope you'll let us close. We are to be family, after all."

It was strange, the ease with which the Montgomery siblings threw that word around. How quickly they were willing to accept a stranger into their family showed some kind of hereditary madness, surely. To avoid answering, Adelaide opened the duke's mouth just a fraction to see if the ice had melted. Then she prodded at the sides of his throat. She had no evidence that she could force a man to swallow by doing so, but it seemed to be the most likely way.

After a moment, the duke's throat bobbed.

"Yes!" Adelaide pumped a fist into the air. Margaret whooped. The two opened his mouth again, and it was empty. "Right, now we have to do that enough times to hydrate him," Adelaide said. Mission one might have been to convince the duke to keep quiet about his failed proposal, but Adelaide had to keep him alive long enough to do so.

Chapter Fourteen

Rhett sat on the floor of his bedroom, his back against his bed, his shoulder resting against the bedside table, the light from the lamp above illuminating the pages of the book he was reading...kind of reading. Not really. He'd get half-way through a page and catch his mind wandering—to his brother, who had shown no signs of waking despite their best efforts; to Meg, who was keeping a midnight vigil; to Jac and Winnie, who were in bed when he last checked on them. It was nearing two in the morning, and he should sleep, but when he closed his eyes, images of a strawberry-blonde conundrum appeared, with soft lips and a hard shell he was determined to crack.

Normally, he would have delighted in such images. His imagination was a constant, reliable source of pleasure that he appreciated, but not now. Not tonight. Not when his imagination seemed fixed on a woman Rhett could not even entertain the idea of having. If Della was an unmarried lady of the *ton*, however delightfully she might curse, that immediately put her out of contention for one of his dalliances. That she was Peter's fiancée added another layer of impossibility.

Whatever his feelings for his brother, Rhett would

not betray him. Besides, what woman would break off an engagement with the duke for Rhett—a second son with nothing to his name other than a series of rollicking good stories and a sense of humor?

No, he needed to put Della firmly out of his mind, so he turned back to the novel, looked for the last thing that felt familiar, and sighed when he realized nothing did, before beginning to read from the top of the page again.

Was it his inattention or something else that dragged his gaze from the blur of words in front of him to the door? It wasn't a sound; the room and the corridor beyond were silent, but the crack beneath the door shone yellow, the shadows on the wooden floor shifting with the rhythm of footsteps.

The servants had no reason to be in the family wing at this hour, and none of his sisters were capable of moving so silently, which left one person. With equal stealth, he climbed to his feet and took hold of the lamp, turning it down until it gave only the barest hint of light, enough to see if you knew where you were going, but not enough to attract attention, *hopefully*.

The sliver of light had vanished. He crept to the door and slowly, quietly cracked it open.

Della was moving swiftly, faster than he'd expected. He was still half convinced she wasn't who she claimed to be. Granted, the discovery of Peter's journals had given him pause. It had been there on the page in his brother's handwriting—he was proposing marriage to Lady Cordelia Highwater, whose blue eyes and red hair would look regal on a future heir, whose hips promised satisfactory childbearing potential, and who appeared of relatively sound mind and sharp wit.

Sound mind and sharp wit, indeed. Della had proven intelligent and resourceful. He had a great deal of admiration for a woman who could so quickly turn to a solution rather than dissolving into her emotions. But despite his brother's words, Rhett could not reconcile the woman he'd seen glimpses of—kissing him in a dockside tavern, swearing in multiple languages, proposing audacious plans to wake Peter—with his knowledge of young debutantes.

And now she was creeping through the house for no good reason. In one hand, she held a lamp, in the other, a small basket that barely swung as she moved. The woman was a bloody ghost. Perhaps she was a ballet dancer, though she seemed too well endowed for that.

Whatever experience caused it, the way she glided silently was one more example that she was not what she said she was.

Snuffing his flame entirely and relying on only the wall sconces and the leftover glow from her moving lamp, he followed her, slowly gaining ground as she turned corners, descended stairs, and strode quickly through the foyer with furtive glances. Every time her head flicked over her shoulder, he flattened himself against the wall. Thank God for the charcoal-colored bed clothes he wore. In the shadows, he was almost imperceptible.

When she crossed the foyer, he expected her to head down the east wing to his brother's study. He'd interrupted her earlier; that much was clear. Perhaps she was off to finish what she'd started. *Which was what, exactly?* Marriage machinations of young ladies of the *ton* rarely involved creeping through their target's home in the middle of the night, unless it was to force a scandal, and Cordelia did not need to do that if Peter had already proposed.

She had been at Peter's desk. Perhaps she worked for one of Peter's business competitors, and she was scouting for inside information. Perhaps she was a spy working for a foreign state. Peter was one of the most powerful men in

England, and she was abnormally good with languages. She might not be English at all.

While he was trying to determine what she wanted from Peter's study, Della turned in the opposite direction, downstairs.

Blast. What the devil was she doing?

He shortened the gap between them to not get turned around. She found her way to the kitchen easily. Too easily. As if navigating belowstairs was second nature to her. No young lady of the *ton* was that comfortable. Upon reaching the kitchen, she hefted the basket she'd been carrying onto the long workbench that ran almost the entire length of the room. The moment she turned, she would see him.

He stepped into the light before he could be caught, swinging the belt of his banyan. "Hungry?"

As she swung to face him, her fists balled. Proper fists. Thumb on the outside, half raised, the right hand pulled close to her chest as though ready to strike.

"Whoa," he said, holding his hands up. "I was simply inquiring about your midnight cravings."

"Rhett." Her shoulders eased, the crease between her brows softened, and she let out a whoosh of breath. "Why are you creeping around the house at two in the morning? Explain yourself."

Explain myself? "Funny thing, that. I was in pursuit of a woman who was creeping around my brother's house at two in the morning. Such suspicious behavior, don't you think? What reason could there be for it?"

Della colored, her hand traveling to the basket beside her. For a moment, he thought she'd take it and flee. Instead, she flipped open the lid. Her nose wrinkled in a charming expression. Charming until the scent of what was inside wafted to him.

He clasped a hand over his mouth. "What the devil is that?" It smelled like horseshit and rotten eggs.

"It's my new plan."

"Plan for what? Gods, woman. Who *are* you? And what did my brother's servants do to deserve such a prank?"

A muscle ticked along her jaw. "It isn't a prank."

"Is it revenge? An assassination attempt?" He swayed away from her as the implication hit him. "What *are* your intentions?" All this time, he'd thought she was trying to ensnare Peter, or take advantage of him—steal from him, perhaps. As he held back a gag, the idea that she could actually mean his brother harm hit as hard as the nauseating package she possessed.

He rolled his shoulders and set his feet. If she meant to hurt his family, she'd discover that he was not above hitting a woman. His stomach churned. At least, he was not above manhandling one. He could detain her without landing a blow.

"I plan to wake the duke. It is time. I just need to add some vinegar and boil it."

"Like smelling salts?" Now that his senses had adjusted to the rancid odor, he realized her idea made far more sense than a murder attempt. "Like vile, putrid, I-want-to-vomit smelling salts."

"Actual smelling salts didn't work," she said, pulling out wrapped packages from the basket and setting them down. "His nose did twitch, though, which gives me hope that if the concoction is vile enough, he will wake."

It was genius. A horrible, mad genius, but still genius. "You plan to boil that here in the kitchens? In one of the cook's saucepans, I imagine."

"Yes," she said hesitantly.

"Oh, the cook is going to *hate* you. Every meal you eat from here on out will be a gamble."

The grimace she gave suggested that the thought had occurred to her as well. "Perhaps you would volunteer to taste test my meals for me for the duration of my stay?"

"Like the queen's bodyguards? Hardly likely."

"But you will not stop me?"

"No." It might work. The gods knew that smell could make even a skunk retch. It reeked worse than the time he'd been spat on by a llama in Greece. He'd been unable to find a bed that night. No one would even let him sleep in the stables.

If there was even a chance her plan might work, he had to take it. Peter needed to wake. "No, I will not stop you. In fact, I'll even help."

He would have been well within his rights to turn on his heel and leave her to it. To escape from it. From her. But there was something about the way her braid hung over her shoulder—raw, innocent, undone—that hooked across his heart and snagged. That was how she wore her hair at night. If they married, that strawberry-blonde braid with its green ribbon and curl at the end would lie on the pillow next to him for the rest of his life.

For some reason that was not reason at all but madness, he wanted that. He yearned for it. For the first time in his life, the thought of going to bed with one woman forever was a vision he wanted to hold on to. And not *any* woman. This one, who swore like a sailor and smelled like lemon, when she wasn't holding an infernal concoction at least.

She smiled and his heart did somersaults. "If you would be so good as to fetch that saucepan, it would be much appreciated." She gestured to the pan tucked away in the corner on the highest shelf. Smart. It was dull and battered and clearly rarely used. The cook might not even notice it was missing.

She frowned as she took it from him. "We need a damn llama," she muttered.

"Excuse me, what?" This was the most blatant example yet of her reading his mind. Perhaps she was a psychic.

"Llamas. They are just...foul. Don't get sucked in by their cute faces. I make it a rule not to get within a hundred feet of one. Not since—" She shuddered. "Just trust me on this."

And in that moment, he did trust her. Whatever, whoever she was, this moment wasn't faked. Like her earlier admission that she had been lonely, this was the genuine Cordelia. Perhaps the Duke of Thirwhestle bred llamas on one of his estates. Perhaps she'd experienced the horror of the llama at a country fair. Both explanations were just as plausible as his being spat on by the beasts at a market that ran alongside the Greek port of Piraeus.

The stove was already lit, coals burning low, ready for the kitchen maid to add fuel to it first thing in the morning. Della ducked out the door that led to the kitchen gardens and returned a moment later with kindling and logs. It took her mere seconds to get the stove firing.

"You know how to do that well."

She arched a brow. "You don't know how to stoke a fire?"

"I—" *Damn.* "I do, actually."

"Then why are you surprised that I'm also in possession of basic living skills? Is it so impossible for a woman?"

Impossible? No. Unlikely? Yes. "I traveled the continent without a valet for years. Self-sufficiency was a necessity if I wanted to stay warm. Where did you learn such a skill?"

She smiled tightly. It didn't touch her eyes. "A housemaid stokes the fire in my chambers every morning. One only needs to watch a handful of times to learn the basic principles."

That was true. If he dragged Jac downstairs and asked her to do the same, she'd do it. She'd complain at him the entire time, but she'd be able to get the stove roiling.

He tried to shake off his suspicions and focus on the task at hand. "What is our first step? Boiling water?"

She shook her head. "I don't want to dilute it."

"Heaven forbid."

"I thought we'd add vinegar and then set that to boil. You check the pantry while I combine the rest." She wrinkled her nose in disgust but got to work.

As Rhett checked the labels of the pretty glass bottles in the pantry, he realized that this was perhaps the most interesting thing he'd done with a woman. When he'd seen Della on the docks, he'd thought her beautiful, a goddess, a creature of sublime perfection. When she'd kissed him in the tavern, he'd thought her captivating, spellbinding, a woman unlike any he'd ever met. Tonight, she was all of these, but also intriguing, capable, and unexpected. She still might be an assassin, but she was a beguiling assassin.

"Thank you," she said as he handed her the vinegar.

She placed it on the counter, away from the edge, leaning toward him as she did so. Somehow, bizarrely, underneath the layers of rotten egg and excrement, the fresh scent of earthy lemon hit him. It warmed his breath and pooled in his belly. He caught himself drifting closer to her.

Was it his imagination, or did she drift toward him as well?

She straightened and poured the vinegar into the doomed saucepan, as if it were the most normal thing in the world to her.

"Truth. How do you know to do this?"

"Boil vinegar?"

"Any of it. From the beginning, you've had a plan for every setback."

A single shoulder hitched, and she did not meet his gaze. "One could argue that since the duke is yet to wake, I don't know what I'm doing at all."

He edged closer to her without planning to do so. It was just an inch. It was only an inch. Gods. "You got him hydrated this afternoon. Even the doctor hadn't done that, and you've had plenty of ideas with solid foundations. How?"

Wrinkling her nose, Della reached for the bowl in which she'd added the rest of the concoction. "Honestly, I practice a lot of things in my head. In fact, I probably spend far too much time thinking about what I might do if certain situations arise."

"Like an unconscious duke."

She snickered at that, and he felt absurdly pleased to have made her laugh. "Exactly, although perhaps not *precisely* that."

He looked around the room for a wooden spoon, spying them in a jug on the bench next to the saucepans. "Have any of these practiced scenarios ever come to pass?" he asked as he fetched one.

"Well, no. But it's good to be prepared in case they do." There was a hint of embarrassment in her tone. There shouldn't be. It was actually quite adorable.

"Give me an example scenario, so I know during what emergencies I should follow your lead."

She held out her hand, and he gave her the spoon. "Earthquakes."

It was his turn to snicker. "Because England is beset with earthquakes."

The vinegar was boiling now, and her brows were knitted in concentration as she poured the contents of the bowl into the saucepan. That was why she didn't notice his visible jolt as she said, "I might not always be in England."

He swallowed hard. "Truly, you would consider traveling?" Gods, there were so many places he could take her.

She gently stirred the concoction. "I want my own home.

I want somewhere I can stay for as long as I want to. But yes, I can see myself traveling."

Rhett smiled giddily. "In what other scenarios could I count on you?"

She returned his grin. "If ever there is a herd of stampeding cows, I have a plan."

This time, it was her who swayed; he was sure of it. The hand that wasn't stirring the mixture edged toward his until it was less than an inch away.

He couldn't help himself; he grazed his other hand across her shoulder. She sighed and sank closer to him, making his heart thump wildly.

A pop sounded from the stove, and she jerked upright, wiping a stray hair from her brow and smiling awkwardly.

"The spoon will need to be thrown out too," she said, turning back to the stove and giving the pungent mixture a stir.

He swallowed hard, trying to push back on the moment. "If this works, perhaps we can gift it to my brother as a memento. I'll tell him you'd be mortally offended if he didn't give it pride of place in his study."

"The stench is never coming out of this."

Rhett waggled his eyebrows. "I know. It's such a shame that keeping it will be the only meaningful way he can show you his appreciation."

Della snorted. "Are you truly the rapscallion you purport to be, or are you playing the part your siblings cast you in?"

"What came first, the chicken or the egg?"

Della frowned. "I—"

He cut her off before she could jab at the truth any further. Those bruises were tender enough without her poking them. "Don't make the mistake of thinking I'm anything other than what you see before you."

"An irredeemable, irresponsible rogue...I don't believe it. You said yourself, you have a hungry soul."

He would make her believe it. The longer she held on to this positive impression of him, the more disappointed she would be when he failed.

He stepped close to her, close enough to see the slight flush that crept up her neck and the bob of her throat as she swallowed. He was close enough to feel the air heat between them and see her gaze lose focus. He brushed the back of his hand against her cheek. His cock shifted as she turned into him, her eyelashes, long and red and soft, grazed his fingers.

He hooked a finger beneath her chin and nudged until she was looking up at him, eyes wide and sultry, lips parted. Her tongue flicked across them, and his gaze arrested on the pink skin. Gods, what he wouldn't do to claim those, press them against his, tease them open with his tongue, explore the parts of her she was determined to keep hidden.

Without thinking, caught in the gravitational pull of her heated gaze, he cupped the back of her head, sinking his fingers into the loose braid. For a moment, he stopped breathing completely, his reason utterly turned around by this inexplicable energy that thrummed between them. He lowered his face. Her lips were mere inches from his when her breath hitched, the slight gasp a gut punch significant enough to cause him to step back.

Only an irredeemable, irresponsible rogue took such liberties with his brother's fiancée.

Then she stepped forward. Damn it. She leaned toward him, a whole body lean that spoke of wanting, needing, yearning. It was a lean that should lead to touching, grazing, kissing. It was a lean that made his cock stand at attention and his heart beat double-time. He flexed his hands, doing his best not to let them drift toward her waist. He had no confidence that if he touched her again now, he'd be able to let her go.

"You're leaning," he whispered.

His words broke the spell. She sprang backward. By reflex, he grabbed her arm to prevent her from backing into the hot stove. Her face turned beet red as she shook him off.

"See?" he murmured. "Totally irredeemable." And it was. He was. He was everything the world thought him to be.

Della dragged a loose hair backward. "I think I've had all the help I need. Thank you." Her voice shook as she spoke and she, usually so fearless and unflappable, eyed him warily.

It was a natural consequence of his actions—overwhelm a young lady with her own, unpracticed senses, and she was bound to want distance from you. It had even been his plan, so why the sudden disappointment? Why the feeling that he'd just scored a goal against himself?

Because you want her. And he did. He wanted her up against him; he wanted her in his bed; he wanted her sitting on the steps of the Colosseum; he wanted her in cramped ship's quarters; he wanted her in the Uffizi Gallery. Hell, he even wanted her swimming in the filth of the Thames.

And that was terrifying, because she wasn't his to want.

He gave a jaunty salute, an expression he hoped hid the maelstrom of emotion he was feeling, but the tune he whistled on the way out the door was an up-tempo version of a funeral march, because that's what each step away from her felt like. He tried hard to not look back. He failed. At the edge of the light that pooled around the kitchen floor, he turned.

His strawberry-blonde assassin was tapping the wooden spoon against her palm, so deep in thought that she was mindless of the muck splattering against her hands.

Chapter Fifteen

As Adelaide trudged down the main street of Berwick, she did so like the walking dead, one foot mindlessly in front of the other, drawn forward by the promise of a coffee—hot, hot coffee—and the perfect Parisian pain au chocolat. After a sleepless night tossing and turning, she'd risen early. Any thought of asking the staff for a hot drink or breakfast was quickly quashed by the venomous looks sent in her direction by the housemaids she'd passed. The smell must have lingered downstairs, despite her best efforts to dispel it. She couldn't tell. She'd placed the mixture by an open window overnight, choosing bitingly cold air over the stench, and still it had burned through her nostrils. She couldn't smell a thing this morning, not even the heavenly scent of the pine trees that lined the streets.

Finding a French bakery in the middle of English nowhere had felt like the only thing that had gone right since Cordelia had fled down the cathedral stairs. Yesterday, in anticipation of a day with the duke and his family, she'd gorged herself. She'd sat at a table outside, bundled up against the cold, and eaten pastry after pastry while she watched the comings and goings of the town.

Now, having spent the past five hours remembering what

it was like to kiss the younger Montgomery brother, imagining kissing him again, getting not a wink of sleep, the only thing that could make her face the day was coffee and a pain au chocolat.

A large coffee. Two, perhaps. And two pastries, even three. Lord only knows you need the sugar, Adelaide.

She pushed open the door to the bakery. No, she couldn't even smell the baking bread. "Bonjour, Madame Moreau," she said with faked vigor. "Le plus grand café que vous ayez, et trois pains au chocolat, s'il vous plaît."

The woman at the bakery counter *tsk*ed while reaching for the largest mug. "Je suis désolée, ma demoiselle. Nous avons vendu toutes les pâtisseries ce matin."

None left? But it is only half seven! Yesterday she'd arrived at the bakery at nine in the morning, and there had been plenty of her favorite breakfast food left. "Y en a-t-il à l'arrière?" she asked. Surely the baker had some set aside somewhere.

Madam Moreau shook her head. "Non, ma demoiselle. Sa seigneurie les a toutes prises ce matin." She nodded to the back corner of the room.

Adelaide followed the woman's gaze. *Damn.*

Rhett sat reading a newspaper, thoroughly consumed by it, a plate piled high with pains au chocolat in front of him.

She could leave now. He hadn't seen her. She could dash out the door and not be forced to reckon with his smile or the way her stomach flip-flopped when he looked at her, or the inexplicable sense of belonging that she felt whenever she was in his presence.

She should leave, but then she would have no coffee and no pains au chocolat, and damn it—he was the reason she needed them so badly. "Je vais le rejoindre," she said to Madame Moreau.

She wove between the tables until she was standing in

front of Rhett, her fingers twisting around the handle of her reticule. "Good morning. Do you have enough food there, do you think?"

Rhett looked up and broke into a wide grin that flooded her with warmth from her toes to her scalp. "Della. This is a surprise."

She arched a brow. "It is a surprise that you're awake so early, when just yesterday you were complaining about mid-morning visitors."

He wrinkled his nose and rubbed his hands over his face. "I didn't get much sleep after I left you last night. Any, if I'm to be honest."

Adelaide wondered if it was the same thing keeping him awake that had kept her up as well. Was he also tossing and turning over the damnable attraction between them, feeling as hot and bothered as she had? Or was that just in her imagination?

Of course it's your imagination, Adelaide. His brother's unconscious, perhaps dying, and he's about to be burdened with a life of responsibilities that he never asked for. How arrogant to think he's losing sleep over you.

She stuffed her disappointment into the furthest crevices of her mind and gestured toward the pile of pains au chocolat in front of him and the very large coffee that sat beside the paper. "I take it you and I share a similar approach to sleepless nights. Caffeine and sugar."

He grinned and nudged the plate toward her, unaware of how her body loosened in relief as he did. "Try one," he said. "These are the best pastries in existence."

"Clearly, if you're buying out the entire bakery." She tried to keep the resentment from her tone. He was sharing, after all.

Rhett stuffed himself with a mouthful. "Someone else

bought them all yesterday," he said, barely intelligible. "I didn't even get a look-in. You cannot imagine my disappointment."

Whoops. That had been her. She could imagine his disappointment. She'd felt it through her entire body not two minutes ago. If she had known Rhett was as attached to these misplaced Parisian delicacies as she was, she would have left him at least a couple.

She shucked her coat and sat, tugging off her gloves and setting them aside. There was nothing delicate or ladylike about the mouthful she took, or the groan that escaped her. She closed her eyes and inhaled. Her sense of smell might be deadened but enough of her taste remained that she was once more transported to Rue de la Lune, to crisp autumn mornings and bustling streets, women crossing the road with arms full of the last summer flowers, and children running alongside men on bicycles, begging for a sweet or a coin or even a tip of the hat.

"It's the most extraordinary thing," Rhett said, interrupting her recollections. "These are exactly the same as pains au chocolat from Boulangerie des Étoiles. It's this tiny, hole-in-the-wall bakery on the corner of Rue de la Lune—"

"In Charonne," Adelaide said, her mouth still half full.

"You know it?" Rhett's excitement was palpable.

Adelaide nodded. "I was there last autumn. Every single thing they baked was divine. I had to let all my waistbands out, and I regret none of it."

"What were you doing in France?"

"I…Uh…We were in Paris to prepare my wardrobe for the season," she lied. "Mother is so preoccupied with having the most exclusive of everything. It wasn't enough to have a French seamstress; the clothes had to be sewn in France. Although the joke is on her. I'm fairly confident the dressmaker was not French at all. The sound of her r's was off."

He snorted as he laughed. "I visited Boulangerie des Étoiles on my last day in France, right before I returned to England. Their pain au chocolat was my last meal, so to speak."

Adelaide pursed her lips. If she was to have one final meal, it would probably be from that boulangerie. "How was Madame Desjardins, do you know? When we last met, her son had just been accepted into la Sorbonne."

Rhett took a long sip of coffee, just as Madame Moreau set Adelaide's on the table. "Yes, Francois is doing exceptionally well there, apparently. In his last letter, he mentioned he was working with Jacques Barbier and that there would be an exhibition in the Musée de l'Orangerie."

Adelaide put a hand to chest, so relieved. "Oh, I'm glad. She was thrilled when he was accepted. I wonder when the exhibition is."

Rhett leaned forward in his chair, toes bouncing against the stone floor. "If you visited that often, you must have met Marco."

"Marco the mime?" Adelaide let out a peal of laughter at the thought of the Italian performer who frequented the street corner near the bakery. Truly, what people could get away with when in face paint was remarkable, although given what she was currently getting away with in the disguise of someone else, she shouldn't be surprised. "He stole a red ribbon from my hat and turned it into a flower, which was so diverting, I didn't realize until I was back in my room that I never got the ribbon back. That cost two shillings!"

"Did you get to keep the flower?"

"For a week, until it died. I would still have that ribbon now."

Rhett leaned back against the wall, crossing his arms behind his head, as relaxed as she'd ever seen him. "He might have stolen your ribbon, but he stole my dignity."

She snorted. "Oh, is that where it went? Clearly, he never returned it."

Rhett rolled his eyes. "Ha ha, hilarious. But in all seriousness, it's hard to look dapper when you're covered in flour."

Adelaide choked on her coffee. She had actually seen Marco play the same trick on a gentleman bedecked in the finest of coats. She was quite sure there would have been violence if it wasn't for the delighted applause of the women who had stopped to watch the performance.

"It was so pleasant to sit at a table outside and watch him interact with stuffy English aristocrats. They did not know what to do with him." For a second, she thought Rhett might have picked up on her slip—stuffy English aristocrats didn't generally refer to themselves as such, but he grinned, too excited by their conversation to mark her error.

"You know, he taught me how to do the wall."

The wall had been one of Adelaide's favorite skits. It was simple but so effective—an ever-shrinking box forcing Marco to fold up into himself. But it was an illusion. There were no cinder blocks or stone, just hands hitting hard against the air. Something about the idea of being trapped by an absence of walls resonated. *She* was trapped by a lack of bricks and mortar, but not for long—not once this absurd situation concluded.

She shook off the maudlin turn of thought. "Show me."

Rhett cocked his brow at the challenge and stood. He tugged the edges of his jacket and stepped around the table to where there was space. The other patrons of the bakery sent him sidelong glances, but he did not seem to care. With an expression of fierce concentration, he held up one palm and then the other, repeating the pattern until he reached the top of his "wall" and peeked over, his eyebrows raised in shock and his tongue poking out the side of his mouth.

Adelaide dissolved into a fit of giggles. "Close," she said.

"You're *so* close. You just need to be more firm with your hand movements. Here, let me show you."

She stood and joined him in the free space between tables. "First, you need to relax your shoulders and make sure they're square, otherwise you'll not get a consistent depth to your wall." She placed both hands on his shoulders, unprepared for the sudden zing that bounced through her, setting her heart fluttering. *Don't be stupid, Adelaide. It was nothing more than static.* With a steadying breath, she eased his shoulders into place and gave him a wan smile that she hoped disguised the immodest thoughts she was having.

His returning smile was brittle.

She took his hand and uncurled it, pressing her palm to his, her fingers too. There was no mistaking the spark between them this time. It wrapped itself around her chest and tugged like an ill-fitting corset, stealing all breath. *Damn it. You should have been wearing gloves.* The warmth from his hand infused hers, skittered across her arms and up her neck as a hot flush. It meandered down her body in a lazy swirl that pooled in her midsection. She would have snatched her hand away if she could, but her body had other ideas. It wouldn't move. It remained locked onto his, like his hand had become an extension of hers, the two of them the same person, same soul, suddenly made whole in this moment.

Don't be such a romantic twit, Adelaide. Act normally.

She cleared her throat. "You need to extend your fingers. If there's even the slightest bend, it will ruin the illusion. You'll be creating a wall of jelly, not brick."

He flexed his hand in response, the muscles stiffening.

Her fingers followed, wrapping around his in a caress she couldn't prevent. She heard his breath hitch and felt his body tense. He drifted toward her, as though pulled by a tide. It scattered her senses, and she could barely see straight. Her vision was simply him. Everything else was obscured by a haze of desire.

He intertwined his fingers with hers with a slight tug that drew her forward. They were close. So close. Too close. There were barely inches between them, and that gap was alive with a beautiful fire she was ready to burn in.

Behind them, a cup clattered on a saucer, and the flame was doused. There were people around. How could she possibly have lost awareness of her surroundings so completely?

"Your wall is leaning more than the Tower of Pisa," she said, stepping out of his reach.

He followed her with another step, trying to maintain their closeness. "Then you will need to continue your instruction."

She blushed and turned back to the table. "We should finish our coffees and return to the house. We have a plan, remember?" She looked pointedly at the crowd watching them, and Rhett's eyes widened.

"Yes." He swallowed. "We have a plan. Speaking of which, I have some ideas. Shall we discuss?"

"Rhett, *come on*," Della said as they started up the long driveway. "She wanted to do more than divine your future."

Della wasn't wrong. The moment the Greek fortune teller asked him to remove his shirt for a proper reading, he'd known how the afternoon would unfold, but teasing Della was fun. Her irritation was cute. She screwed up her nose and gesticulated wildly. There was nothing prim or proper in her frustration.

He *tsk*ed, knowing it would further rile her. "I think you're dismissing Madame Pythia's obvious ethereal talents. She comes highly recommended."

Della reached both hands out as if she wanted to strangle him. "Because she tells the future *half naked*. Of course men will recommend her."

Rhett grinned and spoke with the utmost sincerity. "Clothes impede the communication between her and the otherworld. It is essential that she lay herself bare to the message the universe wants to send."

Della sucked in a deep breath. "She's certainly laying herself bare to someone." She put out a hand to stop him in his tracks. "Truth. Do you actually believe that there are people out there who can tell you your future, fate, whatever they want to call it?"

"Will you give me a truth in return?"

"Yes." She gave him her hand and he took it, surprised by the resolve with which she grasped his. Few women shook hands with men, and on the rare occasion he'd taken a woman's hand, it had been limp, like a dead fish.

He stuck his hands back in the pockets of his coat, and they continued along the gentle incline. "I thought there was such a thing as fate, and that she would find me, but now I've got this awful feeling that I'm going to have to go and find her. But I don't know where to look." He was grateful they were walking. The words would have been harder to say if he'd had to contend with her expression.

Della bumped against him. "My guess is that fate will not be found in an incense-filled den of iniquity, whatever Madame Pythia might promise."

That was probably true. He was half tempted to ask her honestly, *where did one search for a purpose?* But that felt too stupid, too childish to ask. Certainly, a man his age should already be well on his journey with purpose in his grasp.

"Your turn," he said. The firm dirt path turned to gravel and traversed a wide arc. He held out his arm to ensure her balance, and she took it. The sensation of her fingers on his sleeve gave him an internal steadiness he hadn't known he lacked. He coughed, trying to dislodge the sudden frog in his throat. "What would you do if you were a man?"

"Pardon?" Della stopped walking to look up at him.

"Your options are limited as a young lady, even more so than mine. What would you do if you were in my position?" Perhaps she could guide him toward a purpose he hadn't thought of.

Della pursed her lips as she considered it. "I would work for the Home Office," she said quietly.

"As a spy?" Perhaps his earlier guess hadn't been too far off.

"No," she said, resuming their journey. "Recording passenger arrivals and departures."

Rhett stood there, dumbstruck, as she kicked her shoes against the stair rails to dislodge the mud that covered them. "Pardon?"

She had already handed her overcoat to Daunt with an apologetic wince by the time Rhett jogged up the stairs behind her. Rhett, too, expressed regret for his muddy hem and then followed her toward Peter's study.

"You want to record arrivals and departures at the London docks?" he said as they passed a row of dukes' portraits until they reached the current duke, right next to the study. Peter had waited until he was in his twenties to have the likeness captured. Rhett wasn't sure if it was because he didn't want to appear young and inexperienced, or if because becoming the duke at such a young age had been a painful reminder of their parents' death.

Della entered the study and went straight to Peter's desk, retrieving a reticule from the floor beneath it. "Aha," she said, holding it up.

He was pleased. Sure. Whatever. It was a reticule. Mostly, he was interested in the bizarre career aspirations of the *ton*'s most delicate flower. "Do you have a particular tendre for England's most odious locale, or are you a fan of bothersome paperwork?"

Her hip rested against the side of the desk, and her fingers went to the ties of her bonnet, untwisting it until the ribbon was free. "I like stories. It would be interesting to hear why people are coming and going." She tipped her bonnet upside down and tossed the reticule inside. "Whenever I see people board a ship, I wonder what they think they're going to."

Rhett shucked his jacket and hung it on the coat stand by the door. "You would make a terrible records officer. In every country I go to, the queues are horrendous. God forbid you get a chatty records official at the end."

She cocked her head with a jesting smile. "If you're going to make fun of my truths, I shan't give you any more."

"I'm sorry," he said, crossing the room. "It's just that I thought a woman like yourself, daughter of a duke, diamond of the *ton*, would choose a career with more...grandeur. I thought you'd run a country, or become the Gallery Director at the Royal Academy of Arts." He stopped too close to her. Her face was in caressing distance. Why did he do this to himself? Why did he put himself in her orbit? Why did she?

If there hadn't been witnesses at the coffee shop, he might have kissed her. The sensation of her fingers pressed against his had been almost too much to bear. He'd almost let his wall crash down and wrapped a hand around her waist. He'd almost pulled her to him.

He had seen her dressed in nothing but transparent petticoats, for God's sake, but somehow standing next to her, miming, had been more intimate.

"Joy can be found in the mundane," she said. His nearness made her nervous. The pulse at her neck fluttered and her tongue flicked across her lips. The room felt heavy with expectation. There were no witnesses around now to act as guardrails.

"Della."

She shook her head. "It's my turn. Truth." She opened the bottom drawer of Peter's desk and removed those damn sketches. "Why did you sit for these?"

Rhett groaned, running a hand through his hair. "It's wrong for those to be in his possession. They were supposed to be a source of amusement, not shame."

Her brows furrowed. "Is that why you posed for them? To entertain people?"

Rhett strode to the fire so that he could get a better look at them. Entertaining people had certainly been one factor. No one thought less of you when you were distracting them from the tedious reality of life. Knowing it would infuriate his brother had been another boon.

But that wasn't the heart of it.

"I had been told that in order to be a respected artist, I must lay myself bare—show the world the deepest, rawest side of me."

She joined him near the warmth and put a hand on his shoulder, giving it a squeeze. "You posed because you wanted to be seen for who you truly are."

He closed his eyes so that he wouldn't have to look at her. "And all anyone saw in those sketches was a debauched rake. What does that tell you?"

She took his hand and wrapped it in hers. "That no one looked closely enough."

Her words were devastating. They took a sledgehammer to the carefully constructed facade he'd spent a life creating, and there was nowhere for him to hide. This was the nakedness he'd not achieved in Paris or anywhere else. She saw him, and what she saw was not irredeemably flawed.

He cupped her jaw in his hand. Gods, he wanted her. When she was near, he felt whole. But she wasn't his. She intended to complete someone else.

"Truth," he whispered. "Why did you leave Hornsmouth?" He yearned for an answer that would give him some hope.

She swallowed hard. Fear crossed her face, and she gnawed on her lip before speaking. "Rhett, please don't hate me. The truth is—"

A knock at the door broke the moment, and she sprang away from him.

He sucked in a deep breath before turning away. "What is it?" he asked, trying to keep the frustration from his voice.

Daunt entered. "You have callers, my lord. Apparently, Mr. Gray told the townsfolk that you would hear their concerns this morning."

"*Damnation.*" He looked back at Della. Her brows were furrowed in confusion.

"They want something from the duke. From me." He turned to Daunt. "Please ask them to return once my brother wakes."

Daunt didn't leave his post by the door. He stood there with a disappointed frown—the most emotion Rhett had ever seen on the man's face.

Della cocked her head. "What do they want?"

"I do not know." Did it matter? Couldn't he just go about his business? "What they need is the Montgomery brother who has answers. I am not him."

Della pursed her lips. "I think you underestimate yourself. The very least you can do is listen. That is, in itself, more than some lords do."

She looked at him with such a confident, encouraging smile. To her, he was not Lord Everett the Disappointment. To her, he was just Rhett—kind and witty and perhaps even capable.

"You cannot ignore this, Rhett. But I feel as though you'll surprise yourself."

He girded his loins. "Very well. Send them in."

Chapter Sixteen

"My lord, it is a monstrosity, an eyesore, a blight on the landscape. Only a fool with no taste could think painting an entire barn a violent shade of pink would be a good thing."

The young woman who stood next to the furious farmer had a stubborn, mulish glare. "I like flowers. It reminds me of fuchsias."

"Then plant yourself a garden and spare the rest of us."

"Plant yourself a hedge so you don't have to see it."

The farmer's eyes almost bugged out of his head. "My lord, this cannot be tolerated. It is your land, your barn, your duty to make her see sense."

It was not Rhett's land, Rhett's barn, or Rhett's duty, but he had made it through the past twenty minutes of arguing with neighbors. He could make it through this.

"My lord, that barn was old and decrepit. His Grace gave me explicit permission to renovate it as I saw fit."

"His Grace clearly didn't expect that you would lose your damned mind and paint it such an offensive shade."

Rhett rubbed his temples. "There is no need for such language in front of the ladies, Mr. Jones. Mrs. Patterson, is the painting complete?"

She shook her head, her loose curls bouncing furiously. "No. I had only gotten as far as the trim before Mr. Jones got his knickers twisted and dragged me here."

The farmer gasped in outrage, his face turning beet red. "How dare you suggest I wear *knickers*?" The last word escaped his mouth in a horrified whisper.

Rhett put a hand up to halt the exchange. "Then this is what we're going to do. Painting will pause on all sides of the barn that face other properties." The young woman's jaw dropped, and Rhett wagged a finger. He wasn't finished. "Just until I've had time to view it for myself. You want something that will spark the same joy your garden does in the middle of winter? There will be a way to do so that does not offend your neighbor. In the meantime, I give you leave to paint the interior of your house whatever shade you like. Then your winter garden can follow you every minute of the day."

The farmer snorted. "When Mrs. Patterson leaves, you'll have to repaint the entire home before you'll find another tenant."

"And that will be my brother's problem." Rhett looked at his pocket watch and then at Della. She had entered with a tea tray and was standing quietly by the door, shooting him smiles of optimism along with enthusiastic head nodding. It centered him. It gave him the motivation to continue. "Mrs. Patterson, I will be over to scope out work on the barn this afternoon. If you'll excuse me, there is another tenant I must see." He stood and shook both of their hands.

The farmer nodded smugly, clearly seeing the morning as a win. The woman gave a satisfied swish of her skirts as she left. Job done.

"Bright fuchsia?" Della snorted as she lay the tea tray on the desk in front of him. "I love a garden as much as the next person, but some colors should be used sparingly."

"Agreed." Rhett looked at the warm shortbread on a plate next to the teapot. How she had known what he needed in this moment, he could not fathom. He scoffed one down. "Are there many more waiting?"

"Just one. A burly gentleman."

Rhett sighed, relieved that it was almost over. "Send him in. Then we will wake up my brother so he can deal with the next argument."

"It's a plan," she said, smiling.

His heart jerked as she gave his hand a comforting squeeze. As he watched her leave, he realized all his doubts had vanished. He knew too much of her for it be a lie. Which meant maybe he could do this, if he had to, if worse came to worst and his brother passed. If Lady Cordelia Highwater, daughter of a duke, accomplished member of the *ton*, was with him, he was almost certain he could. She was so competent and self-assured and steady. She made him assured. She made him steady, and perhaps he was more competent than he'd ever given himself credit for.

"My lord," a beefy man said, his shoulders stiff as he nodded in deference from the door.

Rhett gestured for him to come in, smiling in the hope that it would make the man comfortable. "Everett, please," he said, holding out a hand for the man to shake.

"My lord Everett." The man shifted his weight from foot to foot. "I need you to talk to my son. He is acting foolishly. Benjie wishes to marry Julia *Smith*. It will not be tolerated."

Two hours later, the entire Montgomery family was crammed into the duke's bedroom. "Are we certain this is going to work?" Jacqueline asked, regarding the jar Adelaide held with suspicion, her hand pinching her nostrils shut.

"No, not at all," Adelaide admitted. There was definitely

a chance. One would have to be pretty close to dead not to react to the sensory overload she and Rhett had planned. He had taken her faux smelling salts idea and run with it, turning it into something better and more terrifying than she could ever have managed on her own. The poor duke.

"Is that stench why the footmen were so cranky at breakfast?" Winnie fanned a scented handkerchief in front of her face.

"Very likely, yes," Rhett said, grinning. He'd been looking forward to this moment since they'd discussed the plan on their brisk walk home from the bakery. Over the top of Winnie's head, he caught Adelaide's eye. Something had changed in the way he looked at her. His gaze was hot but steady, less like a crackling fire and more like a steaming cup of tea that soothed the senses and warmed from within. Even when she blushed and looked away, the steadiness stayed.

She was overcome by wanting, a sudden knowing. Here was a person she could imagine a future with, a future beyond a couple of weeks in a town she was just moving through. When she pictured her home with its walls and heavy furniture, there was now a person in it. Someone who ate at the same oak table, who lay on a rug beneath a tree reading while she planted flowers that lasted more than a few days because they had roots in the soil.

Rhett, next to her, with her, forming a future together. He was kind and funny and loved his family fiercely. His enthusiasm for life was so vibrant, despite all he was going through. The stories he told of his travels were full of color and passion and a vitality that made her yearn for the same. He was open to life and to people. It made her wonder if she shouldn't try to be as he was.

As long as he wasn't the next duke, and as long as he felt likewise, he might be persuaded to put down roots with her. The two of them could lease a house, perhaps here in Berwick with England's finest pain au chocolat a mere stroll away. With a steady home base, she might enjoy travel again.

Who wouldn't want that?

"And so, what is the plan again?" Meg asked from the chair by the window, shaking Adelaide from her reverie.

"Rhett is going to cover Peter's feet with snow," Adelaide said. "Edwina is going to play the violin. Jacqueline is going to tap Peter's elbow with this candle snuffer, right where the funny bone sits, and I am going to uncork this concoction and hold it under his nose."

Jacqueline frowned as she took the candle snuffer from Adelaide with an annoyed glance. "I don't see why Winnie gets to play the violin and I only get to tap Peter's elbow. Surely, as the elder sister, I should be the one to choose."

The youngest Montgomery sibling gave a satisfied *hmph*, looking as smug as Adelaide had ever seen anyone look.

Rhett put an arm around Jacqueline's shoulders, squeezing her until she shrugged and tried to twist out of his grip. "Winnie gets to play the violin because she is an order of magnitude worse at it than you."

Edwina's satisfied smirk morphed into a look of outrage, and, for a moment, Adelaide thought she might toss the violin and leave in a huff, but Meg stalled whatever objection was coming with a sharp "Ah, ah, ah." Even Rhett jerked to attention and snapped his mouth shut.

Nodding her approval at how quickly all three of her siblings ceased their bickering, Meg turned to Adelaide. "Why the funny bone?"

"Because we want him to feel pain, but not too much pain. Plucking his nostril hairs would be better, but the bottle will be in the way."

Edwina leaned over the bed and peered up her brother's

nose. "If this doesn't work, I think we should take tweezers to him, anyway. It's a forest up there. He'll thank us when he wakes."

It was like herding cats. Keeping one of the currently conscious members of the Montgomery family on target was a challenge. Trying to orchestrate all four of them was a feat worthy of a saint or the devil himself. "I will leave the personal grooming decisions to his siblings."

"Why?" Jacqueline looked at her askance. "You're his fiancée. You're the one who is going to have to look at it in bed each morning, and you're as much a part of the family as we are."

The words were said so casually that it took a second for Adelaide's brain to process them. Then she was unable to keep tears from springing to her eyes. Her throat tightened, and all she could manage was a nod.

She turned so the girls wouldn't witness her oversized response to Jacqueline's simple words.

She had never truly had a family. The thought of joining someone else's had not occurred to her. Unconditional love, easy camaraderie, a genuine sense of belonging, even frustration tempered by affection—these were all things Della had thought were tied to blood relations, but she felt them now, for the first time that she could recall.

Even though none of the furniture in this room belonged to her, she sensed a wisp of the feeling she'd been chasing— a home.

Joining the Montgomery family would mean no more holidays spent by herself. There would always be someone she could talk to. She could share a life with them. They had several houses and plenty of space for an ancient chaise longue. Joining this family would mean she wouldn't be alone.

Surely the girls would still consider her a sister if it was Rhett who she ended up marrying. The whole Peter situation could be forgiven once they understood why she'd deceived them.

She swiped at her eyes before anyone could see the tears welling there. When she turned around, Rhett was giving her a funny look, as though he longed for something as much as she did. He stared at her, hot and heavy, and a lump formed in her throat.

Could he read her thoughts? Could he guess how she felt about him? Did he know how much she wished everything was different? *Once the duke wakes, Adelaide. Then you can come clean and beg his forgiveness.*

Meg cleared her throat, and Rhett's attention jerked back to the room.

Adelaide smiled colorlessly. "Let's get to it."

Thirty minutes later, Andrew walked into the room with a stack of papers, took one look at the scene in front of him and walked back out again, shaking his head. Adelaide couldn't blame him. They must have been quite a sight.

Meg paused tapping together the two bells they'd found in Peter's room. The first had come from the wall. Rhett had unhooked it from the rope that called downstairs. The second bell had been found on a table by Peter's bathtub.

"Don't mind Andrew," Jac said to Adelaide, continuing to tap out a beat on an overturned hatbox with the candle snuffer she'd previously wielded as a weapon. "He's been looking for a moment with Rhett for two days. He rather thinks you are avoiding him, brother."

"He thinks that because I am," Rhett said. Once they'd all conceded that the plan wasn't working, Rhett had taken the violin from his sister while Della had corked the foul-smelling salts and tossed them out the window. Now he played a delicate, jaunty tune as he spoke. "At least I *was* avoiding him. He wants to run over the estate finances."

"Does he *know* you?" Winnie asked. "I love you, brother, but finances are not your strong suit."

Della was about to object when Rhett drew an uncharacteristically sharp note. "I am well aware. Hence, why I was avoiding him."

Meg tut-tutted. "This is not another commitment you can shove beneath your bed and hope people forget about. Peter is relying on you to step in while he is unwell."

Rhett's jaw tightened, and Della could see a muscle tighten along it. She ached to reach out a hand to let him know he wasn't alone.

"I will do it," Rhett said. There was anger and frustration in his tone. "I will see Andrew directly once we are finished. I just needed some time to center myself." He looked at Adelaide and smiled. "I've had my time. I will attend to the estate matters this afternoon. Now where were we?"

"Eighth day of Christmas," Adelaide said, and the cacophony of homemade instruments and enthusiastic singing began once more, filling her with a sense of Christmas spirit she hadn't experienced in a very long time.

Chapter Seventeen

Once a footman had hesitantly braved the chaos to say luncheon was ready, Rhett's sisters had each given Peter a kiss on the forehead before filing out of the room. Adelaide hung back, looking as though she had something to tell him, before she sighed, gave a small smile, and followed the girls out.

Rhett needed a moment before he could join them. He needed to process the feelings that had engulfed him as he watched Della sing with his family. It was somewhere around "eight maids a-milking," when Della was twisting Winnie's hair into a fierce Viking braid, that he realized he wanted that moment again, and again, and again. Every so often, she'd caught his gaze, and blushed, and bitten her lip, and there'd been a funny little effervescent feeling in his chest that he hoped would never go away.

Della was beautiful. She was kind. Regardless of how bawdy a story he told, she found it hilarious, not distasteful. She was practical in a way he was not used to. And, to be honest, she was practical in a way that he himself was not.

He liked the thought of being with someone who was

proficient where he wasn't, who could teach him to be better. Perhaps he could do the same for her. Just as she'd shown him he was, in fact, capable, he wondered if he could show her it was, in fact, safe for her to let another person into the lighthouse she'd built around herself.

The song had ended, and Della had leaned forward to whisper something in Winnie's ear. His sister had giggled and whispered something back. That was the merest hint of the vulnerability she could be capable of, if she stayed around long enough.

But with *him*.

He wanted her to belong with the family as *his* wife, not his brother's.

Rhett was slumped in his chair, his feet crossed at the ankles, toes resting on the baseboard of the bed. He looked at Peter, lying there still. Even dressed in nothing but robes, his pallor pale, his expression empty, Peter still looked regal. He had a gravitas Rhett could never, would never, have. His presence commanded attention. It seemed to take up more of the room than his body did.

"I have never wanted your life," Rhett said to him. "I have wanted the respect people give you without question. I've wanted my life to have meaning, as yours does, not that you would know it given my behavior. But I've never wanted the things that you have. I don't want the title, or the estates, or the money. I don't want this." He waved at the richly appointed room, at its grandfather clock and dressing bench covered in snuff boxes and cuff links and pins. "It is too large to carry from city to city. I don't want to inherit it. So, if you could do me a favor and wake, I'd very much appreciate it."

As expected, Peter didn't move. He showed no sign of hearing anything Rhett had to say, which, if Rhett was being honest, wasn't too different from usual. Many times, Rhett had tried to talk with his brother, only to be shut down.

But that was unfair. Rhett had shared nothing even remotely personal with Peter. He'd never mentioned his fear of dying forgotten, as inconsequential in death as he had been in life. There was no way of knowing if Peter would have had a sympathetic ear.

Rhett tried to picture sitting down with his brother in a neutral setting, one stripped of pomp and power, perhaps the local tavern, and telling all the twisted, messy truths that he'd bottled up over a lifetime.

Peter would most likely have reminded Rhett that meaning could be found in the church or in the military. Respect could be found in both too. Both would suffocate him. Surely there was another path yet to be discovered—one that wasn't the army, or the church, or academia. That also wasn't floating around the globe with no purpose. Surely there was a way to float and still feel as though he was achieving something important.

"Maybe Della is that something. Showing her the world could be my purpose."

Peter's nose twitched, and Rhett jumped.

"Brother, are you waking?" He knelt by the bed and took Peter's hand, rubbing it within his own to chase the chill from the duke's skin. "Brother, can you hear me?"

Peter was as still and as silent as stone.

Damn it. He was imagining things. He'd thought about Della and hallucinated Peter's response because Rhett knew Peter wouldn't approve of such thoughts. One rarely approved of having their fiancée stolen.

But honestly, who stole from whom?

"I saw her first, you know. I met her the day she ran from Hornsmouth. She was kitted out with enough jewels to put any princess to shame, and she was standing on a wharf, swearing like a fisherwoman. I knew in that moment she was something different." He'd never met a woman like her. She was real, unaffected, without the airs of their class. She was as close to a kindred spirit as he'd found.

"I saved her life. Did she tell you that? Did she mention that she almost drowned? Of course, she had saved my life just seconds beforehand. This might sound sappy and illogical, but I think she is still saving it. She sees me in a way no one else does. She assumes I am capable and that I am good, as though the possibility of my being a useless, irresponsible wastrel hasn't crossed her mind. When I'm with her, I feel as though I'm everything she thinks I am."

He held his breath. He'd just declared his feelings for Della to the man who planned to marry her. Peter was used to getting what he wanted. Surely, if anything would wake him, it would be the opportunity to whup Rhett's arse for Rhett's temerity.

Still, there was no response.

The maelstrom of fear and guilt and grief in his stomach swirled, its edges creeping like bile up his throat. He gripped his brother's hand. "If you choose not to wake, I promise to take care of her. I promise to take care of them all. I may not know what I'm doing, and I can't promise not to bollocks it up entirely at first, but I have Andrew to help me, and Meg, and Della. I will learn, and I will make you proud."

Rhett swallowed back the lump in his throat. "And if you choose to wake—which, gods, I hope you do—please let me have her. You could have any woman in England. Women would murder their husbands for the chance to be your duchess."

It was true. Women had lied and schemed just for the opportunity to meet Peter.

"I know Della was conveniently placed, and that you didn't have to do anything to find her. I know that's ideal for you. But I have been looking for her for years, without even realizing it. I have scoured the globe for her. In every room I enter, I have looked for her. Please, please wake. And when you do, please, brother, let her choose me."

Chapter Eighteen

Not long after Adelaide and the siblings had piled back into the duke's bedroom, there was a rumble from outside—a coarse, rasping sound Adelaide had only heard a handful of times. "Is that a motor?"

Immediately, Jac discarded her knitting project and jumped from her seat to press her face to the window. "It is! It's a motor!" she said, bouncing on her toes.

Rhett and Adelaide exchanged glances. "Are you expecting company?" Adelaide asked, suddenly uneasy.

"No. Who is it?" he called to his sister.

Winnie climbed up from the floor where she was sitting with her back against Peter's bed. "I don't know why you were the one who went to look," she said to Jac. "You can't see that far without your spectacles."

"So I'm not even allowed to look?"

"I'm just saying, there's really not much point in looking when you can't—ow!" Winnie rubbed her side where Jac had jabbed her with an elbow.

"The motor is green," Jac said, triumphant.

"And the color of the man's hair?" Winnie asked dryly, ignoring the glare Jac sent her and pulling the curtains further aside to look out. "I don't know why you don't just wear your spectacles. Then it would be as clear as—oh, it's Uncle Frank!"

"Uncle Frank?" Rhett and Jac both asked, their expressions perking.

Winnie gathered her skirts and half skipped, half ran from the room.

"Wait, Winnie," Jac said, tripping over Meg's discarded slippers. "Just hold on a minute."

"Uncle Frank?" Adelaide asked Rhett, hoping the worry didn't show on her face. Somehow, over the past two days, she'd become so at home that the anxiety she'd felt over her fraud had melted away. None of the sisters had shown any hint of suspicion, and even Rhett had stopped testing her. She'd felt safe. *Stupid, Adelaide. You are never safe.*

Uncle Frank would be of the *ton*. If he'd been in London at all over the past few months, Frank would likely have met Cordelia, and Adelaide couldn't count on him having the same poor eyesight that Jac did. *Fuck, fuck, fuck.*

Rhett furrowed his brow. "Surely you've met Uncle Frank. He is quite the fixture on the London social scene."

Cold crept over Della, and she shivered. Luckily, Rhett and Meg were too busy bickering to notice.

"Don't be so stuck-up," Rhett said, picking up Meg's slippers and handing them to her. "Uncle Frank has been nothing but kind to us."

Meg shoved them onto her feet. "Uncle Frank is kind when it suits his agenda, and he's a terrible, terrible influence on you. Why is he here? Did you send for him?"

Rhett shook his head. "No, but I'm glad he is. We could use his help."

Meg sniffed. Adelaide couldn't tell if it was in distaste for the uncle or at the suggestion that they needed his help.

"We need nothing from Frank," Meg said, rolling her

neck the way Adelaide had seen boxers do before a fight. "We should thank him for his concern and then tell him it is too delicate a time for guests."

"He's hardly a guest." Rhett peeked out the window. "He's family."

Meg shook her head, closing her eyes as though she could block out what was happening.

Adelaide knew that look. She knew the kind of man who inspired it.

"I'm going to my room," Meg said. "I need a moment to gather myself before I face him."

"Do you want company?" Adelaide asked. Perhaps she could avoid coming face-to-face with a man who might be her undoing. If Uncle Frank had spent so much time in London, he was bound to notice her fraud immediately, and the Lord only knew what he'd do with such information.

Meg shook her head and left, muttering.

"She is just being dramatic," Rhett said. He took Adelaide by the hand. "She blames Frank for the time I got caught painting Lord Weatherington's horse green—but that was a joint idea, if a terrible one. I'm just glad it wasn't both of us who had to endure Weatherington's dressing-down."

Rhett's tone suggested he held no ill will toward his uncle, but Adelaide was getting a sense of the man's supposed bad influence.

"You'll love him. He's great."

As he dragged her from the room, Adelaide cast a glance over her shoulder at Peter. "Now would be an excellent time to wake, Your Grace," she hissed. As she expected, he didn't react at all.

The Montgomery family resemblance was strong. Frank shared his nephews' hazel eyes and sandy hair, but where

Rhett and Peter were both muscular and toned, Uncle Frank was soft. His body wore all the hallmarks of an idle life. He had stripped off his gloves already, and his fingers looked like breakfast sausages. The fluffy buoyant knot in his cravat did a fair job of hiding his sagging jowls. Still, his eyes were sharp, and he'd probably been handsome in his youth. Beneath his puffy skin was fine bone structure, not unlike Rhett's.

When the two men embraced affectionately, they were close to the same height. Frank smiled as he roughed up his nephew's hair, and in that moment, Della could see exactly why Meg declined to spend time in this man's presence. His smile was oily, and it didn't move past the unnatural curve of his mouth. A real smile lit up a person's entire face. A real smile could be felt like it radiated outward. A real smile could be seen in the eyes. When Frank smiled, the pulling back of his lips resembled a snake at the moment it struck.

That venomous reptilian gaze locked onto Adelaide. "Well now, Rhett, who is your beautiful guest?"

Shit. Damn. Fuck. Her charade was over. *You should've told Rhett the truth, Adelaide. You should have admitted it all yesterday. Now, they're just going to think you're a liar.*

"Uncle, this is Lady Cordelia Highwater. Surely you've met before."

Frank properly smiled then, and Adelaide shivered. She was about to be devoured, swallowed whole, digested for months.

She turned to Rhett. "I can explain—" The words were barely out of her mouth when Frank interrupted.

"Forgive me, Lady Cordelia. I'm so used to being dazzled by your finery under the light of chandeliers that I didn't quite recognize you in a day dress."

"I...Oh...Pardon?" *He can't truly think you're Cordelia.*

Yes, she and Cordelia both had red hair and blue eyes and a relatively similar figure, but that was where the similarities ended. No one who had spent significant time with one would mistake them for the other.

He's playing you, Adelaide. You've become a card he's shuffling in his hand, ready to use to his best advantage.

She did not want to be ensnared in his trap. Whatever schemes he was concocting, she wanted no part in. She was about to blurt out the truth, confess all to Rhett, when Winnie slipped her hand into Adelaide's and squeezed tightly. "Della and Peter are engaged!"

Frank's eyes narrowed as he looked at his niece, and then at Rhett, and then finally at Della. "Well, this is a surprise, given the circumstances in which I last saw you." He crossed the short distance that separated them and took Della's free hand. He drew it to his lips—cold, dry, unfeeling.

Her breath caught in her throat, and she waited for him to sink his fangs into her skin.

"Oh. You mean the *wedding*?" Jac whispered conspiratorially. "We don't talk about that."

Della looked at Rhett. He was staring at his feet, his toes grinding into the floor as they always did when the subject of either of Cordelia's betrothals came up.

Did he have little to say on the matter because he had little interest in weddings, or was it because the thought of Della marrying another was too difficult to bear?

How she wished it was the latter.

"It was a beautiful wedding. No expense was spared. I rather think your mother stole every flower in England. How cunning of her. How resourceful."

He was not talking about Cordelia's mother. Not really. It was code. *How cunning and resourceful you are, Adelaide, to fool an entire family.* "The duchess does like flowers."

"Then I'll be sure to send her some. It has been almost two decades since the last bouquet I sent her, on the birth of her child." Not "on your birth."

He knew.

She could see the cogs in his head whirring as he tried to put together all the pieces Rhett's family had missed.

He knew she was not Cordelia. She was not betrothed to the duke. And from the speculative glance he gave his nephew, he knew that there was something between her and Rhett. Frank literally rubbed his hands in glee.

Fuck. Damn. Damn it.

Frank put his arms around Jac and Winnie. "Come on, girls. Take me to see my other nephew. On the way, you can fill me in on all the news."

"The news isn't great, I'm afraid," Jac said as the three of them headed toward the stairs. "Peter has taken a fall. Terrible, terrible thing. Luckily, Della was *right there*."

Frank looked over his shoulder, his gaze locking with Della's. "That was a lucky thing indeed."

As he and the girls left, Rhett crossed to Della, brushing her arm. She couldn't help but lean into him.

"Jac needs to work on her delivery of that news," he said. "She almost makes it sound as though you played a part in my brother's accident."

"I played no part in his fall." *Only the lie that came afterward.*

Just this morning, she'd had a glimmer of hope that it would all work out and that somehow the family wouldn't be furious at her deception, that Rhett would understand why she had lied, and that he'd still want a life with her in England. That they all would want her in their lives.

Uncle Frank's arrival changed things. The outside world, reality, was creeping into the bubble she'd been in.

"Are you well?" he asked, concerned. "You look as white as a ghost."

She swallowed down the lump forming in her throat. "Everything feels so awfully complicated."

Rhett nodded and took her hand. "It is, and it's up in the air. All we can do is wait."

Wait for Peter to wake. Wait for Peter to die. Wait for the truth to come out. The waiting was going to drive her mad.

"Are you coming?" he asked.

She nodded back tears. "I'll be there shortly. I just need a moment."

"Well, then I'll see you in a moment." He squeezed her hand before letting it go and following his sisters.

Bloody hell, fuck, damn. What are you going to do now? The longer she stayed, the more likely it was that everything would fall apart in the worst way. Uncle Frank was a problem she hadn't accounted for. If she stayed under this roof with him, he would have her twisted up like a fly in a spider's web.

But could she leave now, before the duke woke? She would be giving up everything—the money Cordelia promised, Rhett, his siblings, the future home she'd let herself imagine. She gnawed at her thumbnail.

"Lady Cordelia?" The footman she'd spoken to yesterday approached her hesitantly.

She plastered a fake smile on her face. "How can I be of assistance?"

"I asked around downstairs, my lady. The announcement notice His Grace was planning to send to *The Times* was last seen in Lord Everett's bedroom. Another footman put it there so that his lordship could decide what to do with it."

Something inside her loosened. It was a sign. Stick to the

original mission. Find and destroy the betrothal announcement, wake the duke, beg forgiveness, and leave. All she had to do was accomplish all of that without coming face-to-face with Frank again.

"Thank you. Your help is much appreciated."

Chapter Nineteen

"So, Peter is getting married, is he?" Uncle Frank asked once Jac and Winnie had both left the room to find Meg. He pulled a snuffbox from his coat pocket and tapped it three times on the edge of the table by Peter's bed.

How was Rhett supposed to respond to that? *Yes? No, he might die? No, his fiancée might choose me instead?* It would be best to keep his mouth shut. Not that Uncle Frank ever needed a second person's input in a conversation.

"It's unexpected. The boy's shown little interest in women. He barely tolerates them when he's in town." Frank flipped open the lid to the snuffbox and tipped out a small pile of white powder onto a hand mirror. "I'd begun to think that he'd given up on carrying on the family line."

Rhett cleared his throat. "My brother knows his duty. He was always going to marry." And he still would, just not Della.

Frank took a five-pound note from his pocket and used it to straighten the powder into lines. "I'm surprised it took him so long. What spurred him to action, do you think?"

In large part, Rhett thought it was simply because Della was there. Peter had found a bride without having to reenter the marriage mart. But there was another element to it. Rhett shifted uncomfortably. Rhett's adventures on the continent had gotten increasingly wild over the past year as his sense of dissatisfaction had grown. More than once, his escapades had made the gossip section of the newspapers, and not in a way he was proud of. They hadn't been harmless antics. He'd been arrested twice for public indecency. Thankfully, being the brother of the Duke of Strafford meant something, even in Finland. No charges had been laid; he'd simply had to sleep off the drunkenness in a cell, but the impact had been felt in England. Meg had been forced to limit her social engagements, and Jac's first season had been cut short.

Shame crept up his neck, red and hot. He'd been so consumed with women and wine and his own enjoyment that he'd failed his family. It was part of why he'd remained abroad. Coming home would mean facing the consequences and inevitable censure. He would make different choices now.

"I think my brother chose to marry because he finally comprehended the reality of what would happen if the estates and the title fell on my shoulders." But Peter had had that realization far too late. Now he might die, and the future of the estates looked dire indeed.

Frank clapped a hand on Rhett's shoulder. "Don't worry about that, son. Not everybody is suited to such responsibility. You have plenty of other things going in your favor."

"Truly? And what are those?"

Frank chuckled and rolled the note into a tight cylinder. "You've the ability to make half the population squirm with pleasure and the other half let loose all their trappings and have fun. Is that not enough?"

A week ago, he might have been resigned to that. A week ago, he would've prided himself on some of those things. Now they felt hollow. Was that seriously all he was capable of? It wasn't boastworthy. It was embarrassing.

Rhett scrubbed at his face. "I don't think my brother would agree with you. In fact, I'm fairly certain that had he not met with his accident, I'd be getting for a red coat or a cassock as soon as Christmas was over."

Frank leaned over the mirror and snorted a line of powder, brushing his nostrils. "Your brother was a wet blanket. He always has been. He resolutely refused all of my entreaties to show him how to have a good time, and now look at him." Rolled note still in hand, Frank gestured toward the bed. "Of course, he's the duke. He doesn't need a personality to find a wife as pretty as the chit downstairs. They never do."

An old bitterness resurfaced in Frank's words. It was a story Rhett had heard before. Frank would tell it whenever he was drunk, or high, or maudlin—the woman who got away, Rhett's mother, snatched from Frank by Rhett's father, the duke.

"It will never be us, son. The spare is never the first choice, only the last resort. Women will throw you over at the mere hint of a title. But you know that, don't you? Lady Meredith taught it to you." He offered the mirror and the remaining line of cocaine to Rhett.

Instinct was to reach for it, especially at the mention of Lady Meredith, but Rhett hesitated. He and Frank had spent many an afternoon high, commiserating over all the women who'd done them wrong while hoping to bag a duke, but today, Rhett simply didn't feel like it. He shook his head.

Frank raised an eyebrow, but shrugged and snorted the second line.

"Della isn't like other women," Rhett said. She wasn't Lady Meredith. This wasn't some elaborate scheme to become a duchess. It was simply an odd set of circumstances, not a game plan to use Rhett for personal advancement.

"That's for sure," Frank said, snapping closed the snuff box. "She left Hornsmouth at the altar when that title was a sure thing, although I suppose your brother is younger and prettier than Hornsmouth. I still wouldn't trust her."

That had been the tenor of their conversations for decades—*I wouldn't trust her.* But for all his good intentions and the many seemingly correct paths down which Frank had steered him, his uncle was wrong in this situation.

Rhett did trust Della. Sure, she'd refused to give Rhett an explanation for why she'd skipped out on her last wedding or why she'd agreed to marry Peter, but if Rhett had to guess, she'd left Hornsmouth because he would have dampened her spark. She was so very self-sufficient and independent, and Hornsmouth was a controlling ass. Peter would have more or less left her alone after the heir and the spare were produced. Della would have had a freedom she couldn't have had with Hornsmouth.

Rhett would give her freedom. Together, they would roam the continent with no master. They would spend as much time as they wanted at the French boulangerie. Rhett would show her the ruins of Pompeii and watch as she was stirred by the stories that swirled around the artifacts. He could spend a lifetime making a list of places he'd been that he wanted to take her to and then another list of all the places they could see together for the first time.

He'd never been to Africa. If any woman was resourceful enough to explore those lands with him, it would be her.

And if she was marrying Peter for safety, for protection against her father's wrath and society's ridicule following her failed wedding, Rhett could deliver that too. Just let them come for her. He would show them the irresponsible playboy was not here to play at all.

"*Hehemm.*" Uncle Frank had his head cocked and was studying Rhett.

"I do not know why Della left Hornsmouth or why she

chose to marry Peter. I'm certain she had good reasons for both."

Frank tapped on the arm of his chair. "Perhaps she heard of Hornsmouth's mistress. There was an argument the night before the wedding. The stupid strumpet flung a fifty-karat emerald necklace in the duke's face. It is preposterous that she thought Hornsmouth would choose her."

The glee with which his uncle shared the news sat ill with Rhett. He knew the pain of not being chosen. Hornsmouth's rejection would have hurt. "I hadn't heard of the affair."

Frank snorted. "Lady Cordelia clearly had. She proved to be as immature and spoiled as everyone says. Affairs are the way of life. Hornsmouth did well by ending things until he had an heir. Lady Cordelia should have closed her eyes and carried on."

The thought of anybody treating Della so poorly made Rhett's blood boil. "Della is far from childish or spoiled. She's bold, and competent, and kind. She's done more for my brother than even the damned sawbones. Hornsmouth would have been lucky to have her."

Uncle Frank raised an eyebrow, and his suspicion made the illness in Rhett's belly roil. "Well, she certainly seems to play the game well."

"What do you mean?" Rhett asked warily.

Uncle Frank shrugged and crossed a leg casually over the other. "Only that she's maneuvered things expertly. If Peter wakes, she will be the Duchess of Strafford, and if he doesn't wake..." Uncle Frank trailed off, but his gaze was sharp with expectation, as though he was waiting for Rhett to put the pieces together.

Rhett refused. His whole body rejected the thought. "And if he doesn't wake?" he demanded, daring his uncle to say it.

"If he doesn't wake, son, you will be the duke. And if

your passionate defense of her is anything to go by, she will still be the Duchess of Strafford. Clever, clever girl."

No. No, it couldn't be. Rhett's blood turned to ice at the thought. Della was not Lady Meredith. She was not toying with his heart to gain the title. But Uncle Frank had never steered him wrong before, and right now, his mentor was looking at him with pity that fractured Rhett's heart.

Adelaide didn't join the family in the duke's bedroom. She stopped two doors down, bending as though to dislodge a pebble from her shoe. When she was satisfied that no one was watching, she took a deep breath and entered Rhett's bedroom.

It was completely impersonal. She shouldn't have been surprised; Rhett had told her he rarely visited his brother's estates. He also lived as nomadic a lifestyle as she had. He wouldn't be lugging trunks full of personal items across Europe. Hence, the room was empty save a bare minimum of furniture and a small trunk pushed up against the wall with its lid open. He hadn't even bothered to unpack. His clothes were folded neatly inside.

At last, some bloody luck. It would take next to no time to search this room thoroughly. If he had been a man to enjoy fripperies, it might have been a different story. Her heart flip-flopped. A man who enjoyed fripperies was a man ready to settle down in one spot. Hell, it was a man who had one spot in which to settle. Nothing about this room suggested Rhett was that man.

But everybody would give up floating for that one permanent person whom they can make a home with, surely.

Shoving her concerns about Rhett's willingness to settle down aside, she crossed to his desk. It was the logical place for him to put the announcement, so she would start there. But the desk was bare, save a stack of papers requiring the duke's signature. Each piece had been placed facedown, as though Rhett was ignoring their existence. A lease that needed signing, a licensing agreement for some sort of new technology, and a missive from the prime minister, asking for Peter's input on a new bill.

No betrothal announcement. Nothing pertaining to Cordelia. Damnation.

Della opened the drawers of the desk, but they were both empty. The only other personal items in the room were three books by the bedside. Perhaps the announcement was between the pages. Rhett seemed like an agent of chaos who would use a random piece of paper instead of a ribbon to mark his place. Not that the betrothal announcement was some piece of scrap. Using it so flippantly would certainly be saying something.

She sat on the edge of his bed. Her sense of smell must be returning. As she inhaled, she could pick up the scent of citrus, fresh air, and a little salt. It smelled like a spring day by the ocean.

She picked up the first book, one she had read before, and wondered if he was going to be as infuriated by the ending as she had been. He hadn't used anything as a bookmark. Instead, like a heathen, he had dog-eared the pages and scrawled notes in the margins. A quick inspection of the other two books revealed no sign of the betrothal announcement.

She lifted his pillow, but it wasn't under there. She got on her hands and knees and checked under the bed. It was spotless and bare. The only other place it could be was in his trunk.

She hesitated. Going through his clothes seemed a great violation of his privacy.

Really, Adelaide? As though you haven't just thoroughly violated it, anyway?

Feeling sick with guilt, she knelt before the trunk and carefully picked her way through it, lifting each item gently to look behind it, setting it aside so that she could return it to its original position.

His belongings included two pairs of trousers, two sets of long johns, a handful of shirts, a sketchbook, and a small sewing kit. It was the kind of sparse, practical trunk that she was familiar with. It mirrored her own. He was ready to leave at a moment's notice. She lifted another shirt.

Oh. Oh, wow. Oh, Adelaide. Why the devil does he own that? She knew why *she* owned one, and she could have understood his owning such an item if he had different proclivities, but Rhett was attracted to women. At least, she was ninety-nine percent certain he was.

She wrapped her hand around the giant marble cock and held it up for closer inspection. It was exquisite. The artist's attention to detail was superb. A delicate vein ran down the length of the stone. The foreskin had been rendered in perfect clarity. The tip of the cock was so polished and so smooth she could almost imagine a drop of liquid spilling out of it. The marble was hard and cold, yet within a few seconds, it warmed in her hands, as though she were caressing something soft and alive.

Heat swirled in her body, sending a hot red flush up her neck and pooling between her legs. Her heart thudded, and her thoughts scattered as the sensation gave rise to images. Damn her imagination. She could so clearly picture Rhett running his hands across her bare skin. Rhett, trailing his lips in patterns over her breasts, taking her nipples in his mouth and sucking gently, nipping at them, grazing his teeth over them.

She imagined the feeling of him between her legs, his cock pushing up against her as she locked her ankles behind his back. The gentle push became more urgent until he slid into her, filling her, stretching her, making her groan his name. Her grip on the marble cock tightened. With her free hand, she fanned her face.

And it was like that, while she was hot, dizzy, and completely undone, that she heard the door open.

"Della?"

"Rhett?" She spun around, pressing the giant marble cock against her chest. *Damn, damn, damn, damn.* The words echoed the thudding of her heart.

"What are you doing here?" There was nothing light or joking in his tone, nothing that felt like the Rhett she'd shared pastries with that morning. He regarded her with deep suspicion.

Of course he fucking does, Adelaide. He's caught you snooping through his things.

She looked down at the marble phallus, but there was no way of discarding it without drawing attention to it. She snapped her head back up. She had to maintain eye contact and keep him from realizing what was in her hands. "I was looking for a piece of correspondence," she said weakly. "The footman told me he'd seen it in your room."

Rhett crossed his arms and scowled. "You thought *your* correspondence was in *my* trunk?"

She grimaced. "Well, it wasn't on your desk or between the pages of your novels." She tried for a nervous laugh to break the tension, but Rhett wasn't having any of it.

He stalked toward her, graceful, angry. "What do you really want?" he asked when he was just inches from her.

His nearness scattered her senses. The warmth of his body mingled with the fire that burned inside her, threatening to erupt into a full-blown inferno. She tugged at her collar, trying to release some of the building heat. "I really was just looking for a piece of correspondence."

He leaned forward. He was within kissing distance. All she had to do was rise to her tiptoes. But his lips were pursed in displeasure, not desire. "You couldn't ask me if I had your letter?"

She swallowed. "Well, it is a little sensitive."

"Something you don't want me reading."

He stepped back. As he did so, his gaze dropped to her hands, to the marvelous marble cock she was gripping. He stilled, and his face flushed crimson. "I...Uh..." He shifted and studied the curtains, then the desk, then the corner of the wall, the entire time rubbing at his forehead, obscuring her view of him. "Did you ever find that book?"

Fuck, Adelaide. Fuck.

She thrust her hands behind her, fingers pressing against the marble cock as though all her humiliation could be transferred from her expression to it. "Book?" she asked, pretending everything was normal.

"The book you were looking for in Peter's study. I haven't seen you reading it to him."

Double fuck.

What if she told him the truth? All of it? Told him now before his uncle could blindside her with the information. "Your brother had written a betrothal announcement for *The Times* prior to his proposal. He hadn't had the chance to send it before his accident, and I was hoping to retrieve it. That's why I was in the study that night, and why I'm here." There. Part of the truth. She waited for his response.

He faced her with a look that was half anguish, half hope. "Are you planning on sending it?" There was a hitch to his voice and a wariness to the way he looked at her that was colder and more suspicious than he'd ever been.

She took a step backward. "No. I was going to destroy it."

Rhett sighed then, his shoulders sagging. He shook out his arms as though flinging off mud or a bad feeling. "That's good. That's really good. My uncle said...Never mind. He's wrong."

Della tensed. "What did your uncle say?" *It can't have*

been the truth. Rhett would not be speaking to you if it had
been. So, what then?

"He said that you are deceiving me."

Della's heart plummeted. "Rhett—"

Rhett crossed to her, taking her shoulders gently in his
hands. "He said you are determined to be the Duchess of
Strafford at any cost, and that our . . . friendship . . . is a tactic.
But that's not true."

She shook her head, tears welling. Their relationship was
genuine. The circumstances were a lie, but what she felt for
him was sincere. "No, it's not a tactic." She didn't want the
title. She didn't want the duke. She simply wanted the man
in front of her. She was starting to think she wanted him
more than anything else. More than a house, even.

"That's good. That's a relief." Rhett brushed a stray hair
from her cheek, and goose bumps rippled across her arms.
She felt the earth sway beneath her. "I'm glad that this, whatever it is, is genuine," he continued.

He paused for a moment, and across his face flickered
uncertainty, guilt, and then finally determination. He cupped
her head in his hand, his fingers twining through her hair.
Gently, he pulled her closer to him, stopping with his lips
mere inches from hers, waiting for her to make a choice.

"Della." The whisper was a plea. Their breaths mingled,
and her whole body pulsated with the rapid *thud, thud,
thud* of her heartbeat. She reached for him, one hand still
wrapped around the marble, the other caressing his side with
her fingers. He was warm even through the layers of shirt
and waistcoat. She felt his body flinch as she slid both arms
around his waist, and he swallowed. His thumb grazed the
back of her skull.

There were still so many unknowns. Would he forgive her
once he discovered her lie? If the duke woke, would Rhett

want to build a life with her in one place or was his love of travel too strong? If the duke died, Rhett would become the duke, and then a life together would not even be a possibility. A duke didn't marry a lady's maid.

All she really had was this moment, and moments were like people—fleeting. You had to grab hold of them for the short time you had.

Using his stillness for balance, she rose to her tiptoes and pressed her lips to his. He was as warm as the waters off the coast of Syracuse. Sinking into his kiss was like floating in the Mediterranean, loosening in the sun, the smell of the saltwater fixing the memory in her mind. She would never forget this, never forget the way his fingers splayed across her back, or the way he closed the distance between them with a groan, or the way his cock pressed against her, setting off a searing heat between her legs. She would never forget the way his tongue flickered across the seam of her lips, or his soft growl as she opened to him. His tongue explored hers like the most intrepid traveler who wasn't content with the usual tourist locations and wanted to know a city's heart.

The hand on her back traveled lower. His fingers curled around her hip, bunching the silk of her skirt. His other hand curled in her hair, and he pulled, breaking off their kiss and exposing her neck to his curious probing. His teeth grazed her jawline, sending a cascade of shivers down her spine. He took her throat in his mouth, sucking on it and making her vision blur and her knees weaken. His journey downward reached the collar of her shirt. He growled at the impediment, pulling at it with his teeth, caressing it with his tongue, and she tightened her grip on him to keep from collapsing. She would never forget the urgency of his kisses and the way the heat of his breath against her skin turned all of her senses inside out.

She pressed closer to him, moving her free hand to his

head, forcing his lips back to hers. Her own mouth nipped and licked as she took all he offered, now, while she could. In this moment, while it lasted, she could let go of everything that was holding her back from being with him.

There was a *thunk* of marble against the rug, but she ignored it as she frantically yanked at his shirt, pulling it from the waistband of his trousers until her fingers reached his warm, soft skin. Shivers ran down her spine at the feel of him. Her heart beat so hard and so fast it was as though she'd just climbed to the top of Mount Etna and was on the precipice of falling in, being consumed by the boiling, bubbling lava.

Rhett went to work on the delicate buttons that ran from her neckline to her waist. With every inch of her throat exposed, his tongue explored further. Soon, he'd freed enough of the fabric to pull her shirt aside. "Gods, you're beautiful."

Goose bumps raced across her décolletage. Hidden by the firmly fastened corset, her nipples peaked, yearning for his touch. As she dragged in a deep breath, her breasts swelled, straining to be free. Rhett groaned and turned his attention to the parts of her his mouth could access. As he ran a tongue along the worn lace edge of her corset, her knees weakened. She grabbed ahold of his shoulders for support.

She wanted this. She wanted this more than she'd ever wanted any man. If she were being honest, she wanted this more than she wanted a solid oak dining table. She would give up all the bookcases and wardrobes and delicate chaise longues in the world if it meant Rhett's lips would never leave her skin, if it meant this feeling of belonging would stay with her forever.

She groaned at the thought, and he straightened, sinking a hand into her hair, drawing her face close to his. He kissed her deeply, hungrily, fusing them together as if they were one soul.

Impatient, lustful, overcome with desire, she took the

hem of his shirt in her hand and pulled it over his head. He tossed it to the side. God damn, he was beautiful. His tanned skin was flecked with a smattering of honeyed hair. She ran her fingers over it, delighting in the juxtaposition of smoothness and coarseness.

The artists who'd captured him in their sketches had been true in their translation of him. His chest was hard, his body a map of ridges and valleys. When she rested her hands just above his hips, it was on top of long, lean muscles that drew the eye down toward his waistband.

Rhett captured her mouth again, and as he explored her with his tongue, she could feel the tug of his fingers at the laces of her corset. Within seconds, it was free and discarded on the floor. Her skirt followed a heartbeat later, her bustle after that, leaving her in just a chemise and petticoat.

She grinned as she remembered their first meeting and the boasts he'd made of how quickly he could undress a woman.

"What are you smiling about?" he murmured as he ran a trail of kisses down her neck, across her décolletage and to the swell of her breasts. He took a hand to one, kneading gently. In unison, they groaned.

"Nothing," she murmured, too overwhelmed to form a sentence.

He tugged at the edge of her chemise until her breasts sprang free. "I want you more than I have wanted anything in my life," he said.

Her nipples pebbled against the cool air of the room and the soft brush of his breath. She arched, wanting—nay, *needing*—him to take her into his mouth. With a moan, he did so, sucking gently. Heat pooled in her belly, and her core pulsated with desire. She grabbed onto his shoulders, her fingers digging into his bare skin.

He pressed his face more firmly into her breasts, his

hands reaching around to cup her arse. He squeezed it tightly and she could feel herself get wet at his touch. Good God, she wanted him inside her. She wanted to feel the thrust of his hips and the length of him pump into her over and over until they both climaxed.

"Rhett," she whispered, hoping he'd know exactly what she wanted without her having to say it.

He broke away from her breasts and stood, resting his forehead against hers. Their breaths mixed in a tangle of lust. "Lady Cordelia Highwater, I think I'm falling in love with you."

Instead of a rush of headiness or euphoria, icy dread flooded her, washing away every tendril of heat and lust. She stiffened. *Stupid, Adelaide. Stupid, stupid, stupid.* He wasn't falling in love with her; he was falling in love with the person she was pretending to be. Everything he felt was false at its core. He wasn't kissing Adelaide Rosebourne, and that knowledge shattered her. Being crushed by the heaviest bookcase could never be so hurtful.

The future she'd thought so tangible—the breakfast table they both sat at, the summer afternoons beneath a tree they'd planted, the children who ran at their feet—suddenly dissipated like the mirage it had always been.

She stepped away from him, out of the warmth of his embrace and into the cold emptiness. She pulled her skirt up from where it had tangled at her feet, tying the laces quickly. "I should go. Andrew was looking for you. He might very well look for you here."

"Della," Rhett protested. His expression was tormented, but he handed her the corset that he'd discarded. She didn't bother with the laces. She buttoned her shirt and her collar, not caring at all how the fabric bunched where the corset was misplaced.

"No. No, I can't." She took another step backward while

trying desperately to get the last buttons done. Then she tripped. She went down on her arse hard, feeling the sharp thud from her tailbone to her teeth. Flushed with embarrassment, she felt for whatever she'd stepped on that caused her to fall, holding it up in front of her.

Brilliant. Nice work, Adelaide. Way to make an awkward scene worse. The marble cock in her hand was a sharp reminder of what would have been if she hadn't come to her senses.

Rhett also blushed. He grasped her free hand to help her up. "It was a gift," he said, rubbing the back of his neck. "From an artist in Florence. She, um...I sat for...well, I guess lay down for... You know, I should just get rid of that."

Oh, God. It's his. Suddenly, she couldn't peel her eyes away from it. *It can't possibly be to size.* She thought back to the way his cock had pressed against her. It was likely to size. Holy God. "It's nice. Very impressive," she said weakly. What else was there to say?

"Thank you." Rhett found a spot over her left shoulder to stare at, his ears turning crimson. His lips were pinched, and she could see the hurt in his eyes.

"I'm going to go." Managing a tight smile, she curtsied, felt stupid for doing so, and ran from the room. She didn't stop running until her bedroom door slammed behind her and she sank into her mattress.

Why? Why? Why? Why? With every repetition, she knocked herself on the forehead. The solid tap reinforced her self-rebuke. How had she gotten herself into this mess and how the devil was she going to get herself out of it?

It was only once the despair had sunk in and both hands had settled on her chest that she opened her eyes and realized why her forehead throbbed. There, resting right above her heart, was the heavy marble cock.

Bloody hell.

Chapter Twenty

Adelaide lay on her bed, staring up at the canopy, turning Rhett's penis over and over in her hands. She would have to return it, obviously. One couldn't hold on to a man's member forever, regardless of how perfectly shaped it was and how the feel of it reminded her of the lustful boiling beneath her skin whenever he touched her. But how, exactly, to hand it back? Should she sneak back into his room and tuck it beneath the shirt under which she'd found it? Or should she attempt to return it to him in person? Should she hand it over across the dinner table and then ask him to pass the salt?

The truth was, she didn't really want to give it back. It was a highly, highly unusual memento of a person, but in a day or two, it would be all she had of him. A marble penis and the memory of their kisses. She couldn't stay. She was falling in love with Rhett, and Rhett was falling in love with a woman who didn't exist.

No. She needed to avoid him as much as humanly possible. Once the duke woke, Adelaide would sneak out of the house, collect her money from Cordelia, and find an equally hidden town to escape to.

There was a knock at the door. *Rhett.* She should have

known he would not have gone quietly. He would want an explanation. She might as well get it over and done with. She hefted the penis in her hand. *Time to hand you back too.*

She padded over to the door, setting her shoulders in anticipation of what would follow. He would want to know why she had rushed out of the room as though the hounds of hell were on her tail. One moment she'd been throwing herself at him, and the next she was running. That behavior deserved an apology and an explanation. What a pity she couldn't tell him the truth.

"Rhett," she said, opening the door.

"Neither of my nephews, I'm afraid." Frank's smile was more of a leer, and immediately the wrong sort of shudder ran down her spine.

"I'm afraid you have the wrong room," she said calmly, ignoring the clattering of panic in her chest. She swung the door shut, but he put out a hand and entered before she could stop him.

Della's throat tightened. Her gaze went straight to her bed, underneath which an emergency bag was concealed. It was a small pack that carried a change of clothes, her few valuables, a medical kit, and enough hard cheese to feed her for three days. It was her "go-fast" bag, ready to be deployed the moment she felt her safety was in question. *Like right fucking now, Adelaide.*

The only problem was that Frank stood between her and it. The only weapon she had in her reach was the heavy piece of marble in her hands. That would be formidable, assuming she could get a full swing in. But she didn't want to fight if she could avoid it. Frank was bigger than her, by fifty pounds at least, and he had that semi-wild-eyed look of a man who was running on more than a good night's sleep. Cocaine, perhaps, or the wildest mushrooms.

She had two options: turn around and flee, which would get her out of any immediate danger but would still leave her at the mercy of his machinations, or negotiate, assuming he was a man who could be negotiated with.

"What do you want?" she asked with confidence she didn't feel. She knew men like this. They preyed on the weak. They searched for women who kept their heads down and eyes averted. She shot him a piercing stare. His reptilian grin widened.

"I've known Cordelia Highwater since she was born. Her father and I are old friends. You are not her."

That figured. The Duke of Thirwhestle was an unpleasant man. It made sense that his friends were equally unpleasant. "I'm her lady's maid. So again, what do you want?"

Frank walked to the desk by the window and poked around the few items Adelaide had stored there. "Where is Lady Cordelia?"

"Safe." It would take less than ten minutes for him to discover the cottage—too many people had been there after the duke fell—but those ten minutes would give Adelaide time to reach her, protect her.

He looked back at her. "Does your mistress know you are dressing up in her clothing?"

"It was her idea." A bloody stupid one.

Frank narrowed his eyes. "Lady Cordelia barely deigns to speak to those she thinks beneath her—second sons included. She would not tolerate a maid standing in her place."

"Self-preservation convinces us to do plenty of things we otherwise wouldn't." *Like you going along with this idiotic farce, Adelaide.*

He settled himself in her chair and picked up a pencil from her desk, twirling it between his fingers. "Did she hurt the duke?"

"No." The word was quick and as sharp as she could manage. "It was an accident. Peter tripped. Cordelia had nothing to do with it." Della fought the urge to cross her arms; instead she stood with arms akimbo, ignoring how vulnerable it made her feel.

"Pity. I might have had more respect for her if she had." Frank didn't seem even remotely affected by his nephew's current state. He spoke of it as though he were speaking of bad weather, or taxes, or the condition of the road between here and London.

"What do you want?" she repeated. He was toying with her, taking pleasure in her discomfort.

"Trapping my nephews into marriage, was that also Cordelia's idea, or were you simply taking advantage of the situation? Your resourcefulness is admirable." He tapped the pencil on the desk three times, hard enough to crush the graphite. "I respect it."

Della swallowed, still frozen to the spot. "That has never been my intention. I'm not trying to trap anyone."

Frank cocked his head, clearly skeptical. "Interesting, because Everett seems quite besotted."

Her heart soared, then Frank leered, and her heart crashed and burned, caught in the tangle of insurmountable problems.

"What do you want?" she asked, surprised she could get the words out without choking.

"I want what you want." He leaned back in the chair, crossing his legs at the ankle. "I want you and Everett to live a long and happy life together."

That wasn't it. It couldn't be it. It was too easy. It was too kindhearted to come from this man.

"On the continent," he continued, and the other shoe dropped.

"Why?"

"Why?" he murmured. He traced patterns on the desk, glaring at them, leaving smudges in his wake. "Because I want what my brother was given freely but I was denied simply because of the order of our birth." He scratched a line into the polish. "Because when Peter dies, the estates will fall to Everett." Another line. Another deep scratch. "Because with Peter dead, only the boy stands in my way."

Frank looked up, catching Adelaide's stare in a viselike one of his own. "He can saddle himself with the title and all that comes with it and be miserable, or he can choose to live life as he pleases."

"Leaving you with control over the estate, I assume." It made so much sense—if he could get Rhett out of the way, he'd have the power he so clearly lusted for.

Frank shrugged. "Someone has to do it. It might as well be me."

Adelaide shook her head and stepped to the side, leaving a path clear. "Rhett will make an excellent duke," she said firmly. "He's intelligent and kind and just, and he feels the responsibility of the title deeply. He will not abandon his duty so easily." She gestured toward the door.

Frank snorted, showing no sign of moving. "Everett Montgomery? The same Everett Montgomery who was expelled from Cambridge for setting a half dozen pigs loose in the dining hall? Who has made a name for himself tupping discontented married women in ballroom alcoves? Who has spent the past five years sunk so deep in debauchery he formed gills to breathe through the booze?"

It was a picture of a man she didn't recognize. *Perhaps that was who he had been, but it's not him now, and no one can see it but you.*

She set her shoulders and straightened her spine. "I won't do it. I won't encourage him to go back to that life."

Frank smirked. "But you will, because when the duke dies, powerful people are going to want to know why. From where I stand, you look pretty culpable. Cordelia will run and hide behind her father's title, leaving you to take the fall. A life on the continent with the man you're sleeping with is more appealing than gaol, don't you think?"

Adelaide's momentary confidence vanished. He wasn't wrong. If the duke died, she had only Cordelia's word that she wasn't responsible, and Cordelia was a child who could not be relied upon. Adelaide swallowed hard. She could barely force her voice above a whisper. "And if the duke doesn't die?"

Frank chucked the pencil aside and stood. "If the duke doesn't die, you have bigger problems than me. I can't imagine he'll take well to being assaulted. But rest assured, my nephew will die. He's had naught to eat nor a proper drink for days. His body won't hold out much longer."

He's right. God damn it. The handful of ice chips they'd managed to feed him would not suffice for long. "Get out," she whispered. "Get the hell out."

Chapter Twenty-One

Rhett rolled his shoulders as he walked down the hallway from his brother's study, a stack of ledgers and notebooks in his arms and a redheaded woman on his mind. Della hadn't come down for dinner the previous night, or for breakfast that morning, and there had been no sign of her when he rode to Berwick's small bakery. According to Winnie, Della had a splitting headache, but Rhett knew the truth. She was avoiding him, and it cut because he'd been left reeling by their encounter.

All morning, when he should have been concentrating on what Andrew was telling him, he'd been wallowing in the memory of her—the taste of her skin, the press of her hands against him, the intoxicating scent of lemon, the rush of blood through his system as she completely felled him. In all his years, no woman had ever set him so at sea. No woman had ever bewitched him so thoroughly.

All he wanted now was to close the chasm that had opened as she'd fled. He'd startled her. She was a proper young lady. He needed to apologize. Then he needed to do it with her all over again, this time with more care.

Andrew strode next to him, completely oblivious to the

lewd turn of Rhett's thoughts. "That was a lot of information," he said in response to Rhett's silence. "Even if you had stayed in England and been more involved with the family estates, that would still have been an overwhelming amount of information."

With his free hand, Rhett rubbed his face. "I know. I know. But it still would have been easier..."—if he hadn't been gallivanting around the world and had instead taken some interest in the family business. If Peter hadn't thought of him as nothing more than an irresponsible, feckless fool. If Rhett hadn't worked so hard to cultivate that exact impression.

Della had been right; he could no longer ignore this. Now there was a tower of notebooks and journals tucked into the crook of his elbow—light reading he needed to get through today in order to make fairly crucial decisions tomorrow. Light as a lodestone, that is. The only thing that would save him from it was a miracle—Peter waking before then.

Rhett had thought he'd understood the magnitude of just how his life would change if the dreaded circumstance arose—the constant pull of people who would need something from him—but the numbers, in black and red within the ledgers, illustrated it in a way that nothing yet had. Berwick was one of nine estates, encompassing over ten thousand people. The risk of their collective disappointment threatened to crush him. His chest felt tight, his arms were shaking beneath the load of leather-bound books, and he had the early markings of a headache forming at the base of his skull.

"You care. That's not nothing."

When he and Andrew entered the hallway, the constriction around his lungs eased, and he drew a deep, full breath for the first time in hours. She had her back to him and was examining the Caravaggio by the stairs. She must have washed her hair. It was in a long, haphazard strawberry-blonde plait down her back, with a twist in the middle of it where she must have pulled it over her shoulder to finish braiding.

"Della." He put a hand on her shoulder, seeking the comfort of her, seeking her unflappable calm, seeking the now-familiar frisson of energy that sparked between them.

She shrank away as she spun.

Everything in his head shifted, and the books he was holding came to a thudding crash on the floor. "You're not Della."

The woman wrinkled her nose.

Andrew stepped forward and gave the woman a nod. "My lord, may I present Lady Cordelia's maid, Miss Rosebourne? Miss Rosebourne, Lord Everett Montgomery."

Rhett bowed out of politeness rather than protocol. The chit gritted her teeth and curtsied in response. It was remarkable how similar the two women were. Their hair was identical in color and texture. They both had blue eyes, but where Della's were deep and fathomless, sparking with humor and empathy and soul, her maid's gaze was cold and shallow like a midwinter fountain that had yet to be drained.

"My lord." She had the clipped accent of the royal class and the bearing of it too. If Andrew hadn't said otherwise, Rhett would have assumed she was a member of the *ton*, not a maid. But that couldn't be the case, unless...

"Are you a relation of the Thirwhestle family? Della's cousin, perhaps?"

She grimaced. "You might say that."

Rhett was tempted to give her a message for Della—something simple. Something benign. Something that showed that she was in his thoughts without revealing just what those thoughts were.

But before he had a chance, the maid turned her back on him.

Rude.

"Why are things not yet resolved?"

Adelaide jumped. She'd been so lost in thought she hadn't heard the door open. "Cordelia," she said, turning away from the window.

Cordelia stood in front of her, arms akimbo. "Why are you still here? It has been days. I was counting on you having everything sorted by now."

Adelaide pinched the bridge of her nose. She had bigger problems to deal with than Cordelia's impatience. "I thought we agreed that you'd remain at the cottage. I've told the household that the duke's accident overwhelmed you and that you are beset with migraines." The last thing she needed was Cordelia further complicating an already impossibly complicated situation.

"I'm hungry." Cordelia crossed to the bellpull and yanked it. "I cannot believe you would let me and Patches starve."

"Patches?"

"The cat."

Sigh. There was no reason Cordelia or the stray cat should starve. Adelaide had left the cottage stocked with bread, jam, eggs, and some vegetables. Even if Cordelia couldn't pull together a soup, she should've been able to put together a sandwich. The cat, no doubt, could survive well enough on its own.

"You can't be here," Adelaide said, standing and trying to usher Cordelia out of the room. Cordelia refused to move, stubborn as a bloody rock. "Please. If anyone should see you..."

"I am dressed like a peasant." Cordelia gestured to the

dress she was wearing, the one Adelaide had worn to the wedding—her favorite. "If anyone should see me, they will simply presume I'm a maid." She shuddered.

Adelaide gritted her teeth. The compounding stress of the past few days was exhausting, and she wasn't sure she had the energy to shape her words into something appropriate. Thankfully, she was prevented from biting back by a knock at the door. A housemaid entered.

"You rang, my lady?" she asked Adelaide.

Adelaide shifted so that she was standing between the maid and Cordelia. "Could you please bring a lunch tray? Thank you."

The maid gave her a surprised look before adding a quick curtsy and exiting.

Cordelia *hmph*ed. "That maid is impertinent. How dare she look at you…me…like that."

Della took a deep breath and tried to calm the raging frustration within her before turning. "Daisy is likely confused because not ten minutes ago I told her I didn't want luncheon."

She'd eaten next to nothing since dinner the night before, taken in her room because she was too cowardly to face either Rhett or Frank. Everything she'd eaten had tasted of ash. All she'd managed that morning was tea and toast in her room. Even that had made her stomach turn.

She knew this feeling. The nausea wouldn't relent until the threat did.

Cordelia plopped down onto the bed, completely oblivious to Adelaide's discomfort. "Well, that makes one of us. If you are going to stay any longer, you are going to need to stop by the cottage at least twice a day to prepare some food."

Adelaide started to neaten her already tidy room, untucking

and retucking the chair. "Or I could come over once and show you how to prepare food. Teach a man, and all that." The moment she said the words, she regretted them.

· "I don't fish," Cordelia said sternly.

Adelaide sighed. "Fine. You can eat luncheon here, and then I will come around later this afternoon to prepare soup." A large pot. Enough soup to feed a person for a week. Not that she planned on being in Berwick that long. With any luck, she and Cordelia would be gone in a day. "But you can't come here again."

Cordelia's presence posed too many risks. She was loose-lipped and couldn't be trusted not to spill the truth to Rhett accidentally before Adelaide could tell him herself. Hell, her mere presence might create questions about Adelaide's story. Cordelia looked and carried herself more like a lady than Adelaide could pretend to be. It wouldn't take long for that to raise eyebrows. Besides, the danger had gotten far more immediate.

"Rhett's uncle has arrived. He knows I am not you, and he's making threats."

"Lord *Frank* Montgomery is here?" Cordelia put a hand to her throat, her already-pale skin blanching further. "Oh, God. What if he's already sent for the duke? The other duke. My father duke, not my fiancé duke."

Adelaide rested her hip against the desk. "If that's the case, then we have two days before your father arrives." *A day for the news to reach London, a day for the duke to get here. Can you finish it in two days, Adelaide?*

Cordelia threw herself back on the bed, fists slamming into the mattress. "Why is this taking so long?"

Adelaide was not in the mood for her mistress's self-absorbed tantrums. "The duke has yet to wake," she snapped. "Do you understand the implications of that? A body can only go so long without food and water. The longer he remains unconscious, the greater the chance that he will *not* wake."

"The greater the chance that I killed him, you mean?" Cordelia asked.

"Yes, Cordelia. The greater the chance you killed him."

A tear dripped down Cordelia's cheek and onto the pillow she lay on. Adelaide immediately regretted her harsh words. Cordelia was but a child, and one who had been taught entitlement from birth.

"What happens if he dies?"

Adelaide sighed. "I do not know."

"Will his siblings question the circumstances of his death? Or have they accepted his fall as an accident?"

Adelaide rubbed the bridge of her nose. "I don't believe they would have questioned it, but Lord Frank is threatening to allege murder."

"Why would he do that? He and my father are friends."

She pulled out the chair she had just put away and sank into it. Lord, she was tired. "Lord Frank wants the dukedom, or whatever parts of it the law will allow him to have. He wants me to convince Rhett to return to the continent and have his uncle act as his proxy."

"That makes no sense." Cordelia's eyebrows furrowed, and she cocked her head in confusion. "Why would Lord Everett listen to you?"

Adelaide was saved from answering by a knock at the door. The housemaid entered with a tray covered with plates. The maid's eyes darted between Adelaide and Cordelia, who looked perfectly comfortable lounging upon the bed in a manner no lady's maid ever would. Adelaide could see the wheels turning. Their time was running out. Someone was bound to put the pieces together.

As soon as the door closed, Cordelia leapt from the bed and nudged Adelaide from the chair. Within seconds, she was devouring the food. Perhaps she truly hadn't eaten since Adelaide had left.

"So, tell me why Lord Frank thinks you can influence Lord Everett," Cordelia said between mouthfuls.

Adelaide had no good answer to that. She took Cordelia's spot on the bed, pinching the bridge of her nose while she tried to think of one.

"Goodness," Cordelia exclaimed, dropping a forkful of ham. "Does this have anything to do with the reason Lord Everett touched my arm in a *very* familiar manner? Adelaide!"

"We are friends. That is all." But even she could tell her tone was not convincing.

"*Friends?* Men like Lord Everett Montgomery do not have women friends. They have paramours."

"That's an unfair assumption about him." *But not an unfair assessment of the situation, Adelaide.*

Cordelia's hunger clearly overrode her many years of deportment training, because she shoveled more food into her mouth and did not wait to swallow it all before continuing. "He left London to avoid the hordes of angry husbands ready to hoist him by the underclothes he never wears."

"He has changed. You don't know him as I do."

Cordelia was yet another person who only saw the irresponsible, carefree facade Rhett had so carefully created. Cordelia might have been trying to issue a warning, but all it did was solidify Adelaide's feelings. Rhett had gone so many years without being seen, not even by his family. She would not betray him now when he was ready to take off the mask and show the world who he truly was.

Cordelia didn't need or wait for an answer. She waved a

fork at Adelaide. "Regardless of whether he has changed, he is a member of the aristocracy. You are a maid."

"I know!" It was Adelaide's turn to throw herself on the bed, an arm across her face to hide her frustration. The situation was impossible. If the duke died, she and Rhett could never be together. The only chance she and Rhett had was for the duke to wake, a scenario that seemed less and less likely.

"Adelaide Rosebourne, have you developed feelings for this rake?"

"Yes," she mumbled. "I love him. But if you knew him, you'd understand. He might come across as an irresponsible rogue, but he's sweet and funny and incredibly loyal."

Cordelia snorted. "Very loyal, clearly, if he's pursuing his brother's fiancée."

"I'm not his brother's fiancée."

"Does he know that?"

"No."

"Well, there you go." Cordelia reached for the tea that had come with the food. Had she had tea since Adelaide had left? Could she even boil water? "Lord Everett is a man who would steal from his own flesh and blood. Point proven."

Adelaide sat up and looked at her employer. "Peter and I are hardly a love match."

Cordelia threw her hands in the air. "You're not a match at all! Do you hear yourself? Adelaide, you are a maid, pretending to be a lady, trying to get me *out* of marital entanglements, not dumping me into the middle of an even more complicated one. Lord, I can just see the headlines now: Runaway bride leaves second duke for his untitled philandering brother."

She's not wrong. The papers will have a field day if any of this gets out. Which it will, if you don't do exactly what Frank wants.

"I'll fix this," Adelaide said. "I'll tell them all the truth right now."

"No!" Cordelia jumped up. "If you tell them the truth and the duke lives, I will be married off to him to save my family from the scandal. If you tell them the truth and the duke dies, I will be *arrested*. How could you mess this up so badly?"

Adelaide dug her hands into the blankets to stop from pulling her hair out. "This was your idea."

"I didn't know the duke's entire family was going to show up at his bedside. Of all the interfering—" Cordelia was interrupted by a knock at the door. Before either of them could call out in protest, it opened.

Adelaide slid off the side of the bed, her arse hitting the carpet with a thwack. Hiding was instinct, if a completely useless one. If Frank was at the door, her absence would be an invitation for him to confront Cordelia.

"Della, why are you lunching in your...never mind," Jac said. "Are you coming? Andrew has brought the Christmas tree into Peter's room. It isn't Christmas without him, and perhaps the tree will deliver a Christmas miracle."

From where she sat, Adelaide could see Cordelia's confusion. Her brows furrowed. She threw a quick look at Adelaide as if to confirm that events were unfolding as they appeared and then cocked her head.

"Well?" Jac continued. "I have set aside Peter's share of the baubles, but if you don't come now, I can't guarantee Winnie won't steal them."

She doesn't have her spectacles on. She thinks Cordelia is you. Adelaide motioned to her mistress to play along.

"I will be there in a few minutes?" Cordelia said uncertainly.

"Very well. I'm sure I can fend my sisters off for a few minutes, though they are like wild jackals when it comes to the Christmas tree."

Adelaide heard the door shut and dropped her head in her hands.

Cordelia threw her an arch stare. "Well, aren't you on familiar terms after four days? You're decorating their Christmas tree."

"They are very sweet. They didn't hesitate to bring me, you, into the bosom of their family."

Cordelia looked as though she were Vesuvius, ready to blow. "Then detach yourself from the teat and get back to reality. You can't just join a family, especially the family of a duke. Get a grip on yourself, Adelaide."

But what if you could? What if they'd welcome you?

Cordelia folded her hands in her lap. "What do we do?"

Adelaide closed her eyes, wishing she could block it all out. "You go home. I wake the duke and convince him to stay quiet."

"How?"

"I don't know."

Chapter Twenty-Two

"She should decorate Peter's section of the tree, since they will be married," Jac said, hands on her hips as she stared at the giant Christmas tree taking up a good portion of Peter's room. At its base were scattered boxes of decorations filled with baubles and trinkets they'd collected over the years.

No. Nope. Rhett shook his head, arms crossed. He would concede nothing to Peter when it came to the woman he loved. He certainly would not concede this piece of family tradition. "Della needs her own section. She can have this bit next to mine."

"If she's going to have her own section, she should be next to Peter."

"She can be between Peter and me."

"But then who will decorate Peter's section?"

Rhett laced his fingers behind his neck, taking a deep breath and trying to find the joy in his first Christmas home in years. "Peter's section can remain bare...or you could decorate it," he added when Jac opened her mouth to argue.

From the corner, where she sat in the armchair covered in a thick blanket, Meg *tsk*ed. "Everett. Jacqueline. Enough bickering. And you need to wait until everyone else arrives before you start placing anything on the tree."

There was a cough, and Rhett looked to the doorway; Uncle Frank had a mock scowl on his face. "Where is my section?"

Jac flushed. "I hadn't thought..." She trailed off, clearly embarrassed not to have considered their uncle in her plans.

"You don't have one," Meg said bluntly.

Rhett sighed. He would never understand the antagonism between the two. Meg was usually so reasonable. "Take Peter's section of the tree, Uncle. He's not using it."

Frank rubbed his hands together. "That's fine with me. Is that fine with you, Margaret?"

Meg gave a sarcastic smile. "It's just a Christmas tree, Frank. By all means, hang a bauble."

Jac rolled her eyes as she plopped down on the floor and started untying the string that held the decoration boxes shut. "Well, aren't we all in a festive mood? Merry Christmas, everyone."

"Merry Christmas," Rhett muttered. He looked over at his brother. Peter was wearing a fresh nightshirt made of garish cotton printed with holly and mistletoe. It had taken Rhett, Andrew, and Peter's valet a half hour to bathe and dress the duke. Rhett had seen more of his brother naked than he'd ever wanted to see.

The same shirt sat folded on Rhett's bed, a gift from his sisters for tomorrow. They had a ridiculous vision of wearing matching outfits as they drank eggnog and exchanged gifts, which he would acquiesce to, if only from guilt. It had taken the cessation of his allowance for him to return to his family for the holiday. Now that all the siblings were under the same roof for the first time in half a decade, he wished he'd come home earlier. He wished they'd spent a Christmas together with all of them conscious, even if that meant suffering his brother's criticism.

His imperfections—and his family's constant reminders of them—had been all he'd thought about as he was escaping. Somehow, he'd overlooked the fact that they loved him regardless.

It felt so obvious now, even in the smallest of gestures—the way Winnie would shift her chair closer so that she could rest her head on his shoulder even while she complained that he still smelled like a sewer; the way Jac would pass him the salt, sugar, potatoes, and whatever else he wanted before he could express the need and without pausing in her conversation with Della; the way Meg squeezed his hand every time she left the room, as though she were afraid he'd be gone when she returned. It was not an unreasonable fear—hadn't he been planning to do just that the moment he could?

And then there was Della, who loved him; he was sure of it. It was there in the way she would scan the room as she entered, and then relax her shoulders the moment her gaze met his. It was there in the way that her body was always turned slightly toward him, and every time her cautious expression softened as he spoke.

If Peter woke—when Peter woke—what signs of affection would Rhett realize he'd missed?

He reached for a string of bells that Jac had pulled from a box, and he crossed to Peter's bed. "If you're planning to make a dramatic return, can I suggest you do it before tomorrow's breakfast? Mrs. Carlyle has quite the feast planned." There was no response. He sighed and wrapped the bells around the bedposts.

The hairs on the back of Rhett's neck rose, and he smiled. Looking over his shoulder, he saw Della in the doorway.

"Has there been any improvement?" she asked, looking

hesitantly at the two brothers. It was the first time Rhett had seen her since their kiss yesterday.

She'd always been beautiful. Her blue eyes had always crackled with intelligence, and her lips had always been soft and kissable. She'd always stood with a willowy elegance that begged for his hands to slide across her waist and settle on her hips. None of that had changed.

He had changed.

His cock reacted as it always had, but now his heart also jerked, and the breath caught in his throat. A single word ricocheted through his mind. *Forever.* He would do whatever was needed to convince her he was serious about a relationship, that their kiss was not something for her to be afraid of. She wasn't another conquest or fling. There was nothing temporary about his feelings for her.

"No change," he replied.

She crossed to stand awkwardly next to him, ten inches away, her hands clasped firmly in front of her.

He leaned, bumping her shoulder with his arm, trying to defuse the tension. "Perhaps there will be a Christmas miracle?"

She bumped him back, her whole body relaxing. "Perhaps." She looked around the room. "Where is Winnie?"

"Fetching decorations from my trunk."

"From your trunk?" Adelaide hadn't seen decorations in there, but then again, she hadn't gotten past a certain marble object that she had yet to return.

"Yes, my trunk, which is now safe for her to enter since you absconded with my, *ahem*."

Della's cheeks turned delightfully pink. "I have been trying to work out how to return that."

"Don't." The word came out before he could consider it, but then he did, and he agreed with his instinct. "Consider it yours." His marble penis, his real penis. She could have either, often, whenever she wanted.

"I…uh…thank you?" Her pink cheeks turned crimson, and she glanced around as though to make sure no one was listening. She flinched as her gaze landed on Frank, who was watching them closely as he hung a glass ball on a pine branch.

Jac approached and handed over a box. "We split the tree horizontally. Your row is the second from the top."

Adelaide swallowed. "I have a row?" Her eyes took on a shine that made Rhett's chest tighten.

"Of course you do. You're Peter's wife. At least, you will be." Jac leaned over to brush her eldest brother's hair. "He'll wake in time for Christmas. I have that feeling."

Peter had better wake, and quickly. Until he did, Rhett would be forced to endure his sisters' assumptions that Della would join the family in an intolerable way. "Let's get back to the tree," he said gruffly.

"Shouldn't we wait for Winnie?" Meg asked dryly from the corner.

"No," both her siblings said in unison.

Jac looked at Della. "She would hog all the good ones. I told you she's feral."

Della tried not to laugh as she placed the box at the foot of the tree and lifted a painted glass bauble. "Constantinople," she said, beaming.

"Rhett sent us decorations every year that he was on the continent." Jac held up a delicate crepe paper festoon. "This is my favorite. It came from Italy."

"I wanted to be here in spirit, if not in person," he said. That had felt like an excellent compromise then. He would do it differently now.

"And that's what Winnie has gone to collect? More baubles from your travels?"

"This year's are exceptionally interesting. Here, place this one." He handed Della the bauble he loved the most, a delicate glass orb he'd bought in Paris from a glassblower with a workshop on the banks of the river Seine. Five colors intricately intertwined. By happenstance, they were the Montgomery family's favorite shades.

Their fingers brushed as he placed it in her hand, and his heart swelled. He would find another by next Christmas, one that captured the essence of her.

"I found the decorations! You started *without* me?" Winnie's outraged shriek shattered the moment.

"There are still plenty of decorations, and no one has touched your row."

She *hmph*ed and raced to kneel by the tree. Like a starving orphan thrown a few crumbs, she gathered baubles in the crook of her elbow, picking through the boxes to claim those she wanted.

"Are you sure you still want to join this family?" he asked, holding his breath for her response. He couldn't add the qualifier *as my wife*; not now. Not before he'd spoken with Peter. But he did his best to convey it in his expression.

"Very much so," Della whispered.

His heart clattered like reindeer hooves on tiled roofs. "Then you'd best get hanging ornaments, or your section of the tree will be bare."

The next few minutes were spent reminiscing about Christmases past as the five of them hung ornaments, Meg directing her sisters from the armchair where she was happily ensconced. Della was quick to laugh and comment, but she shared none of her own stories, as though she hadn't any happy moments to talk about. Rhett would change that. He would give her another fifty years of merry holidays.

He grazed his fingers across the back of her hand. He

couldn't hold it. Not yet. Not in front of his sisters. Not until the situation with Peter was resolved. His brother deserved to be the first to know that Rhett and Della were in love. If his brother died, his family would need to mourn before they could celebrate such joyful news. So, in public, a passing graze of hands was all they could do.

"I'm so happy you're here," he whispered.

"Me too." She looked around the room. "Your family is—oh my *God*. Winnie, what are you doing?"

Rhett turned, fully expecting his sister to be accidentally setting fire to the curtains with a candle or overloading the tree with ornaments so it listed to one side. Apprehension morphed into humiliation. His whole body flushed hot, and his ears rang like the eleven pipers piping were doing so up close.

"These balloons are terrible. Brother, you were swindled." She held the rubber sheath to her lips—

"No!" Della leapt forward and snatched it from Winnie's hand.

"*Mean*." Winnie scowled as Frank cackled.

"Everett Francis Montgomery." The fury in Meg's tone was palpable. Jac looked from sibling to sibling, her confusion clear.

"That is not a balloon, Winnie." Rhett wished for a sinkhole to form and swallow him whole.

"Then what is it?" Winnie asked.

He couldn't form the words. He knew what they were, but his mouth would not speak, probably because his sister would tear him apart.

"It's a French letter," Della said when no one else would.

Winnie's confusion gave way to horror. As she sputtered, Jac joined her uncle in hysterical laughing.

"Ew! Rhett, how could you? I touched that. I put my mouth to it."

Rhett winced. "It was unused, if that helps."

"No, it does not help. Oh my God, I am never going to forgive you for this. I swear, you'd better lock your door every night, because I am going to get you."

He ran a hand through his hair. "You were the one who took it from my trunk."

"I thought it was for decoration! If it was for *you know what*, why do you have so many?" She picked up the box he stored his French letters in and tossed it at him. The lid was not on it, so the rest scattered in a line as the box flew through the air. Rhett caught it before it could thwack him in the head. As he crawled on the floor to pick the French letters up, Frank's laughing doubled.

"Here," Della said, also on her hands and knees. She gave him what she'd collected. He couldn't even respond, just gave an embarrassed nod.

"Lord, I wish Peter had been awake for that," Jac said. "He would have been mortified."

"Perhaps he can sense what's happening," Meg said.

"No. If he knew what was happening, he would wake just so that he could reprimand Rhett."

"You know, this isn't actually my fault. Wearing protection during sex is the responsible thing to do. Peter might actually approve."

Della went around the room, pressing ornaments into everyone's hands. "Did you know French letters are banned in America? They have the most peculiar laws, don't you think?"

Grateful for the slight shift in conversation, Rhett nodded.

"All countries have peculiar laws," Frank said, setting a star upon the highest bough of the tree, an honor that usually belonged to the youngest Montgomery. "In fact, there's a debate in parliament about steam trawlers and the idea that they should have letters and numbers painted on their hulls.

Some say it would make our waters safer, and others say it's a government overreach. What are your thoughts on the matter, son?"

Rhett froze, keenly aware of everyone's eyes on him. "I wasn't aware of the debate."

"So, you have no thoughts on it? That's a shame given you may be the one voting on it. What are your thoughts on the proposal to pass all responsibility for roads, bridges, and poor relief to county councils and boroughs?"

It wasn't embarrassment that made Rhett's ears burn hot now. It was shame. "I don't know...I haven't heard anything about that."

"And what about the Housing of the Working Classes Act? Have you paid any attention to what's happening there?" Frank's usually jovial tone had hardened. For the first time in their entire relationship, Rhett sensed disdain from his uncle.

"No, I haven't." A lump formed in his throat.

"Those are things a duke should be on top of, don't you think? There is no greater responsibility than running a country. One should, at the very least, be aware of the discussions being had."

Della moved to stand between Rhett and Frank. "If it should come it to, Rhett will inform himself and make honorable choices. He is more than capable of being an excellent duke. You should see him with the townspeople. He's a natural."

Frank shook his head. "There's more to the title than placating individuals on a single estate. Millions of lives depend on the duke's willingness to read the information given to him. He needs to do that while managing all of his estates, not just this one."

Rhett tried to imagine the number of people that would

be. The number of lives counting on him making the right decisions. He hadn't even visited most of Peter's estates in decades. Not since he was a child.

"You're right," he said, hoping his sisters didn't notice how choked the words were, how terribly humiliated he was at his deficiencies being laid bare in front of them all.

Uncle Frank clapped a comforting hand on his shoulder. "It's all right to be daunted, son. Being a peer is not for everyone. Especially not for those who crave adventure. It's a lot of paper, and people, and difficult decisions."

Rhett clenched his jaw to stop himself from snapping, *I know.* The past few days had been a trial by fire. Andrew had practically buried him in paper and warned him of worse to come. The House of Lords was that worst.

Uncle Frank smiled. "Don't fret over it. I'll be there. I can't be your proxy in the House of Lords, but plenty of men don't take their seats, and I can be your proxy everywhere else."

A small part of Rhett felt relief at his uncle's words. Frank was older, wiser, and knew more than Rhett ever would. He could step into Peter's shoes without stumbling over them. But the rest of him was frustrated. Something had settled over Rhett these past few days, wrapped around him like armor, steadying and strengthening him. He might not have a fucking clue how to be a useful member of the House of Lords, but he had the capacity to learn. He was not destined to fail.

The furious, mulish glare Della was currently sending in his uncle's direction was the strap buckling his armor together. She'd had faith in him when no one else had. She would be a good wife, a good duchess if needed, just as he would be a good husband, if she would have him.

"Everett doesn't need a proxy."

Rhett's heart gave way, and his ears rang at the sound of Peter's hoarse voice. "Brother, you're awake."

Chapter Twenty-Three

In an instant, the already shambolic room descended into chaos. Della was frozen to the spot as Rhett's family rushed past her to his bedside.

"Peter, you're awake."

"How do you feel?"

"Are you well?"

"Are you cold? Do you need another blanket?"

"Are you hot? Should we open the window?"

"You must be starving. Someone fetch food."

"Someone fetch the doctor."

"You must be thirsty. Here." Meg poured a glass of water from the jug by his bed and pressed it into his hands.

Della backed away slowly. This was good news. The duke waking meant neither she nor Cordelia were going to prison for his murder. It was excellent news; it was simply *terribly* timed. The entire damned family was there. *Shit, Adelaide.*

If she kept her movements tiny and inched toward the door, perhaps she could escape before the surprise of their brother's awakening wore off and the Montgomery siblings looked for her. In an ideal world, she would confess all to the duke and beg for his cooperation *alone*. Besides, she wasn't ready to face Rhett and his sisters with the truth. They would be angry. They would likely demand she remove her ornaments from the tree, and while that might seem like a trivial thing, she had never had a family Christmas tree. Trees and ornaments were far too bulky to be carried from place to place. The closest she had come were kindhearted innkeepers who'd allowed her to place a trinket or two on the sparse trees that leaned in the corners of tap rooms.

By the bed, Rhett and Jac were helping their brother sit up. The duke grumbled, as men do, but he clearly needed the help. When the pillows were stacked behind him, he closed his eyes and sighed. Meg fussed with the blanket, and Winnie reached over to remove the tinsel crown he wore, throwing it toward the mess of ornaments.

Della was so close to the door. Only a few more steps, and she would be gone.

It would be over.

Peter grasped Rhett's hand. "Thank you for coming home, Everett." The duke's eyes glistened, and a lump formed in Adelaide's throat. Rhett had been so nervous about facing his brother, but the duke's love for him was so clear. She didn't know Peter, but she couldn't believe that someone who looked at their brother with such affection wouldn't want the best for him.

She would whisper goodbye, but they might hear her, and she needed to disappear. But that wasn't her fate.

"God damn it," she muttered as Andrew appeared in the doorway, blocking her escape.

"Peter, you're awake. Thank God."

"Thank God, indeed," Jac said. "It does feel like a Christmas miracle."

"I told you the Christmas tree would work," Winnie said.

"Della, what are you doing all the way over there?" She grabbed Della's hand and dragged her into the circle of family standing by Peter.

Peter smiled at her.

She smiled back.

Jac grinned at them both.

Frank stood in the corner, sniggering, while Rhett kept his eyes firmly on his shoes. His smile was frozen.

"Good afternoon," Della said when the silence became too awkward to bear.

Peter's brows furrowed, and he cocked his head, clearly confused, clearly wondering why on God's earth Cordelia's maid was standing in his bedroom.

Fuck, fuck, fuck. This is it, Adelaide. The moment all your lies are going to crash down on you.

"Apologies. *Who* are you?"

Rhett's head shot up. The girls all gasped in unison.

Meg took Peter's hand in hers, squeezing gently. "Brother, you don't recognize Cordelia?"

Peter shook his head. "Should I?"

"Oh, good God." The words burst from Rhett's mouth as he turned away from them all, his hands intertwined behind his head.

Meg looked at him sideways, but Jac and Winnie were focused on Peter. "She is your betrothed," Jac said. "You don't recognize her at all?"

Don't say anything, Adelaide. Don't say a word. Just wait for the ground to swallow you.

Peter shook his head. "I'm betrothed?"

Oh my God. He doesn't remember.

"Oh my God, he has amnesia." Jac's hand flew to her mouth. Winnie gasped. Meg sank into the chair by his bed, and Andrew pinched the bridge of his nose.

Jac leaned across the bed and grabbed her brother by both shoulders. "Do you know who we are?"

Peter nodded. "Jacqueline, I know who you are. Margaret, Edwina, Everett, Andrew." He looked at Frank and scowled. "Frank." The word came out flat. Clearly, the duke knew exactly who his uncle was. He turned to Adelaide. "You do look familiar."

Winnie sighed and grabbed Adelaide's hand. "That's because she's your fiancée, dummy. You proposed to her just a few days ago."

Peter shook his head and shrugged.

"It's fine," Adelaide said. It was a relief, in fact. The axe was still hanging there, but it wouldn't swing right now. "Perhaps after some rest, things will come back to him. I'll go ask the kitchen for some willow bark tea. He must have a devil of a headache."

With one last look at Rhett, who was staring out of the window shaking his head, she fled the room.

Chapter Twenty-Four

From Peter's bedroom window, Rhett watched Della exit the house. It was remarkable how quickly she had packed her things, changed into outside clothes, and left. She walked the edge of the house toward the stables, her expression stricken. What did that mean? Why was she running? He was about to go after her when Uncle Frank joined him. "It seems her schemes are not going to plan."

"I don't know why she's upset."

Frank shrugged. "Perhaps she wasn't counting on the duke waking. If Peter had died, she'd have the brother she wanted and the title. Now she has to choose."

Nausea swirled in Rhett's belly. For years, he'd been dodging this precise situation. He'd gone to extreme lengths to escape being compared and found lesser.

Della tightened her coat, hugging herself as she rounded the corner, out of his sight. What was she thinking? Was his uncle right? Was she honestly not sure of her choice?

As if sensing Rhett's thoughts, Frank continued. "You'd think that if she had no designs on the dukedom, she would have said so right then."

Rhett swallowed. "Perhaps she wanted a private moment

to do so. She's not the kind to break off an engagement in front of a man's entire family."

Frank clapped him on the shoulder. "Son, she left a man at the altar in front of all of London. If she'd wanted to break things off, she would have."

That was true. Rhett hadn't considered that because the woman who'd humiliated her fiancé in such a public manner seemed like a completely different person from the one he knew and loved. But she had left Hornsmouth with no consideration for the man's feelings. She might leave Rhett just as easily.

"Don't be so morose. It's not the end of the world." Frank gave Rhett a rousing shake of the shoulders. "Now you can go back to hopping from ballrooms to bars across the continent. It will be as if the past few days never happened."

But Rhett wasn't sure that could be the case. This past week had changed him. *She* had changed him. His heart was still set on traveling the world, but he couldn't go back to the aimless vagabond he was. He wanted his travels to have a purpose, and he wanted that purpose to be with her.

As he watched her stride down the drive, he prayed she was leaving the situation and not leaving him, but history was not on his side.

"Her hair is a lovely shade of strawberry blonde."

"He knows what color her hair is. He saw her not ten minutes ago."

"When he failed to recognize his own betrothed."

"Yes, when he failed to recognize her. He has amnesia; he's not blind."

"I simply think that if he pictured the color of her hair, it would bring back a memory of the first time he saw her."

Winnie and Jac stood on either side of Peter's bed, glaring at each other. Meg was still in the armchair, one hand covering her eyes as though that could block out the girls' bickering.

Frank had exited not long after Peter woke. He would be at the tavern in town if Rhett wanted to join him. As his sisters' tit-for-tat continued, escape was tempting, but Rhett would stay until the doctor arrived. Until they knew why Peter woke, they wouldn't know if he would stay awake. Rhett wasn't leaving his bedside until he was confident his brother was well.

Or at least as well as one could be when one was the sole focus of all three sisters' attention.

Peter rolled his shoulders and tried to work out the kinks in his neck. It seemed lying in one place for four days was not the relief Rhett imagined.

"Lady Cordelia's hair seemed perfectly lovely," Peter said. "But I'm sorry. It sparks no memory."

Impossible, Rhett thought. Della's hair glowed. The first time he'd seen it, it had caught in the afternoon sun, making her seem like a fiery goddess.

"What about when she mutters '*verdamnt*' under her breath?"

Peter scowled. "Edwina Abigail Montgomery, you are not supposed to even know that phrase, let alone use it."

Winnie crossed her arms. "Della has been instructing me in the rich languages of the continent. That's why you should marry her. She's incredibly intelligent."

Peter pinched his nose. "I never said that I wouldn't marry her. I don't remember proposing, but assuming I did, I will be true to my word."

Rhett's mouth went dry, and his stomach caved in. He'd been hoping that Peter's amnesia would be the natural end to that engagement. That it would have been broken off without Rhett having to be the one who broke it.

"You can't marry her out of obligation," Jac said. "You must marry her because you love her."

"I don't even *know* her," Peter said, frustrated. He pulled back the bedcovers, as though to extricate himself from his sisters' care, but Jac pulled the covers back in place. He huffed. "I don't recall ever having set eyes on her. There's been no conversation between us that I am aware of. But Jac, plenty of marriages are out of obligation."

Jac and Winnie both had their arms crossed. "No."

"That's awful."

"We will not stand for it."

"Della is perfect for you, and in the time she's been here, she's come to feel like family. Hasn't she, Rhett?"

"Yes." The word was near impossible for him to utter. He turned away to see Meg looking at him, confused.

Jac continued. "So, the next time she comes to visit, you will not be so churlish. You will appreciate the blessing that you have in her, and you'll propose again so that she knows you want this."

"I will, will I?" Peter raised an eyebrow.

Jac's frown deepened, and she kicked the baseboard of the bed. "Yes, because she did her best to keep you alive."

"*And* she saved Rhett's life before they fell into the Thames," Winnie added.

Peter looked at him, brows furrowed. "You fell into the Thames? Were you drunk?"

And there it was. Peter had been awake for less than an hour, and already Rhett was disappointing him. "I was not drunk, and I'll have it known that I saved Della's life in return."

"Because you almost caused her to drown by pulling her

into the river with you," Winnie muttered. At some point, she had ferreted out more of the truth than Rhett would have liked, but not the most poignant aspects.

Peter tossed and turned, and immediately Meg leaped up to adjust the pillows behind him, trying to make him comfortable. "I don't know why you're all making such a fuss about my betrothal." He was vexed. Rhett could hear it.

Meg scowled, first at her sisters and then at Peter. "Because you were a dunderhead, and it's causing no end of problems." Her eyes flicked to Rhett and then hardened as her gaze returned to the duke. "We've heard the full story. You proposed to Lady Cordelia because you needed an heir, and she fell right into your lap. You didn't give any thought at all to the consequences of such a bloodless decision. It was quite stupid."

Peter sat up straighter, hand going to his head as he did. "Margaret..." Rhett recognized that tone. It was usually directed toward him.

"You are so incredibly lucky, brother," Meg continued quickly. "Because despite your calculated reasons for selecting her, your convenient duchess is *perfect*. It's impossible *not* to fall in love with her."

Rhett's heart cracked. It *was* impossible not to fall in love with Della. As unlikely as it might seem, he'd fallen in love the first second he saw her. But Uncle Frank's doubts had wormed their way into Rhett's brain. What if she didn't truly reciprocate those feelings? She'd never said as much. She'd kissed him, sure, but he knew more than anyone that a kiss could mean nothing. It certainly didn't mean a lifetime.

And even if she loved him, would she choose him over Peter now that the option was there?

"Where *is* Della?" Winnie asked.

"She's giving the family space," Jac replied.

"Well, she's being stupid. Family doesn't need space."

"She's not stupid," Rhett said. "And you're wrong." He loved his family, but if Peter married Della, if she chose the dukedom, he was not sure he could live with it. He certainly couldn't live here, in England. He was going to need all the space the continent could offer.

Chapter Twenty-Five

"He's awake? Their asinine Christmas tree plan worked?" Cordelia paused her pacing and stared at Adelaide, mouth hung open.

Adelaide shrugged. "The duke is awake." *And everything has shifted.*

"So, what did he say? Does he blame me for his accident? Is he going to have me arrested?" She gripped Adelaide's hands. "He has, at least, called off the engagement, yes?"

Adelaide winced. "Actually, I didn't quite get an opportunity to talk to him."

"So, I'm still engaged." Cordelia's lips thinned, her expression darkening.

"Technically."

"But he thinks you are me."

"Yes."

"Even though I want no bar of him, and you're in love with Lord Everett Montgomery."

The mention of Rhett felt like a gut punch. "Yes and yes."

Cordelia pulled at her hair, leaving Adelaide surprised her mistress chose to sink her fingers into her coiffure instead of wrapping them around Adelaide's throat. "This is the type of debacle they write about in trashy novels, Adelaide, not real life."

That's so fucking true.

"The duke proposed to me in person, in this very room. How can he possibly think that you are me?"

Both women's glances traveled to the armchair that had knocked the duke cold. "It seems the duke is experiencing minor amnesia. Either that, or the knock has caused some… deficits. You and I do share some similarities. Perhaps that added to his confusion."

Cordelia huffed. "I suppose it is too much to ask that his deficits extend to completely forgetting the past week."

She knew what Cordelia was thinking. Could they just up and leave with no one the wiser? How much Adelaide wished they could. "He will see his journals soon, and his intentions were written clearly in there. I imagine he'll write to your father soon."

"My father?" Cordelia sunk down to the floor, her head in her hands. "I'm done for."

Adelaide sat cross-legged in front of her mistress. She put a hand on Cordelia's knee. "Your father can be counted on to keep this entire mess secret. He will not tolerate a scandal."

"No he will not. That's why we ran in the first place, wasn't it?" Cordelia swiped at her eyes. "He'll say I've failed him again."

"Or pleased him," Adelaide suggested. "What better way to make the *ton* forget your engagement to one duke than betrothal to another?"

Cordelia looked up, face streaked but jaw set. "Only if I were to go through with the wedding, which I can't. Which I won't." She patted her lap, and the straggly cat that was partly responsible for the current situation paced over to her and snuggled into her.

Adelaide sighed. "Would it be the worst thing in the world to marry the duke? You would be protected. You would be well cared for. You would be out of that goddamned house and away from your parents. You would be joining a family who love each other, who would move heaven and earth for each other. The girls are sweet. The duke seems...distant but otherwise unobjectionable, and Rhett is..." Her breath hitched in her throat. "He is a good man and would ensure your comfort and well-being."

"From the continent?" Cordelia gave Adelaide a pointed stare. "Because he is not likely to remain in England. He's a known traveler. He will settle down for no one."

"He might." If Rhett could forgive her for lying. But was she enough to convince him to stay in one place? He planned on returning to the continent at the first opportunity. He lived a vagabond lifestyle and loved it. That wasn't the life she wanted. She wanted walls, damn it. She wanted roots and heavy furniture, and to breakfast every day at the same table. But now, she also wanted Rhett. She wanted to look across that table at him every day. The dream home she'd been picturing for years was feeling empty, and it didn't even exist yet.

But she did want a home. Rhett wanted the world.

Rhett pounded on Della's front door. There had only been so much of his sisters' wedding planning he could take when that wedding was to be between the woman he loved and his brother. After two hours of torment, he'd saddled a horse and ridden hard, praying that the biting air and thundering hoofbeats that resonated through his chest could distract him from the hopelessness that was all-consuming.

Uncle Frank was convinced that, whatever her feelings might be for Rhett, Della would choose Peter. Rhett wouldn't have believed it if he hadn't seen her so distressed, if she hadn't failed to set Peter straight, if she hadn't disappeared completely.

The ride to her cottage didn't help. Passing through the estate he'd finally accepted responsibility for was now a cutting reminder that he was responsible for nothing. His entire world had been turned upside down by Peter's accident, and then when it had finally seemed to settle, it was turned upside down again, and he wasn't sure he'd ever stop falling this time.

He pounded on the cottage door. She would see him, damn it. He couldn't wait until tomorrow to find out where she stood in all of this. She'd been in shock when Peter woke. He couldn't blame her for leaving. He'd also wanted to escape as far and as fast as he could. Perhaps she, too, was feeling like a tumbling weed. Either that, or Peter's awakening had made life simpler for her.

"Della!" He pounded again.

Her maid opened the door with a put-upon expression. "Ad—*Cordelia* is bathing." She went to slam the door shut, but he put a hand out to stop it.

"How is she?"

The maid scowled and crossed her arms. "She is fine, I suppose."

"Truly? She doesn't seem the least bit, I don't know, conflicted?"

The maid screwed up her nose in confusion. "I can't say I pay all that much attention to how she seems. It's been a long day, you know."

Rhett sagged against the doorframe. "I know. Trust me, I know. Can you please tell her I'm here?"

The maid shook her head. "I will do no such thing. It is late, and you are who you are. It would be highly inappropriate."

Rhett crossed his arms. "You're quite impertinent."

The woman turned bright red, and if looks could kill, he'd be skinned and on her plate in a heartbeat.

He heard Della before he saw her. "It's *fine*," she said. She appeared in the doorway, her skin still flushed from bathing, her hair pulled into a rough bun, tendrils at the neck curling from the damp. She gave him a haggard smile.

The maid narrowed her eyes. "He's not coming inside this house."

"We will remain on the porch," Della promised, pulling on her thick coat and nudging past the dragon in her path. She shut the door behind her.

"Your lady's maid is bossier than I'm used to."

Della shook her head. "Forgive her. She has had a difficult couple of weeks." There was a tremor to her voice, and she held herself apart from him. It was only a few inches more than she usually did, but it felt like a chasm. Her body was as stiff as her words were shaky.

Her nails were digging into her palms, and he felt the urge to tease her fingers apart, thread them through his, and provide the relief she needed.

"Della." It was supposed to comfort her, but the word came out thin and desperate. He couldn't shake the dread that had settled over him the moment Peter woke.

She sank to the paved doorstep. "I'm so tired. I know I should...but I just can't. Not tonight."

He sat down beside her. "It has been quite a day."

"Tomorrow promises to be no easier." She sounded exhausted, and resigned, and sad.

He put an arm around her, drawing her close, trying to convince her in that one movement to choose him. "It could be all right," he said. "Peter might be put out knowing that he has to take part in next year's season if he wants a wife, but he wouldn't be heartbroken. He doesn't remember you."

"It's not that," Della said, and his stomach churned.

He interrupted her before she could say anything that might actually break his heart. "The girls will be just fine. They adore you. They won't care which brother you marry."

She stiffened, and he realized it was the first time he'd mentioned marriage. It was the first time he'd even spoken as though their future extended beyond their current situation. But she had to understand that was his intention, didn't she? When they'd kissed...

Her shoulders hitched, and her words came out strangled. "Rhett, things are going to change between us in the morning, and I don't know if you'll ever forgive me for it."

There it was: the confirmation he was dreading. Uncle Frank was right; she was going to choose the title. He hadn't realized just how well his heart had healed until it fractured into a thousand pieces once again. He swallowed to force back the lump that had formed in his throat. His eyes burned hot, but he kept the tears at bay. Just.

"You don't need to explain." He tried to keep the bitterness from his voice. He understood what she was trying to say. He'd understood it his entire life. He was the spare. The back-up plan. The option that was only an option when the duke wasn't there.

She took his hand and looked up at him. A single tear tracked down her cheek. "This friendship, this connection, whatever you want to call it—it has meant the world to me. I had no idea how lovely it would be to let another person close. You showed me a side of myself I didn't know existed."

Hope grasped at her words. "Then don't let tomorrow change anything. You don't have to marry Peter because it's convenient for him or because he can offer you a title. You and I could explore every corner of this world together."

Della swallowed and dabbed at the corner of her eye with her sleeve. "It's not as simple as you think."

To him, it was very simple. She had a choice to make—him or Peter—and it shouldn't be so hard, not after what they'd shared.

"All I wanted was a home," she whispered. She gripped his hand. "No matter what happens tomorrow, I want you to promise me something."

He couldn't get words past the lump in his throat, so he nodded.

"Promise me you'll remember you're a good man who cares about people, who listens, and who can put himself in other people's shoes. You've a quick mind and big heart, and you're worthy of respect. Don't accept anything less."

He knocked his fist against the step, hoping physical pain would detract from his agony. "This sounds like you're saying goodbye."

Della swiped her eyes. "I guess I am." She took his face in her hands and kissed him, slowly. Her lips were soft; her fingers left prickling trails where they grazed him. When he inhaled, there was lemon, and he knew that scent was ruined for him now. His heart thudded, but his body remained frozen—refusing to move if moving meant the end.

"Goodbye, Rhett." She stood and rubbed the heel of her hand across her cheekbones.

He sat there in silence as she waited for a response, sobbed, and ran inside. The door slammed. As he stood, the thousand fractured pieces of his heart scattered like dust, impossible to pick up. "Goodbye, Della."

Chapter Twenty-Six

Rhett had woken early and was too restless to stay in the house. He'd poked his head into his brother's room and had been comforted by Peter's soft snore. The blankets had been tossed aside, so clearly his brother had not slipped back into his comatose state. Rhett's sisters were likewise asleep, so he snuck out of the house and saddled a horse.

He'd been to see Mrs. Patterson to make sure that she had what she needed for her new paint job. He'd also checked in with the estate gardener to confirm plans for Mr. Jones's new hedge. Rhett wanted to feel confident that in the inevitable flurry of activity that would occur the moment Peter could sit at his desk, the agreements that Rhett had reached would be fulfilled.

He'd also stopped past the bakery, hoping to erase the emptiness inside him with coffee and pastry, but no amount of pains au chocolat could fill the void. Not here. Not where he'd shared it with her. He would need to go to Paris to find satisfaction. Or to Germany for its apfelstrudel.

He was swirling the dregs of his coffee when he was confronted by three older, angry men and two younger ones, who'd clearly been dragged in by their ears.

"My son will never marry a Smith." *Hack and spit.*

Benjie's ears had flamed red, and he'd tried to interject before the other father pushed forward, dragging his son with him.

"Julia Smith is betrothed to Gabriel. What kind of man steals another man's bride?"

What kind of man, indeed? "Samson, I presume," Rhett said, remembering his conversation with Gregory at the pub the day after everything had gone to hell. He rubbed his temples to ease the pressure building there. "Do you love her?" he asked Gabriel.

"She's all right, I s'pose."

"All right?" Benjie's outrage was unmistakable. "She is the sun. She is the moon. She is everything that is good and fair on this earth."

"She is a Smith."

"She is already spoken for."

"She is rather talkative," Gabriel muttered.

"Is there a contract in place?" Rhett asked. All five men nodded. Rhett took a deep breath, common sense warring with emotion within him. Common sense won. It had to. Look where emotion had led him. He clapped a hand on Benjie's shoulder. "We must play the cards we're dealt. Another woman will come along. Many, if you play the game right. This one is not for you."

The entire way home, he felt ill. Benjies's outrage had sparked a roiling guilt in his belly, but what other advice could Rhett have given? The girl belonged to another, neither of their families supported the match, and love just wasn't enough. Not in this world.

Rhett kicked his boots against the doorframe to dislodge the snow, then handed his coat and hat to Daunt. "How is my brother?"

"Remarkably spry for a man who verged on death yesterday morning."

"Good. That's good." He was relieved his brother had survived. Had he passed, Rhett's grief would have been long and deep. But strangely, it wasn't a relief that he no longer had to fill his brother's shoes. The idea had been horrific at first, but he'd warmed to it. He'd come to relish the opportunity to show the world his substance. He would've been a good duke. He would've been a great head of the family. Now everybody would go back to seeing him as he was prior to his brother's accident.

"Please tell the family I will be upstairs shortly."

He'd come home the night before and desperately needed something to take his mind off of Della. So, instead of dwelling on how damn much he hurt, he'd prepared notes regarding the proposed law to transfer responsibility of infrastructure and poor relief to local counties. Over the course of his travels, he'd witnessed the best and worst of local and national governments, and, in his opinion, local governments did a better job of meeting the needs of their constituents than federal ones did.

Rhett pulled his notes from his coat pocket. He was half tempted to chuck them into the fire. What a waste of time that had been. But perhaps it would be useful to Peter as he regained his bearings. Perhaps it would show Peter there was more to Rhett than alcohol, women, and a good time. He had thoughts, and they were worth something.

He would leave them on Peter's desk. His brother could read them or not as he saw fit. Rhett pushed through the door and immediately sensed the difference in the room. The air no longer felt oppressive. The walls no longer leaned in.

Peter was in the armchair behind his desk, slouched backward, eyes closed.

Terror tore through Rhett's body. "Brother, are you all

right?" He rushed to Peter's side, crouching down to be face-to-face with him. "Brother?"

Peter opened his eyes. At first, they were dazed and unfocused, and Rhett worried his brother was slipping back into illness. But then they sharpened, catching Rhett in a piercing stare, a stare that might have made Rhett quake in his boots five years ago but that had less impact now.

"You should be in bed," Rhett said.

Peter raised an eyebrow. He wasn't used to anybody telling him what to do, especially Rhett. "I've had enough time in bed over the past week, don't you think?"

"Has the doctor cleared you to be up and moving?"

"The doctor wasn't given a say in it."

"Then, no, I don't think you've had enough time in bed. Come on, let's go." Rhett dumped the notes he was holding on his brother's desk and took Peter by the elbow, urging him upward. As much as they might be of similar size, Peter had been weakened by his ordeal. In a physical battle of wills today, Rhett would win.

"Please," Peter said as he resisted Rhett's tug. It was the first time in memory that Rhett could recall his brother begging for anything. "I'm going to lose my mind if I have to spend one more minute with them."

"The girls?" Rhett asked, letting him go.

Peter pinched the bridge of his nose. "Their obsession with this wedding borders on hysteria. I cannot handle another moment of flowers or fabric or breakfast menus."

Rhett swallowed. "So, you're going through with it, then?"

"The archbishop is on his way. Andrew sent for him the moment he thought I would not wake. I'll marry the chit as soon as he arrives. There's no point stringing it out."

A knot formed in Rhett's throat that words could barely squeeze past. "Congratulations, brother."

Peter didn't pick up on Rhett's hesitation. "Thank you."

"I should leave you to your rest." He should leave, period. The south of France was nice this time of year. Plenty of things there to distract himself with.

Peter shook his head. "Don't. Sit with me for a while. We need to talk." This time, he actually reached for Rhett's arm, welcoming the steady support as they walked over to the armchairs by the roaring fire.

Once he'd seen to his brother's comfort, Rhett took a seat, crossing and uncrossing his legs, waiting for the lecture. "If this is about those sketches…"

Peter frowned. "What sketches?"

"Never mind." If Peter couldn't remember having to round up naked pictures of his younger brother, Rhett would not remind him.

"I need to thank you."

"*Thank* me?"

"Andrew has given me a report of the last few days. You stepped into my shoes and kept the estate functioning. You were a pillar of support for your sisters, and that is not easy. He said you even read through the proposed bills that will sit before parliament next year."

Rhett had been prepared for a thorough dressing-down and more threats of military service, not approval. "My notes about them are on your desk."

"I would like to read them."

"You would?"

Peter frowned. "Of course I would. I'm keen to hear your perspective on these things. I've never heard you comment on politics with anything more than an off-color joke."

Peter wasn't to blame for that. Rhett had never previously ventured an opinion. What would have been the point? He wasn't his brother. His thoughts had had no value. At least, that was what he had told himself. Maybe, possibly, he'd been wrong.

Rhett brought the papers to Peter and sat anxiously tapping his foot against the coffee table, trying to read his brother's inscrutable expression. At one point, Peter looked up with a frown, and Rhett stilled for a whole fifteen seconds.

When he'd reached the end of the pages, Peter folded them and dropped them onto the table between them. "That statement was carefully considered and well executed."

"Thank you."

"I'd like to know what else you have to say. What are your thoughts on the Housing of the Working Classes Act?"

And so began the oddest conversation Rhett had ever had with his brother. They talked for hours on every conceivable matter that could affect the lives of the people who lived on the duke's estates—from new farming innovations, to taxes, to women's rights, to Britain's foreign policy. They did not necessarily always agree, but they found common ground in most places and new insight where they differed. Peter might have more political experience, but it became increasingly clear that Rhett had more lived experience—and that was, in and of itself, valuable.

When the conversation reached a natural lull, Peter pinched the bridge of his nose. "You still need employment."

Rhett sighed and slumped down in his chair. "I know." He could not go back to gallivanting around the world with no purpose. "There just has to be something I'm more suited to than the military, and it can't be the clergy."

"I think there is an alternative," Peter said. "It would take some wrangling, but the prime minister owes me a few favors."

Rhett perked up. He would take any alternative to the paths he'd been shoved toward his entire life.

"Everett, you speak more languages than anyone I know; you've keen political insight and a natural way with people that I could only dream of. You made Mrs. Patterson and Mr. Jones cease arguing in less than a week when I've been trying to negotiate a ceasefire between them for years. You can see all sides of a situation and find middle ground. You would make an exceptional foreign diplomat."

Rhett's jaw dropped. "A diplomat?"

"Think on it," Peter said. "But it would suit you."

Work as a foreign diplomat would still allow him to travel, but his time would be spent doing something meaningful, and it would get him out of England, away from Della. "I don't need to think on it. Sign me up."

It was snowing when Adelaide walked from the cottage to Strafford Abbey. She shook her head every few minutes to dislodge the snowdrifts forming on the hood of her coat, causing it to sink down over her eyes. Her shoulders were likewise dusted, and not even two pairs of stockings could stop her toes from freezing. The rest of her burned hot, and not because of the vigorous walk. Her heart thrummed at the thought of what she needed to do today—admit the truth to the duke and ask for his forgiveness.

Then she needed to talk to Rhett.

She should have done it last night. She'd had every opportunity. And perhaps if she had, he wouldn't have left looking so stricken. But if Rhett had chosen not to forgive her, she might well have been turned away this morning. Then the entire debacle would have been for naught. She needed to talk to the duke first and fulfill her bargain with Cordelia. Only once that was done could she go to Rhett and explain, lay herself bare, and wait for his decision.

"Good morning, Daunt."

Daunt bowed, and it sat uneasily the way it always had. "The family is in the breakfast room, my lady."

Thank God. With Rhett and the girls distracted by food, she could have the conversation she needed without risk of interruption.

"I shan't go in. I was hoping to see His Grace privately."

"Of course." Daunt took her coat and gloves. As she walked toward the stairs that led to the family quarters, he cleared his throat, and she turned. "His Grace is no longer taking visitors in his bedroom."

Embarrassment touched her cheeks. "Of course. That's entirely appropriate. Pardon."

Daunt escorted her to a sitting room. In all the time she'd spent in the house, she'd never visited it. The Christmas tree was planted in the dead center of the room with the chaise longues and armchairs arranged in a semicircle around it. *Damn, moving that must have been difficult.*

"The footmen had a difficult time," Daunt said, noticing her reaction. "But His Grace was insistent that the Christmas festivities be moved out of his quarters."

"I'm surprised they didn't take the decorations off first and then redecorate." She touched the Paris ornament. It was the only thing out of place. Someone had moved it from Adelaide's branch of the tree to Rhett's.

Daunt bowed. "I will let His Grace know you are here."

Too nervous to sit, Adelaide wandered around the room. It had a distinctly feminine touch, unlike the parts of the house she was accustomed to. She wondered who had decorated it. Rhett's mother, perhaps?

The room had large double bay windows that opened out on a garden. Despite the roses having been pruned to bare stalks, there was still color as crocuses broke through the snow. Seeing the burst of purple in the winter tundra made her smile. Mrs. Patterson, as disagreeable as she might have been with her neighbors, had a good point. Color during this season could lift the mood, even her mood—a kaleidoscope of regret, longing, and apprehension.

"I would have thought you'd be halfway to the continent by now." Frank's voice was slimy and made the hairs on the back of Della's neck rise to attention. "Or are you here to salvage what you can of your schemes?" he continued.

Della turned. "There are no schemes, Frank. I'm here to have a conversation with the duke on Cordelia's behalf, as I told her I would."

"And you wouldn't lie?" He smirked.

"Not anymore." The truth would be out, as it should have been days ago. It would no doubt destroy everything, but at least it wouldn't be hanging over her head, ready to drop.

"I'm going to enjoy watching this." He moved further into the room, as if to take a seat to see a bloody play.

Enough. She stepped so close to him that he was forced to take a step backward. "Stay away from me, unless you want me to tell the duke that you knew I wasn't Cordelia from the beginning. I'm sure he'd love to hear what your plans for his brother were."

Frank paled. It was all she could do not to hiss at him.

"*Hehemm.* Frank." The duke stood in the doorway, arms crossed.

Frank quickly plastered a smile on his face. "Your Grace. Della and I were merely discussing the latest gossip to come out of London."

"The family is in the breakfast room." It was a curt dismissal, and Frank's smile thinned.

"Godspeed, my lady." As he left the room, Della realized her fingers were digging into her skirts, and she worked them loose.

"Apologies for my uncle," Peter said, crossing the room and taking a chair, gesturing for her to do the same. "He has all the patina of a gentleman with none of the fundamental structure." The duke's voice was deep and thick like honey. It sounded nothing like the hoarse, scratchy voice he'd had yesterday when he'd woken.

"I've dealt with men like Frank my whole life. There is no need for you to apologize." She took a seat near him. "Should you be out of bed? I can't imagine the doctor having given you leave to roam the house."

The duke raised an eyebrow. "Young women rarely question my decisions."

Adelaide blushed. "Of course. I was out of line. I apologize."

He regarded her for a long moment before shrugging. "I suppose since you were so instrumental in saving my life, you earned the right to question how I'm treating it—in the short term. It would be unpleasant to have it held against me for the rest of our lives."

This was the moment. She took a deep breath, trying not to pay attention to the way her hands shook or her throat pinched together. "Your Grace. I have a matter of importance to discuss with you."

"If it's about the wedding, you are best off talking to my sisters. They have taken complete control over it."

Della shook her head. "It's not exactly about the wedding. Not precisely."

The duke sighed and rubbed the bridge of his nose. "You're not about to cry off, are you? I've heard that's a habit of yours."

She winced. "It's a little difficult to cry off from an engagement you never agreed to."

The duke's brows knitted together, and Adelaide could

see the cogs turning in his brain as he tried to recall his proposal. "I have it written in my journal."

"Which you wrote *before* you proposed."

"Surely you said yes. Your father and I discussed the
possibility of a match two years ago, before he settled on
Hornsmouth."

*Patience, Adelaide. You are not here to correct his
arrogance.* "You didn't actually propose, Your Grace. You
walked in and told Cordelia that she was to marry you
because she was convenient, as though she had no free will
of her own. It was an assumption, an arrogant one, and she
took umbrage with that."

The duke cocked his head, his eyes narrowing. "Why are
you speaking in the third person? I'm confused. Blast, I wish
I could remember that day."

"I wish you did too." Then Adelaide wouldn't be forced
to recount the entire mess. He would have recognized her
charade the moment he woke. "The truth is—"

She got no further before the sitting room door opened.
"Della's here?" Jac asked, not pausing to see if she was welcome before entering.

Meg followed, dropping a kiss on top of Della's head.
"Good morning. We missed you last night. Shove over, Jac.
Give me some room."

*Damn, shit, fuck. The only thing that would make this
worse would be if...*

"I was called to the—" Rhett grimaced when he saw
Adelaide. His entire body swayed in the doorway as if physi-
cally repulsed by the sight of her.

Leave. Please leave.

Frank came up behind Rhett and slapped a hand on the
back of Rhett's shoulder, propelling his nephew into the
room. He winked at Adelaide. The bastard knew exactly

what he was doing—finding the most excruciating way for Adelaide to die of humiliation. "Now the family is all here."

"Almost," Meg said. "Where's Winnie?"

"She will be down in just a moment," Jac said. "She's gone to get the you-know-what." *Wink, wink. Nudge, nudge.* Adelaide wasn't the only one with secrets, apparently. "Has anyone called for tea?"

"Jac, you just had tea not sixty seconds ago in the breakfast room."

"Yes, but has Della had tea?" She called out to the footman waiting outside the door. "Can you bring a pot of tea?"

"Two pots," Meg added.

"Make that three," the duke added.

"And a whiskey," Rhett muttered.

"What have we missed?" Jac asked, turning to face the duke. "Nothing interesting, I hope."

Peter's expression was grim. "Lady Cordelia was just explaining the minutiae of my proposal, since it seems I am missing some crucial details." His tone was cold and sharp like steel.

Jac shook her head. "You should be more friendly toward your future wife, brother. Della is resourceful enough to find a curious way to murder you."

"Maybe she's a samurai," Rhett ventured.

"Both of you, enough," Meg snapped. She, at least, had sensed the ominous undertones in the duke's statement.

The five Montgomery siblings stared at Adelaide.

"It all happened so fast," she said, the words barely making it past the lump that had formed in her throat.

"The accident? You're finally going to spill it?" Jac drew her legs up beneath her, hunkering down for a story.

"We were in hiding. After running away from Hornsmouth, we tried to go to France; that's when I met you." She gave Rhett a small smile, but his was guarded, untrusting. As it should be. "When we couldn't get a ship that morning, we came here."

"Why here?" Rhett asked. "No one knows it even exists."

"I like maps. Berwick is only found on a few. Most maps of Kent don't bother to mark it, so I knew we were unlikely to be discovered. We pretended to be spinster sisters."

"You and your lady's maid," Meg said.

"Me and"—she took a deep, shaky breath—"Lady Cordelia."

The siblings exchanged glances, their expressions displaying various levels of confusion. Adelaide avoided looking at Rhett and instead stared at her hands, lacing and unlacing her fingers.

"Wait. What are you saying?"

"You're not Lady Cordelia?"

"But I saw you leave the church."

"Rhett saw you in that dress by the docks."

"How could you not be—"

"Shush." When the duke raised a hand for quiet, the room fell silent.

Adelaide ventured a look at Rhett then. His face was pale, and his expression inscrutable. More than anything, she wanted to take hold of his hand. She wanted to convince him that not all of it was a lie, because the way he was looking at her caused literal pain, as though it were splitting her in two.

Swallowing hard, she carried on. "When Peter fell, Cordelia panicked. She is young and not particularly sensible, and she doesn't have the mettle to face a difficult conversation, so when the doctor arrived, she told him I was her."

"And you went along with it?" Peter asked incredulously. "That is quite a decision, even for a lady's maid."

"No! Not at first, at least." *Why, why, why did you agree?*

You're a damned fool, Adelaide. "The idea was preposterous. Then she begged me to play along until you woke up so I could keep the situation out of the newspapers. We thought you'd wake in an hour. Neither of us expected you to be out so long, or for your family to arrive. When I agreed to be Cordelia, I hadn't anticipated lying to you all. But then I did, and I didn't know how to undo it." Her voice cracked at the end. She needed them to understand. She'd never meant harm.

Rhett stalked to the window, his fingers gripping the frame. "We don't know you at all. We don't even know your name." Rhett's bitter tone hurt to hear.

She stood, torn on whether or not to go after him. "You know me," she pleaded. "I'm still Della. I'm still who I was these past few days. I just have a different name."

"Which is what?" he asked, still refusing to face her.

"Adelaide Rosebourne." A sense of relief washed over her. The truth was out completely.

"And you're a *maid*?" Jac asked, leaning forward, so clearly starving for more details. Unlike her brothers, there was no anger in her tone, just rampant curiosity. Meg was looking at Adelaide with a mixture of pity and concern.

"I have only been a maid for the past few months. Before that, I traveled the continent. I wrote articles and sold them to magazines." *I'm like you*, she wanted to tell Rhett. *We share something*. But if the shake of his head was any sign, that knowledge didn't help. In fact, that she'd failed to disclose her travels when he talked so openly of his was just another betrayal.

Finally, he turned around, and the agony in his expression elicited the tears she'd been holding back. "So you're a professional storyteller," Rhett said. "That's good. That's better than having been fooled by a novice."

"Rhett—" What could she say to him? Her lies had been indefensible.

"Della, why didn't you tell me?" Meg asked, standing to take Adelaide's hand.

Her throat tightened. "I wanted to—every day, I knew I should—but I was afraid that I would lose you. All of you. I was so alone, and then suddenly, I was a part of a family." She wiped her cheek with the sleeve of her jacket. "I was a sister. I was a friend. I knew it would all come crashing down eventually, but I couldn't give you up. I love you. I love all of you when I don't think I've ever loved anyone."

Meg sniffled and nodded her head, reaching into her sleeve for a handkerchief.

Adelaide took two steps toward Rhett, but he shook his head, and she froze. "I'm so very sorry for lying to you." She willed Rhett to please, please see the truth of how she felt about him. He remained motionless, staring at her as if she was as nasty as the river they'd fallen into.

She had known that telling the truth would be hard, but she had not known that it would shatter her. This feeling was why she refused to become close to people. This was the reason she'd always held herself apart from others.

She'd lost Rhett, and she'd lost his family. Never again.

She would go back to moving from town to town. Roots kept you pinned down, unable to flee the storm.

She swallowed back the lump in her throat. "I should go. It was very lovely to get to know you all." She gave a colorless smile and walked quickly to the door. Her fingers had just closed around the handle when the duke spoke.

"Marry me anyway."

She froze. "Pardon?" She turned and faced the family. Jac was beaming. Frank looked as though he'd bitten into a lemon. Meg was dabbing at her eyes with her handkerchief.

"*What?*" Rhett said, horrified.

The duke shrugged. "I need a wife, and I don't want to spend the next season on the marriage mart having to listen to mindless debutantes parroting my own thoughts back to me. My sisters have spent the past twelve hours convincing me you are perfect. You seem to have a mind of your own. So, marry me anyway."

"But she's a *maid*," Frank spat.

"Barely," the duke continued. "We'll tell people she was Lady Cordelia's companion. Perhaps they are distant cousins. Lord knows Thirwhestle owes me a favor now. He'll maintain that story if he doesn't want the world to know about his daughter's abominable behavior."

"This is perfect!" Jac leaped from her seat to envelop Adelaide in a bear hug. "Please say yes."

"I…" Adelaide was stunned into silence. Her arms wrapped around Jac by reflex. Over Jac's shoulder, she stared at Rhett.

He said nothing, just looked at her coldly.

Jac hopped from foot to foot, jiggling Adelaide with joy. Meg looked apprehensively from Adelaide to Rhett and back again, her lip caught between her teeth. The duke sat there, waiting for an answer.

He's offering everything you've ever wanted, Adelaide. A house, more furniture than you can use, and a family you never even knew to ask for.

When Cordelia had run from her wedding to Hornsmouth, Adelaide's first thought had been *stupid*. Marrying a duke would have ensured Cordelia always had a roof over her head and food on the table. It would have given her position, power, security. Cordelia had been a fool to give that up. *So what does that make you, Adelaide? Are you a fool?*

But was all the furniture in the world worth sitting across from Rhett over dinner as his sister and not his wife?

The door banged open, and Winnie came skidding into the room, almost colliding with Jac and Adelaide. Her arms were full of ruffles. "I have the dress!" She came to an abrupt stop at the sight of Meg's tears and Rhett's angry expression. She turned to Adelaide. "Della, what did I miss?"

Rhett cleared his throat. "She's not Della, Winnie." With that, he strode out of the room, and with him went a piece of Adelaide that she would never find again.

Chapter Twenty-Seven

She wasn't an assassin, or a spy, nor a ballet dancer or an enigma. She was just a liar whose eyes had been on the title all along. Rhett had waited for her to reject his brother's proposal. She hadn't. Instead, she'd looked at him with *please forgive me* eyes. Well, he didn't need to wait around to see it. He'd seen it before.

Rhett bypassed Daunt and went to the coat cupboard, pulling the thick woolen coat from its hanger. What he wouldn't give for his old one, the one with a familiar fit and semi-proficient stitchwork where he'd repaired the sleeve after Pamplona's running of the bulls. That coat had been tossed in the rubbish cart along with Rhett's common sense. For what else could explain the past few days?

His next step was clear. He would return to Europe immediately. Peter's suggestion of a diplomatic posting offered exactly the life Rhett wanted, but it would require time in London to set up. Meetings needed to be had, and a post needed to be found. He would need to be briefed.

Rhett didn't have it in him to remain in the same country as Adelaide for any longer than he absolutely had to. He jammed his hands into his coat pockets. "Have someone pack my things and send them to London," he said to Daunt. He wouldn't waste time going upstairs to collect them himself. He needed to be gone immediately.

Rhett strode out into the cold and slammed the door shut behind him. *Now what?* It would take a coachman twenty minutes to ready the carriage. He was mad if he thought his sisters would leave him alone for that long. His gaze turned to his uncle's car. Rhett had been a passenger a handful of times. Dickey Stevens had even let him drive a motor once. Rhett had broached the idea of purchasing one before he left, but his brother had shut it down. "*Motors are for reckless daredevils and irresponsible wastrels who've no care for their own safety or the safety of others*," Peter had said.

"When the shoe fits," Rhett muttered.

He ran a hand across the hood of the green car. It was ice cold. Uncle Frank had left it unlocked. Inside, the keys were sitting on the driver's seat. No one was going to steal from the duke's residence, so there was no need to hide them.

Borrow. Rhett was going to borrow the car, not steal. He would drive back to London and leave the motor at his uncle's townhouse. Frank could return home by carriage with the girls.

Clutch. Hand brake on. Turn the key. The engine spluttered, as though trying to come to life, but then died. Clutch in. Hand brake on. Turn the key. Pump the accelerator.

This time, the engine roared before settling into a rough hum. He eased off the brake, and, with a little jerking, turned the car around.

In the rearview mirror, he saw Della—Adelaide—race out the front door. She yelled out. He couldn't hear her; instead he watched her mouth form the words. 'Rhett, wait!'

There would be no waiting. Impatient, irresponsible good-for-nothings didn't wait to hear excuses from the women who broke their hearts. He pushed the pedal to the floor and left her in a cloud of dust and gravel.

Della swiped her eyes as she climbed the front steps. Rhett had left. Her instinct had been right. He would never forgive her for her lies, no matter how much she wished he would. He was lost to her.

You have two choices now, Adelaide. Accept the duke's offer and have everything you ever wanted, or go back to floating on the tides, alone.

If she couldn't have Rhett, then she could at least have tables, and tea chests, and a grandfather clock in each room. She would be immovable. She would grow deep into the soil and try to forget the man who had made her feel like she walked on clouds.

She returned to the sitting room.

"Well?" Peter asked, the girls looking up at her with eager expressions. If she couldn't have Rhett, his sisters could be an excellent consolation prize. Perhaps.

"Yes. I'll marry you."

Her heart tore into a thousand tiny pieces with her words.

If you are getting everything you want, Adelaide, then why do you hurt so much?

Chapter Twenty-Eight

"Full house." Rhett rubbed his hands together as the others flipped over their cards. The pots were small this far from London, which meant he had the blunt to buy in with what cash he had in his pocket, but winning enough to fund his way to Europe was going to be a long, hard slog.

"Another ale, please," he said as the barmaid passed. After he'd run his uncle's motor into a ditch, he'd been forced to trudge through snow to reach the nearest inn. His feet were still numb, his nose was red, and he was worried his todger had succumbed to frostbite.

Lord Geoffrey Kingston wrinkled his nose. "Ale? Peasants drink ale. Gentlemen drink brandy."

"I'm no gentleman." Ale reminded him of where he was going—the big cities of Europe where he could disappear in the crowd, becoming only Mr. Montgomery.

"Don't tell the ladies, or there goes half of your charm. All you'd be left with is your pretty looks." Kingston sniggered.

"Plenty of men have lived entire lives based on wit and looks." Rhett would do just that. Peter wouldn't reinstate Rhett's allowance, not now that he'd abandoned the opportunity to take on a proper job. Rhett would have to be more circumspect with the women he entertained. Instead of flirting with the most enigmatic lady in the room, he'd need to look for the one who wore the largest jewels. Generous gifts could supplement his gambling income and any seasonal work he found picking fruit.

"You could run with us for a while," Lord Ainslie said. "As long as you promise not to thrash us at cards every night."

"Are you going to the continent?" Rhett asked.

Ainslie shrugged. "Paris, maybe Rome."

"Cádiz?" The carnival was in a couple of months. It was always a good time—the undulating throng of bodies, the sound of bells and drums, and the wild cracking of fireworks.

Ainslie shuddered. "That's far too close to the heathens, Montgomery. I was thinking something a little more refined."

More refined. More like London society, he means. Rhett couldn't do it. He couldn't be part of the beau monde regardless of what city it was in. There, he would always be the lesser brother.

"Thank you for the invitation, but I'm planning to travel a little farther than that. Perhaps even Africa." There were plenty of opportunities for adventure there. Hell, he was a decent shot. Perhaps he could make a name for himself as a game hunter, protecting settlements from lions, cheetahs, and hippos. Then, when he was forced to come home, he could armor himself with stories so fantastical that no one would think to suggest he settle down.

"There aren't many women in Africa," Kingston said.

"I'm fairly sure Africa has the same proportion of men to women as England."

"There aren't many *beddable* women."

Rhett didn't agree with that. Some of the most exquisite women he'd ever seen had warm, midnight skin. But that wasn't the point of traveling to exotic lands. He didn't want to fuck his way around the African expanse. He didn't want to engage with women at all unless it was purely about money. He was done. After years of protecting himself, he'd once again fallen in love with a woman, and this time, she hadn't even existed.

His mug was still empty, so he reached across the table for Kingston's brandy glass and downed it in one gulp, taking pleasure in the way it burned his throat.

"Hey," Kingston protested.

Rhett tossed him one of his hard-won bills. "Let's just play." Africa was at least another twenty pounds away, and then he'd have an entire ocean between him and a certain redheaded woman who'd taken root in his heart.

"Ouch!" Adelaide winced as the local seamstress Jac had found accidentally jabbed a pin into her rib cage.

"Apologies, my lady." The woman flushed and wrung her hands.

"It's fine," Adelaide said. "It was simply unexpected."

Cordelia, who was watching from an armchair, arched a brow. "Yes, I hear blood red is the look du jour at all the fashionable weddings."

Adelaide tried to silence her former mistress with a sharp glare. A distraught seamstress with a handful of pins was not less likely to make a mistake. Every sharp-tongued crack Cordelia made further risked Adelaide walking out of this fitting as a pincushion. Even Cordelia's high-pitched sneezing caused the seamstress to flinch.

"That dress is decades out of fashion," Cordelia said, sneezing again.

"It was the duke's mother's. Jacqueline and Edwina retrieved it from the attic."

"It should have stayed there, or at the very least, been aired out properly." *Achoo!* "I'm allergic to camphor, you know."

Adelaide rolled her eyes. "I know. It was on the very comprehensive list of directions when you hired me—no camphor in the wardrobe."

"Precisely."

Adelaide sighed. "You are under no obligation to stay. I'm sure Mrs. Beetham is more than capable of refitting this dress without your oversight."

The seamstress nodded vigorously, but Cordelia didn't shift. "I'm fine where I am. Thank you very much."

The seamstress's hopeful look faded, and she turned her attention back to the waist of what was to be Adelaide's wedding dress.

Your wedding dress. She shivered. Rarely had she allowed herself to imagine a wedding. Marriage was a rather permanent step. She'd always known better than to think any relationship would last that long. Even Rhett had left without even a backward glance.

No, Adelaide didn't do permanence, except, apparently, she was about to.

Stupid, stupid, stupid, Adelaide. The plan was for a home of your own. A walled garden and a heavy fucking dresser. You didn't go into this looking for a family to lose.

Adelaide had been on a train once. She'd taken the Orient Express from Paris to Constantinople just for the thrill. The speed at which they'd whipped through the countryside had been exhilarating. In the intertwining mess of excitement and fear, she'd wondered how she could possibly trust this behemoth of a vehicle not to tip over around curves or collide with another train. It moved too fast to stop suddenly. She'd realized it was impossible to get off if she changed her mind about her destination or the train itself. She'd been trapped.

Marriage to the duke felt much the same. It was taking her to where she wanted to go—a home and gardens she could sculpt into whatever secret hideaway she wanted. But it also came with family, and so where she should feel excitement, all she felt was fear.

What if this marriage crashed? What if Peter wasn't like his siblings? What if her secret got out, and the *ton* was vicious? What if she got bored? What if she never got over Rhett and was forced to pine over him at family occasions for the rest of her life?

She swallowed back the thought of sitting across from him, unable to touch him, watching him smile and joke with his siblings, knowing that he would no longer do so with her.

Adelaide's heart rate kicked up a notch, and nausea roiled in her belly. She fanned herself with her hand, praying she wouldn't cast up her accounts.

"Is it too tight, my lady?" the seamstress asked. She pulled free a few pins, loosening the waist, but it did nothing to help Adelaide breathe.

There was no getting off this train. The archbishop had arrived that morning, expecting to perform funeral rites, and was instead readying himself for a wedding. He'd grumbled about the lack of pomp and circumstance but had agreed to perform the service regardless, which meant that in twenty-four hours, she would be the Duchess of Strafford.

"You look awfully morose for a person who's about to be wed," Cordelia said.

"I dare say I look happier than you did, or did you forget that you almost passed out at my feet?"

Cordelia scowled. "I was given no choice in who I wed.

You are free to do as you like. That is the difference between us."

She's right. You chose this, Adelaide. You chose the duke. She closed her eyes against the pain that buffeted her. *Rhett wasn't an option. He wants nothing to do with you. He discovered your betrayal, and he left.*

"It was the right choice. Marriage to His Grace gives me everything I've ever wanted." If she said it loud enough, with enough confidence, perhaps she would believe it. Because it didn't ring true right now.

That morning, she'd stood in a room that would be hers, staring up at an ugly bear's head with gilded teeth that would also soon be, in theory, hers. She had more knickknacks than she could ever have accumulated on her own, and she still felt a lacking. She had the house, but it didn't feel like home. She'd gone from room to room, and not one of them had given her that same sense of belonging she'd felt in that disgusting dockside tavern as Rhett had braided her hair.

"*Does* this marriage give you everything?" Cordelia's tone suggested that she thought otherwise. "I admire your practicality. I can't help but want one particular person to love."

And there it was, the first clue to explain why Della was in this mess to begin with. "Is that why you ran away from Hornsmouth?"

Cordelia narrowed her eyes. "That's still an impertinent question, Adelaide. You're not a duchess yet."

"Will you answer it when I am?"

"Have you never wanted that one person?" Cordelia countered, refusing to answer the question or acknowledge her momentary slip.

Rhett. You wanted Rhett. She pasted an unaffected look on her face. "Relationships are fleeting. One needs to make decisions based on common sense."

You should leave now, Adelaide. Common sense says find another path. This one will hurt too much.

Before she could act on the thought, Jac and Winnie bounced into the room. Their unbridled joy for tomorrow's events should have been a comfort. Instead, it was a sharp contrast to her own hesitation. She could not match their eagerness to be sisters. Losing one's sister would no doubt hurt as much as losing one's love.

"Mrs. Carlyle is far from happy about catering such an important event at the last minute, but I have convinced her to prepare goat's cheese tartlets, as they are Peter's favorite," Jac said.

"Then we realized we do not know your favorite food," Winnie stated. Both girls stared at her, waiting.

"I truly don't mind what food is served."

"That's not an answer to our question," Jac said.

"Technically, you didn't ask a question," Cordelia muttered.

Jac turned her back to Cordelia and prodded Adelaide. "Well, what is your favorite food? We must make sure Mrs. Carlyle prepares it. It's the happiest day of your life. You'll want to be eating your favorite foods."

"Besides, this is the type of thing we should know about our new sister, don't you think?" Winnie added, taking Adelaide's hand.

Adelaide smiled tightly. "Beef cheeks, with butternut pumpkin, potatoes, and gravy."

"Liar." Cordelia snorted.

Jac pursed her lips, ignoring the comment. Once she'd realized Adelaide was not Cordelia, all her memories of Cordelia's ballroom smarminess had come flooding back. She was not outwardly antagonistic, but that was the best she could manage. "Beef cheeks are an odd choice for a wedding luncheon, but we will make it work."

The two sisters left to continue executing the most fanciful wedding they could, given their limited time and supplies.

"Why didn't you tell them the truth?"

"About what?"

Cordelia rolled her eyes. "That you are mad for pastries. Every single stop we made on the way here, you found some excuse to incorporate pastries into our meal."

"You're imagining things." How ridiculous that Cordelia, of all people, had been around long enough to learn this intimate thing about her. That *Cordelia* was, perhaps, her most enduring relationship.

"But I'm not imagining it. You say you want the Montgomery siblings to be your family, but you refuse to be honest with them. I saw your eyes widen when they showed that dress to you. You think it's hideous."

"I—" Adelaide avoided looking down at the dressmaker, who was intently pinning the hem, trying to blend in with the rug. The dress *was* hideous. She'd much rather get married in something simple—light green, perhaps, or purple. Something with less lace and far less bustle.

"If you're not going to be honest with them, Adelaide, you should at least be honest with yourself. These people are annoyingly high-spirited and seem to be very fond of you. Are you capable of returning their affections?"

Della threw her hands into the air. "What would you have me do, Cordelia? Run away as you did? Should I wait until I'm at the altar? What am I to do after that? Go back into service or back to the continent, where I'm not even sure when my next meal will be?

"I want a home, damn it. I want a piano so big that I can't move it and a bed that hasn't been replaced in decades because no one can work out how to get it out of the room.

I want the freedom to stay in one spot for as long as I like. Marriage to the Duke of Strafford gives me that, and I will brook no more conversation on the matter."

Cordelia raised an eyebrow but said nothing further. Instead, she reached into her reticule and pulled out a fistful of jewels from her ill-fated dress. "Here. Perhaps they will bring better luck to your wedding than they did to mine."

Chapter Twenty-Nine

It was midmorning when Rhett packed up what little he was carrying with him to make his way into the cold air of the stable yard. A bus was due to come past, which could take him to the nearest railway station. He would then board the train to London and be out of England within a day.

First, though, he had to send a letter to his uncle to explain the crash and the precise location of the car. Frank would understand. He'd been in Rhett's situation. He'd also lost the woman he loved to the Duke of Strafford. A different Duke of Strafford, but the very same hurt.

"I hope you enjoyed your stay, my lord."

Rhett gave the innkeeper a tense smile. "Very much, thank you." There had been no "my lord"ing when he'd arrived two days ago, but drinking and gambling with Ainslie and Kingston—quintessential aristocrats—had clearly clued the innkeeper in on Rhett's background.

Outside, there were unsettled *harrumphs* from the stables, the creaking of wood and metal as wagons got hitched, and the chatter and clangs from the kitchens as the cook and her maids cleaned up after breakfast. The bang of pots and pans reverberated through Rhett's skull as the aftereffects of a night drinking heavily weighed on him. He'd hoped to escape the thought of Della by drinking himself into oblivion, but the memory of her remained even through the combination of ale and gin and brandy. He'd then hoped the throbbing pain in his head and nausea in his belly would bury the ache of his heart, but it wasn't to be.

Rhett had his hands shoved deep into his pockets. As the bus arrived, full to the brim with passengers, Rhett withdrew the fare from the loose change floating at his fingertips.

The bus came to a stop and people flowed out of it, keen to stretch their legs after having been packed tightly all morning. A handful of people remained, preferring to guard their relatively comfortable spots rather than risk losing them for ten minutes of comfort.

"Just one," Rhett said, handing the fare to the driver.

"I've only got room up top."

He could use his brother's title now and secure a place in the bus's warmth, protected from the cold. If the damned title was going to cost him so much, he should get something from it. But he didn't. Instead, he nodded to the driver and climbed up the footholds to where bench seats had been installed on top.

Only one couple remained on the roof.

"Benjie?"

The lad raised a finger to his lips and cocked his head toward the girl asleep on his shoulder. She was so tightly bundled up that all Rhett could see of her were her eyes, currently shut. She had a scarf across her face and blankets piled on over her coat.

"She doesn't like the cold," Benjie whispered.

"Pretty terrible time to be taking the bus."

Benjie grinned. "Seize the moment when you can. Our parents were so distracted with the duke's wedding, they didn't even notice us leaving."

Mention of Peter and Della's wedding caused Rhett's roiling stomach to heave. "It is today, then?" They had wasted no time. Damn, he hoped there was booze at the railway station. His train left at one, which would be when the ceremony started. His brother was traditional that way.

"I'm surprised you're not there," Benjie continued.

Rhett shook his head. "I have pressing business elsewhere."

"Is it true the duke is marrying a lady's maid?"

Rhett yanked his scarf tighter. "She was Lady Cordelia's companion. A distant family member." That was the official line, and he'd stick to it. Della might have crushed his heart, but he wasn't about to throw her to the wolves of the *ton*. Saying that she was the Duke of Thirwhestle's kin would protect her.

"Was it a love match?"

Rhett snorted. "Hardly. They'd only been in each other's company for a quarter hour." Not that one needed much more time than that to realize Della was something altogether different—captivating, magnetic, spellbinding. Rhett had known almost instantly that she would be someone who shaped his existence; he just hadn't realized it would be by fulfilling the fate he'd been running from.

"She's done well for herself, then."

"*Very.*" Had she even loved him? He'd thought she had at least some affection for him. It had felt like love, though neither of them had voiced it. Perhaps she'd been playing him all along. He didn't know. He shouldn't care.

Rhett slapped Benjie on the shoulder. "I'm glad things are working out for you, though. At least love conquered all for someone. It folded under the weight of opportunity for me."

Benjie looked down to check that his woman was well, and tucked the blanket more tightly around her. When he faced Rhett again, he was shaking his head. "Love helps, but it conquered nothing. Julia would have married Gabriel even though she loved me and barely tolerated him."

"You don't find that manipulative? Calculating? Cold?"

"Not particularly." Benjie shrugged. "Women can't make their way in the world like we can. They need to marry well to be safe. Gabriel was the better choice. His family business has been established for years. Julia could have had a very nice life with him."

Rhett could see the parallel that Benjie was making, even if the lad didn't know he was making it, but theirs was a very different story. "Julia *chose* you."

Benjie's pained expression made Rhett feel like an errant schoolchild. "Because I fought to show her she could. Flowers and pretty words weren't enough. I had to show her the plan, prove that if she chose me, she wouldn't end up destitute. I saved up money; I found a job in London. I showed her she could rely on me. If I wasn't able to do that, then she *should* have married Gabriel. Did your woman know you were a safe choice?"

Rhett shifted uncomfortably, and it was not the hard wooden bench or the frozen wind that made him do so. Did Della know that he was a safe choice? She knew he wanted to be with her, but had he given her any reason to think he could provide for her? He looked down at the coat and shoes his brother had paid for. He didn't even have a pack with him. He was headed to Africa with the clothes he wore and last night's winnings, where he planned to live off his charm.

She had said she wanted roots. Roots didn't grow in tumbling rivers; they grew in steady soil. A diplomatic posting was steady soil, at least as steady as a man like him could manage. It was purposeful. It was tethered. It offered a security he'd never cared for, but that she would find value in.

But she didn't know about Peter's offer. He hadn't stayed around long enough to tell her. As far as she knew, a future with Rhett looked exactly like this moment—imprudent and capricious and unstable.

Shit.

Chapter Thirty

Jac and Winnie had found a musician to play the estate's small chapel organ. The faint strains of a lively tune could be heard from outside, where everyone from the town who hadn't shown up early enough to claim a spot inside was waiting. If the turnout was anything to judge by, the duke certainly had plenty of people who cared for him, across multiple generations. He had history here. His family had history.

The many parishioners wished him well as he walked from the house to the church. Adelaide watched from the carriage parked near to the church garden. She sat hand in hand with Cordelia.

This is what you need, Adelaide. Roots run deep here, and you can graft yourself to them. And if the roots felt foreign now, it was just because she needed time for them to feel like hers. It had nothing to do with the thought worming through her brain that she had already started to form her own, and the tendrils were inextricably tangled with Rhett's.

"Better you than me," Cordelia muttered, looking out at the gathered crowd. Then she grimaced.

"Thank you for being so very reassuring."

Cordelia brightened, as though Adelaide's sarcasm flew straight past her. "You're welcome." Cordelia patted her hand. "But in all honesty, this match is beyond what most women could dream of. London will be perfectly livid when they find out the duke is taken. I'm happy for you. You've done very well for yourself."

This time, Adelaide's thanks were not sarcastic. At least one person in the carriage had confidence in this arrangement.

Once the duke had made his way through the throng of well-wishers, Adelaide exited the carriage with the help of a footman. The crowd *ooh*ed and *aah*ed, even though Della was fairly sure she looked like a seventeenth-century ghost had gotten drunk and cleaned out its mistress's jewelry box. Somehow Cordelia's gift of jewels had made a hideous dress even more hideous.

"Are you ready?" Cordelia asked, fluffing out the enormous bustle.

Are you, Adelaide? This is everything you ever wanted, isn't it?

Cordelia frowned at Adelaide's hesitation. "You must be ready. If your gut tells you this is a mistake, it probably is."

She gripped the garden-sourced bouquet until she could feel the imperfect nubs and lumps on the stems. "My head tells me it's right." Even she could hear the uncertainty in her tone.

Cordelia wrinkled her nose. "You can run if you're not sure. I ran from mine, and there were far more people of consequence there to witness it."

Adelaide's gut, heart, and brain were not in concert, and her feet weren't listening either. Instead, they towed her through the church courtyard, where the flowers and well-wishers provided the distraction she needed to continue.

At the entrance to the church, her feet stopped dead, and the congregation went silent.

Your heart is with Rhett, but he has gone. He is no longer an option. You ruined that opportunity.

The duke stood at the altar, firmly gazing ahead at the archbishop even though he must have known she'd arrived. Perhaps he was the traditional type and wasn't planning to turn until the wedding march played.

Adelaide searched for his sisters. All three were sitting in the first of the wooden pews. Winnie waved, bouncing in her seat. Jac beamed and mouthed the words, 'you look beautiful.' Meg was more subdued, but still she gave a warm, reassuring nod.

If you can't have Rhett, his sisters could be an excellent consolation prize, if you let them.

And she couldn't have Rhett.

The music started. Cordelia was forced to nudge her into action. With a deep, bracing breath, she walked toward her new life, thinking about how heavy that blasted bear's head was, and how it would soon be partly hers. Peter turned. His expression was passive. He neither smiled nor frowned. Did he feel anything at all? She couldn't tell.

The archbishop clearly had feelings. As she settled in front of him, he frowned. She wished Peter would take her hand or do something to make her feel at ease. If he took her hand, she wouldn't be able to run, and Lord, she felt like running.

"Dearly beloved, we are gathered here today in the sight of God—"

There was a murmur from the crowd, a slight ruckus that displeased the archbishop and caught Adelaide's and Peter's attention. She turned, and all breath escaped her.

Rhett was standing there, looking as carefree as he

usually did, but she could see the sharp rise and fall of his chest and the way his smile didn't quite reach his eyes.

"Rhett!" Jac waved him over. "You are *late*." She shuffled into Winnie, who shuffled over into Meg, who shuffled across to make space in the pew. Jac patted the seat next to her. "You almost missed it. Your timing is absolutely atrocious."

Winnie elbowed her in the side, and Meg addressed the archbishop. "Apologies for my siblings, my lord. Please proceed."

But Rhett hadn't moved from his place at the top of the aisle. He didn't acknowledge his sisters in the slightest. Instead, his eyes remained locked on Adelaide.

He is here. He returned. She almost sagged in relief.

Frustrated with Rhett's lack of motion, the archbishop moved on without him. "Dearly beloved, we are gathered here today, in the sight of God."

"I object," Della whispered.

"Pardon?" The archbishop's scowl deepened.

"I object," she said louder, this time with more confidence.

Rhett grinned. "I would have to object too."

The archbishop turned to Peter, scowling. "What is happening?"

"I do not know," the duke said, looking from his brother to Adelaide and back again.

Jac stood. "Rhett, what are you doing?"

Rhett ignored her and instead strolled down the aisle with the same cocky confidence he'd had that day on the docks, strolling down the jetty. He did not acknowledge the increased commotion from the parishioners who had gathered.

"Adelaide Rosebourne," he said when he was only a dozen feet from her, "I know we haven't known each other long, and there is still a lot for me to learn about you, but what I do know, I love."

His words ignited fireworks within her.

"You are unlike any woman I've met. You are kind, brave, and intelligent. I cannot bear the thought of spending the rest of my days without you."

Adelaide put a hand to her chest, checking to make sure her heart wasn't about to literally leap from her body.

"I know you crave a place to belong," he said, "and heavy blasted furniture. You want roots. I can't promise all of that. I do not come with bookcases, but I promise that you can put your roots down in me. I will be the place that you belong. I will be your home."

Adelaide swiped a hand across her cheeks, but the tears continued to fall. This was what she'd been looking for. For so long, she'd believed that what she was missing was connection to a place, that if she could just stay still for long enough, she'd feel the sense of belonging she'd envied in those whose towns she'd passed through. But it was connection to people that she'd lacked. She had a person now. She had Rhett, and that was where she belonged.

Rhett took another step forward, then he gave his brother a grateful smile.

"Peter offered me a position in the diplomatic corps, and that journey will take us across the world. But it will be with purpose. It will be with a plan, and no matter where we are stationed, you will have family." He finally looked over to where his sisters sat, dumbstruck. "I will never stay away that long again. I failed you by giving into my fears. That's the last time that will happen."

Winnie threw her hands in the air. "What is going on?"

Meg yanked her sister's arms down. "Shush, Edwina, for goodness' sake."

Adelaide ignored them both, stepping down from the altar toward Rhett, toward her home. "I'm sorry I didn't trust you with the truth. You didn't deserve that. I should have told you everything from the beginning." She took a deep breath. "Including the way I feel about you."

"And how is that?" he asked, taking another step toward her, close enough that he could take her hands. There was a collective inhale of breath from their audience. She could see his pulse thrum at his neck.

"I love you, Everett Montgomery. I love the man you are. I love the man you're going to be. I love your joie de vivre and your courage to do what's hard. I love how well you love your family. I love the promise of our family. You're going to be an exceptional diplomat and an even more exceptional father. I can't wait for our children to see the world through your eyes."

Rhett grinned and wrapped his arms about her waist. The touch of his fingers along her rib cage lit a fire within her, even through the many layers of petticoats and corsets and the silk monstrosity of the dress.

She took his face in her hands and drew him close, so she could lift onto her toes and kiss him, to the shocked gasps of the congregation. They could be as shocked as they liked. She'd found where she belonged, and no one else mattered. Just him. Just them. He squeezed her tightly, lifting her from the ground and spinning her until the shocked gasps morphed into *ooh*s and laughter.

"So what does this mean?" Winnie asked loudly, causing Della and Rhett to break off their kiss and face the siblings.

Winnie looked thoroughly confused. Jac was watching everything with wide eyes and rapt attention. Meg looked happy-ish. She flicked a concerned look to the altar, and Della froze. She had utterly forgotten about Peter, who was rubbing his temples as if the entire affair was giving him a headache.

Della slid until her feet touched the floor, and she watched the duke apprehensively.

Peter sighed. "I think it means that I'm standing in the wrong spot." He took a step to the side, where the grooms-men would normally stand, and gestured for Rhett to replace him in front of the archbishop, who was shaking his head vigorously.

"No, this is not the ceremony I agreed to."

"It's not the ceremony any of us were expecting," Peter said, sounding tired, as though he hadn't had four solid days of sleep that week. "But let's move ahead with it, anyway."

Rhett's hands tightened on Della's waist. He bent down to whisper in her ear. "Adelaide Rosebourne, will you marry me?"

Her insides warmed at the sound of her name on his lips. "Yes, Everett. I will marry you."

Chapter Thirty-One

Luncheon stretched on for hours. In the space of two days Mrs. Carlyle and her kitchen staff had put together a feast unlike any Rhett had ever experienced. For every country he'd sent a Christmas bauble from, she'd replicated a local dish with astonishing accuracy. With every dish, he and his new wife shared a story of their favorite time eating it—punctuated by comments from Adelaide such as "Pain au chocolat from France. Wait, no. Apfelstrudel from Germany." And "I change my mind, Spanish churros."

"Any form of pastry, then?" Jac said, accepting another glass of lemonade from a passing footman.

Adelaide nodded. "Yes. Any form of pastry and I'm in heaven."

"Good to know, sister. There is an exceptional bakery in the village."

Adelaide popped a mini quiche in her mouth and looked at Rhett. "I am aware."

Standing in the bakery's only empty space, hands pressed against each other's as they built a metaphorical wall, was the moment Rhett had realized they might be soulmates. It was certainly the moment he'd realized they were kindred spirits.

Now he knew why—they'd both been floating the continent, experiencing it alone. Now they could experience it together.

With her next to him, he would be one of the best foreign diplomats out there. Her natural ability to adapt to her environment and fit in seamlessly, just as she'd done this past week, would be an asset. She would have as great an impact as he would, working the often-hidden side of strategic decisions, made by women across tea sets and shared with husbands across pillows.

He'd personally experienced her ability to influence. Together, they would be a powerhouse.

Jac and Winnie—Winnie in particular—soaked in every word of Rhett and Adelaide's reminiscing, with oohs and aahs, and comments like "Can women have a grand tour, or is it limited to men?" and "Peter, when Rhett and Adelaide are set up, the family should visit, don't you think?"

Peter, for his part, managed not a single disparaging word. In fact, judging by the ever-present smile on his face and the way he clapped Rhett on the shoulder, he was both supportive of and happy for his brother. A miracle, or perhaps inevitable if Rhett had been open to seeing it.

"We will go to London to talk to the Prime Minister next week," Peter said. "Though it may take some months before you can settle into a posting. What will you do in the meantime?"

Rhett looked to Della, who had ensconced herself on a settee with Meg, the two women talking animatedly. "If you're willing to loan me the money, which I swear to pay back, I'll buy an empty house in London and watch Della fill it. That way we'll have a home base."

"If it means having you home more often, you have my full support. Talk with Andrew. Work out a budget. He can see to the financial aspects."

Rhett pulled Peter into a hug, having not felt this close to his brother since childhood, except...He had been closer than this, far more recently and with far fewer clothes. He drew back, still holding on to Peter by the shoulders. "I'm truly sorry."

Peter frowned. "For interrupting the wedding? That's all right."

Rhett let out a short, sharp sigh. "For the lengths we went to to wake you. One day, someone will tell you the stories and Gods, I hope I'm out of the country when that happens."

Peter opened his mouth—to object, to interrogate, to forgive, Rhett would never know. He ducked out of his brother's reach to avoid the awkward questions and made his way toward his wife. He'd been out of her orbit for a full twenty minutes now, and that was too long for newlyweds. It was far too long, full stop.

Ten feet from his bride, Rhett was stopped, his uncle sidling up next to him, seemingly from nowhere.

"Congratulations, son. I hope."

Rhett pressed his lips together. He took full responsibility for his actions. He'd left when he shouldn't have. He'd given in to his fears. But still, there was a part of him that resented his uncle for stoking those fears to begin with.

Rhett didn't know what Frank's motivations had been. Perhaps his uncle really was trying to look out for him. Perhaps not. Either way, at the moment Rhett needed support, Frank had not been that. All Frank could see was the person Rhett had been and not the man he was now. Rhett felt a twist of sadness as he realized he'd grown beyond their relationship. Unless Frank also chose to give up his bitterness, there was no room for him in Rhett's life beyond the occasional encounter at a family event. That was sad. They'd once been close. But, as he looked at Della and she caught his smile, returning it with her own sweet one, he was okay with that loss because what he was gaining was so much richer.

"May I have my bride?" Rhett asked Meg.

His sister shook her head. "I'm not finished with her. We have much to discuss."

"You have a lifetime to discuss it. We will be back for every Christmas, every wedding, every birth. I promise." He took Della's hand, wondering if he would always feel this sense of having come to rest when he touched her. Leaning close enough to smell the lemon in her hair, he whispered, "Do you think we can escape yet?"

His sister's ability to throw together a last-minute celebration was to be admired and endured. As the hours had worn on, the tension within him coiled tighter. Intertwining fingers, resting his hand on the small of her back, her thumb grazing his—those moments weren't enough.

He needed her. He needed the taste of her lips and the silk of her skin, and the feeling of her beneath him. He needed to kiss her long and deep, in a way that would scandalize the footmen and send his brother into a conniption, so he had endured with quick pecks on her cheek or the press of his lips to her hair while they enjoyed the celebration.

But enough was enough. He could love his family tomorrow. Right now, he was going to make love to his wife.

"I think we can go, if we make it subtle," she whispered.

They were on the opposite side of the room to the door. "Subtle will take longer," he murmured. He ran his hand down her waist, wrapping it around her hip and pulling her against him.

Her breath quickened. "Not so subtle then."

He tried not to make eye contact with anyone as he steered her directly through the middle of the room at a quick clip, though he could feel all eyes on them.

A red flush crept up the back of Adelaide's neck, but she didn't slow her pace or veer off course. The moment they were out of the room and away from prying eyes she started laughing. "Your family is tactful enough not to mention our quick exit, aren't they?"

"Our family. And they will definitely bring it up when it suits them, probably for the rest of our lives."

She shook her head but grinned regardless, and then wrapped an arm around his neck, twining her fingers through his hair. "We best make the innuendo worth it, then." She pressed her lips against his, her body against his body, her hand on his chest.

It was more than any sane man could take. He lifted her and carried the two steps needed to flatten her back against the wall. His tongue ran across the seam of her lips, begging, pleading, until she opened to him. They explored each other, hands roaming frantically across necklines and waistcoat buttons, and the damned waistband of his pants.

"Gods, I want you."

It was the sound of the door next to them snicking closed and Meg's embarrassed cough that drew them apart.

"While I can understand your enthusiasm, brother, perhaps it's time to take it upstairs." She returned to the room, no doubt to prevent her younger sisters from leaving until Rhett and Della had taken a moment to adjust themselves and depart.

He tried to draw her upstairs, but she pulled back until he faced her, and then she cupped his cheek in her hand. "You're perfect," she whispered.

The words cut through him like the Viking sword of Sigurd. No one had ever thought him perfect. He'd been called handsome, amusing, a skilled lover, an entertaining friend, an excellent shot, a keen gamer with the devil's own luck, even physical perfection by the artists he'd posed for, but never perfect in and by itself. His heart twisted at the thought that Della had seen him for who he truly was, flaws and all, and still thought him splendid.

"No, you are perfect." She was, and she was his. He'd done nothing in his life to deserve a woman with such kindness, intelligence, or beauty. She was not his karma or a reward from the gods. He'd not earned such a prize. She felt like a sign from fate, though, an encouragement from the universe, a sense of divine belief that he would be worthy of her. His future would not be a reflection of his past. They would forge something new.

Finally, he had something to reach for, not run from.

She shook her head. "No, *you* are perfect."

He pressed her knuckles to his lips. "I have never been this happy. I didn't even know it existed."

"Me too," she whispered. It was her turn to drag him toward the stairs and up to his bedroom. He didn't pull back at all.

Chapter Thirty-Two

One year later...

"We are going to be late." Adelaide shivered as Rhett's fingers skimmed over her stockings and up beneath her skirts and petticoats until his hands rested on the back of her thighs.

"Then let's be late," he murmured, his lips pressing into the silk bodice of her gown. He was only half dressed for the dinner they were to attend that night. His cravat was untied, hanging on either side of his neck. His waistcoat was open, and the top buttons of his shirt were undone, revealing a smattering of wiry hair across a chest turned golden from all the sea bathing they'd done on Cyprus the week before. It would be the latest chapter in *A Lady's Adventures*, the travelogue she wrote that had gripped the *ton* and provided Adelaide with independent income with which she bought trinkets and furniture to send back to their London home.

Rhett sat on the edge of their bed, his legs spread wide. Adelaide stood between them, using his shoulders for support as her knees faltered.

His hands trailed higher until only thin cotton drawers stood between him and her arse. He squeezed it hard, and a rush of heat pooled between her legs. "The invitation was for seven o'clock," she said with little conviction.

His strong hands kneaded her soft flesh. "The grand vizier is always late. Make love with me now, and I promise he will never know we weren't there at seven." He nuzzled his face against her midsection.

"You'll put creases in my dress."

"Not if we take it off." His hands shifted through the slit of her drawers, and she felt the warm caress of his finger.

"Oh, god." She wrapped his cravat around each of her hands, using it to steady herself. He increased the pressure of his finger and slipped into that perfect rhythm, the one that never failed to set her entire body shuddering.

"See?" he murmured. "Isn't this worth it?"

Her gaze slipped out of focus. "Yes," she said, pulling away from him so that her brain could function. "But only if we make it quick."

Rhett grinned, and she turned so that he could make quick work of the buttons that ran from her high collar to the gathered skirts at her hip. Carefully, she pulled the loose silk over her head and lay it on the rug as neatly as possible. The petticoats could stay on. No one but her would see the wrinkles in them tonight.

As she carefully arranged her dress, Rhett pulled his shirt from his waistband, unbuttoned the fall of his trousers, and shimmied until they were in a pool on the floor by his feet.

Adelaide raised an eyebrow. "No drawers?" she asked as she tugged at her own until they, too, were nothing but a pile at her feet.

"It saves time. That's the responsible thing to do, is it not?" He leaned back on his arms, studying her. His knees were spread wide.

The sight of his cock, large, stiff, throbbing, wiped all

thoughts of dinner commitments from her mind. She gathered her petticoats in her hands until they were bunched at her waist, her legs and arse exposed to the warm air.

Rhett sat upright, holding her by the waist as she climbed on top of the bed and straddled him, her petticoats settling across them both. She let out a soft moan as she sank down.

"Gods, Adelaide." Rhett collapsed back on the bed, his hands fisting in the layers of cotton around them.

She couldn't respond. Her senses had been completely scattered as they were every time they made love.

Rhett grabbed her hips with his hands, his fingers pressing into her, holding on as she rode the swelling wave that would bring them both to climax.

Afterward, she collapsed onto his chest, dragging in a deep breath, feeling completely at home against the rise and fall of his chest.

Rhett kissed her hair, which was definitely going to need addressing before she left the house. Then he patted her backside. "Come on. We have a dinner to attend. You're making us late."

"*I'm* making us late?" She scrambled off of him.

"The Prime Minister doesn't like to be kept waiting," Rhett said as he stuffed his legs into his trousers and tucked his shirttails in. "And he's been early to every meeting so far."

"Wait. What?" She snatched her dress from the floor and pulled it over her head, not taking the care it needed and pressing creases into the skirt.

"It's all right. I'm sure he'll be understanding when I tell him my wife ravaged me."

He's kidding, Adelaide. He's probably kidding. Damn it. "Buttons. Now."

When her clothing was fastened, he turned his attention

to his cravat, fingers flying. She stood in front of the mirror to repin the strands of hair that had come loose during their lovemaking. Finally, they were both presentable.

"You are a scoundrel," she said as she walked through the door he held open for her.

"You love a scoundrel," he said as he followed.

By the time they'd reached the landing, Winnie was already in the foyer, impatiently circling, tapping a leaf of paper against the pale green dress she and Adelaide had picked out for dinner. "What took you so long?" she asked, waving the letter in the air.

A warm flush crept up Della's neck. Before she was forced to tell a lie, Rhett stepped forward.

"Button issues," he said. "One came loose and I had to help sew it back on."

"You?" Winnie looked at her brother skeptically.

He held a hand to his chest in mock affront. "I'll have you know I am quite handy with a needle and thread."

His sister *tsk*ed. "It's no doubt why you're both late. You should have left it to Della. She's far more proficient than you at sewing. At everything, really."

Rhett pursed his lips, clearly unhappy to be caught between defending his talents and suggesting that he was better than his wife.

To extract him from his dilemma, Della turned to Winnie. "Next time we have a loose button, I will simply choose another dress so that we can remain on time."

While Winnie's expression was approving, Rhett's was heated. "Yes. Next time," he said. "I'm sure there will be many more loose buttons in the future."

Adelaide was all too aware of the embarrassed flush creeping over her, and she elbowed her husband in the ribs.

Oblivious, Winnie furrowed her brows. "If that's the

case, brother, Della needs a better seamstress. Now you have not yet asked about this letter," she said, waving it again. It is from Jac. Cordelia is set to marry again."

"Pardon?" That was the last thing Della was expecting. As far as she knew, Cordelia had been exiled to the Scottish highlands until her father chose to allow her back to London. She crossed to the mail salver and sifted through her own correspondence. The two had stayed in touch following Adelaide's wedding. They had, in fact, formed a friendship of sorts. As impossible as Adelaide may have thought it a year ago, Cordelia had even demonstrated personal growth in her isolation. But there was no letter from her in the pile.

"There was an announcement in today's *Times*," Winnie said. "Cordelia Highwater is betrothed to the Duke of Moorhouse. They are to be wed the moment the season starts. Thankfully, I will, at least, be there to see *this* wedding. "Do you think she'll go through with it?"

Would she? Adelaide didn't know. "I am not sure," she said to her sister. "It depends on why they're marrying."

"Come," Rhett said. "We are late already." He took Della's coat from the butler and helped his wife into it. When she turned to face him, he licked his thumb and rubbed it across the hairline by her ear. "Dirt," he muttered.

Damn. That would have been from earlier. The gardeners at the consulate had agreed that she could have her own garden on the grounds, somewhere she could plant an English tree and tend to flowers. It would be her gift to the country, and a gift to all the diplomats' wives who would come after her—a garden they could tend that would contribute to a rich tapestry of roots, lives, and history.

She rubbed her hairline. "Is it gone?"

Rhett nodded, and gave her a quick kiss. "It is. You are perfect. Let's go negotiate a treaty."

Want more of the England's Sweethearts series?

Don't miss *The Duke's Got Mail*, available in Fall 2025.

About the Author

Samara Parish is an award-winning author and writing coach who has been escaping into fictional worlds since she was a child. When she picked up her first historical romance book, she found a fantasy universe she never wanted to leave and the inspiration to write her own stories. She lives in Australia with her own hero and their many fur-babies in a house with an obscenely large garden, despite her track record of failing to keep even cacti alive.

You can follow her writing, gardening, and life adventures on social media and access bonus content by signing up for her newsletter at her website.

You can learn more at:

SamaraParish.com
X @SamaraParish
Facebook.com/SamaraParish
Instagram @SamaraParish
Pinterest @SamaraParish
TikTok @SamaraParish

Get swept away by Forever's historical romances!

Opposites Attract x Murder Mystery

NEVER BLOW A KISS
by Lindsay Lovise

Emily Leverton has a dark past, which she is determined to leave behind. When she is recruited by a secret network of governesses who spy on the ton, it may be a way to redeem her past. Zach hunts killers for the police by day and attends balls at night. When a saucy governess blows him a kiss, he never expects that he will fall for the woman. But Emily is hiding an explosive secret that could destroy them both.

A GOVERNESS'S GUIDE TO PASSION AND PERIL
by Manda Collins

When governess Jane Halliwell's employer is murdered, the former heiress is forced back into the world of the ton—and to work with the lord who broke her heart. Lord Adrian Fielding never noticed Jane when they were younger, so her icy demeanor confounds him—as does his desire to melt the tensions between them. But first he must find his mentor's murderer and ensure Jane's safety as she insists on joining the investigation. With a vicious killer circling, will it be too late for their chance at forever?

Forbidden Love x Risky Secrets

WHILE THE DUKE WAS SLEEPING
by Samara Parish

When Adelaide Rosebourne has to impersonate her mistress for a few days, it doesn't seem like a difficult task, even if her mistress's supposed fiancé is in a coma. All she has to do is wait until he awakens and then convince him to retract the proposal—thereby securing a tidy reward. She doesn't count on the arrival of the duke's brother and his damned inconvenient interest in her affairs. But does it really matter? She'll be gone before he finds out the truth…

MY SECRET DUKE
by Sara Bennett

Most ladies would be thrilled to receive a proposal from a handsome duke only weeks into their first season, but Olivia is not most ladies, and the circumstances are less than ideal. A scandal has left her family's coffers empty and its reputation on the rocks, which means Olivia must marry someone rich, with an impeccable pedigree. So a man with shaky finances and a taste for risky adventures is exactly wrong for her, no matter how charming his smile…

Forced Proximity x Scandalously Steamy

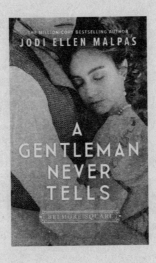

A GENTLEMAN NEVER TELLS
by Jodi Ellen Malpas

Frank Melrose is on the cusp of taking his father's printing business global, and the last thing he needs is the distraction of any woman, let alone the dazzling Taya Winters. A mysterious highwayman is causing havoc in Belmore Square, and Frank's under pressure from the newspaper to unmask the culprit, but his infuriating clashes with Taya keep slowing him down. What's more, he's sure that the highwayman is right under their noses—and that exposing their identity will not only end his story but ruin his family too…

Women's Fiction x Family Secrets

THE GARDEN OF LOST SECRETS
by Kelly Bowen

When Isabelle purchases a crumbling chateau in the French countryside, it's not just a renovation project—it's a chance to reconnect with her sister, Emilie. What she uncovers instead is an intriguing mystery about their great-grandmother Stasia, a children's book author who found herself one of the most hunted agents of the Resistance during World War II. As the siblings piece together the incredible truth, Stasia's exciting story of courage against the Nazis reveals an explosive secret that will change everything Isabelle believed about her family.